PLANET OZ

GALES of CHAOS

PLANET OZ

GALES of CHAOS

RODNEY BLANC

ISBN-13: 9798218835668

LCCN: 2025918636

Cover design by: Rodney Blanc

Printed in the United States of America

DEDICATION

To my family, friends, and students. As always, I dedicate this work to you all. Thank you. Please enjoy and be inspired.

CONTENTS

"Deal with yourself as an individual worthy of respect and make everyone else deal with you the same way."

- Nikki Giovanni

PROLOGUE

"In the world of Oz. The stars bear witness to a land that never heals." -Unknown.

In Oz, the twisters never stop. They have been moving across the surface in large waves for over a century, destroying everything in their path. Whole cities have vanished as if they never existed. Rivers turned into dry beds, and farmlands were instantly destroyed. They continue this destructive pattern to this day.

Nobody understands why they suddenly appeared. Those answers vanished with the old world. They didn't just alter the landscape; they transformed everything about life itself— animals, ecosystems, and more. Only about a third of the Ozian population survived.

When it seemed like everyone had given up, something changed.

Among the survivors were a few rich and powerful families who saw an opportunity for the Ozians. They became known as the Archons of Oz. They built enormous domes, partly underground, by transforming old mines into lively Ozian settlements for those who remained. Inside these settlements, everything was carefully managed— from the weather and seasons to the very air we breathe, creating a safe and controlled environment.

These sanctuary domes were called ArcCities. There were eight of them in the Windland region of EvLand: Emeraldia, Titania, Metallia, Oreiana, Dymania, Saphoria, Rubinia, and Crystallia. Each ArcCity had its own Archon family in charge. These families selected a mayor for their city who made sure everything ran smoothly. The mayors also helped everyone follow the rules and passed along important news from the Archons to all the people living there.

With Ozians now living in domes, the *Ventus Age* started. The old world ended, and a new way of life began. This is the basic story we all learn as kids. But we all knew there was much more to it. The world around us is like a big puzzle, dark and full of questions that no one seems willing to answer.

But it wasn't always like this. There were courageous people who continued looking for the truth. They asked hard questions, even if it made them uncomfortable. They wanted to discover what was truly happening beyond what the Archons had told us. Many have tested their limits but could only go as far as they were allowed.

Now it's my turn to step up.

My name is Dawn Dorothy Vogan, though most people call me Dorothy. I dream of exploring the unknown and taking on the challenges left by those who came before me. I want to understand why the twisters are destroying the topside and whether there's a way to stop them at last. I know it might be an impossible task, but I am committed to trying regardless.

18

CHAPTER ONE

I was only six years old then, but the memory feels like it was yesterday. It's always the same. Mom's hands, warm against my cheeks, and the way her eyes kept filling up with tears even though she was trying so hard not to.

"Please don't send me away, Mommy! I won't sneak on the sky-deck again, I promise!"

She just knelt there, her face all crumpled up. "This isn't forever, honey... This is only for a little while."

I looked at Dad. He was my guy, my hero. He always fixed everything. "Daddy, please!"

He got down on one knee and talked in this quiet voice, the one he used when things were really bad. "My little Dot. There's nothing in this world that could keep us from you. For now, go with Uncle Neel. He'll take care of you."

"We love you, alright?"

I just wanted them to be honest. "Alright... do you promise you'll come back for me soon?"

They both went quiet.

"Dad, you promise?"

He looked away, just a quick hesitation, but it was enough. I knew. I could feel the promise dissolving in the air.

"Mommy?"

Nothing.

Just the sound of their boots fading down the long, dark corridor until I couldn't see them anymore. Then it was just the humming of the air vents and the pounding of my own heart, and the cold creeping into my cheeks.

"Rook... Rook... Rook! Are you listening?"

The memory vanished. Snapped back to reality by Captain Max, our crew lead.

"Oh… Yeah, um sorry, Captain," I said, trying to shake the feeling off. My pickaxe dropped from leaning against the wall with a hollow clang. An awkward silence followed.

"Get your head out of the dust and pay attention," he said, all business. "Okay, team, this is a fragile chamber. Dorothy, you are the rookie, so what's the rule?"

"Weak structure, means high risk of collapse," I mumbled, already sick of this speech. "So the rule is don't use too much force, don't sneeze too hard, and definitely don't breathe wrong."

He gave me a hard look, but I'd said what he wanted. "Good. So, before you go using that special little sixth sense of yours, communicate. We'll be at the far end of the ridge. You think you can handle that, or should we get you back on radios?"

I just gave a quick nod. "No need sir, I understand."

He knew what I could do. He knew why I was on the Onyx Team—the best mining crew in the Southern District. I'm sixteen, which may seem weird, but I'm a huge rock nerd. They had a bunch of names for me, some good and some you probably wouldn't repeat back to your mother.

The one I grew to like was "Gemhawk." It had a little superhero ring to it. Truth is, when I got around them, I could just… *feel* the rocks. I'd touch a wall in these mines, and something would hum in my bones. It's how I got so good with a drill, and why I made it to the Onyx crew, even though I was a nobody.

I turned back to the wall, letting my fingers skate across the cold stone. It felt… different. Not just the usual cold, damp rock. There was a low vibration, almost a song, coming from deep inside. I rubbed a patch of grime away with my glove, and a shimmer of green dust coated my fingers.

Back at the children's home, books about rocks and gemstones were my escape. I'd pore over them for hours, learning about how they formed, where they came from. It was the only thing I cared about. So, I knew what that green dust meant.

Emeralds.

These raw stones are everything. They're our power. Once processed, they keep this whole city running, from the smallest streetlight to the biggest machine. Everyone thinks the emeralds have some kind of special magic, but it's not magic, it's just science.

Better science than what they have in Metallia, that's for sure.

Emeraldia's mining is what makes us the best. That's why they call us 'Battery City.' Our resources, especially emeralds, are unrivaled.

"Here," I whispered to myself, swiping dust off the wall. "This section's solid, green dust… and it feels… hollow."

My fingers traced the rock again. My gut screamed yes, and I didn't need a scanner to confirm it. I grabbed my pickaxe and started chipping.

"TINK! TINK! TINK!"

The sound echoed, and with every hit, a piece of me felt more alive. Finally, something bright sparked behind the rock.

"No way… I knew it! I was right! It's here! I've gotta go tell Max and the others."

I looked down the tunnel. They were still too far off. I wiped the sweat from my brow, and a stupid grin spread across my face.

"Okay, Dorothy, open it a little more. Make it easy for the team. Max is gonna lose his mind. Rookie of the Year? You know it."

I switched to the drifter drill.

"ZZZZRRRRT! ZZZZRRRRT!"

A little while later, while still drilling, a call buzzed in my comms.

"Good stars, Rook! What are you doing?"

It was Jorral. The oldest vet on the team, and a total prick.

I clicked on the comms. "Oh hey, Joe! I'm getting us the haul! You won't believe what's behind this wall—"

"No! Have you lost your mind?" he barked, cutting me off. "Max just told you this area's unstable!"

"Joe, we're in the mines. Everything's unstable. With this amount of emerald ore, we'll go beyond the quota. You have got to see this!"

"That's it," he snapped. "As your senior, I'm telling you now…cease the drilling and report back to the team. You're out of line."

I gritted my teeth. "Look, I get it. You don't want me on the team. Fine. But please... trust me on this. This is the one."

I pressed the drill harder into the rock.

"Besides," I mumbled, "what's the worst that could happen?"

* * *

"Move, move, move!" Max shouted, shoving me forward as the mine echoed with a deafening crack.

We had seconds, maybe less.

A chunk of rock the size of a train car slammed into the floor where we had been standing. Dust exploded everywhere.

"This way!" he screamed, dragging us toward the narrow escape tunnel. I was running, pushing past the smaller rocks hitting my helmet while my lungs burning.

"Cough, Cough."

Behind me, Joe was dragging the drill cart, wheels screeching against the stone.

Miri helped him, her boots skidding on loose gravel.

"This is bad! I didn't think a tremor this big would happen!" I shouted.

"You never listen!" He snapped, "Now keep running!"

The whole shaft was shaking around us. We turned the last corner, and I saw the light from the emergency flare we'd planted at the tunnel entrance.

"Almost out!" Miri shouted.

But another deep rumble followed. More stone grinding, shifting.

"Faster!" Jorral called out.

I stumbled, and Miri doubled back, grabbing my arm.

"Come on, we're not dying down here!"

We left the tunnel, another collapse roared behind us. Dust chased us like a living thing, pushing through the entrance.

"WOOSH!!!"

Then there was silence.

We finally settled into stillness. I fell to my knees, chest heaving. Everyone else dropped around me, coughing, panting, and just happy to be alive.

"We made it," I whispered, half to myself.

"Status report. Is everyone okay?" Max called out into the haze.

"I'm okay!" I coughed out, my hands trembling, covered in green dust.

"Could be better!" Jorral grumbled, his voice full of hate.

One by one, we checked in. No one was missing.

No one was missing. We had survived. But the silence from the team was my sentence. They looked at me like I was a bomb that had just gone off.

I stood up slowly. "I am sorry! I'm so, so, so, sorry you guys. I thought I had a lock on my drill point. Next time, I'll triple-check the structural data before drilling another wall."

"Next time?" Jorral raised an eyebrow, "There's no next time with you! Max, tell her this little tryout is over! She is off the team!"

"Wait, why? That's not fair!" I protested.

"Are you serious right now?" Jorral shouted. "Most of our equipment is buried in the rubble, we can't see a thing, and we almost died!"

"You're right. I screwed up… but hey… there's a ton of emerald ore behind that wall. 3 months' wages. That's a huge payout."

"The rook has lost her mind!" Jorral shouted.

Max tried to mediate. "Jorral, I understand you're upset, but let's try to stay calm."

"Calm down? Max, look at us! We almost died in there! Hey, Rook, let me say what others won't. You're too ambitious and reckless, and you don't listen! It doesn't matter how much potential the boss sees in you, you're not a good fit for us. We don't need rookies, especially not a Vogan! We have a reputation to maintain!

He wasn't finished.

"You know, unlike you, some of us have families waiting at home—"

"Okay, that's enough! Max finally interrupted, "Jorral, can it! The last thing I need is to hear an earful from the boss about your Vogan comment. Go cool out!"

He spat on the floor, kicked a loose pebble down the tunnel, and walked away without another word. His words stung deeply, and the silence that followed was deafening.

"Dorothy," Max turned to me, more relaxed but still stern. "What you did was reckless. That's just not how we operate on this team. You don't get to make your calls out here."

"Sir, I saw the green dust deposits on the wall. And the haul—"

"That's not the point, Rook!" Max snapped, his words echoing down the shaft. "You might be skilled. No one's denying that," he continued, lowering his voice. "But an unapproved dig puts the whole team at risk. This isn't just about finding emeralds. It's about trust… about working together. You've still got a lot to learn."

I couldn't meet his gaze.

"We'll talk more with the boss. In the meantime, take a walk, rookie. Cool off."

"Yes, sir," I answered, barely getting the words out. My throat tightened as I turned toward the shaft lift. The tears came quickly, and I didn't bother hiding them. I continued walking.

* * *

We made it back to base, but my mind wasn't with the others. All I could think about was everything that had taken place. I knew I'd have to face the boss soon, explain myself, and answer for what I did.

But all I could think about was the haul; the proof that I was right.

"I mean, I did my job… didn't I?" I thought to myself. *"We face risks like that every day. Why can't they see it from my side?"*

I didn't say anything to anyone. I had stepped away before they called me into the office. I needed a moment to clear my mind.

I took an early lunch break and climbed up to the upper shafts. It was my favorite spot. I used to sneak up for years when I was younger. From here, you could see all of Emeraldia with the best view.

Some days, it looked like a masterpiece of design. Other days… it looked like an illusion . The green haze from the rigs drifted through the city like low-hanging fog, making everything feel like a distant dream.

Honestly? I liked it that way. A dream you could wake up from.

But right now, the dream could wait. I was starving.

I dug into my pack and pulled out my lunchbox. It clicked open with a familiar snap, and the smell hit me fast. Nothing fancy, only something I'd packed myself, but after the day I'd had, it tasted like gold. First bite? Pure magic.

"So good," I mumbled with my mouth full. I grabbed my drink from beside my gear and took a long sip.

"Man… what a day."

Yet another shift in the emerald mines of Southern District Section 4. We called it home sweet home. And if Emeraldia was known as the Battery City, SDS-4 was known as the *Battery District*.

We worked long hours in tight shafts, breathing bad air, barely earning enough to scrape by. I was only sixteen, but that didn't mean much down here. In poor districts like ours, people rarely ask your age. If you could work, you worked. Simple as that.

That was life. Not just here, but in every ArcCity.

I looked out toward the city again. This massive dome, the elaborate layers of metal pipes and gear. The hiss of steam. The green power runs through those pipes like veins. Emeraldia looked like a living machine.

All my old memories came flooding back. I was about eleven the first time I looked out from here and made a quiet promise to myself: *"One day, I'm getting out of this place."*

A sharp whistle from one of the passing ArcWay trains pulled me back to reality. In the distance, the train's cars thundered through the tunnels, hauling supplies and orders. Another train screamed past, this time with people.

But those rails weren't made for people like me. They were set aside for the high-ups, clean and fancy, patrolled by soldiers. In Emeraldia, most of us live our whole lives in one ArcCity, unable to afford a trip elsewhere. The wealthy have the freedom to travel between all the cities.

Then I looked up.

Above it all, airships floated slowly through the sky, through the haze. It's every child's dream to be up there, flying far above the noise, and seeing everything.

But that "lottery" for two free airship seats? Everyone down here knew it was fake. It just another trick to keep the lower districts dreaming. The winners were always from the North or Central districts, never from areas like the South.

Still, we kept trying.

Hope's a hard thing to kill… much like my boss's dream.

He talked about the lottery as if it were the only thing keeping him going. He wasn't usually a guy who smiled often, but that contest made him light up. The bright lights, music, and food of the upper districts were subjects he'd talk about frequently. He wanted to walk the upper district's polished streets without need of a badge or special permit.

"Hey, Dot! There you are! Get down from there! Break time's over, flinthead!"

That familiar, annoying voice snapped me out of my thoughts. Uncle Neel. My boss. My forever babysitter.

I turned and saw him flailing his arms as always.

"You almost got some of my men killed today! We got lucky with that haul, but if anything else goes wrong, it's coming out of your pay, and I swear I'll stick you back on radio comms!"

"Wait… that's it? No lecture? No speech?"

That's just like Uncle Neel. He always went easy on me, always made sure I was okay. He got me this job. Kept me on the team. Made sure I stayed close.

But after today's mess? I expected him to blow up, maybe even fire me.

"Did you hear me, flinthead?" he barked. "Get down! The screens are about to fire up, and I don't need another flag-salute incident! We're still getting heat from that Peace Parade screw-up!"

That was his real worry… not the money or the work, but the city's watchful eye. He hated drawing attention, especially from the upper towers.

I stood up, dusted off my gloves, and shouted back, "Alright, Unc. I'm coming down now!"

"For the last time, I'm not your uncle… I'm your boss! And stop climbing there like a lost street poet! That green fog is messing with your head!"

I smirked. "Whatever you say."

He grumbled something under his breath about teenagers, but I was already climbing down.

* * *

The whole thing felt ridiculous. I stared up at the bright screen glowing on the side of the building next door. It was just another afternoon in Emeraldia. Everywhere you looked, screens were blaring out public announcements, ads, and reminders through our ArcSys network. No corner of the city was safe from them. And like always, right on time, the daily ArcCity pledge rolled in.

Same empty words. Same fake unity.

Mayor Gulch's raspy voice echoed throughout the city:

"We pledge our allegiance to the ArcCity of Emeraldia, and to the Archons of Oz, one nation, one Oz, for all time. Everlast."

Mayor Mira Gulch was Emeraldia's leader and head figure. She was always smiling and went by the book.

But everyone knew she was just another nicely dressed puppet, a mouthpiece for the Archons. And yes, people whispered. But never loud enough for the city microphones to catch. Talk too much? Ask too many questions? And you'd probably disappear fast.

Every time Gulch spoke, it wasn't just noise. It was a threat hidden in a warm, fake tone. We all understood the real message.

She continued, as always:

"… and remember, while we may live our daily lives differently, whether in the central district or the city's edge, we are still one. there are no enemies in Emeraldia. only the twisters above. May they serve as an ever-present reminder of the dangers of the topside. They are the bane of our existence. Anyone who says differently is delusional and stands against Ozians and our preservation."

Delusional.

Every word she spoke pushed the same idea: the dome is your future. The dome is your safety. The dome is your truth.

But it was never enough for me. It never would be.

I didn't want the same old comfort lines people kept handing me.

I wanted the truth. I wanted to dream. I needed to understand the twisters, like my parents. I had many questions:

"What caused them?"

"Why are they still here?"

"Can they be stopped?"

They believed the answers were up there, topside. They studied the storm patterns as if they were decoding the world's oldest riddle. To them, the chaos held clues. A key. A way to stop the destruction.

That belief cost them everything. They died chasing it from a place called Galesville, a refuge village.

It's where I was born.

That's what made me different. I wasn't just a Vogan, I also wasn't born in an ArcCity like the majority of the other Ozians here. I was born and raised topside.

I'm a Topsider. And I'm an outcast for it. They treated me like a sickness. But I've never forgotten who I am or my parents' sacrifice. I've held their mission very dear to me.

And boy, do I have a plan to finish what they started.

CHAPTER TWO

When I arrived at the office to wrap up some paperwork, something slipped from my bag and landed softly at my feet.

Mom's old journal.

A smile tugged at my lips as I picked it up, my fingers grazing the faded cover. This journal was my link to her... to Dad... to the days before everything changed. I opened it up, and as always, her familiar voice came rushing back.

I flipped to the first entry I recognized, the one that started it all.

Dr. Aeryn Vogan Journal Entry #4, pg.13

The Archons didn't always ban topside travel. At first, they encouraged it, at least for research. My team and I set up our first field base just outside the dome. We called it "Sector G." It was a temporary pop-up for equipment and data drops, but we started to call ourselves the Zephyrs. We were all so different—I was a meteor-ozologist, Neel was our geo-rock specialist, and my darling husband, the chief engineer. Together, we were a family.

We believed we could make a difference up here. We were brave. And a little bit reckless. But we knew that this research was the key to a better future for us all.

"Zephyrs," I whispered, turning the page. "Yeah, Mom would have a jacket with a big 'Z' patch on it… I wished she left that with me."

I kept reading, letting the story unfold as if I were there.

Dr. Aeryn Vogan Journal Entry #8, pg.19

Over time, Sector G stopped feeling like just a code name. The Zephyrs started a settlement, and we renamed it Galesville. The deal with the Archons was simple: share the data, keep the radar working, and maintain order. As long as the reports kept coming in and no rules were broken, they mostly left us alone.

But the Archons gave us AGIS generators, which were supposed to be our protection against the storms. Short for Anti-Gale Intelligent Shields. We accepted their gifts, but we knew they were a way for them to keep a leash on us. It wasn't just about our research anymore. It was about proving to them we could build a life out here.

"I know what happened next," I said to myself.

I remembered the stories she told me about the Munchkin Children's Home, how dad built it to help the waiflings left behind. It was all a big blur now, but the feeling was still there. People began to celebrate their charity and their popularity grew. But the Archons saw them not as heroes, but as a threat. The whispers about my parents becoming "co-mayors" had angered them.

Their influence grew, and the Archons got nervous. They called my parents' research "unreliable" and "too ambitious," and issued a final order: shut down Galesville and come home. But my parents stood their ground.

According to Mom, the Zephyrs believed in their mission and couldn't afford to stop. With defiant hearts, they chose to stay in Galesville.

Years later, I was born.

I turned to my favorite entry.

Dr. Aeryn Vogan Journal Entry #23, pg.34

The storm was a beast tonight. The wind howled against the dome, and the thunder shook our little trailer. But I've never felt such a strange, peaceful calm. My husband held my hand, and for the first time in what felt like a lifetime, the tears weren't from fear. They were from pure, un-adulterated joy. Our beautiful baby girl, so tiny, so perfect.

She never made a sound. While the wind screamed and the sky cracked with thunder, she was completely quiet, just looking up at us with those big, calm eyes. She wasn't afraid of the storm. She was a child of it.

"She's our little Dawn," my husband whispered, his voice thick with emotion. I just smiled, holding her close. We named her Dawn, a new beginning for us both. But her middle name would be Dorothy, after my own grandmother. It felt right. She was a gift from the past and a promise for the future.

I loved this entry. It spoke to me every time. It was my little reminder of how much they really loved me.

By the time I was six, Galesville wasn't just a research post anymore; it was a home. The Zephyrs built it from the ground up, using scrap and salvaged tech, but they built it with heart. It became a haven for those who didn't want to live by the Archons' rules. People came from everywhere, leaving comfort behind or running from fear.

But once they arrived, they worked, shared, and fought to keep our village standing.

I remember the kids I grew up with. Our faces were covered in dust, hands stained red from the clay. We raced between buildings made of junk and rusted steel, chasing each other through narrow alleys that only made sense to us. I was the ringleader, sure, but we still enjoyed ourselves.

We paid little attention to what the grown-ups were doing. We only knew that we had to reach our shelter before nightfall, while they continued working.

Most of my memories feel like a blur, but I remember what it felt like.

It felt like peace.

But peace never lasts. Not when the Archons are watching. They saw Galesville as a full-on rebellion. And they hated that.

First came the rumors. Then, people started vanishing. Then came the threats: "RETURN OR DIE." Some left, scared, and headed back underground. Others just vanished.

But once again, my parents remained. Mom once told me they were brave because of me. That I was their reason for standing firm. That's what made what happened next hurt even more.

I remember our last conversation as if it were stitched into my heart.

"Don't send me, Mommy! Please, I can be good. I won't sneak onto the sky-deck anymore, I promise; just don't make me go."

"It's not forever, honey.... It's just... It's just a short time. Then we'll come back for you."

"Daddy, please!"

It's the same memory that replays over and over. I didn't want to leave them. I didn't care about the risks. I just wanted to stay with my family. But the decision was already made.

They packed a bag with their most precious things. I held onto that backpack like it was my whole world. And there was Mom's bracelet, an old family heirloom she said would bring luck. I never took it off after that.

Their hug was the last thing I felt before Uncle Neel picked me up and carried me away. He did his best. He really tried. But it was never the same. He brought me to the Munchkin Children's Home and started his mining business while I waited.

Every day, I waited.

Then the news came.

A catastrophe.

A mega twister.

They called it the Green-Eyed Twister because two Sentinel spies said it had a weird green glow inside of it. No one believed them, but the name stuck. This twister destroyed Galesville and nearly everyone there. Including my parents.

They never came to get me.

I never saw them again.

Something inside me broke that day. The Archons immediately used the disaster as a warning, a message to anyone thinking about going topside. They banned all outside research, shut down every outpost, and locked the domes tighter than ever. And they made my parents into villains. All the good they did was gone, erased from the records. It hurt so much. Still does.

With tears now in my eyes, I flipped to the very last page of the journal, the one I'd memorized since I was a child. The final entry.

Dr. Aeryn Vogan Journal Entry #66, pg. 108

These storms... are odd. We checked our records. The atmosphere seems to have been... influenced by something else. We even heard legends of a great storm that is still active. Grey and green clouds... Powerful lighting and thunder. The team is coming close to unraveling the truth. Somehow, we have to get to this... spire. The answers must be there. We have to try before they stop us.

The sketch was still there—a rough, incomplete drawing of a towering spire. The other half of the page torn out. Whatever this spire is, I'm sure it was extremely important to them a critical final piece they were reaching for. And now, this half-torn sketch is the only key I have left to figure out what they were chasing.

* * *

By the time my shift ended, my body felt like stone. I kicked my glideboard to life and let it carry me through the narrow, cobbled streets of the lower city. The streets shimmered softly under the skylight above. Omni-scooters zipped by, river-carriages glided along the canal rails, and the streets filled with chatter and bursts of steam.

But tonight, I wasn't heading home.

I took a side street and rolled straight toward Lyman's Dumpling Tavern. The smell of steamed mushrooms and pepper-soaked ginger hit me long before I arrived. My stomach rumbled. I needed to eat and clear my mind.

Inside, the tavern glowed with a warm, golden light. Lanterns blinked on oil-stained wood, and laughter bounced off the walls. It was the kind of place that made the noisy, harsh world outside fade away.

"Dorothy! One of my favorites," Lyman greeted, waving me over. "Rough day? What happened? Did someone drill into a wall again?"

I collapsed onto the nearest barstool, my legs barely holding me up. "You could say that," I murmured, rubbing the grit from my eyes.

Lyman chuckled in his usual friendly way. "Miners are the heart of the Battery District. I swear, if I had a token for every time you walked in looking like you had crawled through dust…"

Before I could reply, someone shouted from the back of the room, "Heard she nearly killed another crew again. The Onyx team at that. Third time's the charm, huh?"

I didn't need to look to know who it was.

It was Tobin.

I turned anyway. His walk was slow and unsteady, but his words were sharp as a knife. He was Jorral's brother. Only a couple of years older than me, but life had worn him down.

"Well, look who it is," Tobin slurred. "Dorothy Vogan. Rookie star of the mines. The little dirt sniffer… heard my older brother barely made it out because of you."

I stayed seated while my fingers gripped the edge of the stool tightly. "Tobin, we were all in danger. Jorral knows that. Just ask him."

He laughed bitterly. "Save it! You're just like your parents! Trouble from the start."

"You think you know anything about them? They fought for something better, for all of us."

"Better?" he barked a laugh. "Look around. Do you really think anything has changed? We're still stuck with their mess. They didn't fix anything; they only made it worse."

Then he dropped one word.

"Toppy."

That one word — a cruel insult for being born topside—followed me everywhere like a curse.

I reached for the bottle next to me. I wasn't really going to use it, but I felt tempted.

"You gonna hit me, Toppy?" Tobin taunted, his eyes flashing. "Well, finish the job just like that green-eyed twister did."

I stood up.

"Okay, he's dead."

"Enough," a calm, deep voice ordered.

Someone interfered and stood between us before I could take any action.

In shining emerald armor stood Lieutenant Logan Ironheart, my best friend. He was the one who always knew how to calm me down when I was on the edge.

Tobin hesitated.

Of course, he did.

Leo never flinched or even blinked; his presence was enough.

"Fine," Tobin mumbled. "But this isn't over. I'm telling you. You don't belong here."

He staggered away, with the smell of his booze trailing off.

I stood there shaking, my hand still clenching the bottle, my blood pumping.

Leo gently placed a hand on my shoulder. "Let it go," he said quietly. "He's wrong. You did what had to be done. Everyone who matters knows that."

I slowly exhaled and let my grip go.

"He called me a Toppy," I whispered.

"I know, Dee," he replied, "but remember what I told you during training. Some people will poke at your peace just to see you flinch. Let their jabs fall beneath you."

Even if Leo was right, the anger still simmered in me. That word still stung. It dragged up memories of my parents and everything we lost.

"Thanks," I said, looking up at him.

He gave me that soft smile. "You'd do the same."

I let out a breath and nudged his shoulder, trying to steer my mind somewhere else. "Speaking of training… where were you the other day? I waited over an hour."

He rubbed the back of his neck. "Yeah… about that. Sorry, Dee. I got pulled into combat drills with the new recruits."

I shot him a grin. "Just admit it. You can't take me in combat anymore, so you went looking for new rookies. The student finally beat the master."

He laughed, shaking his head. "Whatever helps you sleep at night, Dee."

We stepped out of the tavern, the night buzzing with distant chatter and the buzz of glideboards passing by. He offered to walk me home. I told him I had my own ride, but he wouldn't take no for an answer.

Leo had always been the calm one. When I wanted to lash out, he kept me balanced. Sometimes I really needed that help, especially when my past was brought up. In these parts, the name *Vogan* still meant trouble.

Most people forgot what my parents represented. It was as if the city tried to erase them, leaving only silence and shame. All it took was saying my full name aloud, and suddenly I became the villain in someone else's story.

I remember the first time I truly felt that pain. I was just a kid when the city took over the Munchkin Children's Home. They sent in Ms. Gobblewortz, a cruel woman determined to remind me that I didn't belong. One day, she "accidentally" let it slip that I was the daughter of the Zephyrs.

"What are you staring at, stupid toppy?"

"Get away. Nobody wants you here."

"She's the reason her parents are dead!"

"She's a rebel!"

Those words hurt more than anything sharp ever could. The mocking, the blaming, the anger. They all wrapped around my name like chains.

But there was one person who always saw the real me.

Leo.

He never cared about my last name or where I came from. Even when we were just a couple of scrappy kids running through the narrow alleys of our neighborhood, he always stuck by my side. Whenever I lashed out at the world, he was there to keep me relaxed.

Back then, Leo wasn't physically strong. He was skinny and smaller than most kids, but his courage was something incredible.

One day, while we were sitting in our secret hideout near an old tree hidden behind power vents, I was complaining about everything and nothing. Leo looked at me with that familiar mischievous spark in his eyes and said, "Why don't you use your middle name? Didn't you say your parents called you that?"

I hadn't thought of it for years.

Dorothy.

The name brought back memories of bedtime stories, warm hugs, and laughter carried by the wind. That night, I said it out loud: Dorothy. And something inside me changed.

From that day forward, I left Dawn D. Vogan behind. I became Dorothy.

Leo took the change in stride, just as he always did. He was my partner in crime. We would sneak into places we weren't allowed, dodge curfews, and even pick locks on city gates with our homemade tools. Whenever I went off the rails, Leo was always right behind me, sometimes shaking his head, but always sticking with me.

Then one day, I found some blueprints. My father had hidden them in one of his old books. It's a drawing of a tunnel that might be a route to the surface. I showed them to Leo like they were treasure.

His face lit up as he said with a smirk, "You'll never dig through all that."

"Watch me," I replied.

We spent hours sneaking into mines back then. We crawled through old shafts and found the best hiding spots. We thought we were tough.

Then one day, everything shook.

The ceiling cracked. Rocks started falling. And in a blink, Leo shoved me out of the way.

One second he was right beside me. Next, he was under a pile of stones.

His arm was crushed. There was blood. Dust everywhere. I screamed so loud, it echoed off the walls. I thought he was gone. It was one of the worst days of my life. And no matter what anyone says, part of me still thinks it was my fault.

Later, when the medics finished their work, I tried to thank him. He just shrugged and said, "That was my first real act of bravery, huh."

From that moment on, I promised myself that I would repay him. I left the Munchkin Home and took any job I could as a kid—delivery runs, junk hauling, and scrounging for spare parts. Every bit of money I earned went toward taking care of Leo, getting him a new arm, and giving him a real chance to recover.

Years later, Leo was no longer the kid I once knew. He had become a Vanguard and a hero in the city. He was strong, respected, with a reinforced heart and a bionic arm that could crush steel. But his heart never changed. I was still full of fire, and he was still as steady as stone. Somehow, we balanced each other perfectly.

* * *

"I see you got a new haircut; I like the blend," I complimented as we continued walking. "And how's your heart doing today?"

Leo glanced over with an easy smile as the low streetlamps cast a soft amber light on the damp cobblestones.

"First… thanks, I'm glad you noticed. I even made a few updates to my arm and heart. Long story short, I'm now about five percent stronger than I was last month. Pretty wild, right?"

I laughed. "Of course you are. You are always chasing numbers. Classic *Green Dog*."

He groaned, "Not again with that nickname." (It was what people called emerald soldiers, and I loved teasing him about it.)

"You wear the armor, you get the name," I teased.

Rolling his eyes, Leo began, "Speaking of careers, I really think you should—"

"No way," I interrupted, already knowing what he meant. "I'm not switching jobs. I like what I do, even if it gets messy."

"And dangerous. And reckless. And chaotic," he added, raising an eyebrow.

"Oh, so now you think you're better than me?" I shot back with a smirk.

"No, Dee," he said gently, "you know that's not what I mean. I just want what's best for you. Tobin seemed serious tonight, and I'm really worried."

I could feel my temper bubbling up inside me. "Look, I get it, Leo. I really do," I snapped, crossing my arms and standing firm. "But you have to trust me on this one. I have a well-thought-out plan this time. And as for Tobin, he's lucky he didn't get hit with that empty bottle tonight."

Leo exhaled deeply, running his hand through his freshly cut hair. "I know reaching the surface means everything to you, Dee. But remember, there's still a real life down here. You can't just—"

"Real life?" I interrupted. "So, what, that means I'm not living a real life now? You really have some nerve, Leo!"

I stormed ahead, my boots echoing louder on the cobblestones. The cool night air did little to ease my temper.

"Dee, wait!" Leo called, jogging to catch up. "Okay, that came out wrong. You know I worry, that's all."

For a few moments, we walked in silence.

Finally, I slowed down a bit.

"You're not wrong to worry, but I really do have a plan. I just can't tell you about it yet." I grabbed his arm. "You've got to trust me. When the time is right, you'll know. Just be ready."

Leo sighed, half hesitant and half smiling. "Oh, I'll be ready. You know I always have your back, even when you're the most stubborn person in the whole city."

When we got to my pod-home, we both stopped without saying anything. We just stood there in the street, staring up at the dome like we always did. The artificial night sky shimmered above us, trying to look like the stars we'd never actually seen.

If we squinted, the tiny lights almost looked real—like the stars were winking at us from It was our little ritual. A quiet moment before I went inside. A second to dream.

"Thanks for walking me home," I said, breaking the silence. "Even though I could've just used my glideboard."

"Yeah, but you needed to walk off those dumplings," he said with a smirk.

"Wow, so they promoted you to jerk as well, is see!" I snapped, laughing. "

He gasped and clutched his chest like I'd seriously hurt him. "Oh ouch! "And on that note, goodnight, citizen," he said dramatically, saluting as if to a high-ranking officer.

Leo turned and walked off. I stood there a little longer, watching the glow of his bionic arm fade under the street-lights.

That arm.

The same one he lost saving me. The same one that kept him moving forward.

He never asked me to make it up to him. And he didn't need to.

But I still planned to.

I had something in motion. A plan. One I believed in more than anything. And soon, it would all begin.

CHAPTER THREE

"After yesterday's chaos, I'm sure this will be another wonderful day to be at work, I guess…"

I hoped today would feel lighter than yesterday. Usually after a tough dig, my team cooled off with some food, drinks, and bad jokes. Even when we messed up, we laughed about it the next day.

But not this time.

The minute I stepped into the workroom, I sensed it.

Cold stares.

Quiet whispers.

I was used to getting side-eye in the city, sure, but not here. The mines were supposed to be different. This place was my second home.

"Look around you, Toppy. Does it seem better?"

The words of Jorral echoed in my head.

I looked up and caught Ted's eye. He worked with a different crew, but we often chatted.

"Hey, Te—" I started.

"I'm sorry. I've got somewhere to be," he said, already walking off.

That was just the start.

When I arrived at work with Onyx, things felt different. Max wasn't in today, so no one had to pretend. A few gave me lazy nods. Most didn't say anything. Jorral didn't even look at me; he acted like I wasn't there.

It was like I had a warning label taped to my back.

Today's job was simple: collect yesterday's haul and help clear the blocked tunnel path. I tried to focus and work like nothing was wrong, but every swing of my pickaxe felt heavy. I kept hoping someone would say something, anything. But the silence just grew. I couldn't take it anymore.

"I need to fix this."

So, I tried.

I walked around the site, made dumb jokes, checked in with people, and even offered to give up my bonus share.

Nothing.

They didn't want my apology. They just wanted space.

I turned to my usual tactic: contacting Uncle Neel. His office was a mess, littered with papers everywhere, receipts, crumpled notes, and empty snack wrappers. He didn't say sorry for the mess, just told me to sit.

I told him everything.

Uncle Neel just listened, arms crossed, nodding slow like he was chewing on every word.

"Listen, Dot," he said finally, "I've known you since you were in diapers. You've always been a firecracker. We had to keep you in sight every second, or you'd be halfway up a scaffold or halfway to trouble."

He gave a crooked smirk.

"Now you're older, sharp as ever. No one drills faster or knows the shaft routes like you. You've got your parents' talent, no doubt. But sometimes…" He leaned back in his chair, which let out a loud groan. "Sometimes you get so focused on the goal, you forget the people standing next to you."

That one stung more than I wanted to admit.

He rubbed the back of his neck. "Look, I know it hasn't been easy after… everything. I just hope I did right by Ethan and Aeryn. I miss 'em every day." His tone changed. "Maybe it's that spark within you, or maybe it's you striving to catch up with them in your own way. Regardless, ease up a little, will you?"

Then he added with a small chuckle, "But hey, I'm no philosopher. That's for the Ministry of Medicine to sort out."

I nodded, keeping my head low. He wasn't wrong.

"Take the rest of the day off," he said, waving dismissively. "No pay, and don't give me like that look. Everyone's on edge these days."

He sighed.

"With the accident, and now those weird new drill rigs the mayor brought in, people are scared, Dot. They just need time. Give 'em that."

I nodded, not because I felt better, but because he was right.

Little did I know, things would only get worse.

* * *

I rode my glideboard home slower than usual. The faces of my teammates kept flashing in my mind. They looked at me as if I were a walking curse, as if by being around me, disaster might strike again.

But it didn't stop me. Uncle Neel always told me, "Forge your own path. Even if they shut every door behind you." And I tried, every single day.

"Mom… Dad… At least I hope you're proud of who I'm become—."

"Wait, what's that smell?" I muttered, interrupting my own thoughts. I sniffed for clues.

"Burning rubber and steam."

Something was wrong. I slowed down, scanning the narrow street for smoke. Then I saw it.

"Could it be… no, it can't be," I thought, moving toward a crowd of onlookers.

"No. No, no, no—"

My board hit the ground before I did. I was airborne.

The alley curved as I raced ahead. When I turned the final corner, everything slowed down. Smoke filled the sky above, and a crowd was already gathered, whispering among each other.

And there it was… my home… on fire.

Flames licked the sides, and the roof was about to collapse. All I thought about were the things inside, like my parents' belongings. They were the last pieces I had of them.

"No…I…" Tears filled my eyes as I watched my past get swallowed by the flames.

"Don't just stand there! Call the Fire Taskforce!" I yelled, but the crowd barely moved.

Then, noticed it again… the cold stares… the disappointed looks… all my life it had happened and now it had come back to haunt me.

"What did she expect?"

"That Vogan family curse was bound to bring bad luck."

"I knew this would happen."

"I hope she leaves."

"It's better this way."

"Snap out of it, Dorothy!" I screamed inside, forcing myself back to the moment.

I didn't have time to wallow. I pulled my hair back, kissed my bracelet, and dashed toward the flames. Covering my mouth to keep out the smoke, I broke through a shattered window that connected to my room.

I scrambled through the thick smoke, lungs burning and tears streaming down my face. My hands were shaking as I grabbed whatever I could. My backpack slammed against my side as I moved through the room, shoving in anything that hadn't been eaten by the flames.

My personal belongings, tools, and my emergency pouch—whatever wasn't already gone, I took.

"BADOOM!"

My hallway ceiling collapsed behind me.

"Think, think, think," I whispered, crouching low under the smoke. My fingers brushed over burned metal and things that felt familiar. Not everything was saved, but I had to move.

The heat was intense, making it hard to breathe. I could see only dark and bright flashes of orange and black amidst my panic.

Then I saw a light.

I ran toward it with my heart pounding and dove out of the window, smoke chasing me.

When I landed outside, I didn't even feel the fall. All I could do was hug my backpack close and cough until I felt weak.

"CRASH!"

Another part of the ceiling fell behind me.

That was it. What remained of my home was gone.

"Cough, Cough"

I sat in the dirt, holding onto the few things I had saved. My clothes were burned and covered in ash. My whole body was trembling.

"Why… Why me?" I whispered. No answer came.

"Cough, Cough"

I looked over my shoulder and noticed a few neighbors had come forward with buckets of water with no urgency. It was as if they were caught between wanting to help and not wanting to get too close.

"It's always the same thing with these people. It's always the same thing!"

I wanted to scream at all of them so badly, but I was too tired and broken to shout.

Through the haze of my tears, I saw a figure at the edge of the crowd. Even from a distance, I recognized his slouchy walk and the way he held his shoulders.

Tobin… that coward, drunkard.

"Why is he here?"

We locked eyes. Without speaking, he mouthed three words that hurt more than anything today: ***"I… TOLD… YOU."***

"T… Tobin!" I called out, my voice trembling with anger. It was all I had left.

He disappeared into the crowd. I reached out my hand in my weakest attempt to stop.

"No… You—"

Then, Leo arrived at the scene. He rushed in and took charge before the flames caused more harm.

"Everyone, step back! Get behind the line!" he ordered.

He quickly grabbed me and held me tightly, but I couldn't bear it anymore.

"Leo… I'm so done, Leo," I whispered, full of pain. "I'm done with everything."

His face changed, and he knelt beside me. "Are you okay, Dee?" he asked.

"Please, Leo, come with me. Let's leave all of this behind."

He paused, surprised.

"Dee, what are you talking about? You need water. Medical help—"

"You promised!" I snapped, cutting him off. "You said that when I was ready, you'd go with me. Well, I'm ready now."

I watched his face fall as he stood frozen.

"I'm sorry, Dee. You're not in the right headspace. Not right now."

"No… not you too…" I replied. "You must be joking, right?"

He slowly shook his head.

"I have a duty to the city. I… I can't go with you."

That was it.

My heart didn't race or drop; it went numb.

"Protecting the city, huh… way to go, hero…"

Something inside me broke. This place had taken my home, my parents, and now… Leo.

He was no longer the boy from under the cavern tree, the scrawny kid chasing dreams with me. Now, he was a soldier, a citizen of a city that never really wanted me around. He stepped forward, reaching out.

"Dee, please…"

"Don't… call me that," I whispered.

"Dee, I jus—"

"Don't touch me!" I snapped, pulling away. I didn't want his hand, the crowd, or this city anymore.

"Stay in your pretty little bubble and be the hero you want," I cried out. "I'm not a hero. I'm just a villain to everyone. I'm done… I'm—"

My voice cracked before I finally whispered, "Goodbye, Leo."

I grabbed my bag and my board and stormed away from everyone.

* * *

I shot down the path on my board, wind tearing at my face as I put more and more distance between me and that broken district. My home, my past, everything behind me felt like it was turning to smoke. Part of me was furious. Part of me was... hurt.

The farther I got, the easier it was to breathe.

I didn't want to be tied to that place anymore. I never really belonged there. I was tired of tiptoeing around people who only saw my last name as a crime. Tired of trying to fit into a city that never gave me a real chance.

They saw a problem. Not a person.

"Fine. Then let them."

"It's time," I whispered to myself. "I'm getting out of here."

Even Leo with his words and promises. They were becoming empty to me. If he didn't want to come, that was his problem. I wasn't going to wait around anymore.

"Operation: Dawn Rising" was underway.

For years, I explored every corner of that mine while pretending to be another cog of the Emeraldia mining machine. Beneath the act, I was quietly plotting my escape. Every time they handed me a pickaxe, I was digging my tunnel, really studying Dad's old blueprints.

Every time they barked orders, I was paying attention to the secret tunnels and vents hidden beneath the military base. They thought they were keeping me in line, but I was already planning something bigger they'd never expect.

* * *

I went back to the worksite, even though I knew the Emerald Enforcers were nearby. I whispered a quiet promise and slipped through the gate. I kept my head down, careful not to get spotted by our security Otto and Tank. I'd studied their routine for weeks, waiting for the right moment.

"Okay, time this perfectly, Dorothy."

At the first chance, I ran as quickly as possible towards the mines.

Right near the mineshaft entrance, I dropped to one knee and moved the rock I'd hidden so many times before. Cool air rushed out and hit my face. The crawlspace was still there. It was tight, dark, and exactly how I left it. Inside, my supplies were untouched: water, tools, flashlight, rations. I checked them quickly.

I pulled my hair back into a tight braid, strapped my glideboard across my back, and flipped on my light. I inhaled deeply afterward.

Then, I stepped forward, into the dark.

"Here we go." I exhaled.

No turning back now.

* * *

For what felt like hours, I moved through darkness, cramped and tired. My night-visor gave off a weak beam, barely enough to light the way. The walls were cold and coated in dust, which irritated my nose even with my facemask on.

My boots echoed against the stone, and sweat clung to my back. I stopped from time to time to drink or rest, but my mind never slowed down. It kept circling back to everything that happened.

And even back to Leo.

57

Even if I were still mad at him, I couldn't block out the memories. I pictured his smirk after our sparring matches. He said I had real skill and something rare, praising me as a natural talent despite my obvious flaws. Those memories ran deep.

But things had changed, maybe for good.

That thought hurt, but I pushed it aside.

After a grueling four hours of crawling, running, and squeezing my way through tunnel openings, I reached what appeared to be a dead end. Every part of me ached, both physically and emotionally. According to my father's blueprints, I should be slightly above the outer vent panel.

With only a thin layer of rock sediment around me, I set down my pack, took out a handheld diamond-edge drill, and pressed it against the rock face.

"Ping! Ping! Ping!"

The quick sound echoed on the walls. Soon, a crisp metallic thud filled the space. After what felt like an eternity, I reached my goal. There was a cold, thin metal wall that separated the choking mines from the faint promise of freedom in the ventilation system. Each spark from the drill ripped through the barrier, forming the final opening I needed.

I stepped back, amazed at what I was seeing. "Wow… this is it. Dad's vent system."

The opening led into a huge tunnel. Way bigger than I'd pictured. I had imagined something tight, like a crawl space.

But this?

This was massive. Wide enough to fit a whole row of ore carriers. I stood there, stunned.

The walls buzzed with a soft vibration from the engines hidden deep inside. Cool air moved constantly, brushing past me. This was one of the four main vents that pulled in clean air for the city. From far away, I can see my ticket topside.

The transport lift.

I climbed onto my glideboard once again and pushed forward smoothly along the concrete tunnel floor. The air felt colder the farther I went, and vents above let out soft whooshes tugging at my hair. All the while, I was keeping my nerves calm.

* * *

"Thirty minutes in, just like I planned. Told you I had this, Leo." I whispered, almost smiling.

Big mistake.

I must've triggered something, because the ground shook. Green lights lit up behind me, and engines revved up. Then, tires screeched, getting closer.

I couldn't believe it.

"No. No, no—"

I didn't stop to think. I hit the throttle on my board and took off.

Then, a voice blasted from an overhead speaker, full of static.

"TRESPASSER. YOU ARE IN VIOLATION OF CODE 24-87. SURRENDER IMMEDIATELY OR FACE TERMINATION."

Termination... No detention or trial. Instant termination.

They weren't going to arrest me. They were going to erase me.

Yeah, that wasn't an option.

I slammed my foot down, flipped the booster switch, and felt the engine jump. The glideboard roared as it kicked into high gear. My only choice was forward. Faster. Outrun everything before they caught me.

Behind me, loud engines roared as more vehicles moved in.

Closer.

Faster.

Louder.

But I wasn't going to get caught. I couldn't.

Next, the blasters started firing.

I wasn't ready for the sharp hissing sound of gale blasters slicing through the air, with red streaks of light zipping by me. A few blasts hit the vent walls with a sickening crack, sending sparks everywhere. But one of them found its mark.

"Argh—!"

A sharp, burning pain cut through my upper arm. It was as if a hot knife had slashed through me. I felt the heat, the blood, and the rising panic.

But I didn't stop.

My vision blurred, but I held on tight to my board like my life depended on it. Because it did.

"I have to make it. I just have to," I whispered through clenched teeth.

I finally saw the transport lift door ahead. It was so close. In a few more seconds, I was going to jump in, slam it shut, and catch my breath. But the blaster fire kept coming. They wouldn't give up. Each shot, inches away, seared the floor, hit the walls, and eliminated any chance to slow down.

The roar of the engines grew louder.

In a risky move, I looked back.

Three enforcer vehicles, like low-hovering monsters with bright under lights and no mercy, were close behind. They were catching up fast. My glideboard was working at its limit, whining under the strain as the tires barely gripped the metal floor in the tunnel.

"Come on, come on!" I growled, leaning into the wind and forcing every bit of speed from the board. "Just a little more!"

But a shot hit the floor beside me, causing sparks to fly into my face. The explosion made the board wobble, and I nearly lost control.

"No!" I hissed, fighting to stay steady. My injured arm burned all the while. I was running on pure adrenaline and desperation.

"I can see it... the lift... but I'm not going to make it in time—"

"SKRRRRT! CRASH!"

Everything exploded behind me.

One enforcer vehicle slams into another.

They spun out, their engines screaming, scraping against the walls until both became mangled heaps.

"What the—?" I muttered.

Debris fell all around. I could hardly believe what I was seeing.

There was no time to think. "Thank goodness," I whispered, clutching my bracelet.

I slammed my hand on the button on the transport panel.

"BEEP—KSHHHHHHH—"

The door slowly started to open while gears clicked, and green lights flashed. My fingers trembled from blood loss.

Then, a dark shadow appeared from the wreckage. It limped through the smoke.

"No..."

I stepped back, eyes wide, while the door's warning beeps grew louder behind me. Through the haze, the shape became clear, and I knew.

"L-Leo?"

His voice cracked through the chaos over the comms.

"Cough, Cough,"

"WE NEED MEDICS AND BACK-UP DOWN HERE ASAP! WE HAVE AN ESCAPEE!"

I stopped breathing for a moment.

Everything else faded — the blasts, the engines, the smoke — until only he remained. Just us. His voice. The way he gazed.

We locked eyes, and in that moment, everything came flooding back.

The days at the orphanage. The nights chasing stars we couldn't even see. The near-death adventure and the quiet moments of laughter.

The bruises we took.

The shared dreams.

Tears flooded my eyes.

Tears flooded his eyes, too.

"GOODBYE."

He mouthed those words as if they broke him.

I couldn't answer. I just couldn't. The transport door shut with a heavy clang between us, and I slid against the wall, trembling. My arm throbbed with pain. My chest hurt even more.

I cried.

For everything I had left behind. For what I had just lost.

For Leo.

For us.

"I'm sorry, Leo," I whispered, pulling my pack close. "I have to... You know I have to."

I leaned back and stared up at the lift's ceiling while blinking away my tears.

"Mom, Dad... this is it... for better or worse. I'm going to finish what you started."

CHAPTER FOUR

*"*W*hat did you do, Dorothy?"*

That question stuck with me for as long as the transport rattled upward through the shaft. The metal walls closed in around me, and all the gears and pistons groaned under the strain. The air smelled of old oil and metal.

But I felt anxious.

This place… this lift, served cargo and soldiers, not a miner-turned-fugitive chasing the memories of her parents. The worst part? The noisy gears didn't bother me; the quiet from the absent pursuit did.

I sat with my knees pulled up, backpack stuffed with the last pieces of my life that hadn't gone up in smoke. The overhead lights buzzed, casting long shadows across the floor like quiet company.

My mind drifted to the people I was leaving behind.

Chef Lyman, with his terrible jokes and perfect dumplings—he always knew how to lift my mood. Whenever I had a bad day, he'd listen, never judging, only smiling and handing me extra sauce like it solved everything. Sometimes, it did.

Uncle Neel… he was the closest thing I had to family. He looked out for me, even when I made it hard. I left without saying goodbye. That hit harder than I expected.

"He was right," I whispered, blinking fast to fight the tears. "Sometimes I don't stop to think about how my choices affect people."

And then there was Leo.

That hurt the most.

The way he looked at me when I disappeared behind the transport door… I wasn't even sure what I was doing anymore.

"BZZZTT!"

A low alarm buzzed above me. We were almost there.

Suddenly, it stops.

"Is it stuck?" I blurted. "Are they calling it back down?" I stood up, my arms shaking.

The doors groaned open. Then—

"WOOOOOOSH!"

"Whoa… wait… a minute!" I braced myself.

A rush of cold air slammed into me. My hair whipped around, gear straps rattled, and for one heart-stopping second, I thought, *twister*. But it was only wind. Real, wild, open wind.

"…Okay…"

I took a deep breath. I kissed my bracelet for luck, like I always do. Then, I stepped forward. For the first time since I was six, my foot touched the topside.

It felt unreal.

"I really made it," I whispered. When those words came out, it hit me all at once.

"I'm outside! I'm really outside! YES! I'M REALLY OUT-SIDE!"

I spun around, laughing. I jumped, ran in circles, and danced like a little kid.

"Mom! Dad! I made it out. I'm free!" I shouted, my voice echoing across the open land.

And for the first time in my life, I meant it. Not trapped behind rules or rumors or fear. I looked up and nearly cried.

"This sky... is incredible."

I couldn't stop staring as a breeze brushed across my face. The sky burned gold and violet as the sun sank behind twisted shrubs and broken rocks on the horizon. The only sounds were the whisper of the wind and the occasional chirping of desert birds. I didn't know their species, but their songs filled me with joy.

"Windland. It's just like Mom described in her writings," I said with a smile. Another gust of wind kicked up sand, swirling it along the ground.

I dug into my pack and pulled out the map. It was crin-kled, and a bit torn, but still useful enough to give me an idea of where I was. See, Oz was divided into two huge continents. To the west was EvLand, home to all the ArcCities where the Ozians had always lived. But don't get me wrong... nature had a firm grip on these lands, not us.

We heard stories of wild twisters in EvLand that could tear the sky, deserts swallowing towns, and strange creatures roaming empty areas. Our bedtime stories weren't fairy tales but warnings.

In the heart of EvLand was the Windland Region, where Emeraldia stood. Cities such as Metallia and Titania were nearby, but they still felt very distant. That separation wasn't accidental; the Archons intended it that way. It made controlling everyone much easier.

But I wasn't focused on the west anymore.

My gaze drifted to the edges of the map, to the areas that the Archons never mentioned. Between the continents, small islands dotted the sea. Some were known, but many seemed imaginary, just tales from old miners. And then there was the land bridge — thin and fragile — the only link to the eastern continent that no one ever talked about.

"NoLand,"

"How come no one has ever explored or mapped this place?" I muttered to myself. A soft wind tugged at the map, bringing me back to the moment. I turned to shield my eyes from the sand and saw something incredible.

"Whoa," I gasped, my voice almost lost in the wind. "Even as a child, I don't remember this dome being this colossal."

Nothing prepared me for its massive size. It was overwhelming. Even when half-way buried beneath the surface, it was impossible to see over its curved top.

The sun's rays reflected off the iron dome, causing its cold metallic surface to shimmer. In the city, it was always advertised on Viztrons as a marvel of engineering, and I guess they were right. Layers of diamond-steel plates, tightly locked together, preventing even air from entering. There are no windows or doors, only walls.

Sometimes, the wind made a weird whistling sound as it passed over the top, like the dome was breathing. The giant beams at the base dug deep into the earth, holding it in place like they never planned to let it go.

The area around the dome appeared completely dead, with still air, no plants, and an unsettling silence, as if everything nearby had been drained of life. It was frightening to realize we had been trapped inside that enormous structure for so long. Still, I couldn't dwell on that now, not when I finally had an opportunity to move forward.

Every step I took away from that transport made me feel lighter. I smiled as the wind tugged at my braids.

"I wish you were here to see this, Leo."

A small gust pushed me forward, and I welcomed it with excitement. That was until the wind grew stronger.

And stronger.

And then faster.

And then violent.

It whipped against my body, making it hard to stand straight.

"A storm's coming… and the winds are picking up. This might be it," I gasped as I fumbled to open my gear bag. My hands shook as I pulled out the essentials: my visor, stormproof jacket, and knee guards—everything I got from that sketchy guy in District 7.

I quickly did everything, my fingers hurriedly working with the straps. I grabbed my storm line and hurried to the nearest boulder, partly buried in the sand. Heart racing, I secured the line tightly and double-checked the knot, just in case this was truly the big one.

And it was.

"This is…" I tried to say, but the words wouldn't come. I knew what it was. But seeing it with my own eyes?

It didn't feel real.

A twister. Massive. Wild. Coming straight towards me.

It rose from the horizon like a monster made of sky, tearing through the clouds as it spun toward me. The air screamed, the ground trembled, and the wind pulled at everything—my clothes, my breath, everything.

I grabbed my storm line and held on tight, pressing my body against a boulder. My hands were shaking, but I didn't let go. The sound was like a thousand ArcCity trains all at once.

"SNAP!"

My storm line broke.

"No, please!" I shouted.

I felt my body lifted enough to shoot terror straight into my soul. Everything spun. Sand stung my eyes, and debris whipped past my cheeks. I couldn't see and barely managed to think.

Then I saw was a flash of gold. A vision of Leo, Mom, and Dad. My time was coming to an end.

"I can't see... I…"

* * *

"…Wait!"

I yelled before I even realized I was awake. My heart was pounding. I opened my eyes and saw that I wasn't standing. I was flat on my back, staring at fabric.

"Huh…?" I groaned.

I checked my arms, legs, ribs. Everything hurt, but nothing was broken. I was sore, bruised, but still in one piece.

Slowly, I sat up. The dizziness hit me fast, like the ground wanted me to lie back down.

"This… this isn't the storm," I whispered.

Then it hit me… canvas walls, a tent roof, soft dirt under my palms.

I was in a tent.

"No… no, this isn't right," I muttered, dragging my fingers across the floor. "How did I get here? What happened?"

Light filtered through the seams, casting faint lines across the ground. I blinked, still caught between a dream and whatever this was.

"Is it… morning?"

I pushed myself up again and instantly regretted it.

"Ugh—!"

Pain shot through my arm like fire. I clutched it, wincing. "Ouch," I hissed through my teeth.

I looked down and saw thick bandages wrapped tight, dark red spots showing where I'd been hit. So… it wasn't a dream. That storm was real.

I tried to lie back down, but a pounding headache stopped me cold. I pressed a shaky hand to my forehead, trying to piece it all together. The storm, the dust, the roar—flashes of it crashed through my brain.

"I'm alive… but how?"

"How did I get in this tent?"

"Who patched me up? And why?"

None of it made sense. My thoughts were a mess; my body even worse.

Still, I forced myself to sit up and take in my surroundings. The tent was small but tidy. My gear was placed neatly beside me. An emerald lantern gave off a calm green light, and a map was spread out nearby.

But something didn't feel right.

Something about this setup. It was too careful and too quiet. It made the hair on my neck stand up.

I scanned the tent fast, my eyes jumping from corner to corner. Then I spotted a rolled-up map beside the lantern. I grabbed it and unrolled it carefully.

It wasn't just a travel map.

It was marked with lots of red "X" scratched across the land. Big ones. Circles, notes, routes. This wasn't rescue. This was surveillance. A plan.

"I'm not a guest," I whispered. "I'm a target."

I reached for my bag and found the only thing that gave me real comfort. My weapon of choice.

I called it my battle-wand.

The handle felt cold and solid in my hand. I built it myself for this exact situation. It looked rough, sure, but it worked. A reinforced electric mace, with an emerald core at the center. Illegal? Completely. But out here, legal didn't matter.

Survival did.

I'd spent months stacking up tokens, sneaking deals through the underground market. I only picked gear that was light, quiet, and durable for quick escapes... and possible conflicts .

My wand buzzed to life in my grip, its green sparks dancing across the rod and lighting the tent.

Then, I heard footsteps. Very close. Someone was right outside. Coming for me.

It could've been anyone: Enforcers, Topside Raiders, or thieves. I didn't know, and not knowing was scarier than anything.

I straightened up, pointed my wand at the tent entrance.

"If you come inside, you better be ready to lose your life!"

Then came a voice. Soft, calm, and definitely a girl.

"Relax. I'm not your enemy."

That only made me hold my wand tighter.

"Yeah?" I snapped. "How do I know you're not lying?"

My eyes stayed locked on the tent flap. I can feel sweat beginning to form on my forehead. I didn't care how calm she sounded. I'd been burned too many times to drop my guard now.

"Because I saw everything," she said. "I watched you step off the lift. I watched you face the storm. I found your body after it threw you like a rag doll. You should've died. But you didn't."

She paused. Then she began to giggle.

"You're either the bravest idiot I've ever seen… or just naiive."

I gave no response.

"Listen, I saved you. That's why you're breathing right now. Please. Just lower your weapon. I can see the sparks."

My grip didn't loosen. The wand hummed louder in my hand, and every nerve in my body was on high alert.

She stepped into the tent slowly and carefully, like someone who knew just how close they were to getting fried. But she didn't flinch.

"Hey," she said again. "I'm Kassi."

Her voice was calm, and unafraid.

I still didn't say anything. My wand stayed pointed, the tip sparking bright green. I studied her from head to toe. Worn boots. Dust-covered pants. A ripped sleeveless top, and a cloak tied at the waist. She looked like she knew how to survive.

But I wasn't lowering my guard.

"Kassi?" I finally said, squinting. "What kind of name is that?"

She shrugged, smirking just a little. "The kind that sticks."

I didn't smile back. Not yet.

CHAPTER FIVE

Kassi stood there with her hands on her hips and chin up. She was slightly shorter than I, but lean and toned. Her light brown skin had a warm glow in the sunlight, and her short silver hair was marked with red tattoos on the sides.

Her gray eyes were fierce, with a red slash running across them, like someone who'd been through stuff. Both of her ears were full of piercings that caught the light every time she moved. She wore ripped, weathered military pants, a sleeveless hoodie, and a neck guard.

Still, I wasn't about to trust her just because she fixed me up.

"You seem pretty young," I blurted, still keeping a firm grip on my battle wand. "Why were you watching me? Are you with someone? Part of a group?"

"I get it. I'd be suspicious too." She laughed casually, marking something on her map. "I'm eighteen. And yeah... I was spying. But I wasn't watching *you* specifically."

That wasn't very comforting.

"Okay," I said slowly, masking my nerves. "So, how does someone like you survive out here? With all these storms and endless deserts? Are you from Emeraldia too?"

"Someone like me? What do you mean... because I'm a girl? You know, girls from the ArcCities and the topside are two different species. We aren't delicate flowers."

"No, that's not... look, I just meant it's dangerous. Even for adults."

She laughed again. "Relax. I'm just kidding. I've been up here since I was a kid. And you? I didn't catch your name."

I paused, drooping my wand. "Dorothy. You can call me Dorothy."

"Nice to meet you, Dorothy. And no, I'm not from Emeraldia. I used to be a Titanian."

"Titania? Really? That's... far away."

She nodded. "Far enough. Same rules. Different people. ArcCities are really their own mini worlds."

"I know," I said. "The last time I met someone from another ArcCity was when I was little... back in Galesville. People from everywhere gathered there."

Kassi stopped. "Galesville?"

"Yeah, I lived there… well until... you know…"

Kassi shook her head in disbelief. "Everyone knows about Galesville out here. What happened there is the stuff of legend. In Titania, it served as a warning to anyone trying to escape to the topside. The Green-Eyed Twister? They say it was the strongest twister ever. People still whisper about it."

I looked away. "I know."

"How did you survive that?"

"My parents sent me away just before it happened."

Kassi began to study me. "Hmm… You're something rare, Dorothy of Galesville."

We both jumped when the tent flapped harder in the rising wind. Kassi looked at her watch, and her expression changed as she began to pack up her things.

"Listen," she said, tightening the straps on her bag, "wherever you're headed, good luck finding it. I think it's best if we go our own ways now since we both have things to do."

Then I noticed a gale blaster tucked at her side. I hesitated for a moment, gathered my courage, and asked.

"Are you... are you a rebel... or... some kind of criminal?"

She froze.

Her back was turned, and she didn't look at me right away. When she finally did, her eyes were serious again.

"Dorothy, the moment you leave an ArcCity without permission is the moment you become a criminal."

I didn't argue. I couldn't.

She zipped up her pack and slung it over her shoulder. "Now that we're both criminals, what's your big plan out here?"

"I'm searching for... the truth..."

"Truth, huh? Truth about what?" she asked while rolling up her map.

I hesitated. "The... twisters."

She didn't say anything right away. Just turned her head real slow, looking at me. Then, just when I thought maybe she was going to take me seriously, she threw her head back and laughed. Hard. Like I'd just told her the dumbest joke in the world.

"Yeah, laugh. But the fact that you're up here," I pointed out. "That tells me you already know something's off. You know the Archons aren't giving us the whole story about the weather, the topside... maybe even the spire."

"Wait, wait, wait...," she interrupted. "Say that again."

"I said, the Archons aren't telling us everything..."

"No, not that," she waved it off, her eyes peering into mine. "You said... *spire?*"

I nodded. "Uh... Yeah. My parents heard rumors about an ancient spire. They thought this thing had something to do with the changes in the atmosphere. It's just their theory."

I could tell she thought it sounded crazy. I packed up my gear slowly, still feeling tired. "Thanks for saving me," I said sincerely. "If we ever meet again, I will repay the favor."

"Wait!" she blurted as I was about to leave the tent. "Your parents… what were their names?"

"Dr. Ethan and Aeryn Vogan. They were scientists."

Kassi's face changed as if I had hit a nerve. She rushed forward and hugged me very tight.

"Ouch!" I cried, pulling away.

She laughed awkwardly, letting go. "Sorry, sorry! It's just… your parents? They're legends up here, Dorothy… legends!"

I gave her a blank stare. "Legends? Let me guess, you're trying to make fun of me again?"

"Listen! I don't have time to explain now, but you have to come with me," she said, quickly grabbing her stuff.

"Wait, what? Where are we going?"

"You asked earlier if I was a rebel," she called out. "Well… it's complicated. But you'll see. And there's something you need to have. Trust me."

I still wasn't so sure about trusting anyone up here.

Not yet.

But the urgency in her voice made me follow her. We took down the tent, packed it into an old cart, and dragged it to where she kept her ride. A dusty tarp thrown over her hover-cycle.

"Whoa, you serious? This is a Sand-Strider, right?" I asked.

"Yeah, she's not pretty, but she runs well," Kassi grinned. "Climb on. And put your mask on. We're almost out of calm weather."

"You don't have to tell me twice," I mumbled as I put on my facemask.

The engine roared awake as we started moving. I climbed onto the back, gripped the sides tightly, and shouted over the engine, "Where are we even going?"

"Monsoon Hive!" Kassi shouted back. "That's the home base for my crew!"

"You have a crew?" I yelled.

She just laughed again, and we sped off across the desert.

* * *

"Watch out!" I yelled, holding on tight as the Sand Strider swerved, almost losing its balance in the strong wind.

Kassi laughed wildly, grabbing the handlebars as everything around us blurred. The strider roared and shook so much I could feel it in my teeth. It wasn't a smooth glideboard ride at all. This was pure speed and adrenaline.

Sand hit my visor in heavy waves, each grain hitting like a slap. I swiftly ducked my head and squinted through the fleeting gusts. The sky, ground, and mountains appeared distorted under a greenish hue. Faraway mountains resembled enormous, jagged teeth sticking out into the clouds. Nearby, a storm system sparked with lightning, almost challenging us to approach.

I grabbed onto Kassi so hard my hands went numb.

But I didn't care.

I wasn't about to let go. We zoomed past sharp bushes and jumped over cracked spots in the desert that looked like they might cave in. Here and there, I caught glimpses of old scraps half-buried in the sand like old pipes, broken windmills, and rusted pieces of machines.

The wind kept trying to knock us over with the cart in tow, but Kassi was amazing. She twisted and turned, dodging rocks like she'd been riding this Sand Strider forever. Even though I was scared out of my mind, I held on tight, determined not to fall.

But secretly? This was the thrill of a lifetime.

After nearly an hour of riding, we burst through the last line of mountains, the engine struggling but still running. The wind suddenly stopped, leaving a loud silence behind.

I let go of Kassi and lifted my visor. My whole body buzzed from the ride, and sand clung to every bit of my clothes and skin.

As the dust settled, I saw a scene unlike anything I had seen before.

"Here we are, Dorothy, Monsoon Hive!"

RODNEY BLANC

CHAPTER SIX

-LEO-

That was enough instruction for today. I locked eyes with the trainees. "You're tired. You're sore. You're thinking too much and seeing too little. That's normal. Today was about failure. Tomorrow's about learning from it."

Two of them started snickering. Figured I was the joke, and I knew why. We all knew. I walked toward them without saying much at first.

"Out in this city, you don't get a do-over. One breath too early. One second too late. One second of doubt, and someone dies."

I stopped right in front of them.

"Might be you. Might be your partner. Might be someone who never saw it coming."

They got quiet real fast.

"What you're learning isn't just how to shoot. It's how to wait. How to listen to your gut when the wind shifts. How to disappear in a world that wants you dead."

I looked around at all of them.

"So go rest. Stretch. Clean your gear. Clear your head. Because tomorrow, I stop holding your hand. Tomorrow, I stop reminding you to breathe. Dismissed."

They filed out without a word. I stayed behind.

The training bay was empty. It was just me and the virtual obstacles course. I figured I'd run a few drills or something to clear my head. Training always helped.

Still, the few words that always haunted me came back.

"You still don't have the heart."

I never forgot that. Guess it stuck because some part of me believed it. I always felt like something was missing. Like I was built wrong.

From the minute I opened my eyes, pain was already there. I was born with a weak heart. Fragile. Defective. Didn't take long for my parents to make their choice. They left me in hospital care and moved on. Probably figured I wouldn't make it anyway.

They weren't wrong to bet against me.

I never knew them. Not enough to matter. They're just strangers now. Could've passed them on the street and never known. The name Logan Ironheart? That came from a nurse. Maybe it was meant as a joke. Maybe she thought the name would keep me alive. Either way, it stuck.

I shook it off and stood up.

"Alright. Let's do this."

"BUZZZZZ!"

The timer kicked on and I strapped my VR Visor on. First round, Pit Crawl.

I dropped to the ground, belly in the dirt. Gale rifle in hand. Scope already fogging just enough to get under my skin.

Five seconds in, and an emergency siren screamed. I was already moving before the echo faded. Low crawl under steel mesh, barbed wire dragging shadows across my back. Barrel tight.

Muzzle low. Chin in the gravel.

Still, the memories kept coming.

I wasn't the only one who got left behind by my parents. In the ArcCities, kids like me were everywhere. *Waiflings*, they called us. Tossed aside, forgotten. The upper families liked to pretend their lives were clean and polished, but they were the worst offenders. In the upper districts, family quotas meant they could only keep so many kids. The rest? They vanished. Quietly.

Dee's father… Dr. Vogan… he knew what that felt like. She told me once that he grew up just like we did. A waifling, shuffled between work camps and holding centers where no one cared if you ate or slept or stayed alive. He wanted something better for the rest of us. So he built it.

The Munchkin Children's Home.

First place of its kind in Emeraldia. Wasn't pretty. Wasn't high-tech. But it was safe. He named it after some old fable about the Munchkin Zolytes—small, brave people who looked out for each other. That always stuck with me.

"BUZZZZZ!"

The alarm pulled me out of my thoughts. Time for the next round.

Pop-Up Range.

"Alright. First target. Far right tower. Six hundred meters. Wind dragging left."

I adjusted, fired once, and the target dropped. Clean.

I didn't stop to admire it. I couldn't. My mind went back to the home.

By the time I got there, the city had taken control of it. The warmth was gone. Headmistress Gobblewortz ran it like a machine. Kids were expected to find jobs even if they couldn't spell their own names. No excuses. No compassion. Just rules.

"BUZZZZZ!"

Next up—Wall Scale. It was mixed reality obstacle round.

It was twenty feet high with climbing handholds spread apart. I slung my rifle and climbed fast. At the top was a wind tunnel platform. It was a standing shot this time. One swinging target at four hundred yards. Miss it, and you drop back down to the start.

I didn't miss.

But don't mistake that for strength.

Truth is, I wasn't built for this. My body couldn't keep up. Even the smallest fall could knock the wind out of me. And in the Southern district, weakness meant you didn't matter. You learned to hide it, or you didn't last.

And then I met her.

Dorothy.

But I called her Dee.

She didn't belong anywhere either. Maybe even less than I did. People avoided her for reasons that never made sense. Too curious. Too different. Too much. But no matter how hard they pushed, she didn't crack. Or at least, she never let anyone see it.

I still remember the day I told her she should start using Dorothy. She rolled her eyes like it was nothing. She said it didn't matter. But she kept the name.

That's the thing about Dee. she never showed how much things meant to her, but you knew they did.

"BUZZZZZ!"

Next up was the urban crawl.

Old rooms. Tight hallways. The whole place was built to feel like a war zone. Broken furniture scattered everywhere. Lights blinking just enough to mess with your depth. Stairwells rusted over and humming with that low electric buzz that never stops. I had to find the enemy

There was no room for mistakes. I cleared every corner before letting my muzzle lead. Never the other way around.

"Movement on the left. Pop-up silhouette. Two shots. Center mass, then head."

I kept moving to the next corner without wavering. But even with my body in motion, my head wasn't quiet. I still remember the day Gobblewortz pulled me aside after patching my bloodied knee from a fall. She looked straight at me and said the one thing I'd been afraid to hear my whole life.

"The world is too dangerous for someone as weak as you. You could collapse at any moment. You should be scared."

And she was right. I was scared.

After that, I cut back on playing, running, pushing myself, and taking big risks. Whenever Dee came up with one of her wild plans, I'd make excuses. She's complained, knowing I was being overly cautious. But deep down, she understood I was just scared, and it became clear on one dreaded day in the mines.

On that day, we quietly entered one of the chambers as we often did to play with the drill equipment. This time, we ignored the hazard signs above and turned on the drill, pretending to haul something on the wall. It was all fun until the ceiling came loose and showered large rocks and dust. I quickly pushed Dee out of the way and felt a sharp pain in my chest and arm before everything went dark.

When I woke up on that care bed, everything hurt. What hit harder than the pain was the silence where my arm used to be.

"BUZZZZZ!"

Back to it. No time to spiral.

Next round. Gravel hill. A mixed reality course.

It was steep, loose, and torture on your ankles. The goal was to use the uphill terrain while avoiding blasts.

Halfway up— ***"BANG!"***

A flashbang exploded, white light and sound crashing over me. I ducked fast behind a steel drum, my ears ringing and chest heaving. Three quick breaths, then I threw myself forward, rolling into the next spot. My metal arm scraped against the ground, but I kept moving.

For months after the accident, it was Dee who took care of me.

The orphanage didn't spare a single resource. Not one bandage. Not one pill. So, she found a way.

To this day, I still don't know how she got the gold tokens for my first cyber-arm. I never asked. Maybe I didn't want to know.

She never complained. Not once. Even when she barely had enough for herself, she made sure I had what I needed.

And I hated it.

Not her, being weak. Having to depending on someone else just to get through the day. Every little thing felt like a reminder of what I couldn't do. What I'd lost.

I was angry.

At the world. At my body. At myself.

But then I'd catch her smiling.

After everything she'd been through, after all the pain she buried, she still found a way to smile like there was something left to believe in. I never understood how.

Still don't.

But it pushed me.

I figured if she could carry all that and still keep going… then so could I.

And I did.

I pushed myself harder than my body thought possible. Every day, I trained. Whenever I felt my limits closing in, I pushed past them. Then I found the Arc Forces.

They were supposed to be the best, the strongest, the only defense between the ArcCities and the chaos waiting outside. The forces were broken into 3 branches.

First, there were the Enforcers, who kept each district safe; second, the Vanguards, who protected the whole city from big dangers; the third branch is the Elite Task Force, who handled secrets no one was supposed to know about.

There was a fourth branch, the Sentinels, a selection of elites who only answered to the Archons. No one discussed them, but everyone knew they existed.

I joined the Vanguards because they were the toughest. It was where I could prove myself and matter. I won't lie, the training lived up to the hype, but I pushed through. I also saved enough money for a new bionic heart, one that wouldn't fail me.

Later in my career, I led the operation that stopped a plot against the mayor. For the first time, the city saw me. People said my name like it meant something. They called me a hero. I made lieutenant in the Emeraldia Vanguards—something Ms. Gobblewortz always said I'd never survive long enough to reach.

And yet... I knew that in Dee's eyes at this very moment, I was a coward.

I'll never forget her face after the fire, when I told her I wouldn't join. It wasn't anger. It was a quiet kind of disappointment.

I'd seen it before.

We were kids, racing down that hill on our glide-boards. Halfway down, I froze. Couldn't do it. We were disqualified, and the other kids laughed. Dee didn't say anything mean. She just patted me on the back and said it was okay. But her eyes told the truth.

I let her down then, and I let her down now.

So, when I saw her in that tunnel, I knew exactly what they'd do if they caught her.

And I couldn't let that happen.

But the moment that stays with me wasn't when I cleared the way. It was right at the end.

Right before the transport doors closed, she looked at me.

And for the first time, I saw it.

Not her usual fire. Not the push-back or the confident edge she always carried. Just fear. Real fear. And something else: sadness and loneliness.

There was no sound. No words. Just a look that hit harder than anything I'd ever heard.

"Don't leave me alone."

That's what it felt like.

But I did.

I stood there. Frozen. I could've run after her. Could've said something. Anything. I should've let the whole mission fall apart just to let her know she wasn't alone.

But I didn't.

I froze.

Same as always.

"BUZZZZZ! BUZZZZZ! BUZZZZZ!"

That was it.

Timer hit zero.

I failed the course. Too slow. Too distracted.

Didn't matter how many times I'd run it. My head wasn't in it.

All I could think about was her.

Was she safe? Was she even alive?

We both knew the surface wasn't kind. The wind alone could tear a person apart. Add the scavengers, wanted criminals... the Sentinels.

Even for someone like Dee, it was brutal.

And yeah, I knew she was strong.

But that didn't stop the worry.

It never has.

But I had picked duty over friendship. Safety over uncertainty. And it left me with nothing.

"Why didn't I do more?" I muttered, dropping my VR visor to the floor as if the weight of it all had finally hit. "Was it because I finally had authority? Recognition? A place where I actually mattered?"

"I wanted this… didn't I?"

Then why did it feel so wrong?

The past few days at the base had felt like being trapped underwater. No air, no direction. Just pressure. Mayor Gulch's voice still echoed in my head from the reprimand. My unit failed.

I failed.

Everywhere I walked, I felt eyes on me. Nobody said it out loud, but I could feel it in their silence. Filing the incident report was no easy task as well as each word a reminder. Being linked with topside criminals was serious.

Dee's escape quietly shook the city, especially in the Battery District, where desperation was common. But none of that mattered as much as Dee did.

I needed to get out.

I stored my rifle and left the training bay. I didn't have a destination, so I just started walking.

Office corridors stretched out in every direction, all of them the same: cold floors, solid green wall panels, door after door stamped with codes I didn't bother to read.

I wasn't looking for anything. I was just moving, letting my legs do the steering.

Eventually, I ended up at the old lounge. Most people didn't use it anymore. It was half storage now. Boxes. Spare gear. Dust in the corners.

But for me, it had always been a place to disappear for a bit. Not to rest. Just to be somewhere quiet. Somewhere I didn't have to keep my guard up.

That was enough.

Only this time… something felt off.

At the far end of the corridor, one door was slightly ajar. That alone was strange. No one held meetings down here. The official briefings were always on the upper levels. But inside, I heard voices. Quiet, serious.

I slowed, instinct taking over. Something about it didn't sit right.

And against my better judgment... I listened.

"I shouldn't be doing this."

But after everything that had happened, I needed to know what was going on.

I caught pieces of their conversation, muffled but clear enough to understand some words. Then one voice stood out.

"Commander Briggs? Is that you? Why are you here?"

He was my commanding officer.

"What is he involved in? Is this a plot or something?"

I listened a little longer while watching the area.

Their voices… these were our high-ranking officers on duty. I secretly kept listening, hoping they weren't talking about the incident.

Highest-Ranking Officer: *"Let's keep this short. We have other things to deal with, but we need to address the matter at hand quickly. We all know things have been tense since that escape incident with the young mining engineer, Dawn Vogan, or Dorothy as they call her."*

High-Ranking Officer #1: *"I'm not surprised. Reports show she's the daughter of the former rebels who caused trouble that time in Galesville."*

High-Ranking Officer #2: *"Very troublesome family. But she's gone now. We don't need to capture her. She won't last long on the surface. But just in case, we'll make sure she gets on the OWL per the Archons' demand."*

Highest-Ranking Officer: *"Now, what do we do about the lower districts? They might see this as an opportunity to find her route and escape too. Captain Briggs?"*

Commander Briggs: *"We've already secured her escape tunnel. It seems to be something she's planned for some time. It's really incredible that she was able to dig such a tunnel. We are still trying to figure out how she was able to find the city's vent tunnel. Could she have been aided?"*

High-Ranking Officer #2: *"We've also been working on plans to monitor the lower districts. We need to select our best men and have them blend in with the people in the district to gather information on possible dissent."*

Highest-Ranking Officer: *"Fine. Choose your men and have them connect with influential people in the district."*

Commander Briggs: *"On another note, preparations have been made for the topside to secure our radars. Our ETF (Elite Task Force) team is almost assembled, but we will need to train them for the tough conditions. By the time we are done, our mapping systems will rival even those of Metallia."*

Highest-Ranking Officer: *"Despite our progress, we still have limited information about our enemies topside. That pesky Mirage. Between the twisters and the rebels destroying our radars, we need to act fast. Not to mention, our informants are getting expensive and reckless. Make sure they're trained quickly."*

As soon as the meeting ended, I slipped out, a normal pace, making no sudden moves. Just another soldier heading back to work. Nothing that would make anyone look twice. By the time I got to my office, I was calm, but I couldn't stop thinking about what had happened.

I closed the door behind me and dropped into my chair, tapping my fingers against the desk. Over and over.

"The mission. A new team for special operations above ground."

We all knew what that meant. Dangerous territory with enough risk to keep most soldiers underground. The kind that made people vanish. I'm sure most wouldn't dare to volunteer.

But if Dee was up there…

"I'd face all of it. Every single risk."

That thought hit me harder than I had expected. I sat back, staring at the ceiling.

If I wanted to find her, there was only one way.

I needed to join the team. No doubts. No fear. I had to get up there.

"Yeah, I'll find a way to join this mission. Hang in there, Dee. I'm coming for you."

94

CHAPTER SEVEN

"Here we are, Dorothy, Monsoon Hive!"

I was shocked. I imagined a large village like Galesville, but it was a fortified cave in the hillside. Desert vines and ferns hung over the entrance like a curtain. The weathered steel beams and rusty supports framing the arch told me its past use.

"So, is this Monsoon Hive… where the rebels live?"

"Yes," Kassi replied calmly. "It's the home of the Monsoon Fighters."

I nodded and looked around again. "I can tell this used to be a mining site," I said, running my fingers over the rusty metal beams.

Kassi smirked. "Nice eye. It was turned into a military outpost during the Second Great Oz War almost a century ago. But enough about history, let's go inside. There's a lot to explain."

As we moved, I noticed something else. "Wait, a minute… Is that a shield generator?" I asked, pointing at the gentle shimmer of energy around the entrance. "How did you get ArcCity to sell one of those?"

"We didn't," Kassi replied with a shrug.

I blinked, surprised by how casually she said it. "Oh… right. Of course, rebels." I mumbled while scratching my head.

Kassi chuckled at my reaction.

"Hey, Kassi, what if… what if the rebels don't trust me?"

She stopped just before the entrance and turned to face me. "Dorothy, trust isn't given here, it's earned… But you're with me, so you're fine! You'll have a chance to prove yourself."

I nodded, hoping she was right.

Outside, fighter soldiers guarded the entrance. They looked about Kassi's age. But their tough, worn protective jackets and gale rifles showed that they were always ready for anything. Their full-face masks and goggles protected them from harsh weather. They quickly greeted us with a salute.

"At ease, fellas. This is Dorothy. She's an ally and a friend to our cause," Kassi said.

"Copy that, Commander Mirage, we will inform the others," one of the rebel soldiers responded.

"Wait, what?... Mirage?"

We walked past fortified iron walls when I noticed Desert-pod vehicles too. Leo was crazy about these things. He had spent countless hours telling me about the latest military tech, like better weapons, faster engines, or new targeting systems. He knew every detail and made sure I did too. It was one of those habits that both annoyed and amused me.

Seeing the Desert-pods now, I could almost hear his voice listing off specs and improvements. I looked up, and I spotted more soldiers nearby, watching me carefully.

"Don't worry, they're just doing their job," Kassi confirmed. "We're heading to the entrance over there."

"Okay... *Commander Mirage*," I joked.

"Yeah, about that," Kassi scratched her head.

* * *

"The inside of this fortress is something else," I marveled.

There was so much going on. It was a maze of tunnels lit by old electric lanterns, with wires and machinery running all over the base. Most of the walls were covered in faded posters and the Monsoon insignia. Inside, soldiers saluted Kassi while moving with purpose.

Kassi turned to me, holding my shoulder. "Think of this as a shelter for those who refuse to obey those rotten Archons. Like Galesville once was. We've spent years building this place. We have many smaller sites, but this is our headquarters."

"And obviously, you're the leader of the whole operation?"

"Right. I'm Commander Mirage of the Monsoon Fighters," she answered. "Mirage is just a codename."

"Why didn't you tell me before?"

"It wasn't important at the time," she said.

"Well, I'm pleased to meet you formally, Commander—"

"No, just call me Kassi," she cut in. "Sometimes I like to feel normal, you know."

"Hmm… okay," I said, caught off guard.

"That was... different."

"Uh, let's go this way," she mumbled, clearly trying to change the subject.

We moved through the main corridor. The armory was the first stop. There were rows of clean, high-powered weapons lining the walls like they meant business. Next were the barracks. Nothing fancy, but a solid place to rest.

The mess hall surprised me the most. People were actually laughing, playing cards, joking around. It seemed to balance the tension around the base.

The further we descended, the more I was impressed. The communication room was lively, filled with activity and calls from other outposts checking in and strategizing.

Everywhere we turned, soldiers were moving, working, talking. And they all had a story. Fighters, survivors, wanderers… each of them had faced the storms and made it out. Now they were here, building something real. Something that felt… hopeful.

Just like I wanted.

"Here in this room, we plan and work together for our cause," Kassi continued.

Next, we went into a war room full of maps and plans. The mood made it clear they were getting ready for their next fight against their enemy.

"I wonder. Are they fighting soldiers that were sent by the Archons? Which military branch?"

"And here we are!" Kassi blurted, interrupting my thoughts.

It was Kassi's private room. It was a small space, not much bigger than a simple pod-room. The walls were lined with old mining planks holding maps, books, and battle plans. In the middle of the room, a strong war table was crowded with scattered papers filled with carefully drawn plans.

Weapons hung above a tidy bed, and next to the desk sat an iron chest with a heavy lock. The room, lit by one lantern, felt very much like the room of a strategist. Kassi invited me to sit and relax while she put away her equipment.

"So now it's my turn to understand. When you found me, you were scouting near one of Emeraldia's surface ports. And you're part of a fighter group where everyone listens to you because you're the commander, right? Am I missing anything?" I asked.

"Just that I'm really good on a sand-strider," Kassi laughed.

"This is serious. How did you manage all this?"

"Dorothy, you've heard their stories. Every one of my soldiers are young, but we've lost a lot... families, homes, and our old lives. I'm not sure what they told you in Emeraldia, but it's been like a war zone here for a long time."

"Warzone? … I mean, I knew things were bad up here, but only because of the storms. I didn't think there was any war," I replied.

I paused, observing the marked maps around the room. "How do you fight when twisters and mega-storms tear everything apart?"

"We've learned to adapt." She answered, leaning back in her old, squeaky chair. "Fighting in chaos is what we do best. That's why we're called the Monsoon Fighters."

Then she shot me a look. "Honestly, I'm surprised you know so little about it."

"How could I know? I was just a kid when I lived up here. In Emeraldia, they never told us about any of this. They just said the twisters were dangerous and that the Archons kept us safe by keeping us away from the surface."

"That sounds about right." Kassi's voice changed as she leaned forward with her elbows on the desk. "They want people to see them as heroes, but the truth is much darker."

She reached over to a cooler and handed me an Aquacapsule to drink. The cold bottle clinked in my hand as her tone grew sharper.

"The Archons don't just spread lies. Sometimes, they send Sentinels.

"Wow, I always figured they those Sentinels were more than just Archon's personal guards. I overheard my parents mention them once."

"You don't even know half of it." Kassi added, her face creasing to a more serious look. "It's worse now. The Archons no longer take prisoners. They burn refugee camps down, killing innocent people who just want to live free from their control. These people have nothing—no resources, no protection, and still, they fight to survive."

She took a breath. "We help who we can, when we can. Sometimes that means smuggling food into blockaded refugee camps. Other times, it means sabotaging a supply run or intercepting satellite comms. Every little thing chips away at their control."

I sat there stunned. "This is all so much. But how can you guys actually stand against them when they have numbers, technology, and power. How do you even go the war against that?"

She nodded toward the map pinned on the nearby wall, marked with worn edges and countless hand-drawn routes. "We know these lands like they know their fancy boardrooms. Sand paths, broken rails, old storm channels—things they forgot or never learned. That's our edge. We know where to hide, where to strike, and how to vanish when we need to."

She then gives a smile. "Not to mention, control is expensive. And the Archons are bleeding resources trying to tighten their grip. Every surface radar, every outpost they build topside, costs them more than they want to admit. That's why they keep pushing propaganda inside so no one questions where all that power is really going."

I looked down at the map, noticing how closely it matched the one I saw back in Kassi's tent. My voice came out quiet but certain. "I think I'm starting to get it."

"Are you?" she asked, softer this time, her tone carrying weight. "Dorothy, how much do you *really* know about your parents?"

I blinked, caught off guard. The question stung a little.

"Seriously? I've told you everything I know. They were scientists who were part of the Zephyrs. They were trying to understand the storms, trying to help—"

Kassi shook her head and cut me off. "No. Not the public version. I'm talking about the truth. The *real* story."

I blinked at her, confused. "What are you even talking about?"

Before I could say anything, Kassi stood up and crossed the room. She opened a small, dust-covered safe in the corner and pulled out a metal capsule. She set it down in front of me with care.

"COUGH, COUGH."

I waved the dust away, coughing. "What is this?"

"Something that belonged to someone you know," Kassi she answered in a more serious tone.

I hesitated. *"What could this be…?"*

I opened the box slowly.

"Oh… my stars."

Inside were a worn notebook, some folded papers, and an old photo.

My knees buckled. I sank to the floor with my eyes locked on the picture. A younger me standing between Mom and Dad. The edges were faded, but the moment was clear. Tears blurred my eyes.

"Mom… Dad…" I whispered. "I've never seen this before."

I ran my fingers over their faces. Dad looked proud. Mom had a gentle warmth in her eyes. I gripped the photo as if it would vanish if I let go.

"How? How did you get this?" I asked, wiping my tears.

Kassi, who hadn't been quiet up to this point, seemed almost hesitant to speak.

She sighed. "Your parents gave it to my brother," she said. "He was just a kid back then... but he was their youngest soldier. They trusted him to protect it."

"Soldier?... Kassi, that doesn't make sense." I shook my head. "My parents weren't soldiers. They were scientists. They led the Zephyrs; it was a research group. They just studied storms."

Kassi looked me dead in the eye. "Dorothy... no. That's only part of it."

She stepped closer. "The Zephyrs weren't just a research team. Yeah, by day they studied the storms. But by night? They fought back. Your parents didn't just observe the twisters; they used them."

I blinked, trying to keep up. "Used them?"

"Your parents started the first true rebellion against the Archons," Kassi said, her hands clutching my shoulders. "The original rebel army."

I froze. "What...?"

"They built gadgets that ran on storm energy. Wind-powered weapons, portable AGIS shields... stuff that shouldn't even exist. They found ways to survive and fight in the worst conditions. And they trained others to do it too."

Kassi picked up the notebook again, flipping it open to a diagram. "They were the first Gale-runners, Dorothy. Your parents didn't just want to survive topside. They wanted to teach the world how to live free again."

My heart thumped so loud, I barely heard the rest. I quickly sat down in a chair.

"Okay… whoa." I took a shaky breath. "This is a lot. Are you saying my parents… lied to me?"

I looked down at the photo again, gripping it tighter. *"Mom and Dad… rebels? Fighting?"*

Kassi stepped closer, shaking her head gently. "No. I don't think they lied. I think you were just too young. They probably wanted to protect you.... Just like my brother did with me."

"So... your brother... what was his name?" I asked, noticing her sad expression.

"Fynn," she said, glancing toward the wall.

She walked over to the faded photo framed in rusted metal. Her fingers brushed the edge of the with care.

"For as long as I can remember, all I ever did was try to survive. Fynn and I were always running. See, there were these shadowy bounty hunters… they were creepy, fast, far from normal. They may have been cyborgs. They chased us for years."

Her voice dropped lower.

"They haunted my dreams when I was little. After we escaped Titania, we ended up in a small refuge village with our Uncle Ciro. He was the only family we had left."

I glanced at Kassi, then lowered my voice. "What about your other family? I mean… your mom and dad?"

She didn't answer right away. Just stared ahead, like she was filtering through pieces in her head.

"We never met our father," she said finally. "Fynn knew more. He never liked talking about him, though. He would tell me the guy wasn't worth remembering."

"And your mom?"

A pause.

"I barely remember her. Just flashes. A warm voice. Holding my hand once, I think." She tugged at the chain around her neck and showed me a small charm. "This is the only thing I have from her. It has my name on it."

"*Kassi O*," I read aloud, then smirked. "So, you do have a last name."

"Not really. I don't know what the '*O*' is for," she answered with a tiny laugh. "It's just what's on the charm. My brother always said we needed to keep our full names hidden… in case bounty hunters tried to find us. After our mom was killed by those hunters, Uncle Ciro took us in. Told us that she was on the OWL."

I knew what that meant. Everyone did. The Ozian Wanted List wasn't just for criminals. It was for rebels, dissenters, anyone who defied the Archons. Once your name was on it, it stayed.

"I'm sorry," I said quietly, not really knowing what else to say.

Kassi gave a small nod. "Thanks," she whispered. Then her eyes drifted off.

"When the Sentinels raided our village, they didn't just show up; they wiped it out. My brother and I hid in this tiny basement space beneath the floorboards. Uncle Ciro had built it for emergencies. He told us to stay put, no matter what."

She paused.

"I remember the crash... I remember the glass shattering, boots pounding the ground. Then a shout... Uncle was urgently telling us to stay hidden. Moments later... a loud thud. It was heavy, and we heard him crying out."

Kassi lowered her head, jaw clenched.

"We stayed down there, shocked and scared. Every creak above felt like it was coming straight for us. I tried to stay quiet, but I was shaking so hard. I was sure they'd hear me crying. Fynn wrapped his arms around me and whispered, 'I won't let anything happen to you.' Over and over again."

It was difficult to imagine what she and her brother had experienced. The fear. The silence. The darkness.

"But then..." she continued, her voice picking up slightly, "the noise changed. At first, we thought we heard the sound of violent wind gusts. We thought the coming twister saved us. In reality, we heard shouting and orders being barked. Then Gale blasters...then... something else.

She raised her hand as if she could picture it all again.

"Chaos, but not from the Sentinels. Someone was fighting back."

"Someone else?" I asked.

"Yes, and they were fast. Really fast. The Sentinels started falling back. You could hear the panic in their comms. And then... there was nothing."

She looked straight at me now.

Fynn grabbed a sharp object and pried the trapdoor open to check. That's when we heard a voice. A woman. Calm, commanding. She asked if anyone was down there.

Kassi gave me a small, almost disbelieving smile.

"She introduced herself as Captain Aeryn Vogan. It was your mom, Dorothy. She found us."

"You met my mom?... She was a captain?" I blurted. "This is... I don't even know what to make of all of this."

She looked away again. "Dorothy, I'll never forget her voice. She was fierce, with her hair tied back by a green band and carrying a Gale sniper. She had beautiful gray eyes with red paint down her right eye, which is why I have this," she said, gesturing to the red slash on her face. "She's my hero."

I couldn't speak. I could picture only her. Her description of my mom, and her eyes was spot on.

She continued. "But don't get me wrong, she looked tough, but your mom had a heart of gold. Gentle. Kind. Especially with kids."

"Your dad, Commander Vogan. Tall, bald, thick beard. Eyes like stone, always thinking five moves ahead. You could tell he carried a lot on his shoulders, but never showed fear. He made the calls that kept us alive."

I felt a lump forming in my throat.

"They placed me and Fynn with a survivor caravan after the raid. They said it wasn't safe to stay. Before we left, your mom hugged me... wiped the tears from my cheeks."

Kassi paused, then added, "Looking back now, I think I reminded her of you. Maybe an older version."

"Ha, yeah... You probably did," I said, trying to keep my emotions in check. I didn't want her to see how much this was hitting me.

"I didn't get it back then," Kassi continued. "But now? It all clicks. Still hard to imagine someone like your parents being so gentle. But they were. Fynn and I looked up to them. Big time."

She paused again, just for a second.

"When he got older, he joined their cause. Left me with the village, but he always came back. He'd tell me stories about his adventures… bits and pieces. He was mentored by your parents and spoke very highly of them."

I listened quietly.

"The Monsoons actually started as a youth branch of the Zephyrs. Just a bunch of young, scrappy, passionate groups that were sick of being afraid. Fynn formed the group with the blessing of your parents. They started as a relief group for other refugees.

During the Green-Eyed Twister, he and his team were out on a mission. When they came back…" She hesitated. "It was all gone. The village, the people… everything."

"Including my parents," I said, the words landing like stones.

Kassi nodded, eyes heavy. "The few who survived told him what happened. He buried what was left. Gave them a proper marker. Never talked about the details… he wanted to protect me. But I knew it broke him."

"Fynn recovered the capsule box your parents gave him… some tools, journals, and relics. He used them to keep their legacy alive. He trained me, trained others. He believed in what they stood for… in what they started. Freedom. Truth. A world not ruled by fear."

She balled her fists again. "But he never got to see that world. He died a few months later. Caught in a fight with the Sentinels. He went down… my brave big brother."

She blinked fast, then straightened up a little.

I couldn't say anything. I just sat there, clutching the photo tighter in my hands, wishing I'd known him too.

"SMASH!"

Kassi's fist slammed against the table. Her whole body shook as the tears finally came. "So here I am," she choked out, "leading a bunch of fighters without my brother. Even though he promised he'd always protect me!"

I didn't say anything right away. Just reached over and rested my arm gently on her shoulder.

"Your brother sounds like he was a strong leader," I assured her. "Someone who truly loved you. I think, no, I know he'd be proud of the person his baby sister has become."

She touched my hand, her fingers trembling as she tried to pull herself together. "That means a lot. Thanks, Dorothy."

It was a lot. Way too much to take in at once. In just a few minutes, I had learned more about my parents than I ever did growing up in Emeraldia. It felt like my life had shifted, and there was a lot to sort out. But I didn't say that out loud. Not yet. Right now, I just want to be here for Kassi. She had opened up to me, and I owed her that.

Still, the question nagged at me.

"Kassi… do you really want to lead a rebel army? Do you actually want to be in this war?"

She didn't answer right away. I watched her face change.

"There's what you want to do," she said finally, "and then there's what you're meant to do. Only one of those really gives you a choice."

Then she pointed toward a pair of loose papers near the notebook. They must've fallen out during the whole emotional episode of ours.

"Careful with those," she blurted out, snapping back to her normal self. "They're important."

I picked them up and noticed something strange right away. "Wait… these aren't the same color as the notebook pages. Were they added later?"

Kassi nodded. "Yeah. Someone slipped those in. And this…" she tapped the corner of one page, "… this is actually the second reason I needed to show you that notebook. Go ahead. Open it."

I opened the notebook carefully, my hands already shaking.

"This is... this is!" I stammered.

"Yep," Kassi answered. "It's exactly what you think. Those pages? That notebook? They came from your parents. Listen, it's not just some diary either. It tells the story of their time as Zephyr rebel leaders. I believe your father wrote it. It is our history."

I knelt down to grab my other book from my bag.

"So let me get this straight. They had two notebooks? One from Mom about their discoveries, and one from Dad about their campaign battles?"

"Oh wow, it seems that's the case!" Kassi replied, examining my mother's book.

"But why not give me both? I still have so much to learn about you two." I felt like my memories of them were already fading, and now there's this entirely new aspect of their lives I had never seen.

She knelt beside me and pointed at the edge of one page. "What's also important is that in your father's notebook, this page mentions the great spire you spoke of at the tent. Unfortunately, I don't have any more information. We searched my brother's old records for the rest, but it was gone. So, when you mentioned the spire earlier, I thought maybe you knew.

"But to find out you're a Vogan…" She shook her head, overwhelmed. "These pages… maybe they're not much. But they could be what helps you start to understand."

I stared at her, then at the pages again.

"Kassi, you have no idea what this means to me," I beamed. Without thinking, I flipped to the back of my mom's notebook, held up the loose pages.

"They match!" I shouted. "These were ripped out from this journal. This is it."

Kassi's eyes widened. "Wait… are you serious? You actually have it? Dorothy, we thought this was lost forever. After the Green-Eyed storm, we assumed it was gone for good."

I nodded slowly. "I think I finally get it now. They sent me this journal when I was little, my only link to them. I read it over and over, even when I didn't understand half of it. I thought it was all they left me."

I looked down at the spire sketch again, then back at the worn cover of my mother's journal. "But maybe… they wanted me to figure the rest out on my own."

We spent the next twenty minutes piecing together notes from both journals and those loose pages. The deeper we got, the more real it all felt.

Kassi's voice finally broke the quiet. "This part talks about a giant, oddly shaped relic... That has to be the Spire."

"Yeah, definitely," I said, pulling one of Mom's pages out and sliding it next to the others. "Check this out—when you line up these diagrams, they actually connect. It makes a full spiral."

Kassi leaned in, her eyes narrowing with focus. "You think these are sketches of what the Spire looked like? Or maybe how to find it?"

"Could be," I murmured, heart racing. My fingers hovered over the page like they could feel the answer if I touched the right spot.

Then Kassi pointed at the bottom edge. "Wait—Dorothy, look. There's writing under the drawings!"

I squinted and read the faded words aloud:

"Power of old... unfolds the road... made of gold?"

"'Power of old... made of gold? What?'" I repeated, squinting at the words. "Is that some kind of riddle?"

Kassi didn't answer right away, just watched me as I fumbled through mom's notebook.

Then it clicked.

"Wait, hang on," I called out, flipping fast through the pages. "Page 24... yeah, here!" I pointed to a line that was underlined twice in red ink. "Mom wrote something about riddles and some compass."

Kassi leaned over my shoulder, reading along with me.

Dr. Aeryn Vogan Journal Entry #31, pg.39

"... when our archaeologist team discovered the old time-capsule, we saw that its outside was covered in ancient writing written as riddles. At first, we thought it was just to confuse us. But when we opened the capsule, we found an ionic compass that was made long before the twisters came. Today, dramatic changes in our atmosphere throw off all compasses and satellites. Yet, these special compasses were known to find the nearest Ionic field, no matter the condition. The problem was that this compass didn't work on an emerald charge. But what energy source could it be?"

I dug into my bag and felt around until my fingers hit cold metal. "Oh right, the compass!" I pulled it out and held it up. "Here it is."

Kassi leaned in and took it from me. Her eyes went wide as she turned it over in her hands. "Wow... so this is an ionic compass? Look at the detail... the carvings, the weight... it's old. Really old."

I agreed. "It's beautiful, but... without power, it's just a paperweight."

She rubbed her chin, thinking. "So... what are you gonna do with it?"

I shrugged, honest and tired. "No clue. I wish we knew someone who actually understood this kind of ancient tech."

That's when her whole vibe shifted. She stepped back, her face clouding over like she'd just She started pacing, muttering under her breath like she was arguing with herself.

"Hey... Kassi?" I asked again, my voice cautious. "You good?"

"Just... give me a second," she answered, holding up a hand.

I stayed quiet, watching her eyes dart back and forth, clearly wrestling with something. Whatever it was, it had her tense. Real tense.

"Kassi—"

"Ugh, alright," she finally sighed, rubbing her forehead. "I might know someone who can help you with the compass. "But…" She paused. "I don't know if he'd actually want to."

I leaned forward, eager for more details. "Well, if we tell him what we're trying to do, maybe he'll help us."

Kassi crossed her arms. "Now, Dorothy, just… don't go trusting people too easily up here, topside. A lot of them are only out for themselves. Survival makes people weird. Friendships here usually come with conditions."

I couldn't help but ask, "Is that how you feel about me?"

She shook her head fast, hands up. "No—no. You're not like them. You're not like the people from ArcCity either. I just… haven't figured you out yet. You're different."

She paused like she was choosing her next words carefully.

But the person I'm talking about goes by the name SKR// CRO, or just Cro. He's… well, he's a genius, but he can be really annoying. He's great with hacking machines and programs, but very interested in old tech though."

I tilted my head. "Okay… then what's the catch? Why are you hesitant to call him?

Kassi let out a sigh. "A while back, we teamed up for a mission, hacking into one of the ArcCity's surface radars. Everything looked solid until it wasn't. It was a disaster and one of our outposts got exposed.

I could see it in her eyes, she was reliving it.

"We fought hard, lost good people. Then they sent in reinforcements, and we were forced to flee. We didn't stop running for a week. When we finally made it back to the Hive... Cro blamed me, and I blamed him."

She shrugged, bitter. "Haven't heard from him since."

I raised an eyebrow. "So... whose fault was it then?"

"Honestly? Both of us. Cro was reckless, sure, but I was too harsh. He's a good kid, just... gets in over his head. And I know he has a hard time trusting anyone. I probably made that worse."

"Wait... kid?" I blinked. "He's younger than us?"

She nodded. "Yeah. By a few years, at least. But don't let that fool you, he has the mind of an old, crazed scientist. Whatever he did in the past, has the Sentinels hunting him to this day. I still don't know the full story. He never told me. Just vanished."

"Well... maybe... you two could fix things. Say sorry, clear the air."

Kassi snorted. "Say sorry? Dorothy, do I look like someone who just... apologizes? Especially to a pre-teen hacker with a bad attitude?"

"Listen, Kassi, we have to try. This Cro kid might be the only one who can help us figure things out."

She didn't answer right away. "I never said I wanted to get involved," she finally muttered. "Don't get me wrong. Your parents were incredible. I mean that. They were my heroes. But what if all of this is just a story? What if the Spire is just some old myth?"

"You don't believe that."

She looked at me, a little harder this time. "So, you think you really know me now?"

"Why else would you show me all this?" I said. "The head-quarters. The book. The Spire pages. You could've kept it to yourself, but you didn't."

Kassi opened her mouth, then closed it again. For once, she didn't have a comeback. She stared at the ground like it might offer her a better answer.

"I don't know," she finally mumbled.

"Be honest. Why did you share all of this with me?"

Moving to her worktable, her fingers quickly played with a small tool from her pocket. "Maybe... it's because I saw a new topsider trying to figure out a new world like an innocent child. Maybe it's pity," she admitted.

She then paused and groaned, "Maybe I did it because the more I learned about you, the surer you seemed about your purpose. And... well, now I'm not so sure about mine."

Her confession struck a chord with me. I stepped closer and gently placed a hand on her shoulder. "You don't always have to be sure. Sometimes you just have to move forward even when the paths blurry. I've seen how your soldiers look at you. They believe in you. They follow you because they trust your leadership. You don't have to fill your brother's shoes. Your worn-out boots are enough."

Kassi chuckled while wiping her eyes. "Ha, I didn't know you had it in you. I probably would have put you to work with my men."

Then she made her decision. "Listen, I will help you. But my soldiers come first. If something happens with them, I will leave immediately."

"Agreed!"

"Good," She smirked. "Now, about Cro, my last intel said he went into hiding in a real sketchy spot." She grabbed the map on the table and pointed to a small "X" in the region called Deadroot Valley. "Here. Hollow Wyck. It's a place full of outlaws. Honestly, I don't even know how Cro managed to stay alive out there."

I looked at the map. "It looks pretty far. How long will it take us to get there?"

"That's the next problem," she responded, tapping the map again. "The storms in this area are unpredictable. Sand-striders would get torn up trying to pass through. And going on foot? We'd be crawling through the desert for days. Which leaves us with one option—you need to know how to ride the winds."

"Ride the winds?"

She nodded and pointed to a shaded region on the map, marked with ridges and storm symbols. "Twister Alley. Dozens of twisters hit this corridor every hour. That's why we don't just rely on vehicles. We train to be Gale Runners, people who can move with the storm instead of against it."

I blinked. "You're telling me we're going straight through that?"

"Exactly," she said. "And if you're serious about finding Cro and solving what your parents left behind, then it's time you learned how to move like the wind."

"Gale Runners? You mentioned that before. You said my parents invented it, but I never read anything about it in the notebook. What exactly is a Gale Runner?"

She laughed. "You're going to love this. Now, grab something to eat and get some rest. We've had a long day."

"Well, it looks like I have a lot of work to do," I thought to myself.

"Zephyrs… My mom and dad… real rebel fighters… real heroes?"

CHAPTER EIGHT

Commander Vogan Journal Entry #21, pg.25

"*The hot desert sun was beating down on us as we walked through the dry wasteland. We were all vigilant, knowing our mission was to rescue the innocent people trapped in this encampment destroyed by the Sentinels.*

As we got closer, there was a sense of unease. Before we knew it, chaos erupted with explosions and gale blasters. The enemy prepared for our arrival. Powerful blue lasers whizzed past us, kicking up clouds of sand. We engaged in a fierce battle. Sweat and dust covered us, but in the end, we won. We were lucky that day."

A few months after moving into the Hive, I spent every night buried in Dad's old writings. His journal entries had turned into exciting stories of missions under the moonlight, last-minute escapes, and fights with Sentinel soldiers. It was like an action movie, and he was the main star.

They all were.

My parents weren't just scientists; they were rebels and leaders. It definitely explained why they were away "working" late nights. What really surprised me was how often these fights happened topside. It made me think about Leo for a moment. *"Has he ever been part of those missions? Did he know this whole time and just never say anything?"*

I sat back in my bunk, staring at the wall.

"Kassi… Mom and Dad… They all had double lives. Secrets. Whole lives that had nothing to do with the world I thought I knew. Leo was probably no different."

A knock rattled my door, pulling me out of my thoughts.

"Hey! Wake up! You ready or what?" a voice called out.

It was Kassi, loud, full of energy, and way too excited about how early it was. Mornings were sacred to me. I liked them quiet, with just the sound of pages turning in my journal and maybe a sip of tea if we were lucky enough to have some. But Kassi? As soon as the sun touched the edge of the camp, she was already running drills, shouting updates, or dragging someone out of bed for a stretch.

And as much as I wanted to roll over and pretend I didn't hear her, I couldn't. She meant well. And if I were honest, her fire was kind of contagious.

With a yawn and a long stretch, I pulled myself out of bed and started getting ready. The others were already gathering for morning drills.

Training out here wasn't a choice; it was how we survived. I was learning new ways to combat, how to drive desert vehicles, and how to use all the Monsoon calls and signals. I was becoming a solider-in-training, soaking it all in.

Over time, I'd earned a codename from the squad.

"Hey, Lady G!"

"What's up, Lady Gale?"

"Let's see what Lady Gale's got today!"

At first, I thought it was just a joke, but the name stuck. They called me "Lady Gale," after the mythical Ozian goddess of wind and storms. My mom used to tell me and the other kid's stories about the goddess' great adventures around the campfire.

The name felt different now. Not just because of the stories, but because I was actually getting good at riding storms.

They called it *Gale-running*.

I just learned from Kassi that my parents were the first to do it as a simple experiment. They used magnetic boots and special glide-boards, called *Storm-Gliders*, to ride twisters using boosters for control. According to their journals, they failed dozens of times and nearly died before they finally figured out how. Then they taught all of the Zephyrs. And now, we were learning too.

* * *

"You sure you're ready for this, Dorothy? You could always stick to the Dusties on the kiddie side," a soldier blurted at me as I walked toward the training zone.

"And miss the fun? Nah, I've got bigger things to chase."

He chuckled and gave my visor a final check. "Alright, Lady Gale. Can't say I didn't warn you. Good luck out there."

I grabbed my red boots, slid them on tight, and headed out toward the training grounds.

I'd been riding a glide-board for years, so I knew the basics: balance, direction, staying upright when the wind wants to throw you like a paper doll. But gale-running? That was a different beast. It wasn't just about staying on the board. It was about syncing with the storm, letting the wind move you without tearing you apart.

And yeah, I wiped out. A lot.

Kassi couldn't hide her laughter the first few times I got tossed by a "Dustie", the smaller, more playful twisters we used for practice. The soldiers had a running joke about how I always got "bumped out." But the bruises didn't bother me. I was learning fast. Every fall taught me something new.

But today was different.

I felt ready.

Weeks of crashing, stumbling, and pushing past my limits led to this moment. I snapped on my visor, pulled on my red storm-glider boots, and zipped up my protective suit. The wind whipped through the area filled with dust, and I could feel the storm coming before I even saw it.

And then, there it was.

Not a Dustie.

A real twister.

It was my first time trying to ride something like that.

I was very nervous.

I could hear them from far away: Kassi and the others up on the ridge, shouting over the roar of the wind. Their cheers mixed with laughter, bets, and that reckless kind of hope only rebels carry. To them, this wasn't just training. It was me proving I belonged. It was me defying every rule the Archons ever laid down.

I tried not to let it shake me. But yeah, the pressure was real.

I took one last look at the swirling wall of dust and air ahead of me. This wasn't like the little dusties I'd crashed into a dozen times.

But I trained for this.

My goal was clear: ride the twister up to its midpoint, catch the downdraft, and glide back down using the boosters. Simple in planning. Terrifying in real life. Any higher, and I'd get sucked into the super-cell zone, and no one comes back from that.

I took a deep breath. The wind tugged at my suit and whipped through my hair. My Wind-Strider was locked in place on my boots, the glide engine buzzing.

"Do it afraid," I told myself. "If you feel fear, let it push you."

"Mirage to Lady Gale, can you hear me clearly." Kassi asked through the comms in my visor.

"Radio is good, and so am I." I answered, shaking the jitters off.

I kissed my bracelet, then stepped forward and launched towards the heart of the twister.

"Wow… it felt just like the first time."

The wind was screaming, wild and furious. It shook the air so hard I thought it might rip me right off the board.

I couldn't hear the crowd anymore. All I could hear was the wind and the storm. It was just me and this fight to stay on my feet.

The gusts came hard and fast. I gritted my teeth, crouched down low, and leaned into the board. My foot pushed on the controls. I hit the boosters, and the board jumped forward with a careful tilt.

I could feel everything. The storm pushed, but I pushed back. Every move had to be perfect. Every second counted. I shifted from side to side, keeping my balance, dodging the drag.

"You've got this girl … You've got this!" Kassi said.

Minutes dragged like hours while I fought not to get bumped out of this beast. But something strange started to happen.

"This feeling… is…"

My nerves began to fade.

My movements got smoother.

I don't know how to explain it, but I felt… connected. Like the storm was talking, and I was finally starting to understand like when I sensed the rocks in the mines.

Immediately, the gusts pulled me upward, straight toward the dark belly of the super-cell cloud. The danger zone. I used my booster to resist the pull.

"Alright, Kassi. Made it to the midpoint," I reported.

"Great!" she said, "Now, find the downdraft."

I shifted my weight and angled my board, trying to catch the flow back down. But the wind had other plans. The updraft pushed me way harder than I expected. My boosters were working, but they weren't enough.

And I kept rising.

Higher.

And even higher.

"Lady Ga ... Dor...."

Kassi tried to contact me, but she cut off. I could barely see anyone on the ground anymore. They looked like tiny dots below, fading fast as clouds began to cover them.

"Wait… no. This can't be. I'm not supposed to be this high."

I hit the comms. **"Lady Gale to Hive. Someone, help!"**

Static.

"Come on. Lady Gale to Hive. Please respond!"

Still nothing.

Panic crept in fast. "I'm in the danger zone. I'm gonna die. I'm actually gonna die up here."

Then, something changed.

"Wait..."

The same strange feeling from before came back, but stronger this time. It felt like a soft shiver in my bones. A glow filled the surrounding air. My knees loosened. I released the booster pedal without meaning to.

I looked up. The sky didn't even feel like the sky anymore. It felt like a different world.

"I can't... believe this is real..."

Lightning danced through the clouds all around me. Thunder cracked, loud and deep, and it even seemed to disturb the wind. Water droplets stuck to my face and arms. Bright flashes of light lit up the mist, showing swirling currents of raw electrical energy.

It was wild. Beautiful. Terrifying.

"This feels incredible... peaceful..."

I wasn't scared anymore. I was excited. Mesmerized. I wasn't thinking about the Archons or the city or anything.

This was supernatural.

This was what gale-runners called being *storm-drunk*. Getting lost in the sky. Losing track of everything. It was risky. If you stayed too long, the storm would take you.

As much as I wanted to float here forever, I knew I had to move.

I had to come down.

I let my instincts take over. Everything I had learned kicked in like muscle memory. I scanned the surrounding air, looking for the wind shift. The drop in pressure that would mean a downdraft was close.

"There." A chill brushed my cheek.

I adjusted my stance and aimed at the ground below. I tilted my strider into the wind, letting it guide me lower, little by little. The clouds started to get thinner, and the roar of the storm softened behind me.

Finally, I managed to break through the storm.

The sky opened up all around me. That beast of a twister was a distant roar now, swirling far behind me. My breathing became calm, and the pressure on my chest was gone. I could see the cliffs again, and the soldiers below. I saw their shoulders relax as they looked up at me.

And when my boots finally hit the ground, a grin spread across my face without me even thinking about it.

Every muscle in my legs felt like jelly, like I was being held up by threads. I could barely breathe. Then, I heard it… faint at first, then louder.

"LA-DY GALE!"

"LA-DY GALE!"

"LA-DY GALE!"

The guys were chanting, cheering like I had just pulled off the impossible.

It felt unreal.

But the moment didn't last long.

Kassi came sprinting over. Before I could completely regain my balance, she pushed me with such force that I almost lost my footing.

"Hey, what was that for?" I called out, still catching my breath.

"Are you out of your mind?" she snapped. "You could've died up there! You flew straight into the danger zone!"

I didn't answer right away.

My head dropped, partly from exhaustion, partly from guilt. The wind picked up again, brushing past us in silence. Everyone stood still, waiting to see what would happen next.

I knew I'd scared them. I knew I had gone too far.

But even with all that... I didn't regret it.

I lifted my head, met Kassi's eyes, and gave her a tired smirk. That was all I had left in me.

She narrowed her eyes, but I saw the smile tugging at the corner of her mouth.

"You were storm-drunk, weren't you?" she said, finally letting the tension go.

I nodded.

We both laughed.

"LET'S HEAR IT FOR LADY GALE!" Kassi shouted. The camp cheered as everyone rushed to celebrate with me.

"LA-DY GALE!"

"LA-DY GALE!"

'LA-DY GALE!"

This was everything.

I felt real genuine pride. As everyone chanted my name, something lit up inside me. I got enough newfound energy to raise my strider into the air without thinking. For a moment, I imagined my parents watching me, and I wished so badly they could see what I had become.

The walk back to the base felt like a victory lap. Rebels clapped me on the back, called my name, shouted things like "That's our Lady Gale!" I soaked it in, letting myself enjoy it. I had earned their respect. I could feel it. They didn't see me as the new kid anymore. I was part of this now.

"I could stay here forever."

Still, underneath all the cheering and praise, I felt a small ache. It was like something wasn't fully settled. I knew this wasn't the end. I hadn't even reached the hardest part of my journey yet.

After I freshened myself up, I went straight to Kassi's office. I found her hunched over her messy desk, studying a map of a place called Twister Alley. She didn't look up right away, but when she finally did, her face softened.

"So… Superstar! How are you feeling?" she asked.

"I'm fine, actually. That ride… it was wild, but I felt like I was in control and lost control at the same time. If that makes sense."

She smiled warmly, as if pondering about her time in my shoes.

"You know, riding twisters can really mess with your head… makes you see the world differently. But I've never seen anyone pick it up as fast as you did. You went into the danger zone and came out calm and in control. That's not normal. It's like you've got some connection up there."

"Hmm, I never thought about it like that," I admitted. "Maybe it was just beginner's luck."

Her words caught me off guard. But when she said it, something clicked. It's like mom said in her writing. Watching storms through the window while she held me close. It never scared me. As I got a little older, I loved it.

Maybe Kassi was right. Maybe something did change up there.

"You know, my first time trying to gale-run was a total disaster," Kassi laughed. "It freaked me out so badly I nearly quit right there. And my brother? He stayed away from it as if it were cursed."

I smiled, feeling a weird kind of pride bubble up inside me. "Honestly, I was nervous too at first. But I think I'm ready now. No more second-guessing. I think I really got this."

"That's the spirit. It might take a while to get where you're going, but I'm glad you stuck around. You've only been here a few months, but you've changed things. Your curiosity and guts make the hive feel alive again."

She walked across the room to grab her jug of water as she continued.

"We used to be on edge all the time, watching for the Sentinels or other Arc Forces to show up. That's why we were always checking the old surface port. But now, it's been quiet. And we're not looking to poke the beast again unless we have to."

I heard what she wasn't saying. This fortress and the guys in it mattered more to her than just strategy or orders. And I finally felt that too.

"I didn't think I'd find family out here," I replied, looking around the room. "But I did. And I'm not just fighting for the truth anymore. I'm fighting for all of you too."

Kassi smiled, then her face turned serious. "Dorothy, listen… I just got confirmation from a scout. Cro's still at Hollow Wyck. He was seen leaving a tavern."

"So, do you think it's time for us to go?"

Kassi sighed, a hint of caution in her eyes. "It's up to you, Dorothy. But if we go, I think it should just be the two of us. I can't afford to risk my men getting hurt."

That made sense. This was our mission to take on.

"Then let's do it."

"Great!" She said as she stood up, already switching into planning mode. "We pack light. I'll make sure the rest of the soldiers stay back and keep the Hive secure."

The next few days moved fast. We prepped for the trip, checked our gear, and reviewed every map and detail we had. As we set out toward Twister Alley, I couldn't help but feel a lot of anxiety. But this was the path I chose.

And whatever waited for us out there, whether it was twisters, bandits, or even Cro, I was ready to face it.

I had to be.

132

RODNEY BLANC

CHAPTER NINE

Twister Alley is a nightmare!

The stormy sky was furious, with thunder crashing and lightning flashing through dark clouds. The dry, rugged terrain faced strong winds and swirling dust, while the constant roar of the twisters echoed across the empty wilderness.

"I don't know how I let you talk me into this, Kassi!... I feel like... I'm being pulled apart!"

"Ha, you're doing fine!" Kassi responded through her comms. "Besides, you need the practice! Those small-time twisters were doing nothing for you."

Gale-running takes a real toll on the body when you are not used to it. I don't think I'll ever get comfortable with how loud a twister really is. Even with my visor on, the roar still found a way in. While we were riding the twister, I kept myself low and held on tightly to my strider, making sure I didn't make any mistakes.

Just behind me, I spotted Kassi cutting through the chaos like it was nothing. She moved as if the wind was just another part of her body.

But me?

I was stiff.

This wasn't like my first trail run. This wasn't a single twister. Twister Alley had a whole row of them moving at once.

Still, I wasn't scared. Not anymore.

Somehow, fear didn't have the same hold on me as it used to. These twisters weren't just monsters to run from anymore; they had become something I could understand. Something I could tame. They had become my rivals, and every time we stepped into a storm, we learned more about how to use its power instead of just surviving it.

"Dorothy, are you good? Time to leap."

I focused on the approaching twister.

"Yeah, let's do it."

Back during training, they taught us an advanced technique to travel between twisters—*leaping*. In short, it's when you use the pull from one twister to fling yourself into another, using your boosters to give you just enough push to survive it.

The trick is timing. Too early, and you get bumped out. Too late, and you spiral into the danger zone, and I knew what that felt like. I wasn't going up there again.

I kept moving, scanning the air for the downdraft, searching for the moment to leap.

"Come on, stay focused!" I told myself.

I waited a few seconds longer.

"…Ok, now!"

In no time, we made our leap to the next twister. It was exhilarating every time.

Twister Alley really lived up to its name.

Looking at Kassi, I could tell how locked in she was. Her focus never wavered. She knew these storms like the back of her hand, and I trusted her.

"Get ready for the next leap, Dorothy," she replied on the comms. "We have only one more twister to push through before we reach the safe zone."

As much as it drained me, gale-running was starting to feel like my thing.

"This might actually be better than mine drilling," I mumbled with a grin, the wind still buzzing in my ears.

And just as that thought crossed my mind, everything went sideways.

Literally.

Even as a rookie, I could tell something was wrong. The wind shifted weirdly, the pressure changed, and every instinct screamed we were off track.

"Hey Kassi, I think we drifted too far from our next jump point."

"You're right," she answered quickly. "Good eyes. A simple boost should fix that."

"Got it."

We adjusted, lining up for our third leap and then

"BOOM!"

Out of nowhere, a chunk of debris slammed into Kassi, sending her off course.

"Kassi!!"

Her board wobbled and stuttered as she fought hard to stay airborne. But she was dipping too low. She was straining to catch the updraft, but it kept slipping out of reach. Without that updraft lift, she was done.

"Heading your way now." I charged.

She waved me off, clearly trying to tell me not to come closer. But there was no way I was backing off.

I needed to adjust my boost just enough to keep from yanking her arm out of the socket. I had to get the angle right and match her momentum. One wrong move and we'd both be toast.

"Dorothy, move away! We'll knock each other out of the stream!"

"Kassi, I can do this!"

Ignoring her warning, I pushed myself as close to her as I could. It was a bold, reckless move, but I had to try.

"Come on, come on..." I muttered, carefully tilting my strider just right. Finally, I boosted just enough to get even closer.

"Kassi, quick! Grab my arm!"

"Dorothy, this is insane!"

"Just grab!"

"Alright. Here goes."

We locked arms and aligned our boards. We shifted our weight in sync and lined up perfectly with the drop in the current. Suddenly, I could feel the pressure changing, the wind dipping. We had found the downdraft.

"In all my years, I can't believe this is actually working." Kassi said, shocked at our streak of luck. But that wasn't all.

In a quick, almost amazing moment, the twister started to get weaker. The wind didn't let us go easily, but it loosened its grip just enough for us to break free. With one last burst from the boosters, we shot out of the storm's edge.

I finally saw open desert below.

"We did it, Kassi! We're out!" I shouted.

"Not yet, Dorothy. Brace yourself—"

"Oh nooo--!"

"PSHHHHH!"

We slammed into a mound of sand, rolling and tumbling. I landed flat on my back, coughing and laughing at the same time. Kassi hit just a few feet away, sprawled out, covered in dust.

We both lay there, staring up at the sky like we had just cheated death.

"Are you dead?" Kassi called out.

"Yes!" I answered.

There was a pause. I turned to Kassi, and she smiled back, and soon we both burst into laughter. We couldn't believe we had made it.

"You really are crazy, Dorothy!" Kassi shouted, playfully throwing some sand in my direction. "You've got to admit, you enjoy this a bit too much."

I wiped sand from my visor and started laughing. "Maybe, just a little."

* * *

After we dusted ourselves off, Kassi noticed my red glider-boots.

"You know, I never asked, but why did you pick red boots for your storm-glider?"

I smiled as a memory bubbled up. "When I was little, I used to see my mom wearing these bright red desert boots. I once asked her why, and she said it was so I would always know where she was.

Kassi's eyes lit up. "Now that I think about it, she was wearing red boots when she rescued my brother and me."

I nodded with a smile. "Yeah… Red was her thing. She really was something else."

We kept riding, our gliders skimming over the uneven ground, catching little gusts of wind off the edge of Twister Alley. It was peaceful. But too quiet. I glanced over at Kassi and saw her staring out ahead, her face all tight and serious.

"You're thinking about the Hive, huh?"

She looked at me and sighed. "Was it that obvious?"

"Yeah," I answered. "You've been quiet. And honestly, it makes sense. You care about your soldiers."

Kassi gave a small nod, but I could tell her mind was still with them.

"Listen, your team's tough. You trained them better than anyone else could. If they're anything like you, they've got this."

"I just worry," Kassi voiced. "Every day, I have to stress about what new trick the Sentinels will throw at us next. I can't afford to get comfortable. Not in this job."

"You're right. But also… look at me. A few months ago, I could barely stand up on a board in a dustie. Now I'm gale-running with the best. That's all thanks to you. Trust me, they will be fine."

"Yeah, you might be right." she smiled.

But her smile faded. Not all the way, just enough to show she was thinking hard about something again. "So, this compass and spire… how do you know we can actually stop the twisters with these things?"

I hesitated for a moment. "I don't. Not yet anyway. I haven't worked that part out. But if we can figure out what's really behind them, maybe there's a way to stop it. Or at least understand it."

She looked at me sideways. "You know, you sound kind of naïve, right?"

I scratched the back of my neck and gave a crooked grin.

"Yeah. Maybe I am. But I figure we won't know for sure unless we try."

There was a short silence before Kassi asked, more casually than she probably meant to, "So... have you been thinking about your friend? Leo?"

I blinked. "Where'd that come from?"

She shrugged. "Just curious. You mentioned him a lot when you first came to the Hive, but not as much anymore."

"I don't even know if he thinks I'm still alive. For all I know, everyone probably thinks I'm gone for good."

Kassi's eyes softened, and she asked gently, "Did you ever… have feelings for him or something?"

"No… of course not. He was my best friend, that's all. Listen, he risked a lot for me, more than most ever would."

I looked down. "But that doesn't matter right now. What matters is what's ahead."

"On that note… Looks like we're close." She pointed out. "But we aren't finished discussing this," she teased.

* * *

"You said we made it to the area. So, how much longer until we reach this valley?" I asked, brushing the dust off my visor while keeping my balance.

Kassi glanced over, eyes scanning the horizon. "Hmm… Not too far now. Like I said back at HQ, you'll know it when you see it."

Over the past few months, Kassi filled me in on how the topside worked. I knew by now that it wasn't just a place for rebels and runaways. Some people up here were full-on criminals like smugglers, ex-soldiers, thieves, and bounty dodgers. And places like this? These were their hideouts. *Wycktowns*, as they called it, were off-the-map settlements that gave them a place to disappear.

She also told me that leaders of Wycktowns usually took a cut off whatever loot came through, offering protection in return. There were no real laws here, but there was still a code. A dangerous one. If you broke it, the whole town could turn on you.

Hollow Wyck was no different.

Kassi told me it was tucked away in the Deadroot Valley region, surrounded by dry hills and rocky cliffs. She said you'd never know it was there from a distance. The whole town stayed hidden until you climbed the final ridge, then bam, there it was. She described some huge old clock tower sticking up like a warning.

And boy did I finally see it.

"Here we are, the infamous Hollow Wyck," Kassi introduced. "It's like I described, right?"

She wasn't wrong.

We hopped off our boards and started walking through an open gate. We moved slowly and carefully.

"So, no one is gonna try to stop us at this gate? Hmm... Maybe that was planned."

"Yeah, Kassi," I whispered, glancing around, "you definitely weren't exaggerating."

This town was exactly how Kassi described it.

A bandit's dream.

The main road was just packed dirt, lined with old saloons and workshops. The storefront buildings were patched together with mismatched metal sheets and canvas awnings that snapped with every gust of wind. Cables stretched between rooftops, powering dim lanterns that swayed overhead.

"Kassi, I won't lie, Hollow Wyck gives me the chills."

"I know," she replied, scanning the area. "But if we're going to find Cro, we've got to be smart. These people aren't exactly thrilled about strangers poking around asking questions."

It's true. The people here looked rough. Worn leather, cracked goggles, pieces of metal and gears patched onto their clothes and even their skin.

"I figured there'd be more people out," I blurted.

Kassi checked her watch. "It's still early. Maybe most of them are asleep."

"Or probably watching us," I said, noticing glares peeking through windows.

We kept walking. I scanned the buildings as we passed, reading the old signs hanging above the doors. One had a blinking sign that read *Whiskey and Wire*. But the light kept cutting in and out, like it couldn't decide whether to stay on or give up.

I stared at it for a second, wondering what the "Wire" part was supposed to be. Seemed like a strange combo, unless you were planning to drink and fix something at the same time.

That's when the clock tower pulled me out of my thoughts.

"There it is," I called out, pointing.

It stood tall at the end of the street, groaning as the wind pushed through it. Around its peak, small mechanical birds spun in circles, their little gears clicking like ticking clocks.

Then came the sound.

"DONG!!!!"

The clock tower bell rang out slow and deep, like a warning to the whole town. Right after, the doors creaked open, and people started coming out, one after another, going about their usual business. They all stared at us with cold, unblinking eyes. No one said a word, but their stares felt like knives.

"Umm… Are we really sure a preteen lives here?" I muttered mostly to myself.

Kassi must have sensed the tension in my voice because she quickly changed the subject.

"Hey," she said, nodding toward a building up ahead, "why don't we check out that tavern first? Grab something to eat. You've got to be starving after all that flying."

I shrugged. "Yeah, let's do that. As long as you're buying."

"Yeah, yeah. Whatever," she said, waving me off.

Food always works for me in times of stress.

* * *

Kassi and I locked our wind-striders onto a board rack and stepped into the tavern. The place was packed, but the second we walked through the door, the noise dipped. Heads turned. People stared.

"Yeah," I muttered, "feels like this is gonna be the vibe all day."

We were still in our gale-runner gear, dusty and wind-burned. Nobody here knew us, and it showed. Reminded me a little of Lyman's Dumpling Tavern back in Emeraldia—only this place had a lot more suspicion and a lot fewer dumplings.

"You still okay eating here?" Kassi asked, glancing around.

I took a breath. "I just flew through half a dozen twisters," I said. "I'll be fine."

She nodded, her hand resting easily near her gale blaster. We found a table and sat. The lighting was low, and the décor was mostly used vehicle parts. Metal mugs clinked and the murmur of voices slowly picked up again. "

A robotic waitress rolled up to our table. Her frame was scratched but well-kept, like someone still cared enough to shine her now and then. Her optics blinked with a soft whir, making a sound like a lens snapping into focus.

"Hey there! I'm EZ-39, but you can call me Miss E. Can I get you started with some drinks?"

We gave our orders and then looked over the menu. Kassi didn't waste any time. She ordered two lunch specials before I even got past the appetizers. Her stomach let out a growl that turned a few heads.

"So, you were hungrier than I thought," I said.

She gave a sheepish laugh. "Guess it hit me all at once."

I leaned in a little. "So. About Cro…"

"Shhh! Keep your voice down," Kassi whispered quickly, leaning in.

A few more eyes looked our way, but didn't say anything.

"Sorry," I whispered back. "So, about Cro… what if he doesn't want to be found?"

She didn't hesitate. "Cro always finds trouble, one way or another. But honestly? He might already know we're here. It wouldn't shock me if he saw us the second we landed in Hollow Wyck. He's big on intel and surveillance. Runs a whole network of drones."

I raised an eyebrow. "Seriously? Hard to believe someone that smart would live in a place like this."

Kassi let out a quiet laugh. "You've got to stop judging a gem before it's polished. Remember when you thought I couldn't make it topside because I was a girl? Look how that turned out."

I rested back a little, thinking. "Wow… I didn't realize I did that."

"You're still new out here, so it happens," she replied. "But yeah. Something to work on."

She paused, then added, "Cro made it this far because he's resourceful. Between his hacking skills and his knack for building gadgets and bots, he's been a real asset around here. Word is, a lot of folks owe him."

I was about to respond when Miss E arrived beside us.

"Here are your drinks and order! Is there anything else I can help you with?"

"No, thank you Miss E. We are done here," I replied.

Our conversation stopped as the plates hit the table. I didn't waste time. That sandwich looked like it had been waiting just for me.

We both dug in, not saying much for a few minutes. Just chewing, savoring, and trying to act like we weren't being watched.

* * *

As we were finishing up, I glanced out the window and spotted a cog workshop just across the street. The sign was faded, but the gears in the window were still turning.

"Hey," I said, nudging Kassi, "what if we check out that cog workshop over there? If Cro's into building stuff, maybe they've heard of him."

Kassi looked out the window, then back at me. "Not a bad idea," she said. "But let's keep it low-key. Not everyone here might be a fan of his."

After we wrapped up our meal, Kassi covered the bill. I told her I'd get the next one. She rolled her eyes but didn't argue.

As I turned to thank Miss E, I caught her staring. Not blinking, just watching us with the same fixed smile. It wasn't hostile, but it didn't feel friendly either.

"That was weird," I thought, trying not to show it on my face.

We crossed the street toward the workshop. A rusted sign above the door read *Cogsmith's Corner*. Inside, the clang of metal and hiss of steam hit us right away. The air smelled of soot and hot iron.

I pushed open the door. It creaked as if it hadn't been used in years, though the noise inside said otherwise.

The place was alive with activity. Artisans in stained aprons and thick goggles moved between their workbenches. Their hands were busy with gears, wires, and strange steam machines I couldn't even name. No one looked up as I walked by.

I walked over to a nearby cogsmith. He had broad shoulders, a huge red beard, soot-covered arms, and a face like a clenched fist.

"Excuse me," I said, trying to keep my tone polite.

He glanced up with a hard stare. "What do yer want, stranger?"

"My name is Dorothy. This is Kassi. We're looking for someone. His name's Cro. We heard he might be around here."

His eyes narrowed, studying me like he were trying to read something behind my eyes.

"Cro, huh? Yer not the first to come asking this Cro person. What's yer business with him?"

"We need his help," Kassi blurted, straight to the point. "He's known for his skills, right?"

He snorted and turned back to his work, tightening something with a wrench.

I stepped a little closer to get his attention.

"Look, we're not here to cause trouble. Truth is, I'm just trying to learn more about my parents. Cro might be the only one with his skills who can help. We came a long way."

For a second, something shifted on his face. The scowl didn't quite fade, but his eyes softened just a bit.

"Yer know," he said, voice lowering, "I had fourteen daughters back in Oreiana. Yer kind of remind me of my seventh. Or maybe it was number four. Hard to keep track after a while."

He scratched his chin, gears still turning in the background.

"Yer think Cro can help yer with that?" he muttered. "Maybe. I can't promise anything. But word is he's been holed up in that there old factory on the edge of town. Looks abandoned, but it's not. That's what I heard anyway."

"Now get moving," he grumbled. "Before someone else starts asking questions about yer two." Then, just like that, he turned back to his work—like the conversation never happened.

Kassi and I exchanged looks. "Umm… Thank you," I said, confused, but grateful. Kassi rolled her eyes as she looked back at the cogsmith with a hint of disgust.

"Well, on the bright side, at least we didn't have to ask everyone in the village about him," I said, trying to sound positive.

"Yeah, the fewer people we have to ask, the better," Kassi replied.

We left the workshop and made our way toward the edge of town.

The factory came into view fast. I was skeptical.

"Yeah… Maybe we should've asked a few more people…"

The factory was tall, grim, and impossible to miss. Rust streaked down its sides, and the paint was flaking off in chunks. Some windows were broken; others were boarded up. Vines and weeds crawled across the walls as if they were trying to pull the whole place down. The front gates were heavy and half open, and scrap metal and busted machines littered the yard.

"So, we're really supposed to believe Cro lives in this ghost factory?" I asked, eyeing the building like it might blink. "How do we know that old cogmith didn't just set us up?"

"Geez, relax, Dorothy," Kassi said. "Just stay alert. If it is a setup, it's probably not the kind you're thinking of. Instead, it may be Cro's doing. He's paranoid about visitors. He could be watching us right now. Might've even set traps."

Right as she said it, a loud burst of caws echoed above us. Circling the rusted roofline.

"You're right," I muttered. "We have to try. This is the best lead we've got."

We knocked on the large, rusty iron doors. Oddly enough, it was slightly open… maybe on purpose, we weren't sure.

"What is it about this town and open entrances?"

"Come on," Kassi said, hand on her weapon.

"Right."

We pushed the door the rest of the way and stepped inside. Our footsteps echoed against the concrete floor. I raised my charged wand, its soft glow cutting a narrow path through the darkness.

"It's way too dark in here," I whispered. "We need to find some kind of light source."

"Let's split up," Kassi advised. "Not too far. Just enough to cover ground."

I stopped in my tracks. "Why would I ever want to do that? Sorry, but I'm not splitting anywhere."

Kassi sighed. "Dorothy, I'm not asking you to go explore some dark underworld. Just a few steps. Find a power switch, a fuse box, anything. Just put your comms on."

"URGH, fine," I grumbled. "But if I die, my ghost is coming for the whole hive."

We split up just a little, close enough to keep the comms open. The room was still dark, and the air had that heavy, old-dusty smell.

"No power source yet," I said, moving my wand across a wall of rusted panels and busted wires. "But this place is eerie. I just found a crate full of robotic heads. Like… a lot of them."

"Same here," Kassi replied. "There's a conveyor belt on my side with metal limbs piled up. No doubt about it… this used to be a robotics factory."

That's when I heard something. A faint shuffle. Not the wind. Not machinery. Something else.

"Hello?" I called out. "Is anyone here?"

No answer.

"Cro, if that's you trying to pull a fast one, just know we've got blasters. Don't be dumb."

"Kassi!" I snapped. "We're not trying to scare him off."

She laughed softly. "I'm just kidding… mostly."

I kept moving when I spotted a doorway tucked behind a row of crates. It led down, deeper into the building. The air felt colder there.

"Hey, Kassi," I said, stepping closer. "I found something. It looks like—"

Nothing but static.

I stopped. "Kassi? Come in. Kassi?"

Still nothing.

I turned around and froze.

Two lights… No, optics. A bright and a shiny body.

"This one is aliv—" I barely got the words out.

The robot charged.

"Nope. Not today," I muttered, raising my battle wand.

It lunged, and I met it halfway, jumping in and swinging my wand hard. A burst of electricity shot through it, lighting up the room for a split second. The bot sparked and then dropped to the floor with a heavy crash.

"Kassi! Come in!" I shouted, panting. "Where are you?"

"Dorothy!" her voice finally came through, crackly. "I'm over here. Comms got jammed. I'm coming to you now. Hold tight."

That's when two more robots stepped out of the shadows. I was ready for round two. Between the combat drills Leo put me through and the Hive training, I knew I could handle at least a couple of basic bots.

"Here we go," I whispered.

The first one swung at me. I ducked, slid low, and swept its legs out from under it. It crashed to the floor, and I hit it with a quick stun blast.

The second bot loomed closer. I took a step back and raised my voice.

"Come on! What are you waiting for?" I shouted, trying to bait it.

It hesitated, sensors blinking. Just then, something shot from above—a drone shaped like a crow. It fired a net straight at me. My wand flew from my hand as the net slammed into my chest, knocking me to the ground.

I hit the floor hard, knees burning. The second robot started moving in.

"Kassi… URGH… where are you?" I called out as I struggle to get loose.

No answer. No footsteps. Just the buzz of the drone and the heavy steps of the bot closing in.

"Okay," I muttered. "Guess I'm figuring this out on my own."

The robot jumped.

I rolled to the side and braced for impact, hoping I had one more move left in me.

It tried to jump again but—

"BLAST! BLAST!"

Two sharp blasts dropped the drone-crow, and the robot's head popped clean off.

"You okay, Dorothy?" Kassi called out, lowering her smoking gale-blaster.

"Yeah. Thanks to you. Right on time."

She stepped closer, scanning the wreckage. "You've gotten pretty good with that lightning rod."

"It's a battle wand," I corrected. "I made some upgrades back at the base. Now, any chance you could get me out of this net? You know whenever you feel like it."

She raised an eyebrow. "What, no manners now?"

"Yeah, yeah..." I said, brushing off the sarcasm. "Look—I don't think someone wants us poking around in here. But I think I know why."

I pointed across the room at a door tucked behind some fallen beams. It looked like it led down.

We started walking toward the door when suddenly a loud voice boomed from the speaker above us, sounding deep, scratchy, and quite annoyed.

"GO AWAY! I'VE GOT PLENTY MORE WHERE THAT CAME FROM."

Kassi straightened. "Cro? Is that you? It's Kassi! Remember, our radar incident?"

"WHAT DO YOU WANT?"

"We need your help," Kassi said.

"LAST TIME I HELPED, THINGS DIDN'T EX-ACTLY GO WELL!"

I stepped in. "Look, Kassi wants to apologize for what happened."

"I DON'T KNOW WHO THE SECOND VOICE IS, BUT THAT DOESN'T SOUND LIKE A BAD IDEA."

Kassi scoffed, "I'm not apologizing."

I jabbed her in the arm.

"Ouch! What was that for?"

"Get over yourself, Kassi. We need this," I whispered.

"I'M WAITING," Cro said through the speaker.

Kassi crossed her arms. "Fine. I'm sorry, you annoying brat."

"MIND YOUR WORDS! I'M NO BRAT. I'M A 12-AND-A-HALF-YEAR-OLD GENIUS AND I RUN THINGS HERE." Cro snapped.

I jumped back in. "So, can you help us or not? We even found some old tech that might interest you."

A beat of silence.

"I told you," Kassi muttered. "He's impossible."

We started to turn away when Cro's voice came back.

"FINE. GET READY."

The factory roared to life. Lights buzzed on overhead. Conveyor belts jolted into motion. Gears turned, and steam hissed through overhead vents.

"Whoa..." I gasped.

"Okay, yeah," Kassi said. "The kid's got some flair."

We moved through the factory slowly, our steps echoing across the metal floor. Steam hissed from pipes. Water dripped from somewhere high above. Machines clanked and spun, building... more bots.

Cro's voice returned, calmer now. **"THE BASEMENT DOOR IS OPEN. HURRY UP BEFORE I CHANGE MY MIND."**

Kassi cupped her hands around her mouth. "Lose the fake voice already, Cro!"

We ran toward the door. The stairs behind it creaked as we made our way down, deeper into the lower level. Along the walls, mechanized crows perched on thick metal pipes. I noticed the camera lenses behind their eyes.

"Cro really doesn't like visitors. You think he ever comes out?"

"Only if it's important," Kassi answered. "Even then, he'd probably just send a bot."

I looked at her, surprised at how well she understood him. At the bottom of the stairs, we reached another door, but this one bigger, reinforced with metal bolts. A blinking red light pulsed above it, and a small camera followed us as we stepped closer.

I stood there for a second, eyes locked on the door.

I couldn't wait to see what kind of kid this Cro really was.

CHAPTER TEN

"STATE YOUR NAME, PLEASE,"** Cro called through a speaker by the door.

"Come on, man, you know who we are already," Kassi said, sounding annoyed once again.

"I WASN'T TALKING TO YOU. I WAS TALKING TO YOUR FRIEND," the voice replied.

Surprised by the comment, I answered, "Oh, I'm Dorothy. I come in peace."

"AFFIRMATIVE. NOW, CAN ONE OF YOU SHOW ME THIS OLD-TECH DEVICE YOU CLAIM TO HAVE?"

"Oh, come on, really? We've come this far. Can you let us in?" Kassi protested.

"SHOW ME, OR MY CROWS WILL SHOW YOU THE WAY OUT," the speaker warned.

"Okay, okay. No problem," I said as I searched through my bags for the artifact. "Look, I've got it here. See?" I held up my compass near the surveillance camera.

There was silence for a moment.

"Well?" Kassi said impatiently.

Suddenly, the light turned green, and the mechanical door creaked open while its gears turned.

"Come on, let's go," Kassi urged.

"Please be nice," I said, giving Kassi a look as she offered me a tight, forced smile.

We stepped inside, expecting finally to meet Cro face to face, but the room was empty.

Instead, we walked into what looked like a full-blown security hub. It reminded me of the rebel surveillance center, only messier. One wall was lined with blinking panels and monitors, each flashing with data or camera feeds. A long desk sat underneath, cluttered with wires, handheld devices, and gadgets I couldn't even begin to name.

In the center of the room was a massive worktable covered in tools and robot parts, like someone had been mid-project and just stepped away.

The biggest screen was across the back wall. It looked like Cro's main station. Maybe it was where he did his hacking. The screen cycled through dozens of camera angles. Some were outside, showing parts of the village and the factory grounds. Others were inside buildings.

"Well, would you look at this…" I called out.

One of the feeds showed the tavern, the same table where we had been sitting. The angle was low, about eye-level. Then I saw a faint reflection on the screen. It was coming from inside the waitress bot.

Miss E had been the camera.

It hit me like a punch to the gut.

"That's why she was acting weird," I whispered under my breath. "Cro's been watching us the whole time."

Kassi folded her arms and looked straight at the big screen. "Alright, kid. We're here. Enough hiding."

The screen glitched. Static buzzed for a second, then the image shifted to a large robotic face, crudely animated and blinking slowly.

"HA-HA! YOU THOUGHT I WAS ACTUALLY IN THERE? PLEASE. UNLIKE YOU TWO, I BELIEVE IN CAUTION," Cro declared through the speakers.

Kassi rolled her eyes again. "You already pulled that trick once. Come out, you wannabe villain."

The screen went black.

"UGH. FINE! YOU'RE RIGHT."

A panel in the wall hissed open. Smoke poured out, and a shadow stepped forward.

"Prepare to be amazed by the great and powerful Skr// Cr0... or just Cro," he shouted, striking a pose.

And there he was.

Cro stood barely five feet tall. Scruffy, sure, but confident. His spiky white hair stuck out in every direction, and his goggles glowed like twin moons. He wore a tech bodysuit with an oversized lab coat with the sleeves rolled up to his elbows. He also had thick gloves, heavy boots, and a utility belt that clanked when he moved.

I clapped slowly, pretending to be impressed.

Kassi didn't bother. She just kept her arms crossed and stared Cro down like she was ready to drag him out by his coat.

Cro narrowed his eyes. "The least you could do is show a little respect."

"Okay, gadget boy," Kassi said, stepping forward. "Let's skip the theatrics. We need your help."

I nudged her elbow again. Harder this time. She shot me a look but stayed quiet.

"At least someone here knows how to show manners," Cro responded, turning to me with a smug nod. "Greetings, Dorothy. Now, whats this you brought me?"

"Its-"

He grabbed the compass quickly but gently before I could fully respond.

"I already know what this is," he replied, flipping it over in his hands. "The real question is... how did you get it?"

"It belonged to my parents," I answered. They entrusted it to me before they passed away.

Cro's eyes locked on mine. "And how did *they* get it?"

"They were the Vogans of Galesville," Kassi cut in. "Maybe you've heard of them."

Cro paused. "The Vogans? As in the leaders of the Zephyrs?"

Kassi nodded, blowing her hair out of her face.

Cro stared at the compass, then back at me like he'd just discovered something unusual. "They had a kid?"

I gave a small shrug. "Yep. That's me. Dorothy Vogan. Resident begotten child of legends."

Cro started pacing, muttering under his breath.

"They were brilliant... both of them. When would they have had time for a child? That does not compute. How old are you, exactly?"

I raised an eyebrow. "Don't you think you're a little too young to ask that?"

"Nonsense," he dismissed. "My brain's older than I am. Plus, I'm twelve and a half. It's a reasonable age to learn about the breeding—"

"WHOA, OKAY, I get it!" I interrupted, "I'm sixteen,"

He stopped pacing and gave me a look that somehow explained everything.

"Hmm... I understand. Your parental units provided this artifact prior to the Galesville incident. What transpired with them... that was quite unfortunate. You have my sympathies. At least they left you a memento to recall them by."

Cro adjusted a small microscope on his desk and held the compass under it, his goggles glowing brighter as he worked.

"Judging by the chassis, the design, and the materials, this is, without a doubt, a pre-Ventus Age relic," he said, adjusting his glasses. "The engravings meticulously match the older schematics from that era. This apparatus is of an authentic nature. It could be worth an extravagant sum on the trade circuit—"

"It's not for sale," Kassi cut in.

"Yeah. It's not," I added, backing her up.

Cro didn't flinch. "I was going to say, if it were in a state of pristine condition. But it is not. Furthermore, it is not broken either, merely drained. All it requires is a sufficient charge."

"We figured that out already, detective," Kassi said.

"Kassi!" I snapped. "Can you not?"

Cro sighed. "Do you want my help or not?"

Kassi turned her head away. "Fine. Keep going."

He spun back to his terminal and typed rapidly. "As for the power source… it's a long shot, but…"

He trailed off.

"What?" I asked.

The screen blinked. A line of strange symbols appeared next to the image of a glowing crystal. The markings were eerily similar to those on the compass.

"What is that?" Kassi asked

"This, I have determined, is *Amberinium*. It is a lost mineral and energy source. I have been researching it for precisely two years. The only known deposits were supposedly eradicated ages ago. People still persist in the irrational belief that it is merely a myth."

My eyes were fixed on the screen. "That's incredible. I've never even heard of it."

"But why are you surprised?" Kassi asked Cro. "The compass is ancient. Makes sense it would run on something forgotten."

Cro let out a slow, creepy laugh. "I'm surprised," he giggled, turning toward us, "because I'm the one who rediscovered it."

"What?" Kassi and I said at the same time, both of us caught off guard.

"Yes, but…" Cro drifted off. He started pacing in tight circles, muttering to himself. Then he stopped cold.

"We might be able to help each other," he said, turning back toward us.

Kassi sighed. "See? Knew it was too good to be true."

"No," I said quickly, "let's hear him out."

"Thank you, Dorothy," Cro said, nodding. "There is only one method by which I may provide a satisfactory assistance. A few days prior, a group of unsophisticated bandits escaped with a exclusive item. An item upon which I have expended several months of labor. I had previously upgraded a weapon for them, and they, in their simplistic minds, presumed it wasn't a single, one-time favor. When they return for more items, my cooperation was not forthcoming. They confiscated my special item as an act of reprisal."

He paused for a moment with a tightened expression and serious tone.

"I would've negotiated, but they weren't interested. They don't get how much that possession meant to me."

Kassi narrowed her eyes. "So, how does that help us?"

He relaxed his tightened face and smiled. "Let's just say… that item might be exactly what you need for your compass… hahahaha!"

Both Kassi and I felt a little creeped out by Cro's laugh.

"Sorry," he added quickly, seeing our faces. "I get a little excited sometimes."

"Sometimes?" Kassi muttered under her breath.

"So, you want us to track them down and bring it back?" I asked. "What do we have to lose?"

"A lot," Cro said seriously. "These bandits are well-armed and unpredictable. I could have sent bots, but I'm lying low. People are still looking for me. Sending drones would bring the wrong kind of attention."

Kassi gave him a look. "So instead, you send *us* to do your dirty work, so you stay squeaky clean?"

"Affirmative!" Cro replied bluntly.

"Yeah, no thanks. Dorothy and I will pass."

"Really? Because if I remember right, you still owe me after that mission you tanked."

"I tanked it?" Kassi shot back. "If your hack hadn't failed, we wouldn't have gotten caught in the first place!"

"And if you hadn't turned it into a battlefield, we wouldn't have had to run for weeks," Cro fired back. "I've been stuck in this rusted bunker ever since."

"Enough!" I yelled.

They both stopped.

The room went quiet.

"Look," I said, "you both messed up. That mission was a disaster, but you made it out. You're alive. And right now, we've got bigger problems. A shared goal. A shot at something that could matter way more than a grudge."

I turned to Kassi. "I know you have doubts. But I've already decided; I'm in. I'll risk it for this. You said you'd have my back."

Then to Cro. "If you can give us support, protection, a plan that actually makes sense, we'll do it."

As I spoke, I saw the mood change. The anger between Kassi and Cro, which had built up from past conflicts, began to fade. Their angry looks softened.

Kassi lowered her arms and sighed. "You're right, Dorothy. Let's just get this done. No more dragging the past around."

"Affirmative," Cro replied.

* * *

"So, what's the plan?" I asked, already feeling the buzz of the next adventure kicking in.

Cro adjusted his goggles, the lenses catching the light as his eyes lit up. "The operational plan is simple. I have meticulously tracked the bandits for a duration of several weeks. I possess comprehensive knowledge of their behavioral patterns, their weak points, and the precise location of their contraband storage. Your singular task is to adhere to the designated route and strictly obey my instructional directives. If you perform those tasks, no one will sustain injury, and no one will be apprehended."

Kassi narrowed her eyes. "And how do we know you won't flip on us the second we're out there?"

Cro gave a lazy smirk. "You don't. But let's be real… I need that item just as much as you do. So, what would I gain from stabbing you in the back?"

I watched him carefully. His voice was calm. His tone? A little smug. But not dishonest.

"Think, Dorothy. He's smart, sure. But is he dangerous? Would he really pull something on us? On Kassi?"

I didn't come up with the perfect answer. But I had a gut feeling.

"Okay, we're in," I responded. My decision wasn't complicated. It felt right.

Cro's face lit up. "Excellent! Now let's get to work. I'll share everything I have on the bandits, and then we'll start planning. It won't be easy, but together we can do it."

Cro began pulling up data on the screens at his surveillance headquarters, while Dorothy and Kassi sat down with him. And so, the unlikely trio began preparing, united by a shared goal.

* * *

"Okay, I'm here," I whispered.

It was nighttime, and we had just arrived at the bandits' camp. Two guards stood by a nearby tent, wearing worn black storm-jackets decorated with old patches, and their faces were hidden behind red night visors. I signaled for Kassi to come closer. She moved silently on her wind-strider, carrying a large package wrapped in sackcloth. As she got nearer, we heard the guards laughing and joking about something earlier.

Dorothy: "Lady Gale to Red Fist. Come in, Red Fist."

Kassi's voice popped in my comms. "When did we agree on these code names?"

Dorothy: "Well, we can't exactly use *your* usual codename, can we? Just go with it."

Kassi: "*(Sigh)*... This is Red Fist... over."

Dorothy: "Red Fist, I've reached the east opening. There's a large tent in the center. Heavily guarded. I think that's where they're keeping the target."

Kassi: "Copy that, Lady Gale. These guys really know how to tuck things away."

Cro: "That sarcasm is going to get you in trouble one day!"

Kassi: "Hey Lame-Brain, can you confirm?"

Cro: "*Grrrrr... the codename's Gizmo.* And yes, Lady Gale is correct. Target location confirmed."

Dorothy: "Right. But let's not get cocky. We might be underestimating them."

Kassi: "We'll see. Stay sharp. I'm moving toward your location with the package."

Above us, a few of Cro's mechanized crows circled silently, their lenses scanning every angle of the camp. One of them sent us a live schematic of the layout, which Cro patched directly into our new night visors.

The bandit camp sat in a place called Skull Clearing. Quiet and tucked just outside of town. It was fenced in with sheets of rusted metal and loops of barbed wire. Their tents were patched together with old desert-sheets, clustered around a smoking bonfire in the center.

We stashed our striders on the west side and eased through a weak spot in the fence on the east. The path ahead wasn't easy, but the goal was clear.

Get in. Get the item. Get out.

The center tent was our mark.

And we were getting closer.

Cro: "Red Fist, confirm the package is still intact."

Kassi: "Yes, it's all in one piece, like I've told you before."

Cro: "I'm just double-checking to prevent any slip-ups."

Kassi: "I'll show you a slip-up if you keep questioning me."

Dorothy: "Alright, calm down, you two. Let's stay focused."

Cro: "Affirmative. Your entry point is just a few yards away. As we talked about, the main entrance is heavily guarded. But the south entrance has a weak point."

Dorothy: "Got it. We're heading there now."

Kassi: "Are you ready for your part?"

Cro: "Affirmative. Once you make the switch, I'll launch the plan."

Just as Kassi and I reached the fence's edge,

"CLANG!"

Bandit #1: "Did you hear that?"

Bandit #2: "Yeah. Go check it out. Let me know if you need backup."

"Uh-oh," I whispered, barely moving my lips. "They heard the package clipped the fence."

"I know," Kassi murmured. "Hold. Maybe they'll chalk it up to the wind."

Cro: "You see, this is why we need no mistakes; you guys need to hurry — the winds are picking up."

Dorothy: "Not now."

As one of the bandit moved towards the noise, we could hear the crunch of his boots against the ground. His shadow stretched long across the ground. He was right on the other side of the gate, charging his blaster.

Bandit #1: "Who's there?"

He started climbing,up; and we were right under him. I held my breath. Kassi quietly reached for her weapon.

Bandit #1: "Whoa!"

"CAW, CAW!"

The bandit flinched, ducked, then dropped back down.

Bandit #2: "Did you find anything?"

Bandit #1: "No, it was just those stupid noisy night birds."

Bandit #2: "Well, hurry up with your rounds. The winds are picking up, and the boss wants us ready to move."

Bandit #1: "Yeah, yeah, I got it. I'll be there."

I let out the breath I'd been holding. Kassi gave me a look of relief.

Dorothy: "Area is clear."

Kassi: "I guess I owe you one, kid."

Cro: "You're welcome. Now keep moving."

We finally reached the opening near the south entrance.

Cro: "Is the opening large enough for the package?"

Kassi: "Yes, it should go through. Your move."

Cro: "Affirmative."

Kassi and I crouched low near an empty tent, the wind starting to howl through the trees. We tightened the sackcloth over the package, holding it down as it threatened to flap free.

Dorothy: "Is something wrong?"

Kassi: "Yeah, what's the hold-up? We're in position."

Cro: "Just give it another minute. I'm triple-checking the codes."

Kassi whispered quietly, "Please let it work this time."

Cro: "I can still hear you! And for your information, the programming is all green. We're good to go."

Kassi: "Finally."

I looked up, scanning the sky. "Wait… what sign were we supposed to see again?"

Kassi didn't take her eyes off the camp. "He never told us. Just said, 'Look up at the sky.' That's it."

"Great," I whispered flatly.

But then I noticed small orbs of light drifting in from the far distance, slow at first. Floating like fireflies, but brighter.

Then they grew larger.

They were coming this way and coming in fast.

"Are those…" Kassi began,

"CRASH!"

She was cut off as a light smashed into the middle of the camp, exploding in a burst of flames.

Bandit #1: "Hey, what was that?"

Bandit #2: "Boss, it looks like fire!"

Bandit #3: "Look up, there are more in the sky!"

Red Eye: "Grab your weapons, all of you! We're under attack. You four, secure the north and south entrances. The rest of you, move! Locate them and take them down!"

All around the camp, boots hit the ground and chaos exploded. Most of the bandits rushed out through the north gate. Others scrambled toward the armory, grabbing whatever they could.

Kassi and I ducked lower, eyes wide.

"Fireballs?" I blurted, stunned. Kassi and I exchanged glances.

Kassi: "Are you serious right now? When were you going to tell us you had Blaze cannons?"

Cro: "That knowledge wasn't vital to the mission."

Kassi: "Clearly it is! You expect us to sneak in while the sky's exploding? I knew this was a suicide mission."

Cro: "Do not be absurd. I have the entire situation under my complete and total control. The cannons are precisely concealed deep within the desert prairie. By the time they have a chance to formulate a solution, the impending sandstorm will have already entrapped them. One of my crows is currently observing your designated positions. Merely keep your heads down."

Dorothy: "This feels reckless, Cro. But I guess we're already in it. Just tell us when to move."

More fireballs hit the camp, sending up another round of explosions.

Cro: "You're clear now. Hurry up and get to the tent. You have a small window."

Dorothy: "Copy that. We're on the move."

Kassi and I sprinted toward the center tent, dodging flames and leaping over broken crates as explosions rocked the surrounding camp. The whole place was chaotic with bandits shouting, fire lighting up the sky, and debris flying.

We reached the tent, breathless and tense. It was empty except for a few crates and scattered supplies. Right in the middle, something sat beneath a draped sackcloth.

I peeked outside to make sure we weren't being followed.

"Hey Dorothy, this must be it."

She pulled off the cloth, and we found what we were after.

"I see," Kassi remarked. "A robot. Definitely unique. Let's hope this thing's worth all the trouble."

"It has to be," I replied. "Cro's throwing everything he has into this."

She agreed. "Alright. Let's make the switch."

We carefully picked up the new robot and replaced it with one of the dummy bots from Cro's factory.

Cro's voice came through: "Lady Gale and Red Fist, have you secured the package? My cannons are almost out of ammo, and the bandits are coming in fast."

Dorothy: "We've secured the new package and are now making the exchange."

Cro replied, "Got it. Now hurry up and get out of there."

Kassi: "What makes you think they won't notice the difference?"

Cro: "You'll see. My crow found a weak point in the west gate from one of the explosions. It's your closest exit. Your striders are just beyond it. But move fast. The sandstorm's closing in, and the bandits are trapped for now."

Dorothy: "Got it. We're moving."

Kassi and I double-checked that the robot was secure. Then we slipped through the broken section of the gate, staying low. Most of the remaining guards were too busy trying to control the fires to notice us.

We sprinted across the clearing and reached our striders in seconds. Kassi clipped the board with the strapped-down robot to her rig while I powered mine up.

Just as we were about to ride, Cro's voice cut in again.

Cro: "Wait, look at this before you leave!"

We turned around just in time to see another barrage of fireballs streak across the sky. They came down hard, hammering the camp.

"BLAST!"

One hit square in the center tent—the one we'd just left.

Flames erupted as the tent was blown apart, the dummy bot inside burning to ash. Bandits scattered, shouting orders, completely thrown off.

Dorothy: "Yes! Genius! Now they'll never know that it wasn't the real one."

Cro: "Precisely!"

Kassi: "Very clever. Way to use that big brain of yours!"

Cro: "Thank you. Now hurry up and head back to base. The bandits are pulling back, and the storm's not waiting."

We kicked off, speeding through the rising wind. By the time we reached the old factory, the sandstorm had already passed through the bandit's area. But we'd made it, robot intact, mission complete.

Cro met us at the door, practically glowing with excitement.

"Ouch! What was that for?"

Kassi gave him a playful punch in the arm. "That's for not warning us you were going full war zone back there."

Cro winced. "Noted."

I couldn't help laughing.

CHAPTER ELEVEN

Back at the old factory, the three of us met in Cro's messy work lab. In the middle of it all was Cro, totally focused on fixing the recovered robot. He sat over the repair table with careful, precise movements that only someone as detailed, and almost obsessively, as he could make.

But boy was he excited. He spoke to the robot as if it were a long-lost friend. Every time he connected a wire or adjusted a part, he paused dramatically, almost as if he expected the robot to thank him.

"Yes, yes! Be amazed by my brilliance, my dear friend," he said, holding up a circuit board like it was a rare treasure. "Soon, you'll be a symbol of my unmatched genius, completely different from those who just don't get it."

Kassi snorted next to me.

"Has he always been like this?" I asked, giving him a sideways glance.

"Who, Cro?" she replied, gesturing at him as he busily muttered something about quantum servos. "Nope. This is even stranger than usual."

Cro didn't seem to notice that we were talking about him.

I cleared my throat. "Hey, Cro? I know you love this whole robot resurrection idea, but shouldn't we worry that Red-Eye and his gang might figure out we trashed their camp?"

He straightened up, looking a bit offended. "Worried? Please, Dorothy, the emotion of worry is reserved for amateurs. My plan was a masterclass in clandestine operations. I have left no clues that could possibly lead back to my person or this laboratory. Red-Eye and his intellectually challenged crew would sooner blame a natural atmospheric occurrence than deduce my involvement."

"Right. Sure." I wasn't completely sold, but I went with it, anyway. He continued his one-sided conversation with the robot.

Kassi shook her head and sat on the nearest couch, fishing a snack out of her bag. "You know, you're really attached to that hunk of metal. Is there a robot love you are not telling us about?" she teased between bites of a snack.

Without seeking clarification, Cro responded, "While I acknowledge your humor, Kassi, explaining my profound connection to this creation would be akin to explaining advanced science to a cactus-plum. Your understanding would not comprehend it."

Kassi then raised her eyebrow at me. "Did he just call me a dumb cactus-plum?"

"Looks like it," I giggled, munching on my snack.

"How long would this take?" I asked, interrupting his train of thought.

Cro didn't even look up as his hands worked through the robot's wiring. "Ah, a solid question from a curious but slightly uninformed observer," he said with a touch of drama. "To answer: about seven hours. Efficient work demands patience. Luckily, my previous fixes are still in place from well before the Sentinel incident."

"Which Sentinel incident was this?" Kassi asked.

Cro straightened up. "Well, let me tell you a tale. A long time ago, relative to my younger days, I was scavenging in the topside junkyards near Metallia. As you both know, I have a knack for finding treasure among the trash."

"I didn't know trash digging was a talent," Kassi muttered.

He ignored her, of course.

"That day," Cro continued, slipping into full theater mode, "I found something special. Buried in a pile of tech over a hundred years old. It was like stepping into history itself—every piece had a story, singing a melody of possibility to anyone who could hear it."

Kassi rolled her eyes. "Let me guess. You were the only one listening?"

"Exactly!" he replied, completely unbothered. "One piece stood out. A robot, half buried. Its frame peeked out from the wreckage, and its worn metal showed signs of a glorious past. It was magnificent. I knew I had to bring it back."

He paused, like he was waiting for applause.

"And then?" I asked, pushing him along.

Cro sighed, "Then, I brought it back to my workshop and started restoring it. The robot was surprisingly well-preserved. I couldn't resist, so I hooked it up to an emerald battery I had lying around. That's when I discovered its secrets. It wasn't just running on one power source; it had two! One was an enhanced emerald, which was expected. But the other?"

"Wait… Amberinium!" I guessed.

"Ha! Now you get it!" Cro responded. "But there's more. The coolest part, was the energy converter built into its back. Even when it was new, which was rare, it could switch emerald energy to Amberinium and back again."

"Okay, that is pretty cool," Kassi admitted.

"Yes, I'm very cool, aren't I?" he gloated.

"I wasn't talking about you—"

"Anyway, even though the converter is damaged, it confirmed what I suspected. This isn't an ordinary machine. This is a prototype, probably one of the fully intact models made during the renowned GEM Age. In short, I found a piece of history… a true marvel of engineering."

"The GEM Age? What's that supposed to be?" Kassi asked, arching her eyebrow as if Cro had just claimed to be a famous tap dancer.

"The Great Energy Migration Age," I answered casually as all eyes turned to me. "It's one of Oz's five big ages. The other four are the Proto Age, the Enchanted Age, the Hundred Years Storm, and the Ventus Age… where we are now."

I glanced over and saw Kassi giving me a blank look, like she was stuck listening to a history lecture she never signed up for.

I continued. "The GEM Age came just before the storm and changed everything. That's when the people of Oz discovered that raw gemstones could be used as energy. It changed technology, medicine, industry… everything. Before that, they had little understanding of energy. They figured it was powered by magic or some fable."

Kassi gave me a look and shook her head.

"What can I say? I read a lot of history and was a drilling engineer from the Battery City," I shrugged, trying to sound modest.

Cro snickered and added, "Back then, people used gemstones like diamonds, rubies, and sapphires for their special energy."

He approached his display screen to showcase different properties of various gems. "Rubies are still used to control heat in the ArcCities, while sapphires regulate cold, and diamonds are used for shields."

He then switched the display to show examples of each gem's use and continued explaining. "They each have unique properties and are quite impressive, but simply put, they couldn't store as much energy as emeralds."

He zoomed in to display the emeralds' properties. "That's why the leaders of Oz chose emeralds as the standard energy source. But there's also *Amberinium*, a rare mineral with even greater energy potential than emeralds. Because it was so scarce, only top scientists and leaders used it. But, it was later banned, destroyed, and then forgotten for reasons we don't know."

Kassi rolled her eyes. "Great. A history lesson about shiny rocks. You two are like walking codex for rock geeks."

Cro smirked. "We forgive your ignorance, Kassi. But try to keep up. It was an experimental model built to test energy conversion in the field. A marvel of its time. I was nearly finished updating its system when the bandits hit me."

"You? Without your tech on hand?" Kassi raised an eyebrow. "That's hard to believe."

Cro shrugged. "I admit, I wasn't used to being in that state. But I didn't let them get away clean. I'd already installed a tracker. Just didn't expect a freak storm to scramble the signal."

He sat back for a second, staring past us like he could still see it happening. "Months passed. Nothing. Then one day, my crow picked up a conversation between Sentinels. They mentioned a 'package' and its description sounded just like my bot. I needed to be sure, so I did some hacking."

He gave us a proud, unapologetic grin. "And I was right. Turns out, they made a trade with the bandits around the same time my bot disappeared. So... I did what needed to be done."

As he spoke, Cro started waving his arms like he was reenacting a scene from one of his own stories.

"Picture it... desert heat rising, a twister building on the horizon. The Sentinels were scrambling to get clear. Right then, I hit them with an Energy-disrupter. Boom! Shut down every vehicle they had.

Kassi and I glanced at each other, trying not to smile as Cro went on with his dramatic story.

"They panicked and ran for shelter in a nearby cave. They had to be new since they had left everything behind. When the storm passed, their equipment and packages were everywhere. I picked through the wreckage. And there it was… my precious prize."

"But then," Cro went on, "a Sentinel spotted me and tried to stop me. Luckily, I was ready. My trusty strider still worked, and I made a daring escape."

"By 'daring,' you mean 'lucky,' right?" Kassi asked.

Cro straightened his collar like he were adjusting a royal medal. "Luck is for people who don't prepare. I call it strategic brilliance."

I stepped in before their back-and-forth caught fire again.

"So, Cro," I asked, "is that why the Sentinels are after you? Why have you been hiding?"

"Yes, that's just part of it," he answered. "After a... let's call it 'not-so-successful' mission with some rebels, I decided to make Hollow Wyck a neutral zone. Helped rebuild it. Supported the locals. It actually worked for a while."

His voice softened as his tough talk went away. "While it's been a constant struggle, I don't regret it. But sometimes... I feel like I've been on the run for my short time being here."

His words hit close to home. We all knew what it was like growing up in a world that chewed up kids and didn't care about them.

"In this tough world," Cro said quietly, "the rich and powerful control everything. And kids? We're just expendable. Labor, experiments, whatever they need. It's always been this way," He stopped, as if his own words were too heavy to speak further.

The room went quiet.

Kassi broke the silence with a yawn. "Well, I'm gonna get some rest. It's been a long night. What about you, Dorothy?

"I'm not quite tired yet. Maybe I'll stay up and do a bit of journal reading. Keep Cro company.

"Oh, you don't have to, but it's much appreciated," Cro said, scratching the back of his head.

"Yeah, Dorothy, you *really* don't have to," Kassi added with a grin.

Cro groaned. "Grrr, the disrespect never ends with you. Good night, already."

Kassi laughed as she wandered off toward the office, dropping onto the couch like she'd been waiting all day to sink into it.

Not long after, Cro was back at it, completely locked in. I sat nearby with my journal open, half-reading, half-dozing, the words starting to blur. But even through the haze, I noticed how hard he was working.

He didn't stop eating. Didn't stop to talk. Just kept tinkering with the converter box, his tools clinking softly in the background.

Even with everything he knew, everything he had, he still couldn't get the bot to fully charge. That frustration showed in the way he adjusted the same wire three times in a row.

Still, he didn't give up.

And watching him... I had to admit, Cro was a lot of things. Loud. blunt. Definitely a little arrogant about his genius.

But unmotivated was not one of them.

* * *

"It is *finished*!"

Cro's voice blasted through the lab, jolting me awake. I scanned the room, trying to remember where I was. Kassi didn't even flinch; she was sprawled out on the couch like she was made of stone. For someone who used to waking up at the break of dawn, she could sleep through a hundred storms without batting an eye.

"She probably hasn't slept without the need to be alert in a long time."

Cro stood over the bot, practically glowing. His hair was wild, his goggles fogged, but he looked more alive than ever. After hours of work, he'd finally done it. The converter box was rebuilt.

Now all that was left was the charge.

He reached for the power lever.

"Uh… Cro?" I asked, sitting up straighter. "Is this safe?"

"Of course," he answered without hesitation.

Even I could tell he was putting on confidence, not real certainty. It wasn't very reassuring..

"Cro, wait—"

Too late. The lever clicked into place with a solid *"thunk"*.

A blinding burst of electricity shot out from the converter. Cro flew backward, slammed into the wall, and let out a grunt as he hit the floor.

The cables lit up instantly, glowing hot as energy surged through them. The robot's eyes blinked a bit to life, burning with a bright orange light that filled the room.

Cro quickly got up and ran over to the electrical gauges, checking the readings like a mad scientist proud of his experiment.

All the lights around the room blinked repeatedly. Then I noticed something else.

"Cro," I called out, stepping to the window. "It's not just here. All of Hollow Wyck is blinking."

Cro laughed a wild, excited laugh that made me wonder if he was losing his mind.

"Isn't it great? I diverted most of the town's energy to this generator."

"Great? You could black out the entire town!"

"That's a minor sacrifice for what we are doing here." He replied, waving me off.

The surge continued. Cro raced around the lab, taking notes and muttering to himself. The static in the air grew so strong that papers flew everywhere. Even my hair stood on end.

He turned to me.

"Yes, that's it! Dorothy, quick... get to the lever! I need you to shut it down on my command!"

"Yeah, I'm actually okay just being over here... un-electrified," I said, backing away from the sparking mess.

"Dorothy, I implore you," Cro pleaded, eyes wide behind his glowing goggles. "This is of grave importance. If my calculations are right... and they should be... I just need to offset the electrical load while starting the converter at exactly the right moment. Please. Just this once."

"Uhh... will this kill me?" I asked, eyeing the sparks shooting off the machinery.

"I'm... sixty percent sure it won't!"

I groaned. "Not helpful, Cro!"

I grabbed a scarf from my bag and wrapped it over my hair, just in case. Then I started toward the lever, keeping my face turned slightly away from the sparks

"Okay! Ready?" Cro shouted. "Shut it down... *NOW!*"

I lunged for the lever and yanked it back up.

Instantly, the power went off. Papers floated gently to the floor, and the lab was lit only by soft backup lights.

I looked across the room and met Cro's eyes. He was breathing hard, a little singed, but there was still excitement on his face.

"Well… Did it work?" I asked.

Cro tilted his head slightly. "I'm sure it did. I mean… it had to, right?"

"Hmmm… what was that just now…" I thought.

We waited in silence, watching the bot. Seconds turned into minutes, and then to half an hour.

Nothing happened.

I looked at Cro, and when our eyes met, my heart sank.

"That's what that was… he's… not sure of himself."

He didn't look like the confident boy genius anymore. He looked small and vulnerable, sitting on the floor with his knees pulled to his chest mumbling technical terms I couldnt understand.

For a moment, I just saw a kid who was scared and alone.

"His face… it reminds me of… me."

I couldn't ignore it.

"Hey, Cro… Apart from him being so rare and valuable… why is this bot so important to you?"

Cro stopped mumbling for a moment and looked at me, his eyes shining with almost-tears behind his goggles. "Because I didn't want to be alone, anymore…"

His lips trembled as he admitted, "You know, Dorothy, I realize you might not understand, but it isn't always easy being considered a genius."

I raised an eyebrow. That stung a little. But I let him talk.

"When I was younger," he continued, "I really wanted a sibling. I don't know why it mattered so much... but it did. My father, he was the Head Minister of Technology in Metallia. Strict didn't even begin to cover it. Everything had to be perfect. I was expected to follow in his footsteps, no matter what."

He looked at the wrench in his hand and tossed it. "I was good at it all. Tech, code, engineering—you name it. I was praised for being a prodigy. But it wasn't real. I was just a tool. I was always trying to prove my worth to adults who didn't really care about me."

He wiped his eyes quickly, pretending it wasn't happening. "I used to watch other kids playing outside with their siblings while I was stuck in a lab, solving problems for people who only saw me as a tool."

He leaned his head back, eyes on the ceiling. "One day, I asked my father why I couldn't go play too. He shouted at me and said I didn't have time for friends because my duty to the city was too important. It scared me to see him upset, but not enough to kill my curiosity."

"What do you mean?" I asked.

He smiled as he rested his legs and went on. "Sometimes, I'd sneak out, anyway. I'd try to show the other kids my inventions. I thought maybe they'd think I was cool. Instead, they'd laugh or just push me away."

"Boy, that sounds familiar to me." I added.

He clenched his fists. "One time, I went into the poorest district, seeing how bad it was with faulty structure and cracked streets. It didn't seem survivable, but kids did it every day, taking any job they could find."

"Just like Emeraldia and every other city." I muttered.

"Exactly," he nodded. "I saw a group of kids trying to fix their glide-boards. They were struggling, so I offered to help. One kid looked at me like I was a weirdo at first. But once I fixed his board... he knew I was the real deal.

His name was Xaven. Smart, quick with people. He spread the word, and soon kids were lining up. We had something good going. His network and my skills... together, we built a small business. We called it Gadgets and Goggles."

I raised an eyebrow. "Catchy."

He chuckled. "We went all over the district helping people with tech repairs for tokens. Some of the kids even insisted on paying me with the little tokens they earned that day. I wouldn't take it. We charged only adults. But I never kept any of it. I gave my share to kids who had it harder than the rest."

"Wow, Cro, you really have a great heart." I said.

He smiled a little, lost in the memory.

"It felt good. Not because I got to show my skills. But because, for the first time, I felt like I mattered. Not to adults or leaders or instructors. Just... to them."

His voice softened.

"Xaven and the others eventually figured out I was from the upper district, but they didn't care. I kept going back, fixing whatever I could. Answering their questions."

"What kind of questions did they have for you?"

He had a lighter expression and tone.

"They'd ask me what it was like, living on the rich side. I told them, there are good things. But they had something else we didn't. More fun. More freedom.

"'*This isn't freedom, Cro. The grown-ups just don't care.*' That's what Xaven used to say," Cro murmured. "I didn't understand it at first. But now I do. Those kids taught me more about the world than any instructor ever could. We spent so much time together. And it meant everything to me."

"Then... everything changed. I was heading home, just another day, when I saw this armored Metallic force vehicle roll into the street. The doors flew open, and soldiers jumped out, chasing every kid they saw. They were all running. Xaven shouted for me to run too. He said it was another cyber-harvest."

"Cyber-harvesting?" I asked as a memory surfaced. "Taking subjects and using them to engineer or upgrade cybernetic parts? In Emeraldia, we've heard whispers about missing children in Metallia. There were conspiracies about what was happening, but cyber-harvesting was the strangest of all."

"It's all true," he replied. "And it's worse than you can imagine. Once Xaven told me what was happening, I had to find out for myself. So, I hacked into the Ministry's most secure files."

He took a breath. The next part was hard for him to say; I could tell.

"What I discovered… was something called Project Brainchild. To improve their new military A.I. chip, they were testing it on live subjects. Just to see how far they could push the brain before it or the chip gave out."

"But… why children? Why not grown soldiers?"

"Because children adapt more quickly. Their brains are more flexible and easier to reprogram, with less resistance." He looked away briefly. "Easier to control."

I didn't say anything. I just listened.

"The Archons approved all of it," he continued. "Every document. Every trial."

He paused, visibly upset. "Then I realized who was behind it… my father. He used my code and chip design. When I developed it, he claimed it was just for a simulation… I didn't know."

He turned to me with tears in his eyes. "They used my work to hurt people. To hurt kids… the friends I made."

"*Cro…*"

"I confronted him. He yelled at me, calling me weak… said I was just like my mother… She passed away when I was little, but I remember… her as kind and gentle… everything he isn't."

I could see how much pain those memories caused him, but then he straightened up quickly, wiping away the tears.

"So, how did you end up topside?"

He laughed to keep from tearing up again. "I destroyed the entire program. I snuck into the ministry one last time with my access card, wiped everything out, and freed the remaining children. I knew what would happen if they captured me. So, I disappeared. I didn't even have the guts to face my friends and tell them goodbye… not even Xaven. I just felt it was all my fault."

Before I could reply, Kassi's voice broke into the dim light. "But it wasn't your fault. You really are a one-of-a-kind trouble-maker, kid. And that's my favorite kind."

As the generator started back up, Kassi stepped forward, showing that she'd been listening the whole time.

Cro grinned. "What, no teasing me about being a top-district brat-hacker?"

"No, Cro. Dorothy is right. I give you a hard time, but you really have a good heart. And even if this robot doesn't work, you aren't alone anymore."

Cro chuckled and reached for the kill switch.

"BZZZT!"

A hard jolt cut him off. Sparks spat from the bot. The lever was down, but the machine jumped to life.

"No way," Kassi whispered.

"It's…" I stuttered, too shocked to finish.

"ALIVE!" Cro shouted in triumph. "HE'S ALIVE!"

The lab filled with a bright glow as the robot stood up, its limbs moving smoothly.

"It's really alive!"

As the giant bot powered up before us, we couldn't help but marvel at its impressive size. Towering over both Kassi and me, it had two large, glowing orange eyes behind round lenses and synthetic white hair at the very top.

"It finally happened! I did it!" Cro exclaimed, jumping around the bot with pride.

Standing tall and still, the bot looked like it was waiting for instructions. Cro made a big gesture toward it.

"Ladies and gentlemen, I am pleased to introduce the Terabot Nexus, designated as T//N. You may refer to him as Tin. He is equipped with a rare graphene-infused steel chest plate and reinforced iron limbs, granting him the strength to lift Metallia's mecha-tank blasters. Furthermore, he possesses sufficient speed to match a sand-strider for brief intervals, and his sensors ensure the proper functioning of all systems."

Cro pointed at Tin's glowing optics. "These optics are capable of processing nearly the entire wave spectrum and have the potential to perceive at distances surpassing any existing technology. The amber light comes from his Amberinium cores. It's beyond anything I can even calculate right now."

"Wow, Tin, huh?" I said, stepping closer to look at the lights on his limbs.

Kassi smirked. "You really went all out with the details. And the hair? Was that just for style?" She reached out playfully to touch the white strands.

"Affirmative," Cro replied.

"Does he talk?" I asked, curious.

"I… CAN… SPEAK," Tin answered, his voice a bit slow but clear.

We all froze, wide-eyed. Then, Tin's voice grew louder as he announced a sequence of messages: "Internal data updating to match current time—system log processing for programming registration. Variables acknowledged. Booting Nexus artificial intelligence. Registering dual cores…"

"Uh-oh, is he already broken?" Kassi teased.

Cro shot her a look. "He's not broken; you are. He's just updating. He's been offline for over a hundred years. I installed new patches in his memory bank, but it'll take a while for him to sync completely.

He turned back to his data screen, dismissing us with a wave. "Now, excuse me while I review the patches in his pro-gramming."

Tin suddenly took his first steps. He gradually approached Cro with his arm outstretched, but it didn't look friendly.

"Tin, watch out!" Kassi shouted, raising her gale-blaster. I quickly grabbed my battle wand.

Tin turned his head sharply, suddenly shifting into a defensive stance.

"I am designated to safeguard Master Cro," he stated. "You are not registered members under Master Cro. Please lower your weapons. This is a cautionary notice."

Kassi held her ground, trying to ease the tension. "Hey, Tin, relax. We're not a threat."

Cro whirled around, clearly surprised by what was happening. "Tin, stop! First, adjust your speech pattern and add Kassi and Dorothy as friends. They need to be protected, too."

Tin's optics dimmed. "Processing command… adjustments made."

"And don't call me 'master.' Turn on your learning mode functionality.

"Understood," Tin repeated. His tone softened as he turned back to us. "My apologies. I was programmed to—"

"We know," Kassi and I said at the same time, sliding our weapons back into place.

I sat down, still a little shaky from the scare. But I noticed he kept staring with a strange gaze at my arm.

"This is uncomfortable. What is he doing? Is really functional?"

He stepped toward me, his movement now a lot slower and disarming.

"You're Dorothy, correct?" he asked in a more natural voice.

"Yes, Tin…. How are you feeling?" I replied cautiously.

"I'm fine, thank you," Tin answered, then nodded toward my bracelet. May I inquire about the origin of that artifact?

I looked at my wrist, puzzled. "This? It's no artifact, just an old family keepsake. My mother gave it to me."

"And from whom did she acquire that? I presume it was her mother." Tin asked.

"Uh… yes and her mother before… Why do you ask?"

Kassi folded her arms. "Yeah, what's the deal with the bracelet, Tin? You're acting weird again."

"I don't mean to pry," Tin said, pausing like he wasn't sure if he should go on. "However, during my scan of you, my memory identified the artifact on your bracelet. I was able to correlate it with one I encountered over a hundred cycles ago."

I glanced down at my wrist and tried to play it cool. "Oh. You're probably thinking of something else. Mine's not that old. Maybe fifty years, tops."

"Possibly," Tin replied. "However, I recall specific events associated with a bracelet of that nature."

"What do you mean?" I asked, a little uneasy now. "It's just a plain bracelet."

Cro, catching the weird moment, explained what was happening. "Tin's still getting used to the world again. He's probably dating everything he sees."

"Correct," Tin confirmed. "I am currently processing a substantial amount of stored data spanning a century. When significant information becomes available, I will ensure you are promptly informed."

"Uh, okay… sounds good," I said, then reached into my bag. "Speaking of relics, would you mind taking a look at this?" I held up the compass.

Tin's optics immediately fixed on it. "This is an ionic compass. The unusual design bears resemblance to an antiquated data key module. According to my records, this compass is deemed obsolete."

"That's where you come in," Cro cut in. "Tin, it needs amberinium energy to recharge. You're the only one who could do it."

Tin gave a small nod. "Acknowledged. According to Cro's system logs, it seems you rescued me from enemy capture."

"Yeah, well, we actually—" I started to explain.

"Absolutely!" Kassi jumped in with a grin, bumping me with her elbow before I could finish.

Tin took the compass from my hand. His amber-colored eyes pulsed brighter, and a current of energy flowed into the device. The gears inside the compass slowly coming back to life.

I couldn't help but feel a great deal of emotion. We were finally going to have a way to find the truth.

CHAPTER TWELVE

-LEO-

"*Okay, I can do this.*" After months of completing my duties and training new recruits, I finally faced Captain Briggs. My heart was racing, but I composed myself. This was my chance to secure my dream assignment after Dee's incident, which had damaged my record. This topside mission could be the redemption I needed.

Cap just stood there, stone-faced arms folded, and not giving away a thing. I started talking anyway. I laid out why I wanted this assignment and what it meant to me. Loyalty, commitment, everything I've poured into the force. I can't lie, I felt the judgment, but I didn't back down.

Little by little, I saw it. His expression shifted… not much, but enough to catch.

"Lieutenant," he finally said, "I'll be straight with you. That escapee incident a few months back raised red flags even among my superiors. But your overall record stands strong. You're still recognized for your leadership during the Emerald Peace Parade. That took courage. Strategy. Nerve. You made the right call when it mattered."

That hit me hard. Not because it was praise. But because it meant maybe… just maybe… he still saw something in me.

Memories of that huge incident came back: the unhappy miners, their fight against the mayor's deal, and the dangerous plot that followed. I had moved on from those memories, but now they rushed back.

*　*　*

The city's deal with Metallia became the only thing anyone talked about. Mayor Gulch's plan was simple: trade our miners for unmanned drill mechs. It looked good on a data sheet— faster work, fewer injuries.

But for the miners, it was the last straw. They refused to accept this and chose to protest in the streets.

"*Show Respect, No Mechs! Show Respect, No Mechs!*"

Their lives were being thrown aside for metal that could do their job effortlessly. I could see the anger building in their posture. It wasn't about the jobs; Their way of life was being erased without a single discussion.

Dee was always the loudest among them.

"How could they make this decision for us without even giving us a seat at the table. They know it's wrong! This plan needs to stop."

Even Mr. Neel, the owner of the southern mining company and a man who never voiced opposition to the city, simply shook his head. He didn't need to speak; everyone knew what was coming.

Mayor Gulch knew the lower districts didn't take the news well. So instead of delivering it plain, she turned it into a big show.

"As mayor, I understand that many of you might feel uncertain about the upcoming changes affecting our districts. Rest assured, we care about your concerns. In Emeraldia, we work hard to foster unity across all districts, but we also value our relationships with our sister cities. To celebrate both our district unity and our new partnership with Metallia, we will host a city-wide event called the Emerald Peace Parade. This is the first of its kind, and we are all invited!"

Many residents were excited about the all-city parade, while others, not so much.

Up north, in the rich districts, the residents didn't care for the idea of mixing with us. Storefronts went on lockdown, and private security forces patrolled the streets. People made plans for when things "got out of hand." It didn't take a genius to see how little faith they had in this so-called unity.

And then, the whispers started.

Talk of something bad, an attack maybe.

It was just rumors, but enough for Command to take it seriously. As a Vanguard, I was given the assignment: find the truth about the threat.

I spent days in underground bars and back alleys, listening without being seen. Then, one night at Lyman's, an informant gave me a name that led to three high-level miners. He also shared a video of their meeting with me. I was surprised by who appeared.

That's when I realized this was genuine. Something was on the horizon.

Something big.

I watched them for days, tracking their movements and conversations. They were careful, but I gathered enough to confirm their plan: sabotage the drill mechs at the parade. I didn't have enough to make an arrest, but I had enough to bring to Cap.

I laid it all out for him and the rest of the unit. Every detail, every observation. He listened with a straight face. He made his decision right there: I would lead the counter-unit. That was a huge moment for me.

Later, the mayor's security team looked over my report and gave me a promotion. I was now in charge of the special joint team. I met with both city forces and the MSF outlining our plan.

"The plan is simple," I said, showing the schematics of the mechs on a screen. "We know they will wait for the right moment during the event to attack. It will probably be when they reveal the mechs. For the MSF team, make sure you get the disruptor gun we've been asking for to stop the mechs."

I then put up a map of the event location outside the city hall.

"My team here will cover the most important spots among the crowd. The rest of you, make sure all the exits are watched and secure from high places. I will be in the crowd with everyone. Do you all understand your jobs?"

"Yes, sir!" everyone replied.

On parade day, the city lit up with music and speeches. The streets were packed, and everyone was filled with a sense of excitement and celebration. The theme was *"A Faster, Safer, Better Tomorrow."*

The crowd had no idea.

I took my position as my team spread out across the area. We blended in with the crowd, watching and waiting. We had prepared for every outcome, and if something went wrong, we were ready.

The moment of truth arrived. After all the speeches and performances, they wheeled in the main event: four massive drill mechs covered in ceremonial cloth. The crowd held its breath. For me, the moment felt heavy.

"Drumroll," the mayor shouted.

I tapped my comm. "Anything?"

"All clear," my enforcers responded.

The cloth dropped.

Towering giants of steel and precision, their frames polished to perfection. Light danced off their armored bodies.

The crowd roared.

To them, it was the future, standing on a stage.

And for a split second, I almost believed it too.

"Dee," I whispered to myself, thinking of her. "It's everything we used to dream about."

As kids, we often dreamt of huge machines that could help everyone. But Dee wasn't here to see it. She had sided with the miners. I understood why, but a small part of me wondered if she had a point.

Then, something happened that shouldn't have. The mechs twitched. A slight motion at first, then another. They moved with a strange, unnatural purpose. One turned toward Mayor Gulch. The others scanned the crowd as if picking their targets.

Mayor Garlit barked a code. Nothing.

"All units, move now!" I said into my comm.

My team split instantly. Two officers covered the mayor. The rest of us triggered our disruptors. Bright pulses hit the mechs, frying their standards receivers. Sparks shot from their joints as they fought the interference.

The saboteurs made a moved.

I spotted them in the crowd, the same faces from surveillance. One slipped into a side alley.

I was on him in seconds.

He reached for his gale blaster, but he never got the chance. I fired.

The weapon flew from his grip and skidded across the pavement with a sharp clatter.

One down.

That's the thing about my gear. Every weapon I use links directly to my cyber arm. Instant fire, no delay. Just precision. Dee likes to call me Green Dog when she's in a mood, but out here, in the field, I was nicknamed *Iron-Sight*.

The rest of the team was fast. One saboteur tried climbing a fire escape. Another ducked through food stalls. They all ran, but none got far. We caught every last one.

By the time the mechs were fully shut down, the saboteurs were in cuffs. We found two gale blasters and a scrambled controller. That was all the proof we needed.

The crowd was still cheering. Most didn't even realize how close it had come to a disaster. To them, it was just part of the show. The drill mechs clanked back into standby mode as if nothing had happened.

Later that evening, the mayor's team found something we hadn't expected: additional control antennas hidden inside the drill mechs. The truth came out. Someone had planned to weaponize those machines to strike down Mayor Gulch and blame Mayor Garlit. It would have been the spark to start a war. We stopped it.

For that, I was given the Emerald Honors Badge and called a city hero.

* * *

I'll never forget that day. The lights, the noise, the way my hands didn't stop shaking after it was over. It's all still burned into me. But even with the medal on my chest, things changed after Dee's escape. I stopped feeling like the hero everyone thought I was.

Now here I am, finally called up for the mission I'd been hoping for. Captain Briggs finally agreed to bring me in as the rifle-blaster marksman and strategist. Next thing I knew, I was sitting in a briefing room, face to face with some of the best soldiers in the force, gearing up for a topside mission.

Every single one of them had a rep.

Lt. Cobalt was sitting across from me, a combat specialist, brutal in close quarters. He'd been training longer than I've been alive, and yeah, he'd even taught me some of what I know. All focus and no nonsense.

Next to him was Lt. Copperton, our vehicle and terrain guy. If it had wheels, wings, or legs, he could drive it. Probably blindfolded, too.

Lt. Rhynes, Tracking Specialist, was quiet and efficient, leading more topside ops than anyone else in the room. He spoke only when necessary.

And then there was him. Lt. Brass, Weapons and Communications Specialist. Self-proclaimed rival. Ever since the Emerald Peace Parade, he's had it out for me. Probably couldn't stand the idea that someone from the lower district climbed the ranks faster than he did. And after the whole Dee's situation, he never missed a chance to bring it up.

The moment he saw me in the room, he walked over, already wearing that smug look he always had when he thought he was being clever.

"Well, well, well. Looks like they'll let just anyone on this team," he said loud enough for the others to hear.

"Great to see you too, Brass," I said, keeping my face calm and my tone even.

"Good thing Copperton's here. After that little tunnel fiasco, I wouldn't trust you to steer a lunch tray."

"Yeah? How's that junkyard duty treating you?" I asked just loud enough.

I knew that hit home.

That mission was low-tier. Digging through confiscated tech and sorting smuggled parts. Brass hated every second of it, thought it was beneath him. His face turned red before I even finished the sentence.

"Why bring that up now?" he snapped, stepping in close.

I didn't move. If he wanted a fight, he'd have to go all in. And if he did, I'd make sure he regretted it.

"Come on, not the time," Rhynes said, slipping between us.

"Yeah, save it for the real enemies," Cobalt added, rubbing the back of his neck like he'd seen this play out before.

"All right, lieutenants, calm down. We're all on the same team," Captain Briggs said, cutting through the tension.

"Yes, sir," we all answered in unison and took our seats. The energy in the room was still tense. Brass kept glaring at me, but I let it slide. He wasn't worth it.

Cap didn't waste time.

"Listen up. We've got a lot to cover before deployment. Some of you will support the specialists near the dome. Your job is to keep everything secure. There's a high chance we'll run into hostiles."

He waited, letting that sink in.

"As you know, most of our topside radar scanners have been destroyed. Some by storms, others by sabotage. We believe the rebels are behind it."

He stepped forward, arms behind his back.

"Our mission has two objectives. First, install the new scanners. Second, secure the nearby outposts. Our techs will handle the setup. Your job is to protect them. We don't want a firefight unless we have no choice. We're a small unit, and our gear is limited. Move smart."

There it was.

The rumors about the radar station going dark weren't just talk. The public noticed, but the mayor stayed quiet because she didn't want to stir panic.

He continued. "We don't have much information about their current locations, although we have run into them a few times before. What we do know is that they call themselves the Monsoon Rebels. They have been operating near our port station and are very dangerous. They shoot on sight and take no prisoners. If you are captured, there will be no rescue mission. Our mission's success comes first. We cannot risk one soldier for the entire team."

No one said a word after that.

"They have the advantage up there," Cap continued, "but we have better weaponry."

A soldier raised his hand. "Sir, what about the twisters? Will we get a weather tracker?"

"No, we won't. That's why Lt. Copperton will lead navigation through the storms with our armored vehicle. Look, nobody said this mission would be easy. We all knew what we had signed up for. Now, let's focus and prepare to execute our plan."

I hesitated before speaking. "Um, sir… I have a question?"

"Go ahead, Lieutenant."

"It's about the recent escapee… Dorothy Vogan."

Brass' face twisted into a smirk. "Ah yes, Vogan, the runaway fugitive. What are the orders for her, sir?"

Cap's tone turned serious. "I highly doubt that Vogan survived topside. I'm afraid she likely shared the same fate as her parents. But if, by some chance, she is still alive, our orders are clear… we eliminate her on sight."

Brass's smirk grew as he turned toward me knowingly.

"What? Eliminate? When did this happen?"

I forced myself to continue. "But, sir, just a few days ago we were told to capture her if we saw her. Has something changed?"

"Yes, Ironheart. New orders came in today from the Archons. Dorothy Vogan is now on the OWL for immediate execution. Shoot to kill."

"What could have changed their orders so quickly? Did Brass know this?"

"But sir…"

"Orders are orders, Lieutenant. Drop it," Brass cut in, still grinning like he had just scored a win.

I clenched my jaw and stayed quiet. But inside, my mind was spinning.

Cap kept talking, something involving supply routes and patrol rotations, but I wasn't really hearing it anymore. I kept thinking about Dee.

She was on the OWL now, marked for immediate elimination. This list was usually for high-level threats like rebels. Real threats.

Not Dee.

It made no sense. I kept going over it in my head, trying to find what I had missed. What could she possibly have done to deserve that kind of order?

I didn't have answers. All I had were questions that burned hotter the longer I sat there.

She was smart. Quick on her feet. But even someone like her couldn't stay ahead of a kill order forever. Not when they were sending people like us after her.

Maybe it was guilt. Or maybe it was something else I couldn't name. All I knew was that if she was still out there… I had to find her.

Before they did.

"Dee, I hope you're safe. If you are, please… stay safe."

"Lionheart! Did you hear that?" Brass's voice snapped me back.

"Sorry, I must've missed it."

He folded his arms. "While you were daydreaming, Captain made it official. I'm leading this task force. And you? You're my second-in-command. I told you your recklessness would catch up with you. Just don't slow me down. Follow every one of my orders and we all will be fine."

I glanced at Cap, knowing full well I couldn't afford any mistakes; otherwise, I'd be sidelined. Despite my differences with Brass, I had to play along.

I nodded calmly and said, "Understood."

Brass leaned closer with a threatening whisper, "And remember, if she's out there, I'll personally take care of it. Understand?"

I didn't answer.

After Cap ended the briefing, I stayed behind, feeling the weight of my boots and my thoughts even more heavily.

The mission was already complicated. Now it was personal.

* * *

As I headed towards my office, the Archons' decision kept digging at me.

"Dee on the OWL? Marked for execution? It doesn't add up."

There was more to this, and I needed answers.

I was deep in my head when I heard footsteps behind me.

"Hey, Iron-Sight."

I turned. It was Sergeant Rhynes.

He glanced around, then spoke low. "Sucks you didn't get to lead the op. Everyone knows Brass isn't right for it. He's reckless. All egos. But just so you know, we've got your back… whatever happens."

"Thanks, Rhynes. Let's just keep the mission solid. No room for mistakes out there."

He gave a short nod and walked off.

I made it to my office and logged into the OWL network, typing in her name. The file popped up fast.

"Dawn D. Vogan. Status: Eliminate on sight."

No attached charges. No context.

I dug deeper, but then… blocked.

"Access restricted. Senior officer clearance required."

I sat back, staring at the screen.

"What is this? Why lock her file unless they're hiding something?"

At this point, I knew digging deeper might set off alerts. Still, I couldn't stop. I widened the search and kept scrolling through linked files for hours, chasing breadcrumbs. Then something popped up.

"No way," I whispered.

There it was. A name I didn't expect: Dr. Aeryn Vogan.

"What is Dee's mom doing on here?"

I opened the file.

"Whoa."

That alone hit hard. But then I saw something worse. She wasn't just flagged. She was labeled a rebel.

"The Zephyrs?" I muttered, reading fast. "I thought they were a science expedition… not a secret army."

Line by line, the truth started to surface. Dr. Ethan and Dr. Aeryn Vogan weren't just rogue researchers. They were rebel leaders. The Zephyrs weren't just explorers; they were soldiers in hiding. Fighting back. They were leading a secret war against the Archons.

"They never told us the full truth about this… Dee, I didn't know it was this bad."

None of this had ever been shared with the lower ranks or the public. The official story painted them as rogue scientists who had run away from justice. But this was something completely different.

"I mean, did you know this, Dee? No, she couldn't have. If she had, she probably would have told me."

The more I searched, the more the truth unraveled. Battle logs, sabotage reports, intercepted messages pointed to one idea: the rebels weren't just attacking; they were protecting something. Records showed the Sentinels launching offenses, only to be pushed back by the Zephyrs or severe weather.

"So, the Zephyrs were protecting these villages from secret Sentinel attacks?" I murmured. "This completely goes against what we've been told."

But in the end, the law was the law. Digging into this without Archon approval can be flagged as espionage. My mind was racing. Dee's entire life had been built on lies. We had grown up in the lower district, unaware of the truth, while her parents waged a secret war.

One final detail stood out. Dee's father was listed on OWL as a capture target, while only her mother was marked for elimination.

"Just like Dee," I murmured.

Then a knock at my door.

"Come in," I said, still trying to process everything.

A firm voice answered, "Lieutenant."

I stood fast and saluted. "Sir."

It was General Zark, the leader of our entire platoon and my captain's superior. I hadn't seen him since the day he pinned the Emerald Honors Badge to my chest. And now he was here in my office.

This couldn't be good.

"At ease," he said, walking in like he owned the place, which, technically, he did. He stopped in front of my wall to look at the city plaque I had received.

"I came to make sure you fully understand the nature of this topside mission." He touched the frame of the plaque with his gloved finger before turning to me. "Lt. Brass mentioned your concerns about his leadership. Is there an issue?"

"No, sir. I don't have any problem with his choice. I'm grateful for the chance to be a part of this mission."

I couldn't show any doubt… not now. I had to make it clear that I was fully committed. My chance of reaching the topside depended on it.

He studied me for a moment. "That's good to hear." Then his tone changed. "Lt. Brass also mentioned your concerns about the recent fugitive escapee, Dorothy Vogan."

He fixed his gaze on me. "The decision about her execution is final. There will be no debate."

His eyes locked onto mine. Testing me.

I gave the only answer I could.

"Yes, sir."

"Listen," he said, stepping closer. "I want to be perfectly clear about what I'm about to say."

I nodded, bracing myself.

"We are aware of your upbringing with that... criminal."

That stopped me cold. My mind went blank for a second.

"Imagine our thoughts," he went on, "when things went sideways during her capture."

"Sir, my link to Vogan is minimal. We only grew up together at the same orphanage, and that's all." I maintained a calm tone. "If my conduct has caused concern, I take full responsibility. However, I have never betrayed the Force."

Zarkov held my gaze for a long moment.

"We know you would never work against the ArcForces or the Archons." He paused before adding, "That would be treason."

Then, just as suddenly as he had come in, he moved toward the door.

"Anyway, good luck to you all. Let's make sure we succeed out there."

"Absolutely, sir," I answered, standing tall.

Before leaving, he glanced at my computer. "And Lieutenant… always remember, we're watching."

I maintained my composure and saluted him once more. "Yes, sir."

He stepped out, and the door clicked shut behind him. Only then did I let out the breath I'd been holding.

So, that was it. This wasn't just about Brass's ego anymore. Someone higher up had been tracking what I'd been doing… monitoring what I'd been reading, digging into, questioning. My search for the truth about Dee and her family hadn't gone unnoticed. But that didn't matter. Not anymore. I turned back to the screen, fists clenched.

"Dee… I'll find you before they do. I swear it."

CHAPTER THIRTEEN

"**Y**ou did it, Tin! Thank you so much!" I shouted, I closed my fingers around the compass. It buzzed against my palm, like it was finally awake.

"Power reserves are at maximum," Tin added. "Output remains consistent. It should continue to operate effectively throughout the duration of your journey."

"Appreciate it, Tin. Really." I turned the compass in my hand. "Now… do any of you actually know where this thing is leading me?"

Cro input a few commands into his tablet. "Let's check it out." A holo-map appeared between us. "This combines pre-collapse data with fresh scans from AF radars."

"Wow, this is so much better than my old map."

The terrain looked like what I expected: endless dunes, large wastelands, and more canyons than hope. But then something unexpected caught my eye. A patch of green, just past a ridge.

"Here is where we are, just north of Twister Alley," Cro gestured, zooming in on a blinking dot. "And there's where the pointer wants you to go…"

He trailed off.

"What?" I asked, narrowing my eyes. "Why the sudden hesitation?"

His finger hovered over the screen. "Dorothy… you might want to rethink this path."

Kassi stepped in, frowning. "Here." She pointed. "That green patch isn't just trees. It's the Ironwoodlands."

My brow furrowed. "Wait… there's an actual forest out here?"

"Yep," she muttered. "The Great Ironwoodlands."

I stared at it. "I've never even seen a forest in real life. Growing up in Emeraldia, the closest we had was the moonmoss and nightwood trees that grew around the city."

"Yeah, but Dorothy this is different. That forest is dangerous. It's where the Kalidahs roam. It's probably what has the brainiac here in a frenzy." Kassi said, offering a smirked.

"Kalidahs?" I asked. "Are those actually real?"

"Yes," Kassi answered. "They're native to the forest. Bandits go there to try and catch them for their fur, and don't return."

"Whoa... so, if we're heading that way, we might actually see one?"

Cro, frustrated, shook his head. "Did you hear her? That place isn't a sightseeing stop. It's dangerous. And not just because of the Kalidahs. There are rumors... old tribes have lived there for generations. Violent ones. Even Sentinels avoid the region. It's pretty much off-limits."

"Tribes?" I asked, trying to piece it together. "How would they even survive the storms all this time?"

Tin expressed his concern. "Their survival remains uncertain; however, some hypothesize that the ironwood trees are remnants of ancient magic prevalent in the old world. In reality, with adequate shelter, it is plausible that a small society could have endured through various cycles."

As he spoke, something lit up inside me. My imagination kicked into gear: ancient forests, lost tribes, exotic animals, Kadilahs. I couldn't help it. The child in me shrieked for joy. I glanced down at the compass again. Its soft vibration felt like an invitation.

"Oz to Dorothy," Kassi called out, waving a hand in front of my face. "You've got that wild look again."

"She's clearly daydreaming," Cro muttered.

I shook my head. "What? Sorry. It's just... the Kalidahs, the tribes, the forest—there's so much we don't know. And I think we should find out."

"I knew you were a little crazy," Kassi sighed. "Listen, there's a reason no one goes into that area. In one hit, those beasts could take your life. The thick forest makes them hard to spot."

"Well, we have Tin," I said, grabbing his cold, metallic hand.

"No way!" Cro blurted, pulling my hand away. "What do you mean you've got Tin? Dorothy, I think you're confused… we already completed the deal."

"You're right," I said, slightly defeated. "But I figured since we've made such a solid team so far, you'd want to be part of wherever this leads us. After all, we all want to discover what lies behind the storms. The compass is our biggest clue that something big awaits us."

"Dorothy, you're not listening," Cro replied, more seriously. "We're talking about bandits, wild beasts, not to mention, possible Sentinels along the way. They're all out there waiting. One wrong move, and it all falls apart. This isn't just a stroll through the dunes."

Kassi scratched her head. "I told you, Dorothy, you're being naïve--" .

"No, I'm not naïve!" I said, cutting her off. "I'm just done being scared of what *might* go wrong."

They didn't say anything, so I kept going.

"I get it, okay? You're both worried. But I'm not walking into this blind. I've lived through hard days before… most of my life's been hard. I just finally want it to *mean* something. That's all."

It got really quiet again.

In that moment, I realized that maybe what I was asking for might have been too much for them.

"I'll go."

"Wait, what!" Cro shouted.

Breaking the silence, Tin spoke up and continued, "If you wish to follow the compass, I shall accompany you. My skills may prove to be quite beneficial on this journey."

"Tin…" I sighed.

"I'm programmed to protect you. I'm also curious about the artifact on your wrist and its connection to my past. Maybe my travels can help me understand it better. Our chances of survival increase significantly if we all stick together."

"Really, Tin?" I said excitedly.

"Wow, you even convinced the bot," Kassi laughed.

"But what about me, Tin? Am I not important?" Cro asked.

"Traveling as a team enhances safety for all individuals involved." Tin replied.

Cro looked a bit shocked. "I just had to add you guys to his program." After pacing and muttering under his breath, he finally, but reluctantly, agreed. "Fine. Tin and I will come with you. But any useful tech or supplies we find will be mine. Agreed?"

"Affirmative," I said.

"Don't get smart! That's my line," Cro grumbled as he held out his hand for a shake. Instead, I pulled him into a hug like a little brother. When I went to hug Kassi, she held up her hand.

"You know our deal, Dorothy," she said firmly. "I'm with you, but my fighters come first."

"Sure, I get it! Now come over here," I replied, pulling her into a hug.

Once we made our decision, we began getting ready. Cro packed food, water, and other supplies we might need. Tin did a final check of his systems to be sure he was ready for any challenge.

"Are you sure you won't mind closing up the factory?" Kassi asked.

"Affirmative," Cro replied. "This is just one of my safe houses. It's not a big deal. People around here usually keep to themselves."

"Guys, I really can't thank you—"

"We know, Dorothy! Let's just make sure we don't run into too much trouble," Kassi said.

"Exactly," Cro agreed.

As we reached the edge of Cro's old factory, Tin suddenly froze mid-step.

"Tin? Everything fine?" Cro asked, concern written all over his face.

Tin didn't answer. He spun toward the village, sensors glowing faintly as he scanned the horizon.

"What's… what's wrong?" I asked, hesitantly.

Kassi's smile faded. Her hand drifted toward her sidearm. "Cro, should we be worried?"

"Tin's still scanning. No clue yet," Cro answered.

Then Tin snapped upright. "Threat confirmed. There are fifteen hostile individuals. They are approaching rapidly."

Cro didn't waste a second. He pulled up his spy-bot feed on his tablet, and we see bandits tearing through the clearing east of town on overpowered sand-striders, engines roaring, weapons locked in. Dust spun up around them like a cloud of fury.

Cro's eyes went wide. "That's Red-Eye's crew! No... they must've figured us out!"

Kassi already had her gale-blaster drawn. "Let them come."

"No," Cro cut in fast. "We can't bring a fight here. Not to Hollow Wyck. We need to go—now!"

We bolted.

Tin scooped me onto my cycle with a quick, practiced move, and I grabbed his waist tight. Kassi and Cro jumped on their own striders. Engines roared to life, and we tore through the outskirts, kicking up a storm of dust behind us as the village disappeared from view.

* * *

Ten minutes in, and this chase wasn't just brutal; it was terrifying. The bandits were closing in fast, their turbo-striders howling like beasts let loose. Tin weaved through the wasteland with impossible speed, but even his precision couldn't shake them.

Kassi tore ahead, blazing through the terrain, but even she kept glancing back. Cro's rig bounced hard across the rocks as he managed his speed.

I held on to Tin tighter, my heartbeat hammering in sync with the roar of engines behind us.

The desert blurred into chaos: twisting paths, sudden cliffs, scattered debris. Shouts rose from behind and blaster fire cracked past us, one shot sizzling right over my shoulder.

"They're gaining!" I shouted.

Tin kept pushing harder, every turn more violent than the last.

One wrong move and we'd be dust.

Red-Eye's crew started shouting behind us, full of rage and closing in fast. They were out for blood. Gale blaster fire lit up the air, and Tin jerked the cycle hard to the left, dodging the bolts by inches. My stomach dropped.

"We can't let them catch up!" Cro said through his comms.

"We've just gotta keep them on defense!" Kassi yelled, already unleashing a barrage of shots. One blast slammed into the dirt right next to a bandit's strider, sending it spinning out of control before it crashed in a spray of dust and sparks.

"Kassi, that was insane!" I called out.

"Please hold firmly Dorothy," Tin instructed.

He didn't have to tell me twice. I tightened my grip around his waist as the cycle zigzagged between jagged rocks and narrow passes, the wind clawing at my face. Everything blurred.

Through the haze of dust and engine roars, I glanced down at the compass. Its digital pointer jittered from the vibrations but stayed locked in one direction.

Forward.

"There's a cliff dead ahead. They're trying to corner us!" Cro shouted in the comms.

With a sharp turn, he veered toward the canyon wall, skidding across loose gravel as shots whizzed past us, lighting up the rocks around our heads.

"We have reached a edge," Tin stated as he brought the cycle to a halt.

Kassi and Cro pulled up beside us, faces tense.

We were surrounded.

Red-Eye and his gang had us right where they wanted.

"Okay, maybe if we keep cool, everyone. We will make it out."

Their engines revving, boots crunching over gravel, and laughter echoing off the canyon walls. The tension was high.

A tall guy climbed off his cycle, boots hitting the dirt with a solid thud. He was all sharp edges, long coat, dark shades, and a scar slicing down his face. He spat to the side and walked like trouble in boots.

"Well, well, well. Ain't this a cute little reunion?" he drawled. "Thought ya could outsmart us, huh, boy genius?"

His crew cackled behind him, engines still growling. He lifted a hand to quiet them, clearly enjoying the spotlight. Then he looked my way.

"Oh, pardon me. Didn't realize we had a couple of little ladies in the group. Where' my manners?" That smug grin spread wider. "Name's Red-Eye. I run this outfit of fine gentlemen."

"Yeah, we know exactly who you are. Now tell me why you're chasing us." Kassi spat without a flinch.

He let out a low chuckle and turned to his crew. "Feisty one. I like her."

He faced us again, with a colder expression. "Funny question though, don't you think? Yer the ones who started running. Makes me wonder what yer guilty of."

Kassi didn't answer. She just stared him down as if she were ready to take his head off.

I shifted slightly, fingers tightening around my wand. Next to me, Tin's stance had changed. None of us were buying his little performance.

Cro cleared his throat. "We thought you might've been Sentinels."

He locked eyes with Cro.

"Cut the act, brain boy! I've watched ya long enough to know how this goes… Always leaving behind a trail of broken things with yer name carved in the wreckage."

Cro adjusted his goggles. "What's that supposed to mean?"

Red-Eye took a slow step forward. Tin shifted to match him, falling into place beside Cro. Red-Eye didn't stop, just gave Tin a passing glance with a smirk before zeroing back in on Cro.

"Figured you could blow our camp to the sky and vanish into the dust? Think again."

"Destroy your camp? I would never do that," Cro protested. "I've always done only what you wanted, so you'd leave me alone."

Red-Eye reached into his coat, pulled out one of Cro's shattered spy birds, and tossed it at his feet. The thing hit the ground with a sad little clink, wings busted, eye lens cracked.

"Yer blasted spy bird, Cro! This little pest was what led me to you. Think I wouldn't notice? My camp's torched. Our prized bot was destroyed. That's yer work. And yer gonna make it all up for me."

Cro ignored him for the moment and crouched, brushing dirt off the broken bird.

"So, what now?" I asked, stepping forward before Cro could start digging a deeper hole with his mouth. "You dragged us out here, opened fire like it's a party, and now you want him to work for you?

"Oh no, you've got it wrong. Those were just warning shots. I don't want to hurt yer little engineer. Not yet. He's still worth something. He just needs to pay up. I'd say it's only fair he builds me a new camp, all new gear, and a fresh bot, since he toasted the last one."

"No."

He turned slowly towards Cro. "Come again?"

"I said no," Cro answered. "You rigged the parts I built for you to fail, then tried to use that to keep me on a leash. That was mistake one. Then you sent your lackeys to harass me every week. That was mistake two. But then you had to take my bot... my friend... as 'payment' for your sabotage. That was the last straw for me."

He looked Red-Eye square in the face, hands clenched at his sides.

"So yeah. I burned it all down. And no, I'm not rebuilding a thing for you."

Red-Eye's grin dropped. He slid his glasses off, revealing his namesake. That cybernetic red optic in his left socket glowed in the light, whirring quietly.

A silent standoff between them ensued. Cro was smaller but the kid had heart.

Tin stepped between them. "I suggest that you concede and allow us to proceed peacefully. Your likelihood of success is quite minimal."

Red-Eye barked a laugh. "Think yer something special, robo-boy? We've put bigger threats in the dirt. And we're not alone."

Kassi aimed her blaster at Red-Eye. "I guess we have no choice then."

The second Red-Eye finished talking, they started closing in, figures peeling out from the rock shadows, weapons drawn, eyes hungry. All around us.

Tin's voice broke through the comms in our ears. "Please close your eyes now. The forthcoming experience may involve increased brightness."

No hesitation. We all shut our eyes tight.

The flash hit seconds later, searing white behind my lids, hot enough to feel on my skin. The bandits weren't so lucky. Shouts rang out, chaotic and panicked.

When I blinked back into the world, Tin was already gone.

Wind tore past me. Just a gust at first. Then the sound of something heavy colliding with something.

Tin moved like lightning. Punches slamming, legs sweeping, metal limbs cutting through the crowd. Bandits dropped before they knew what hit them, too stunned or blinded to fight back.

"Where is he?" I whispered, spinning to keep up.

Another bandit flew across the sand and hit the ground. I caught a blur of Tin's frame before he vanished again, already onto the next.

Kassi was in disbelief. "Cro… what is he?"

Cro didn't take his eyes off the scene. "He's a Terabot. Built for high-speed combat. Precision offense. Even after hundreds of years, he seems not to have missed a beat.

The last of Red-Eye's crew hit the sand, groaning and out cold. Tin stood at the center of the wreckage with his shoulders squared. The fight hadn't even scratched him.

Red-Eye's hand twitched toward his belt. "Yeah? Well, think fast—"

He fired.

Too slow.

Tin moved before the shot finished. With one swipe of his arm and Red-Eye was airborne, weapon gone, crashing into the dirt like a sack of junk. Dust exploded around him. We turned away, shielding our faces as the grit flew.

When it cleared, Red-Eye was on his back, coughing, trying to pull air into lungs that weren't cooperating.

But he laughed. Of course he laughed.

"No matter," he wheezed. "The ArcForces are topside now. Hey Cro! Word is they're making contact with your old friends. What were they called again? Ah—right. The Monsoons."

Kassi froze.

He smiled. "Oh, Monsoons ring a bell? Commander Mirage?"

Her whole expression changed. "No. That's not possible."

Tin turned to Cro. "Monsoons? According to my recent ArcSys data, this pertains to a rebel faction, correct?"

Red-Eye cackled. "She is the Monsoons. Or at least, she was... Your little sharpshooter over there? That's Commander Mirage, their leader."

"You've said enough."

"ZZZZZZZZZTTTTT!"

"Urgh!!" He shouted before passing out.

I silenced him with a mild shock from my wand. He will be alright.

"Tin… I am the leader of the Monsoons," Kassi exhaled slowly, trying to get her words out. "If the AF is about to confront my crew… then I have to go."

"Then we go back. Together." I interrupted. "We help them hold the line. We show the AF exactly who they're messing with."

"I can have more bots ready by the time we get there. My factory's still intact." Cro added.

Kassi turned to us, and for a second her usual fire dimmed.

"Thank you, all of you. Dorothy, I know you're worried. And I am too. But you have to keep going. There are still answers waiting to be found. You can't let this pull you off your path."

She walked up to me and grabbed my hand.

"I made a promise, remember? That we'd face every challenge side by side. But now… I have to break that. My crew needs me. Preparing them for what's coming, because that's on me."

The wind started to rise again, curling around us in dry waves. The sky was shifting, bruising darker by the second. A storm was coming, and it wasn't just the weather.

I looked at her, really looked, and understood.

"Go. We'll keep moving. And when the time comes… we'll find each other again." I said.

She gave the smallest nod. Then she hoisted her blaster and gave me a hug.

"Be safe, Dorothy. Find the answers you're chasing. And remember—we'll meet again soon."

I couldn't hold my tears.

She turned to Tin with a crooked smile. "Hey, kiddo. Tinman. Keep an eye on her, will you? She's got a wild streak."

"Affir… no problem," Cro replied. Then, he dug into his pack and pulled out a spare transponder synced to his factory bots. "Take this. Just in case."

Kassi gazed at him briefly before pulling him into a tight hug, as if he were her younger brother. She held on firmly, despite Cro being stiff as a board. She didn't release him until she had to. I could've sworn I saw a tear behind his goggles.

She gave Tin a small punch on the shoulder to show respect. "You did great today, big guy."

With one final wave, she rode off, disappearing into the distance. My memories flashed again.

She was the first friend I found up here.

I was lost, untrained, barely hanging on. But she didn't hesitate to pull me out of danger and into something that felt like purpose. Her base became home. Her crew became family. She even taught me how to be a gale-runner, how to read the wind, ride with it.

I owed her everything.

I watched the empty horizon for a few seconds longer, then wiped the tears from my face. The wind picked up again, stronger this time. Tin looked toward the west.

"We need to find shelter," he said. "Storm's closing in fast."

Without another word, we turned away from a defeated Red-Eye and followed the compass into whatever came next.

Kassi was gone for now. But I knew we'd meet again. We weren't finished yet.

CHAPTER FOURTEEN

Commander Vogan Journal Entry #30, Pg.35

"*It was a night I would never forget... the night the flying creatures arrived in Galesville. At first, we all thought they were just drones, perhaps some new surveillance technology the ArcCity had sent to monitor us. But that illusion was shattered when the eerie loud screeching pierced the air, and we saw them for what they truly were... real, living creatures. Their long arms and tails were like nothing we had ever seen before, and their swift movements filled us with fear.*

The chaos that ensued was unlike anything our village had ever experi-enced. They attacked the guards and trashed some of our homes. The auto-mated emergency siren blared, warning us of the danger, but it was too late. The creatures seemed to vanish as quickly as they had appeared, leaving us all shaken and bewildered. Aeryn and I huddled close, trying to make sense of what had just happened, but there were no answers, only uncertainty.

What other dangers lurked topside that we were kept in the dark about by the Archons? It only gave me more reason to uncover the mysteries that lay beyond the ArcCity."

It seems morning finally decided to show up, peering right into our little cave. I'm sitting here on my sleeping roll, holding my small green lamp tight. Its light is pushing back the spooky darkness just a little. It's been four long days since we took off from Hollow Wyck, four days of dodging terrible twisters and running on empty.

My body aches so badly, every muscle screaming from all that wind.

But at least for the first time a couple of days, we aren't flying in a panic. We just stumbled upon this cave that was tucked away and set up camp. I hadn't even stood up yet when I reached for the journal. Their journal... my parents'.

I turned the pages ever so slowly, as if going too fast might make them just crumble away.

"Time to eat, Dorothy! Get out here before I eat it all!"

Cro's voice echoed through the cave. He sounded cheerful, like he hadn't just survived a near-death experience two days ago. I closed the journal and stood up, still heavy with thoughts that had no answers. Outside, the cool breeze felt nice against my cheeks. I stepped into it, looking at the gray sky that stretched forever above us. No walls. No ceiling. Just open air and mountains far away.

"This will never get old to me."

After all our traveling, I hadn't noticed until now that the land was less like a desert and a bit greener. It wasn't a lush forest, but it wasn't dead either. As I admired the scene, I spotted Cro crouched nearby, putting something warm on a plate. The smell hit me first: savory, smoky, and definitely edible. My stomach growled.

Cro glanced up, and I smiled before I even meant to. He had that effect lately. He reminded me more of a little brother now than the brainy kid he was back in Hollow Wyck. A little awkward, sure, but still sharp.

And his food? Honestly, better than half the Monsoon ration bars we'd chomped down on the way here.

"Oz to Dorothy," he called, waving a spoon in my direction. "What's with the staring? Come eat before I assume you hate my food."

I shook myself out of it and sat down across from him, gratefully accepting the plate.

We ate for a while without saying much. It was peaceful, in a weird, between-disaster kind of way. Cro looked over my way.

"You've been quiet. What's on your mind?"

I poked my food. "Nothing. Just thinking about how amazing this meal is."

"Uh-huh. Sure. That's completely believable."

"I'm okay, Cro… Just… trying not to think about the Hive. Or Kassi."

"Look, I know she gets under my skin sometimes, but she's tough. Smarter than most, and stubborn in the best way. If anyone can handle what's coming, it's her."

I agreed, thankful he said out loud what I'd been repeating to myself in my head all day.

"Wait… Where's Tin?"

"Out there, scanning the perimeter and likely checking wind patterns as well."

I let out a soft laugh. "What would we even do without him?"

"Right," he replied.

I wiped my mouth, then reached into my pack and pulled out the journal again. The spine was starting to fray, but I didn't care.

"So, this morning I read about something… weird. Dad wrote about a night when flying creatures attacked Galesville. He said they had long arms and tails. But something scared them off before they could finish whatever they had started."

"Its odd, I don't recall that day."

Cro paused mid-chew. "Flying creatures? With long arms? Besides my crow spybots and a few scavenger birds, I've never heard of anything like that. You sure that's what it said?"

"Based on my archived data, you may be referring to *mo-bats*. They are long-limbed, winged creatures thought to be extinct by the twisters."

Cro and I turned at the same time, wide-eyed.

"Mobats?" we echoed almost in unison.

Tin stepped into the clearing, dust trailing off his frame.

"Yes," he said. "Mobats look like ancient primates but have long limbs and strong, feathered wings. They can glide at high altitudes across long distances. Usually, they are curious and playful, but attacking a village is rare."

I stared down at the journal in my lap, fingers brushing the ink where my dad had written about that night. I wanted to believe it, but it still sounded like something out of a storybook.

"Do you think we'll see anything like them in the Iron-woods?"

Cro looked up. "Dorothy, I can handle machines, drones, even unstable tech. But flying jungle monsters? That's a hard no for me. Let's not go looking for them. Let's try our best to avoid those creatures or any creature for that matter."

"We'll be careful. Besides, Tin has our back."

Before Cro could reply, Tin's head tilted slightly, the way it always did when his sensors picked something up.

"There's something else."

Cro groaned, pushing his plate away. "Please don't say more beasts."

"No. Not creatures. It's about your bracelet, Dorothy. I've been analyzing its data signature and comparing it with what remains of my archives."

I sat up. "You found something?"

"I believe so," he said, reaching carefully toward my wrist. "This artifact… it may have been the reason I was destroyed the first time."

Everything stopped.

Cro stared at Tin, confused. "That's… impossible."

"Yeah, Tin…" I added. "How could *this* be connected to the destruction? It's just a bracelet."

He released my wrist. "I understand your confusion. That's why I'd rather not explain it."

"You're not?" Cro asked.

"I'm going to show you."

Cro's eyes brightened. "Are you activating your visual projection mode?"

"Precisely."

"So, he's a walking viztron now, too. Is there anything this guy doesn't do?"

Tin turned and led us back into the cave. The light dimmed behind us as we moved deeper inside, the walls hugging close. He stopped at a clear stretch of stone, adjusted his stance. The cave went dark around us.

"Core projector activation commencing," he stated.

A thin beam of light shot out from Tin's core, cutting through the black and lighting up the cave wall. The recording began to play.

On the wall, the sky was a mess of storm and dark smoke from Tin's point of view. Dozens of robots that looked just like Tin were fighting near a huge factory. But they weren't fighting each other. They were all looking up at something in the air.

"Wait, is that… a bot… in the air?" I asked, my voice barely a whisper.

"She's no bot," Tin responded.

"She?" I said, drawing closer to the wall.

The video zoomed in on the figure. It was a person in a hooded cloak. We couldn't make out anything beside that because of the zoom quality. They were hanging there perfectly still like some kind of deity. The sound of rain on the recording turned into a hard, scrunching noise.

The figure raised an arm, and the sky violently ripped open. Giant, unnatural chunks of glowing hailstones came crashing down, slamming into the bots like war hammers from the clouds. Each one exploded with a burst of electricity on impact.

"What in the…?" I mumbled, my mind scrambling to understand what I was seeing.

"Tin, how is this possible?" Cro wondered, wiping his goggles down.

Each blast sent robots flying, their arms and legs ripped off. Sparks showered the ground like a thousand dying starflies. The view jerked and jumped as Tin dodged the attack. He rolled and ducked behind a piece of metal to hide from wind gusts so strong they made the steel around him bend.

We could hear the frantic whir of his systems over the wind. As the gusts died down, he looked up, and that's when the figure dove. The impact was a massive explosion.

A surge of electricity burst outward, freezing the nearest robots in place. Tin fell back, his systems glitching. An automated voice repeatedly issued warnings: **"Power failing, systems compromised**."

But the hooded power-user didn't stop.

She tore through the robots like they were made of paper. Quick and brutal. Tin tried to fight, but watching the video, I could feel it... he was no match. The hooded attacker flashed forward, delivered a powerful hit straight to his chest, and launched him over the edge of a crumbling platform.

For a second, she was there in full view. A woman, standing with her shoulders straight and her head held high.

Everything spun as Tin's power level dropped, and the screen went dark like he was slowly passing out.

Just before the image cut to black, only one thing was in focus: a bracelet on her wrist. The metal was dull, the pattern familiar.

I was stunned. *"The bracelet... it looks similar to mine."*

"End of data transmission."

The recording ended with a burst of static. Then silence.

Cro was the first to speak. "Tin... are you sure this is real? A flying supervillain? What if your internal AI system just created the memory?"

I can confirm that the incident did occur. The individual in question, who was concealed by a hood, demonstrated significant expertise and appeared to possess an unusual capability that rendered me out of commission. It seemed as though my energy was suddenly depleted.

I stared at the wall where the projection had been. My mind raced with questions.

"So, what does it mean? Why was this person after you? And why was she wearing this?" I asked, holding up my wrist.

Tin hesitated. "I am not sure. The recording is my only remaining evidence."

This was the first time I had sensed emotion in Tin.

He took a seat on the ground, contemplating quietly. "Although I have recovered most of my memories, I remain uncertain about the reasons for my past conflicts or the purpose behind them. I am eager to gain a deeper understanding of myself. Perhaps I was a benevolent robot, perhaps not. It is an aspect I must explore."

"Tin…" I started but didn't know what to say.

Cro sat down beside him. "I never knew that's how you felt, buddy."

Tin rose to his feet. "It's time to go. My scans show the Ironwoodlands are near. We can get there before nightfall."

That got us moving.

We packed in silence. The memory of the video was heavy, and it felt like we were each chewing on it. Tin's past, the bracelet, the figure in the sky—it was all hard to shake off.

After putting away our gear, we climbed onto our striders. Cro's strider hesitated for a second before it roared to life.

* * *

We got closer to the Ironwoodlands, and I was excited.

"Hey Dorothy, are we headed the right direction" Cro asked.

"Yup," I replied, pointing ahead. "The compass is showing this is the way."

After a few minutes, we could see the greenery on the horizon. It was completely different from the landscape behind us.

A low whistle slipped from Cro. "Well, that's not what I expected."

"Whoa…"

Tin slowed down, scanning the terrain. "Dismounting will be necessary. The ground ahead is too unstable for strider travel. Once I collect a scan of the area, we may resume."

Cro slid off his seat with a groan. "Auto-glide it is, then. We'll walk them through until you finish your mapping."

Tin glanced at me. "Dorothy, do you approve of this change in plan?"

I barely heard him, but I nodded. I had already dismounted the strider. I was too caught up in what was unfolding in front of us.

"Wow, this… is incredible."

"Don't worry, Tin," Cro said, shaking his head, "I'm sure she will be fine. She is still new to real trees topside."

I never imagined an ecosystem so rich could exist.

How wrong I was.

We walked under trees so tall it looked like they were holding up the sky. Their branches had a strange, metallic shine in the light. Large green leaves covered us, making the sunlight glow in a softer way. Birds chirped from above, and the bushes rustled with unseen creatures that probably had claws but sounded pretty cute.

"Wow," I muttered. "This is straight out of a storybook."

Cro didn't respond. He was too busy scanning every shadow as if it might jump out and bite him. His hands twitched near his tool belt, and every snapped twig had him turning his head.

"Cro, are you okay?" I called out.

"I'm fine," he muttered, clearly not fine. "Just... forest stuff. Too many unknowns. I prefer places where the threats explode. Not sneak up on you with predatory silence."

Fair enough. But I couldn't help it. I was completely taken in.

Tin, of course, had already switched into guided tour mode. "...The metallic minerals found in this region play a crucial role in influencing the strength and development of the ironwood trees. Over centuries, their root systems have adapted to absorb and stabilize these minerals. This serves as a rare example of natural engineering evolution in response to environmental challenges..."

We kept walking. And Tin kept talking for two hours. I stopped trying to retain every fact he rattled off and focused on what I could see.

A pair of maned squirrels zipped across the branches above us. Iron-speckled frogs blinked at us from the edges of tiny ponds. I nearly tripped when a little owl-fawn peeked out from behind a rock, looking at us with those round eyes.

"Real forest animals…I just can't believe it…"

Then Tin pointed up to a cliff.

Badger-wolves. A whole family of them. Massive, quiet, watching us with interest, I didn't quite trust it. We kept our distance.

"Do you know where we're going?" Cro asked as he looked around carefully.

"Not exactly," I admitted, double-checking the compass. "But it's still pointing this way."

"Well, at least we haven't run into anything awful yet. I'll take that as a win. Though… I can't shake the feeling that we're being watched."

I was about to tell him he was just being paranoid when it happened.

"RARRRRRRR!"

"What in the world was that?" Cro whispered.

"I don't know. Sounded small," I said, already turning toward it.

"Yeah, probably small and frightening," Cro added.

Tin jumped in. "My sensors are picking up signs of a creature caught in a trap. It's injured."

"Well then," I replied, already picking up my pace, "we're helping it."

"Dorothy, that might not be the wisest—" Tin started.

"Come on!" I shouted back.

"Dorothy, wait!" Cro called after me, scrambling to catch up.

I rushed toward the sound through the buzzing and chirping. I pushed through branches and undergrowth until I reached the clearing.

"So, it was you." I whispered.

I dropped to my knees as the others quickly joined me.

Cro bent over, trying to catch his breath.

Kassi warned us about this kind of thing," he huffed. "Dorothy, you can't just take off into danger like that—"

"Is this it?" I cut in, pointing.

Cro took one look and nodded. "Yeah. Going off the fur pattern and size, that's a Kalidah cub."

"Confirmed," Tin added. "Female. Likely no older than a few weeks."

She whimpered again, flinching as I inched closer. Her eyes were wide with fear, her breathing shallow.

"This trap has her leg. We have to get her out."

Cro grabbed my arm. "No. Dorothy, think this through. That cub might have been calling for its parents. Or worse… a whole pack. We don't want to be standing here when they show up."

"I've already scanned the area," Tin chimed in. "There are no predators nearby."

"Ugh, Tin, don't encourage her!"

I lowered myself slowly with my hands open. The cub hesitated at first, legs trembling, but I didn't reach for her just yet. I just let her see me and tried to feel relaxed.

Then, once her eyes met mine and she didn't pull back, I reached for the trap.

She looked up at me, eyes wide. Like she'd been waiting for someone to show up. There was no growling, no snapping, just small whimpers.

I reached down, slowly loosened the trap, and slipped it off her leg. The moment she was free, she pounced. Her tiny claws pressed against my chest. Her little tongue going straight for my face.

"Hey, hey!" I laughed, trying not to fall over. "Easy, girl."

She snuggled into my arms. I didn't know what made her trust me so fast, but I wasn't going to question it. Holding her, I saw something I hadn't expected. It was a look I knew too well.

Lost.

Hurt.

"This is gonna sound ridiculous," I whispered, brushing her fur gently, "but you remind me of me."

She continued to rub against my face.

Cro groaned behind me. "Oh, come on… you're naming it already in that head of yours, aren't you?"

I smirked. "How about… Ursa?"

She licked my chin again, tail flicking.

"First try. Look at that. Ursa it is," I said, scratching the soft spot behind her ear.

"No signs of nearby threats," Tin reported, scanning the tree line. "It's likely this cub was abandoned."

Cro crouched next to me and gave me *that* look.

"I already know what you're thinking. No. Just no."

"I know, I know. You're right," I replied. "But… maybe we just help her recover? Just until she's strong enough to survive on her own."

Tin joined in. "Optimal support would boost survivability without greatly disrupting progress."

"Ugh! Kassi, why'd you leave me with these two?" Cro sighed, rubbing his head. "Fine. But once we find a safe place for her, she stays."

I turned to Ursa with a grin. "Hear that? Uncle Cro cares."

He muttered something rude. I pretended not to hear.

We pressed on, deeper into the forest. Ursa kept close, trotting alongside with a slight limp but surprising energy. The canopy above grew dense, casting moving lights that played tricks on our eyes. The wind picked up just enough to rattle the branches in a way that felt… off.

"GRRRRRR."

Ursa stooped low to the ground, ears pinned back. I knelt beside her. "What is it? Do you hear something?"

Cro stopped walking. "I told you I've been feeling it. We're not alone out here."

I looked around, the hair on my arms rising. "Yeah… I'm feeling it now, too."

"Danger detected from afar and overhead," Tin announced. "Several enemies are incoming."

That was it. We were being followed. I slipped the compass back into my bag and slowed my pace, eyes scanning the trees. Everything looked the same, but we all could feel it now.

Then, a whistle echoed. Then, multiple whistles.

Cro reached for his wrist-blaster when he caught his boot on a root buried in the undergrowth and went down hard, landing with a grunt.

"Cro!" I ran to him, but Tin was already there.

"I've got him," Tin said, lifting Cro up with one arm. "They are closing in. Prepare yourselves."

I nodded and set Ursa gently behind me, grabbing my charged wand.

"They are here," Tin declared.

Masked, hooded figures dropped from the branches above, ropes hissing as they descended.

Before we knew it, masked, hooded figures jumped down from high branches on ropes. Each one carried a spear that pulsed with strange blue electric light.

They all spread out, circling us.

Nobody moved.

Nobody spoke.

Once again, we were at a standoff. And none of us were backing down.

CHAPTER FIFTEEN

"So, the rumors were real after all."

As the masked and hooded figures crept closer, I began to worry a bit. We were cornered, with no way to flee. The eerie whistle we'd heard before made everything feel even creepier. I tried to hush Ursa's low growls, but I was so shaky I couldn't keep still.

One of the figures stepped forward, and with his deep voice echoing through the forest, he demanded, "Who are you? How dare you intrude on our sacred land?"

"We mean no harm!" I answered. "We're just travelers seeking a path through the Ironwoods. We didn't know it was sacred ground."

The masked man's eyes narrowed, and he lifted his spear, its glowing light casting a dark shadow on his face. "Ignorance is no excuse. Our sacred land is not to be trespassed upon, especially by outsiders."

"We apologize for the misunderstanding," Tin spoke up. "We'll leave right away and won't disturb your land again."

This didn't seem to convince them.

"We are the Gilkin Guardians, warriors sworn to protect these lands. We've been watching you since you entered the forest. You trespass on our land and take what is ours. Now you must face our High Chief for your actions. He will decide your fate."

Before I could get a word in, Cro interrupted, "Listen, if this is about the cub, she was injured and we're just helping her until we can find a safe place for it here."

The scout leader paid no attention to Cro's words and swiftly ordered his men to tie us up with strong ropes before we could even react.

Tin said through comms, "We should go with them for now. They seem sharper than Red-Eye's men. They could take one of us hostage if we resist."

We agreed. Our best bet was to surrender for the moment and try to plead our innocence to the chief. We were completely at their mercy. They even looped a rope around Ursa's neck, making her whimper.

* * *

We were led deeper into the forest, and I couldn't help feeling terrible for causing this predicament in the first place.

"I'm sorry, guys. My stubbornness got us into this."

"Yes, it's mostly your fault," Cro whispered, trying to console me. "But they were against us the moment we stepped into the forest. Don't worry, we will find a way out of this."

Cro's words were a little comforting, but I still knew the truth. I've been moving too fast. I needed to be more cautious, like he said earlier. I started to get lost in my thoughts again.

"This is why Leo always called me drill-headed."

A gentle rub on my leg interrupted my thoughts.

Ursa.

She had grown surprisingly calm after the confrontation. She brought a smile back to me. Regardless of everything, I knew rescuing her was the right thing.

"Wait… why are we slowing down?"

I looked up through a gap in the towering trees…

… And wow…

"The Gilkin village…wow… as long as I have been topside, I didn't think anything like this could be real," Cro whispered.

It was beautiful. I immediately felt a sense of awe as I noticed these enormous trees all around me, creating a stunning natural wall.

"This is much larger than I expected. All of this was really here…"

The village was a big circle, with houses built from woven vines and tough ironwood around a central area. Since the houses were huge, I figured multiple families lived in each one. I looked up and saw sunlight shining through the trees and into the middle clearing.

This shared area was full of life. Music floated through the air, people traded food, and kids played a game of tag that involved a lot of yelling and a ball made of some kind of threaded material. But all that happiness stopped the moment we walked in.

Everyone's eyes were fixed on us, and conversations stopped right in the middle. It was not a friendly welcome at all.

"Hmm…like Hollow Wyck," I muttered under my breath. "We're definitely quite a spectacle, huh?"

"Spectacle, sure," Cro added. "But not the fun kind. More like 'watch these outsiders get judged into the dirt' kind."

"The Gilkin exhibit strong patterns of religious zeal," Tin's voice came through the comms, "their worship centers around a green-eyed deity."

"Tin, you are right," I replied, glancing at the strange eye-spiral symbols painted on houses, clothes, jewelry, and faintly glowing on tree trunks. They showed deep devotion to their worshipped figure.

"Yeah, great," Cro replied, nodding toward the biggest structure near the clearing. "But can we focus on that? Pretty sure it's a tribunal. And I don't love the fact that we're being led straight into it."

Tin confirmed it. "You are correct."

They guided us inside. They weren't rough, but they definitely weren't casual either. The moment we stepped in, I realized this was no regular meeting hall. The place looked like it had grown from the ground up, literally.

Tree roots formed massive benches. Moss-covered stones served as chairs. Carvings lined the hollowed-out, wooden walls, that seem to tell stories of forest spirits, hunts, rituals. At the center was a giant tree stump, smoothed flat into a raised platform.

Sitting on top of it was a man who looked like he'd stepped right out of one of the carvings. His robe shimmered with very elegant fabric, woven with dark leather and stitched in green. Right on his chest, the same eye-spiral symbol stared us down.

"Guessing that's the guy in charge," I whispered.

Surrounding him were tribe members, their faces painted in green swirls. Each held an ironwood weapon made with sharp-edged gears. The craftsmanship looked more ceremonial than practical… but still dangerous. Their eyes were locked on us, filled with distrust.

People were chattering all over.

"Let the court proceedings begin," a voice said in the dark.

Then the chief raised his scepter, and the room went quiet.

"I am High Chief Terp, Sovereign of the Gilkin. You outsiders stand accused of trespassing upon our hallowed grounds and poaching from our sacred hunt. How do you answer these charges?"

I took a small step forward. My voice wobbled just a little. "Uh… Oh Great High Chief, we plead innocent," I answered. "We come in peace. We didn't know thou woods were sacred. We are simply travelers trying to pass through thou Ironwoods. We also only meant to heal the hurt cub thou see before… uhm, thee."

Cro gave me a look.

There was a pause. A long one.

"Your ignorance," he replied, "does not absolve your offense. You have defied the divine decree of our Most Holy Master, Vortarion the Green. For such sacrilege… the penalty is death."

"Wait… what?!" I blurted.

Cro and Tin stood stoically by my side.

Cro leaned toward me. "Dorothy, we really might have to fight our way out of this."

"Highly likely," Tin added, already calculating something in his head.

"Just… hold on," I said. "I'm thinking. There's got to be another way out of this that doesn't involve us having to fight."

"Wait!"

An unfamiliar voice called out, interrupting the court proceedings. Soon, the crowd began to murmur. Just when all hope seemed lost, a young man stepped forward. He looked about my age and wore a cloak that caught everyone's attention.

"What business do you have with us, son of Chief Kalimba?" demanded Chief Terp.

"May I request the floor, Honored Chief Terp?" the young man asked.

"This is highly irregular, even by your standards," the Chief replied slowly, "but… speak, if you must. Make haste."

"People of this tribunal," Marimba began, "I am Marimba, Chief-in-waiting and son of the late Chief Kalimba of the Winki Tribe. Though many of you may not know me, I will soon lead my people. I come before you with urgent concern. The cub now in the hands of these outsiders is of our lands, our protection. One of our scouts witnessed the young girl rescue the cub from an unlawful snare set by Gilkin hunters. Thus, this matter falls under Winki jurisdiction."

People around began to chatter again, while voices called for them to be silent.

"Therefore," he continued, "we will reclaim the cub and release the outsiders with a warning, out of respect for their courage and mercy."

We were shocked by this. You could feel the tension between the chiefs as the room fell silent again, waiting eagerly for Chief Terp's reply.

"I shall not permit you to release these interlopers," Chief Terp said firmly.

The crowd gasped.

"Must I remind you," Marimba sharply replied, "that to set snares for our kalidahs is to violate the peace agreement between our tribes? These creatures are sacred to the Winki. They are majestic, revered, and under our protection."

"Yes, yes, we are aware of the so-called peace accord," he replied, dismissive. "But these outsiders have set foot upon consecrated land unbidden. That cannot go unanswered."

"Once more, would you please reconsider and extend mercy?" Marimba pleaded again.

"Once more... NO!" Chief Terp responded, angrily.

"So be it... You leave me with no choice," Marimba declared. "By my right as Chief-in-waiting, I invoke the Ozaruku."

His words stirred a wave of whispers through the crowd.

"How dare you!" Chief Terp thundered.

"Your Holiness, may we speak for a moment?" a Gilkin councilman asked.

Chief Terp glared at him, clearly not thrilled by the interruption, but gave a short nod. The council huddled together and began to talk things over.

As the crowd's voices grew louder, I took the chance to approach Marimba, the mysterious young leader. I figured that was our only window.

"Marimba, right?" I asked. "Hi, I'm Dorothy. Thanks for stepping in back there. But... what exactly is an Ozaruku?"

Marimba offered her a nod and a respectful smile. "Dorothy, you are welcome among us. And you have my gratitude for saving the Kalidah cub. As for the Ozaruku... fear not. It is simply a trial by combat. A tradition."

Cro and I both turned at the same time. "Trail by what?!"

I rubbed my head. "So, you're telling me we settle this whole mess by… fighting?"

"Indeed," he replied, unfazed. "One warrior from the Gilkin. One from the Winki. It is how disputes are settled. And between us… Our warriors rarely lose."

"A decision has been made. We will accept the combat," Chief Terp declared.

"Very well!" Marimba agreed. "We will accept."

Chief Terp continued, "One of the accused will face a Gilkin warrior. So, it shall be."

A council member added, "And because of the young boy's injury and the robot's advantage, we've chosen the girl."

"The girl? That's me!" I yelped, my voice jumping an octave.

Marimba panicked. "Wait, no! That's not how this is meant to go!"

Chief Terp raised an eyebrow, clearly enjoying himself. "My, my… how bold you've become, young heir. In your desperation to impress, you seem to forget the ancient customs. When an Ozaruku is invoked, it is the challenged who dictates the terms. These are ours. Accept them, or declare war upon your fractured, faltering tribe!"

Marimba's face crumpled. He hesitated, clearly stuck between bad and worse. Then he nodded.

The crowd erupted.

Marimba turned to us, his face full of regret.

"What have you done?" Cro snapped, hands clenched at his sides.

"You've completely miscalculated this," Tin added.

I shot a glare at Marimba. "Seriously? Why mess with the trial at all? What did we even do to you?"

He winced. "I just… I only meant to help… to ease the burden on you."

"Yeah," I muttered, "great job with that."

He tried to smile. "Don't worry. They'll likely choose a novice… someone untested."

* * *

I stared at him. Then at the crowd still cheering like they were about to watch the event of the season.

"Sure," I said flatly. "Rookie. Can't wait."

Gilkin Announcer: "WELCOME, ESTEEMED MEMBERS OF THE GILKIN AND WINKI TRIBES, TO THIS SACRED ARENA OF THE IRONWOODS!"

The announcer's voice boomed across the clearing, echoing through the ironwood trees as if he were calling a storm. He was tall, dressed in full Gilkin gear, with a feathered headdress and tribal paint swirling across his face. The crowd roared back, ready for a fight, or at least a good show.

The arena was simple: just a wide-open combat platform in the middle of the forest, surrounded by hundreds of villagers from both tribes. They sat on wooden benches placed around carved-in hills surrounding the arena. The sky above was clear and open, and the noise from the crowd was deafening.

Cro, Tin, and I stood near the edge of it all, watching.

The fierce Gilkin ceremonial warriors gathered together. They wore matching evergreen battle gear decorated with spiral jewelry, iron gears, and animal hides. They carried spears and shields that glowed with green energy, and their faces were painted in detailed familiar patterns.

The Winki ceremonial warriors stood across from them. They wore more colorful gear with bright yellows and reds, decorated with gems. Their warriors had paw prints painted on their cheeks and foreheads instead of the green eye symbols. Their bows and shields were decorated with vines and charms that looked handmade but showed signs of being used often in combat.

"Don't worry, Dorothy," Tin said, his hand gently resting on my shoulder. "I'm here to protect you, no matter what. If things go badly, I won't hesitate to step in."

"Affirmative," Cro added, his goggles shining in the light. "And I've got a few tricks up my sleeve. They won't know what hit them."

"Thanks, guys," I told them, trying to sound more confident than I felt. "I know you've got my back. But I need to do this. I want to respect their customs… and, more than anything, I don't want Ursa getting dragged into this. They're using her to keep us in line. I won't let her be the one who pays for it."

From where we stood, I could see Chief Terp and Marimba up on a raised ironwood platform at the far end of the arena. Chief Terp looked smug, clearly proud of whatever twisted plan he thought he'd pulled off. Marimba… not so much.

Guilt was written all over his face. Our eyes met across the clearing. He didn't say anything. His expression said it all: *I messed up.*

Gilkin Announcer: "WE GATHER TODAY TO WITNESS OUR FIRST OZARUKU IN A DECADE, TO SETTLE A DISPUTE BETWEEN OUR TRIBES. REPRESENTING THE WINKI TRIBE, AN OUTSIDER FROM THE WINDLINS. I PRESENT DOROTHY!"

The crowd exploded. Some cheering, some booing, all of them way too excited for what was about to happen. And there I was, smack in the middle of it again. The outsider. The one who didn't ask for any of this.

I took a breath and tried to focus.

"Come on, you've got this."

I thought back to Leo, who taught me the basics of fighting, always reminding me to be quick on my feet. I also remembered my training with the rebels. I wasn't a hardened warrior, but I was smart and knew how to use every little advantage.

Before I could think too much, the booming voice of the announcer introduced the Gilkin champion.

Gilkin Announcer: "REPRESENTING THE GILKIN TRIBE, WE HAVE A TRUE CHAMPION, A WARRIOR OF UNMATCHED STRENGTH AND SIZE. HE IS THE MOUNTAIN OF THE IRONWOOD-LANDS, THE HERO OF GILKIN, MY TRIBEPEOPLE, I PRESENT TO YOU... GRIMMMMMBOOOOL!"

Suddenly, a massive silhouette filled the arena entrance, and everything went still.

"Oh... my *stars*," I whispered.

The crowd went wild, cheering, stomping, shouting a name I didn't recognize. Meanwhile, my stomach dropped straight into the dirt.

"Grimbol."

He stepped into the light like a walking mountain. Easily twice the size of any other Gilkin warrior, wrapped in met-al-plated armor polished to a shine so bright it looked unnatu-ral. His shoulder plates were shaped like open beast jaws, and the way they glinted made him look more monster than Ozian.

He held a massive sledgehammer, its huge head humming with red energy. Every part of him radiated raw strength and confidence, and his Gilkin markings made his fierce eyes burn even brighter.

I felt tiny.

"What is that creature?" Cro asked, taking a step back.

"Currently calculating our odds," Tin muttered.

"That Marimba," I hissed, eyes narrowing.

As if he heard me, his voice suddenly cut through the noise. "Enough! This contest is not just. It places our challenger at a grave disadvantage!"

The crowd hushed.

Chief Terp didn't miss a beat. "Oh? Are these not *your* terms? And yet you seek to bend them the moment they no longer favor you. Tell me, what kind of leader undermines his own challenge? You've yet to secure the blessing of your elder council. Do not play chief before the title is yours."

He took a breath and stood tall. "Then so be it."

He turned to face the crowd and shouted, "I, Marimba, Promised Chief of the Winki, claim the right to fight in Dorothy's place!"

"What?"

Gasps rippled through the arena like a wave. All eyes locked on him. Even Cro and Tin looked stunned.

Chief Terp and the council did not seem surprised by Marimba's decision.

"A chief may not take the place of another in combat, not even one promised the title," Chief Terp replied with a cool head. "Sit down, young aspirant. Watch. And learn."

And just like that, Marimba's fight was over before it began.

He sat defeated, and our eyes met again.

*"**I'm sorry**,"* he mouthed.

I nodded. "Thank you, Marimba," I said softly. "But it looks like this one's mine."

Gilkin Announcer: "WELL, NOW THAT THE DE-LIBERATION IS CONCLUDED, LET'S GET START-ED!"

The crowd erupted, all noise and heat and pressure crashing over me like a wave I wasn't ready for.

I stood there, staring up at Grimbol. He really was tall. His broad shoulders cast a shadow that made me feel about three feet tall. And his eyes locked on me as if I were his prey.

I wasn't.

And as scared as I was deep inside, I needed to prove that I wasn't very early. I held my battle wand and gave my bracelet a quick kiss.

Grimbol's deep voice rumbled across the arena. "I'll make this nightmare end quickly for you."

I didn't answer. No trash talk. No last words. Just focus.

"Watch over me, Mom. Dad."

Then the ground rumbled. I barely flinched before that giant hammer came swinging at me. Wind blasted my face as it cut through the air. I twisted and stumbled, barely getting out of its way, and the thing hit the ground with a boom so loud it shook my bones.

The crowd gasped. Even Grimbol looked thrown off.

Another swing. Another dodge. I dropped low, rolled, and turned, moving before I could even think. I was very nervous. The hammer slammed down again and again, carving huge chunks out of the arena floor. I was nimble, but I had to be smarter.

Leo's voice echoed in my mind. *"If your opponent is bigger, let them get tired. Use their power against them. Don't fight their way; fight yours."*

So, I didn't stop moving. I ducked, leapt, twisted, anything to keep him swinging. If I were lucky, he'd tire out.

The cheers turned angry.

"BOOOO!!!"

I could feel the crowd's disappointment. They wanted real combat.

"Is that all you've got, outsider?" Grimbol growled through clenched teeth. "All you do is run."

I let a small smirk slip through. "Not running. Just improvising for now."

"Fine. Have it your way!"

In an instant, he spun his huge hammer, and bright, scorching flames burst along its length.

"You have to be kidding me." I mumbled, already bracing myself.

"Isn't that just cheating?" Cro's voice came through the comms.

"If Dorothy was allowed to bring her own weapon," Tin replied, "then this technically falls within their combat rules. The council appears unconcerned."

Easy for him to say.

I shifted back a few steps, thinking fast. "Alright. Just keep your distance. Let him wear himself out."

"Wait... what is that smirk? Is he up to something?"

Too late. He brought the hammer down again, and this time it spat out a glowing fireball the size of my torso. I dove into a roll, heat licking at my arm, and landed hard on the ground. My sleeve was scorched, but I was still breathing.

"Ahhhhh!" I shouted, patting the smoke away. "Now, fire-balls? Seriously?"

Gilkin Announcer: "AND THERE HE GOES, WITH HIS AMAZING BLAZING SPITFIRE ATTACKS!"

I didn't have time to yell at him.

Grimbol came at me again, swinging like a machine. Blow after blow, each one faster, hotter, more dangerous than the last. I ducked, spun, flipped… my whole body running on instinct. My arms were sore, legs shaky, and every second I could feel how badly I was outmatched.

"Okay… I finally can catch a quick br — wait, I see it now… It's happening."

The way his breathing became heavy between strikes.

The way his footwork got just a little slower.

He was burning out.

This was it. This was my moment. A tranquil, almost dreamlike clarity washed over me. The wind rose, grazing my skin, and for the first time during the match, I felt truly in control.

"I've got you now," I murmured. Locking eyes with Cro and Tin, I offered a sly grin.

"Watch closely, boys."

Tin nodded, while Cro waited anxiously.

"Please tell me this isn't one of your weird plans."

I didn't answer. I shot forward in a zigzag, kicking up a cloud of dust. Grimbol's flames roared past me, close enough to feel the heat on my cheek. I nearly slipped, but I didn't slow down. Just kept moving fast and low. He swung again, and I leapt high, vaulting into the air, my wand buzzing with stored energy.

"Not gonna work." Grimbol growled, bracing himself.

"I know."

I didn't go for a head-on strike. I landed beside him with a tight somersault, rolled over the gritty arena floor, and drove my wand straight into the thick armor on his shoulder. It made a loud zap, releasing a burst of electricity that made my teeth buzz.

"RAHHHHH!"

He howled in pain as his huge frame buckled from the sizzling shock of electricity that exploded through his armor. He sank to one knee.

In that single move, you could feel the whole crowd take a deep pause.

Well, everyone except Cro.

"Oh-ho YES! That's what I'm talking about!" he shouted, clapping like a crazed fan. "Metal armor? Dorothy, you genius!"

Grimbol turned, slow and furiously, locking eyes with Cro

Cro fixed his goggles with a smirk. "Oh dear. Did I strike a nerve?"

"YAYYYYYYY!"

The crowd cheered loudly for me.

"I'm not finished."

I jumped back in with quick hits, darting around him like a pest he couldn't swat. Every jab sent more voltage ripping through his gear. His roars echoed louder each time, but his movements were slower, sloppier. I could tell he was wearing out.

Finally.

I paused, catching my breath just as he tried to do the same.

I quickly looked up. Marimba was practically dancing with excitement, while Chief Terp looked like he was ready to chew through his fancy robe.

Tin's voice came through the comms. "Dorothy, your analysis of Grimbol's movement patterns has resulted in highly efficient counterattacks. Well done."

"Impressive?" Cro added. "No, it's exceptional! A tactical masterpiece that shines as brightly as my own genius."

Before I could react, Grimbol laughed and pushed himself back up.

"What is he up to now?"

He let out a beastly growl as he lunged forward with his giant hand clamping down on my arm like a vice.

"Gotcha," he barked, and in one swoop, slammed me into the ground like I weighed nothing.

"UHGH!"

The impact ripped the air from my lungs. My body screamed in pain, and I could taste blood in my mouth. The whole arena spun like a bad dream, the edges of my vision going dark.

"No… I… I can't give up yet."

I rolled just in time as his hammer came down with another explosive crash, missing me by inches. I gritted my teeth, forced my arm up, and jammed my electric wand right back into that cursed shoulder of his. He bellowed in pain and dropped his weapon.

We were both a bloody mess, winded and wobbling.

I pushed to my feet, barely hanging on. He looked like a mountain ready to collapse.

I knew why.

It was his armor. The color. The shine. The conductivity.

I knew it very well. It's *Vanta-metal*. A special grade of metal that's usually mined alongside other igneous rocks. Very durable, but also very conductive of electricity. That's why my wand hurt so badly.

He knew it too. And he hated it.

Gilkin Announcer: "PEOPLE OF IRONWOOD, THIS IS UNBELIEVABLE! I CAN'T BELIEVE WHAT I'M SEEING! OUR CHAMPION IS BADLY HURT BY SOMEONE HALF HIS SIZE! ARE WE WATCHING HISTORY?"

He turned to look directly at the announcer, then at Chief Terp, who nodded at him with a smug little smile in a specific direction.

"No…no way… He can't…"

Grimbol's sneer cut right through me as he locked eyes with Cro. I couldn't believe what was about to happen as he raised his huge sledgehammer again and flames ignited on it.

The fireball came straight at me. I twisted out of the way and coughed a bit of blood when I hit the floor. But it was only a distraction.

His gaze snapped to Cro.

"I knew it!"

"No, Cro, move!" I screamed, lunging forward instinctively. But time slowed, and I knew it was too late.

Grimbol swung again, sending an even larger fireball speeding right at Cro.

I ran on pure instinct, legs pumping harder than I ever had before. But no matter how fast I went, it wasn't nearly enough.

"Cro!!!"

"BLAST!!!!"

The fireball hit. The explosion erupted in a wave of heat and smoke, swallowing Cro in its terrifying burst.

"No!!!!!"

The crowd's gasp echoed around me, hollow and distant.

I fell to my knees in horror.

Grimbol stood over the chaos with a menacing laugh.

"What… have you done?" I called out, still in shock.

Gilkin Announcer: "IT LOOKS LIKE WE HAVE A FEW UNFORTUNATE INJURIES. SAFETY ATTENDANTS ARE COMING NOW…AND…NO… WAIT A MINUTE. THERE SEEMS TO BE SOMEONE… STANDING?"

A silhouette formed in the dust.

When the smoke cleared, Tin stood, his metal body completely normal. Cro was safe. In a split second, Tin had stepped in and created a shield. Something I didn't know he could do.

Angry boos and shouts filled the arena as the crowd turned against Grimbol for his unfair move.

Marimba protested loudly, but Chief Terp waved it off with a smirk.

"Merely an accident," he said.

"You guys…" I whispered with a shaky voice.

I felt both relief and anger as tears streamed down my cheeks.

No.

It wasn't just my tears.

I felt… a raindrop.

I looked up in the sky and saw darkened cloud quickly and the slight pickup of the wind.

The audience shifted nervously, sensing a storm was coming.

I didn't care.

I was pissed.

"We're fine, Dorothy!" Cro called out in the comms.

"Cro! Tin, thank you!" I whispered.

Tin scanned Cro to make sure he was fine, then began walking back toward the combat platform.

I knew what he planned to do.

"Tin, stop… I have to do this," I said firmly, standing between him and our enemy. Tin paused for a moment and then nodded.

Grimbol laughed, ignoring the boos of the crowd. He started removing his scorched armor, showing his bare, muscular body.

"Your little tricks won't save you anymore, girl."

"You coward!" I shouted.

"Coward? Ouch!" he mocked, "Don't get it twisted, kid. I do whatever it takes to win. I could never lose to an outsider and her weak crew. I'm the Mountain of Ironwoods. These people worship my strength! Now let me end it with this."

Thunder rumbled above us like it agreed with him, and the wind kicked up hard. I could see some of the crowd starting to back away as the first drops of rain began to fall.

Grimbol adjusted his weapon once again. The head of his hammer clanked against the arena floor and fell off. I barely had time to process it when a whip uncoiled from the shaft, flames blazing along its length.

He just grinned, smug as ever.

With a swift swing, he sent a fiery whip flying toward me.

"Too fast—"

"URGH!!"

Pain exploded through my leg as the whip lashed around it. I yelped and stumbled, the burn biting deep.

"Dorothy!" I heard Cro yell, already scrambling for his tech gear.

Tin stiffened, about to move.

"No!" I called out, waving them off. "Stay back."

I hobbled a few steps, holding my wand tighter, trying to breathe through the pain.

Grimbol laughed. "Come on, girl. Show me your little tricks!"

Overhead, the sky had gone full fury. Dark clouds began to roll with lightning flashing between them. I could feel something in the air. Something strange.

"It's like that time…"

And something in me snapped. I began to mouth off words without thought.

He cracked the whip again, but I was already moving, dodging it by pure instinct.

Then it all slowed down.

The droplets of rain came to a pause.

The sound of the crowd disappeared.

Even the thunder fell silent.

All I felt was the storm. The raw energy buzzing through the air, pulling into my wand.

Instantly, lightning tore the sky and dropped hard. I lifted the wand on instinct, and the bolt hooked mid-fall, slamming into Grimbol.

"HAAAAA!!!!!"

I let out a yell that came from somewhere deep, letting everything go.

BZZZZZZ-BOOM!

The blast hit with a sound that split the forest open. Light exploded across the arena, blinding everyone. Electricity tore through the air, slamming into Grimbol like a boulder made of pure voltage.

"AAAAHHHHHHH!!!!!"

His whole body convulsed, then crashed to his knees.

The lightning lit him up. He had scorched paint, and pure agony etched across his face. The light faded with a soft crackle, leaving behind smoke and sizzle on the singed fabric of his clothes.

I stood there, somehow still upright, my wand still sparking in my hand. I was untouched by the phenomena.

Everything around me was silent.

No cheers. No jeers. Just a frozen crowd trying to figure out what they'd just witnessed.

Grimbol hit the ground, face-first. A limp heap of muscle and metal, smoke curling from his armor like a dying fire.

The "Mountain of Ironwoods" was down.

The same guy they'd worshipped like a war god now looked small and broken in the middle of the arena.

Even the announcer, who couldn't shut up five minutes ago, had nothing.

I didn't stop to think about what had just happened. The lightning, the timing… all of it blurred in my mind.

But I really didn't care.

"Cro! Tin! Are you okay?"

I took off limping towards them, but that didn't last long. My legs pushed past the pain until I was sprinting. I crashed into them, nearly knocking Cro off his feet.

Tin caught me first. I gave him a hug. Cro just gave me one of his crooked, sheepish smiles.

"We're fine," he said. "Sorry, I scared you. I was, uh… too busy celebrating to—"

"Don't," I cut in, dragging him into the hug. "You idiot. It's not your fault."

Tin paused as he looked me over. "Dorothy… during the end of the battle… your energy level output spiked beyond recognition. For a brief moment, you were radiating like an ionic storm."

"Tin, what are you talking about—"

"YAAAAYYYYY!!!!"

Suddenly, the whole crowd exploded. They were loud enough to shake the trees. Just seconds ago, they were dead silent. Now they were shouting like their lives depended on it.

"Whoa, look at this…"

All around me, people stood, stomped, clapped, hollered. That's when reality hit me. The wind had died down. The storm had moved on. And somehow, I was still standing.

Then came the sting.

It was small at first, like pinpricks on my arms. I glanced down and saw the burns… it was faint, but definitely there. Thin red streaks where the fire had brushed against me. I hadn't even noticed them until now.

"Heh… would you look at that." I wiped my forehead with the back of my hand. "From the cheers we are hearing, guess the big guy was wrong. They don't need his strength anymore."

Cro chuckled, and Tin nodded in agreement.

"You know," I said slowly, "as terrifying as that was… there were moments, like little flashes, where I felt like… I don't know. Like I wasn't just fighting. I was becoming something else."

That made both of them pause.

Tin looked at Cro. Cro nodded back.

"I'm sure you notice it?"

"Absolutely," Cro said.

I narrowed my eyes. "Notice what?"

Gilkin Announcer: "CAN YOU BELIEVE IT? CAN YOU BELIEVE IT? THIS IS THE MOST EPIC AND HISTORIC BATTLE EVER! PEOPLE OF THE IRON-WOODS, I ANNOUNCE YOUR NEW OZARUKU CHAMPION! FOR THE FIRST TIME, AN OUTSIDER BY THE NAME OF DOROTHY!"

The noise was unreal. Cheering. Chanting. People shouting my name like I was someone important. It was odd to se after everything we'd been through. For once, it felt like the whole world was on our side.

I looked out over the crowd and smiled. Just a little.

"We did it," I whispered under my breath. "I wish you could see this, Kassi… Leo."

On the platform, Chief Marimba remained stunned, having not moved for minutes while staring at the arena like he was trying to replay the fight in his mind. Meanwhile, Chief Terp was furious and could not hide his disappointment.

When his eyes landed on Grimbol's crumpled form, he mouthed one word: ***"Pathetic."***

"This is far from over," he growled vengefully. "By the sacred name of Vortarion the Green, I give you my word outsider."

And with that, he stormed off, council members scrambling to keep up behind him. Dramatic exit and all.

Before I could even roll my eyes at that nonsense, a low, familiar roar echoed through the clearing.

"Ursa!" I called. "There you are, girl." She shouldered through a crowd of people and bumped her head against my arm.

Her breath was warm on my sleeve. I scratched the spot behind her ear and felt the shake of her chest settle. I grabbed her large head, checking her to make sure she was unharmed.

"How are you girl? Are you ok? Oh, I'm so sorry you had to go through all of this!'

She responded with a subtle hum that told me she was happy to be here.

But our moment was quickly cut short when Tin hoisted me onto his shoulders in one smooth lift. The world rose with me.

Cro pumped his fists and whooped so loud the nearest birds burst out of the canopy. Around the ring, people clapped the flats of their hands on bark drums. Shoes hit the ground in time.

I looked out over the faces. Painted stripes. Sawdust on shoulders. Kids on their parents' hips, grinning like they witnessed somthing special. I caught Marimba near the front, arms folded, chin high. he didn't smile, not fully, but he gave me a small nod that landed harder than a cheer.

I closed my eyes for a second and let it sink in. Sweat, smoke, blood, the sting of my scraped bruises. The weakness in my legs.

It all led to this.

"I did it. I really did."

And for one fleeting moment, standing on Tin's shoulders with Ursa by my side, it felt like all of Ironwood was shouting with me, not against me.

CHAPTER SIXTEEN

-LEO-

"Watch out!"

Gale-Blasters lit up the sky with a loud, piercing sound like lightning hitting a steel drum, creating a dramatic and electrifying scene.

"Take cover! Stay in formation!" Brass barked.

We dropped fast, diving behind whatever cover we could find. Blaster smoke punched into my lungs. The heat clung to my skin, burning past my armor.

This was real.

I gripped my storm rifle-blaster tight and dropped behind a busted barricade. The world around me roared with shouts, energy rounds, and explosions.

No time to think.

I fired back through the dust and chaos, following every move from muscle memory.

But part of me was somewhere else.

All I could think about was how this mess had even started.

* * *

The radar kept pulsing with the same solid beat. There was nothing out there but wind and dust. We had finished setting everything up and locking down the site. Our mission was technically done.

Brass crouched by the comms dish, playing with the frequency to try and reach our informant out by the edge of the area. Rhynes stood watch, holding his rifle firm, his eyes fixed on the ridge. The wind picked up, but he didn't even blink.

Copperton was in the recon rig, with a half-eaten ration bar in his mouth. His fingers moved quickly over the monitors. He had already sent a signal to ECHO command that everything was "all clear."

But I knew he was also working on a side job for me.

Cobalt and I stayed near the gear cart. I sat against a warm rock, letting my thoughts wander.

"Too easy, right? I told you all to follow my lead!" Brass shouted.

I didn't answer. My mind wasn't here. It was with Dee.

Somewhere out there, she was still fighting. I couldn't explain it, but I felt it. She was too smart, too stubborn to disappear.

"I know you're out there, Dee. Probably facing down some mega machine or chasing another one of your wild ideas."

The corner of my mouth twitched. It was almost a smile.

The wind kicked up again, pulling sand through our camp like the land itself wanted us to leave. I looked around. This was the real world. No screens. No filters.

The sand rolled like broken waves. The sky was so big it made you feel tiny. In the distance, dark, heavy storm clouds gathered, like a giant waiting to wake up.

As beautiful as it is, I can also see the dangers of being up here. They called the topside a graveyard, and I can see why. This place could kill you if you blinked at the wrong moment. The sharp wind-dust could tear your skin, and the storms could wipe you out. There were even desert creatures we didn't know about lurking.

And yet... it was still amazing to see for the first time.

The wind tugged at my scarf, and I pulled it closer. I took another deep breath under this open sky, just to feel small and to remind myself that I was still alive.

The techs were already heading back to the city. They didn't wait for the coming storm.

We had to stay until everything was completely secured.

Then the call came over the radio.

"ECHO COMMAND: COPY THAT, DUSK TEAM 4. YOU ARE NOW FREE TO RETURN TO BASE."

I headed for the recon rig. Copperton was still there, with static on the screens. One hand rested on a monitor; the other clutched what used to be his lunch.

"Anything?" I asked.

"Not a single signal.No tags. Nothing. It's like trying to track a ghost with a brick."

That sucked. I hoped there would be something, anything.

"Well, we tried."

I turned to leave.

"Ironheart…"

His calm tone caught me off guard.

"You know I'm here for you, but it might be time to be honest with yourself. She's been topside a long while. If she's still alive, she's surviving on her own. Trust that she's managing."

He paused.

"And if she didn't make it... chasing shadows won't bring her back."

I didn't respond. I simply grabbed another box from the rig and kept moving.

"I hear you, Lieutenant…and thanks for keeping this between us."

He gave a short nod. But I saw the look.

Pity.

But he was right.

I hated that.

He wasn't wrong. The odds were bad. Dee's chances were razor thin. This desert doesn't offer second chances, and the Monsoon rebels don't spare anyone.

But logic wasn't keeping me in this... hope was.

And when hope finally burns out, you hold on to whatever's left.

I had a *Plan B.*

"Here it is, boys. We've got it," Brass broke in over the comms.

Static cracked through the line before our informant's voice came through. He called himself Red-Eye.

RED-EYE: "THE LOCATION WAS CONFIRMED: A MONSOON OUTPOST A FEW CLICKS WEST OF YOUR POSITION."

Brass quickly ordered, "Lieutenants, we're departing now."

"You sure about this?" Rhynes asked, squinting at the storm brewing on the horizon.

"We just got return orders," Copperton added. "You plan to ignore those?"

Brass grinned like he was untouchable. "We'll say we ran into enemies on the way back. No big deal."

"You're kidding, right?" I called out. "You want to send us into Monsoon territory with half a squad and barely any gear?"

"That intel changes everything," Brass shot back. "This mission is bigger than us. We're the best, and you don't win wars by playing it safe."

I took a deep breath to calm myself. "With all due respect, sir, this wasn't the original plan. We install, sweep, extract. Minimal conflict. This isn't our fight."

"Orders change," he replied. "Ten minutes. Move."

Then he came closer to me.

"And remember, Iron-child, I give the orders. Not you."

I gave a stiff salute, gritting my teeth.

For the team, I kept moving.

I turned and headed back to the rig. The others were quick to pack up. No one liked this, but orders were orders, even ones we didn't agree with.

***

Now, everything was falling apart. Suddenly, our comms burst to life.

COPPERTON: "DUSK 3 TO COMMAND. I RE-PEAT—COBALT IS DOWN. OVER."

RHYNES: "GET DOWN, DUSK 2! THEY'RE MOV-ING TOWARD YOUR AREA FOUR LOCATION. I'M ON MY WAY. OVER!"

Sweat trickled down my back as the heat from my blaster pulsed through my hand.

Suddenly, a shot zipped past my ear.

It was way too close for comfort.

Another blast exploded nearby, spraying sand into my face.

RHYNES: "SONIC GRENADE!"

"BANG!!!"

The shockwave hit hard. I flew backward. My vision blurred, and my ears were ringing so badly that it felt like my skull was splitting. I tasted blood.

I turned around. Rhynes was yelling, but I couldn't hear him. His mouth was moving quickly, and his face was tight with urgency.

He grabbed my shoulder hard.

"Ironheart, snap out of it! The rebels broke into Area Four. What's the plan?"

My vision cleared just enough to see Cobalt down in the dirt. Motionless.

"Okay, uh—" I blinked fast, forcing myself to think. "We save him. Then we fall back."

"Negative. Brass said hold position. You know this was a one-way…"

"No. That was his call, not ours." I locked eyes with him. "Are you really gonna sit here and watch our guy bleed out?"

Rhynes paused for a moment. "That's insubordination."

"Our comrades' life matters more. We save him. Now."

"But Ironheart…"

"He just had a kid, Rhynes. Remember that?"

He hesitated a bit. Then he softened up until he finally agreed.

"You're right, Lieutenant. Let's go."

He pressed a button on his comms.

RYHNES: "DUSK 4 HAS FALLEN. REQUESTING PERMISSION TO RECOVER, OVER."

The response was cold.

BRASS: "STAND DOWN. FOLLOW THE MIS-SION. REMAIN IN POSITION."

"That bastard…"

Rhynes turned to me. "It went just as expected. Now what?"

"We move forward. I'll take the responsibility."

Losing one friend was enough. I couldn't handle losing another. I immediately flashed Rhynes our old academy signals. We crouched, hid silently, moved fast, and made no mistakes.

The battle was getting close, but we were edging closer too. And this time, no one was getting left behind.

Rhynes grabbed his blaster close and nodded once. For a moment, we held our positions, our muscles ready to move.

Then we saw an opening in the enemy fire.

We ran for our lives.

"Let's... keep... moving," I called out, trying to catch my breath.

Adrenaline hit me like a rush of fire. The battlefield turned into a blur of sounds, flashes, and the deafening roar of energy rounds.

"Come on, Leo…Keep moving."

All that mattered was reaching Cobalt. We had to get to him and drag him to safety.

We sprinted through the chaos with sand ripping our gear and laser blasts whooshing past.

Out of the corner of my eye, I saw movement… a projectile moving too fast and too close, headed straight for Rhynes.

There was no time to think.

I tackled him sideways just as my cyber-arm sparked when it deflected the shot. It ripped through my sleeve, but I didn't feel a thing.

"Wow…Thanks Lieutenant!"

"Run!" I shouted. "They know we're here!"

There was no time for stealth. It was either run or die.

Rhynes and I reached Cobalt in seconds, grabbing him by his uniform and dragging him toward safety. He was heavy and unconscious, bleeding badly.

I collapsed near a rocky hill, chest heaving, my vision still a little off. Cobalt stirred, coughing hard. His face twisted from the pain, but he was awake.

"I... I'm alive?" he rasped, barely above a whisper.

"Yeah," I said, pressing a med-cloth to his side. "Barely. But you're with us."

Rhynes checked the pulse on Cobalt's wrist, gave a slight nod.

"Should we report this to Brass?" he asked, not looking up.

"No." My voice came out cold and flat. "We've got bigger problems."

Cobalt let out a shaky groan and tried to lift himself. "Thanks... for saving me..." His voice barely made it out.

Rhynes and I moved quickly, working together to patch the wound and stop the bleeding. My hands knew exactly what to do; all my training took over. Soon, Cobalt's breathing became stable, and his face got its color back. He wasn't out of danger yet, but he had a chance now.

Then our comms burst with static.

BRASS: "DUSK 2 AND 3, CONFIRM POSITIONS. WHERE ARE YOU?"

IRONHEART: "WE HAVE THE INJURED. SE-CURED AND STABLE. OVER."

BRASS: "YOU DISOBEYED DIRECT ORDERS, LIEUTENANT. WE'LL DEAL WITH THAT LATER. OVER."

And that was it.

Silence.

I was too deep now. I didn't care.

I turned to Rhynes. "Stay here. Watch him."

Rhynes narrowed his eyes. "Where are you going?"

I charged my cyber-arm and connected it to my blaster. "To end this."

Without waiting, I sprinted back into the battle.

Smoke filled the air, and a storm was coming soon. Blasters fired above me, and explosions shook the ground.

"Ping... Ping... Ping..."

My heart monitor buzzed like a live wire in my ear.

I was moving!

Through the haze, I spotted it the AGIS generator near the enemy's west wall. That was their weak spot.

If I could get close and plant the smart bomb, I could knock out their defenses and maybe even win the fight.

I ducked behind a broken barricade and slammed my hand onto the radio.

IRONHEART: "COMMAND, THIS IS DUSK-2. I HAVE A PLAN. REQUESTING A DIVERSION."

Static filled the radio. Then Brass's voice came through.

BRASS: "DUSK-2, REPORT."

IRONHEART: "I CAN PLANT A SMART BOMB AT THE WEST WALL. IT WILL TAKE OUT THEIR SHIELDS AND LET THE STORM DO THE REST. IT'S RISKY, BUT WE HAVE NO OTHER CHOICE."

BRASS: "… THAT'S A HUGE GAMBLE, DUSK-2."

IRONHEART: "SIR, I CAN PULL IT OFF."

BRASS: "DUSK-2, YOU'RE TO STAY PUT—"

IRONHEART: "I CAN'T DO THAT, SIR! WITH ALL DUE RESPECT—IF WE STAY HERE, WE ALL DIE. THIS IS OUR ONLY CHANCE."

BRASS: "…"

BRASS: "… DUSK-2… PROCEED. BUT IF THIS BLOWS UP IN YOUR FACE, YOU'RE ON YOUR OWN."

IRONHEART: "COPY THAT."

I held my tongue.

It was typical Brass.

If I succeeded, he'd take the credit. If I failed, it would all be my fault.

Fine. As long as my team got out safely, I could accept that.

I looked out at the battlefield and ran.

"PIIIING… PIIIING… PIIIING…"

"Ahh!" I shouted. At this point, my heart monitor screamed in my ear. I tuned it out as much as I could.

The battlefield closed in, all smoke and wreckage. I kept low, slipping through broken structures and shattered rocks. The shadows were my cover.

Up ahead, I saw the west wall and the AGIS generator buzzing actively.

I set a quick-impact bomb, with my hands locked on the trigger. There was no room for mistakes. One slip and it would be over for me, the team, and everyone counting on us.

As soon as it was armed, I took off running.

"This has to work."

My thumb hovered over the trigger.

"Please..."

I hit it.

"KABOOM!!!!!"

The blast punched through the sky, sending shockwaves under me. I didn't stop moving.

Screams followed. Rebel voices scrambled in panic.

"The shield is down! The shield is down! Fall back!"

And just like that, everything changed.

We had our chance.

We all rushed toward the rig. Lasers shot through the smoke, lighting up the air as the wind finally shifted. It became impossible to tell who was who. Everything was just noise, shadows, and movement.

I kept going. My legs felt like haul of iron. My head was spinning, and every breath stung my lungs. I was heaving.

"Don't stop. Keep moving."

The wind howled around me, and dust blinded my eyes. Then I noticed movement... a figure. In an instant, I raised my blaster, but I was too late. A cold blaster barrel pressed against the back of my head.

"That's it... It's over."

Slowly, I let my weapon fall from my hand and raised my hands. My breathing came in rough gasps.

"Dee... Dorothy..." I whispered, louder this time. "I'm sorry; I couldn't find—"

* * *

"NO, WAIT!!!" I yelled, snapping awake.

My heart racing, breath short, and everything too loud.

"It was all... a nightmare?"

"Ouch!"

"Where am I?" I croaked, the words scratching my dry throat.

I have no idea how long I'd been out. My head felt like it had been hit with a steel beam, pain rolled in heavy waves, and I couldn't focus. My vision kept fading in and out. I blinked hard until I could finally see my surroundings.

It was a cold, dim cell. The walls were made of damp, rough stone, stained with grime and something I didn't want to think about. A weak bulb hung from the ceiling, casting yellow light on the stone floor. Water dripped from a crack, echoing in the stillness. The air was stale and smelled like dust and mildew.

My limbs were stiff, and the cold went right through my uniform, making my bones ache. Metal cuffs were locked tightly around my wrists.

"Great."

I tested the restraints, and they wouldn't move. I looked around and saw no windows, no clues about where I was. I was still alive, for now.

"This has the be the work of the rebels… but why am I imprisoned?"

We were told the Monsoons didn't waste time with prisoners. If they spared me, it was for a reason. Either I had something they wanted, or they just liked watching people break.

Whatever the case, I wasn't planning on making it easy for them.

* * *

Days dragged by, and I lost track of time. The only reminder that I was still alive was the food and water they slid through a narrow slot in the door. They never spoke. They never asked me any questions. They just left me to rot in that cell, waiting.

By the fifth day, I couldn't wait any longer. I slammed my fist against the wall.

I slammed my fist into the wall hard enough to make my knuckles bleed. "WHY ARE YOU HOLDING ME HERE?" I shouted. "WHAT DO YOU WANT?"

Of course, there was nothing. Just the echo bouncing off steel and stone.

By the tenth day, I stopped asking questions.

It didn't matter.

I had no secrets to give up.

In my mind, I was already a name on a memorial wall back in ArcCity.

Then, on the eleventh day, everything changed.

"Did they tell you we tried negotiating with your team?" A distorted voice broke the silence from somewhere in the dark room.

I snapped awake.

"We tried to send you back. Guess what?" The voice laughed. "No one wanted you. Your squad leader marked you as a '*Killed in Action*' and left it at that."

At first, I wondered if this stranger was trying to get under my skin, but it was clearly having an effect. The fact that they wouldn't try to rescue me, knowing I'm alive… my so-called brothers… that cut deep. It didn't seem too far from the truth, especially with someone like Brass taking the lead.

"It's happening again… Everyone abandons me…"

But I needed to be certain. I couldn't let this stranger see that I was ready to break down. I had to stay strong and keep my composure.

"Did you hear me? Your own team would rather see you buried than work with us desert savages."

"Yeah. We knew the cost. So… what now?" I asked in a hoarse voice. "Are you going to kill me now that negotiations have failed?"

The mysterious voice didn't answer right away. Instead, it continued, "Before the conflict, some of our scouts noticed you."

I paused, confused.

"They said you were the only one who seemed to make sense, the only one who tried to stop the fight, the only one who hit our shields just hard enough to make our men fall back."

I didn't respond.

"So, tell me… why? Why did you take on a mission that was doomed from the beginning? Was the title of a deceased hero really worth it?"

I gave a bitter laugh. "Ha, ha, ha…Hero? No, that was never it. I don't care about any of that."

"Then why?"

There was a long silence.

"I was… I was looking for someone."

"Yeah, about that. They told me what you said before you blacked out. That name you called out. Would the person you're looking for be… Dorothy?"

"Dee!" I shouted as my energy shot up. I clenched my hands against the cuffs, and my breathing got faster. I tried to push forward as far as the restraints would let me.

"Tell me! What do you know? Do you have her? Did you hurt her?... Is she… alive?"

No words were said.

Finally, out of the shadows, a figure stepped forward.

"You're… a…" I started, before the words just fell apart.

"So, how do you know Dorothy?" She asked. This time when she spoke, there was no distortion.

"Wait… what?" I responded, still shocked.

"How do you know her?" She repeated.

This wasn't a question just out of curiosity; it felt more like a threat. I was confused and had many questions, but only one came out. I locked eyes with her.

"The real question is... how do you know her?"

CHAPTER SEVENTEEN

"*This is incredible!*"

Marimba led us deeper into the Winki village. It was a peaceful place that felt like a breath of fresh air after the chaos of the arena. Instead of crowded circles, their homes lined a winding river. We told him a bit about our journey, and what we hoped to find out about these terrible storms. But I'll admit, my mind was still on the community they've built here.

I couldn't help but be in awe of it all. The houses were built on strong ironwood stilts and had roofs made of woven leaves. Some were even built high up in trees. Small boats floated nearby.

"This is where our community holds its feasts," Marimba said, pointing to the smoke rising from the nearby trees.

As a gentle breeze drifted in, the delightful aroma of fresh fish, warm spices, and herbs filled the air, creating a cozy and inviting atmosphere.

At the center was a relaxed marketplace. Baskets were filled with fruit, herbs, and carved trinkets. Kids ran between the stalls, laughing. Elders sat in circles, playing drums and flutes, making a calm rhythm that mixed with the gentle rustling of leaves.

Out of nowhere, I felt a tug on my shirt.

"Here you go, Eshanu!" A little girl handed me a beaded necklace. She had a flowery headdress and a kalidah paw print on her cheek.

"Oh my, thank you, sweetie. My name is Dorothy. I love the flowers in your hair."

"Ok, Eshanu Dorothy!"

"No, it's—"

By then, she had already taken off, giggling with her friends.

"Haha, it's okay, Dorothy," Marimba said. "'Eshanu' means champion."

Oh, I see... Eshanu," I said, smiling. "Cro, I think I'd like you to start calling me Eshanu."

He rolled his eyes and shot back. "Yeah, sure, I'll add it to the list of titles you already have, like 'Great Stubborn One' and 'Lady Hardheaded.' Oh, and..."

I quickly stopped him with a laugh, saying, "Okay, okay, I get it!"

As we continued, I noticed that the clothes here were very different from what the Gilkin tribe wore. Just like the warriors from the arena, the Winki wore bright, vibrant colors. They wove feathers, beads, and stones into their braids or sewed them onto their sleeves.

"Oh, before I go, I just have to stock up on hair and clothing accessories."

Marimba then took us to an animal sanctuary. "This is where we care for all our injured animals. We have great honor and respect for every creature in this forest."

I could tell.

It was a peaceful clearing where injured or orphaned animals were getting better. Birds sat on low branches, unafraid. River boars grazed near the edge, and the kalidahs were treated with kindness and respect by the Winki healers. According to Marimba, these healers were called *Omakra*, or Soul-weavers.

As we turned a corner, Marimba pointed out ahead. A wide-open field stretched before us, with its tall grass blowing in the breeze.

"This is where we keep our orphaned kadilah cubs," he said.

I couldn't help myself.

Their fur gleamed in the sunlight, and one cub let out a lazy yawn that showed its tiny, sharp teeth. My heart practically turned to mush.

"Wow, they look just like Ursa. They're so cute."

"Only you call a ferocious baby beast cute," Cro teased, shaking his head.

"Oh yeah?" I said, "You forgot how you gushed about Tin?

"Hey, Tin is a beauty," Cro beamed, "in both engineering and craftsmanship. Right, Tin?"

Tin, ever the stoic, offered a thumbs-up.

"Fine, Tin is cute," I admitted with a grin. Then I turned to Marimba.

"What about Ursa's parents? Are they still alive?"

"Sorry, Dorothy. Just like the others, Ursa is an orphan. The Gilkin hunted her parents. Much of the recent conflict began over these special creatures. They sought to purge the Ironwoods of them, believing them to be spawns of evil."

"How could they?" I asked, "Were the Gilkin always like this?"

Marimba took a deep breath. "My father was honored among both tribes. He forged a peace that held for half a century with, Chief Sanza, the former Gilkin leader. But seven years ago, Terp arrived. Not long after Chief Sanza mysteriously fell ill... and the Gilkin changed forever. Once joyful, they became rigid, ruled by harsh codes and hollow piety."

His fist was clenched on his knee. "I have never trusted Chief Terp. We don't know where he originates. He simply appeared cloaked in prophecy, bearing strange resources. The error of Chief Sanza was making this stranger an advisor. But the Gilkin were drawn to his charisma. He wove his beliefs into the ancient ironwood ways. Now the Gilkin worship *Vortarion the Green*, an ancient god of storms and the sky."

"That name... Green... the spiral symbols with the eye..."

"I'm not sure why I didn't make that connection before. So would this... Vortarion the Green... happen to be a literal twister?" I asked.

Marimba shook his head. "Yes, Vortarion the Green, the original twister that never ends. Chief Terp claims this land was spared by choice and that he was chosen as it's divine prophet."

"But why make the people worship a literal destructive twister?" Cro asked.

Marimba gritted his teeth. "Power and resources."

I can tell he was frustrated by Chief Terp's ambitions. He continued.

"His worship is no devotion. It's a tool. A means of keeping the Gilkin under his rule. He seeks war between our tribes, all to seize dominion over the ironwoods. He knows its worth. He is not the first outsider to covet it... but he may be the most dangerous."

He began to scratch his head nervously. "I confess, I played on the tribe's old rivalries when I called for the Ozaruku. It was the only leverage I had to force his hand, but I did not expect him to go to such extremes.

Grimbol was once a Xamu, a group of special forest guardians chosen to be our strongest defense. My father, however, believed their strength had made them corrupt with power and greed, and so he dismissed them. Many of them left our forests, and I now suspect Grimbol, in his vexation, found it convenient to work for Chief Terp as an act of revenge."

He turned to me apologetic expression. "Dorothy... you have my deepest apology."

I shrugged, trying to brush it off. "It was still crazy to do, but I get it. And hey, trying to take my place in the fight was pretty bold of you."

Cro gave a polite cough. "Yeah, yeah, thanks for the heartfelt moment. But looping back to this Vortarion... do most people here really believe there's been a twister that lasted for generations?"

Marimba rubbed his chin. "In truth… yes. Many of our record keepers have spoken of a great twister—marked by green winds, fierce and unnatural. For some, it is not merely a storm, but a spirit. A force of reckoning from the old world, sent to purge and purify."

Cro nodded at his response and gave me a look.

"You said some believe that. What about you?" Tin asked.

Marimba gave a small shrug. "As chief-in-waiting, my duty is to honor our ways,, to tell the stories, to pass down the lore. And I do. But deep within… I question it. I've seen what reason, what science can accomplish. And the tales of these twisters… something in them has always unsettled me."

Marimba looked at me. "Dorothy, are you okay? You seem tense now."

I looked down. My hands were shaking, just a little. I didn't want to talk about it… not again… but Cro gently placed a hand on my shoulder.

"You don't have to," he said, voice low. "Not unless you want to."

I took a breath. Let it out slow.

"That twister...this... Vortarion as you call it… it destroyed my home," I said. "It killed my parents. Everything I had was gone."

"Is this true?... I'm so sorry, Dorothy," Marimba expressed.

Tin stepped closer. "You have my sympathies as well."

"Thanks," I whispered.

Marimba looked off toward the trees, like he was trying to make sense of something bigger than all of us.

"If there is truly a force behind this storm," Marimba said, "then everything changes. The Gilkin's blind faith in their false chief could falter. And perhaps… our tribes might draw closer once more. We must uncover the truth about this storm, and Chief Terp's so-called god."

* * *

It was getting dark and we had a very long day touring the village. We sat around a crackling fire, warm and worn out. My muscles ached in a good way. Somewhere behind us, the Winki village was settling in for the night. I kept thinking about the baskets of fruit and trinkets they had given us.

"Why is everyone so nice to us here?" I asked, holding a wooden necklace. "I know we are considered Eshanu, but I just thought they would be suspicious of us, too."

Marimba gave a small smile. "Among my people, kindness is not taken lightly. News spreads swiftly through the village. And when they learned of what you did for our cub, the risk you took… they were moved. Such deeds are remembered."

I turned to Cro and gave him a smug grin. "Told you."

Cro crossed his arms. "I was all for saving her from the start."

I slugged him in the shoulder, not too hard. "Sure, you were."

"Ow!"

Marimba laughed, and I shot him a quick nod of thanks.

"But seriously," Marimba said, "your weapon, that lightning spear. How did it summon such immense power?"

I was in quiet thought.

They were all staring weirdly at me now.

I shrugged. "I honestly don't know. The storm hit, and I just… felt something. I grabbed my wand, and it kind of… charged itself. The rest just happened."

Marimba looked confused. "The lightning… it answered you. That is no ordinary thing."

Cro spoke up. "I think Dorothy's bracelet played a part."

"Her… bracelet?" Marimba asked.

Tint raised his finger in agreement. "I can confirm what Cro is saying. During the battle, we observed a glow amidst the storm. It closely resembled my own experience."

"No way!" I replied, "You guys are making it sound way more dramatic than it was—"

"Dorothy, it's true," Cro said, grabbing my shoulder.

"They look serious… But how?... Is it the same artifact Tin fought against?"

I stared at my bracelet, watching the faint glow dancing in the firelight.

"…artifact… artifact…"

"Hold on! That reminds me…" I said, reaching into my bag and pulled out the compass. "Marimba, can you please take a look at this?"

He turned it slowly in his hands, studying every line with care. "Yes… a compass, but not a common one. These etchings… they bear the signature of something I have seen before."

"So, you recognize where this compass might come from?"

"Not its origin, no… but these markings, I know them well. This is *Quadsi*… the written language of the Quadling Tribe."

"Quadling? So… there's another tribe around here?" I straightened myself.

Marimba nodded. "They are wanderers, nomads of the old world. It has been decades, perhaps longer, since they were last seen. They're skilled in music and metalwork. They left their touch across the land. You'd be fortunate to find them. To the Quadling, crafting is sacred."

He paused, eyes narrowing with intrigue. "Tell me… how did this come into your hands?"

"My parents picked it up on their journey topside." I answered.

"Are other tribes still around?" Cro asked.

"All of the tribes once roamed far and wide, scattered like seeds upon the wind. In time, each tribe found its path and its craft. The Gilkin were once esteemed traders and masters of fabric, dye, and fine adornments. But they followed Terp and lost themselves in a new spiritual fanaticism. Other tribes turned more… dangerous. We rarely speak of them."

"It's still incredible that any community topside survived this long," I said.

Marimba agreed. "We survive because of these sacred ironwoods. They shield us in ways you can't always see."

"Hmm…does he mean—"

Cro jumped in. "So, what about the Winki? What are you guys known for?" Cro asked.

Marimba smiled. "We are the keepers of Oz's legacy. The ones who do not forget. From the moment we take our first steps, we are taught to remember. Every tale, every relic, every whisper of the past. It is our sacred charge to gather the history of all the lands and preserve it for those yet to come."

He looked toward the fire, and the flames reflected in his eyes. "Beneath our village lies a place hidden from all but the worthy. A sanctuary of knowledge. There, we have preserved the collective wisdom and secrets of our ancestors gathered over millennia. It is the heart of who we are."

"This compass is pointing us in a direction beyond the Ironwoods," I said. "But it would be good to know more about where it came from. Is it possible to find more clues about this compass's origin in this cave of knowledge?"

"Hmph… It's not so simple," Marimba said. "Only the Great Elder can grant passage, and such permission as this is extremely rare. We've protected it across generations, bound by duty and tradition. Only a select few among the Winki are allowed to enter the sacred grounds. No outsider has ever set foot inside."

I understand," I replied softly, gently tucking a loose strand of hair behind my ear. "It was worth trying to ask. If we could at least have some shelter until morning, that would really mean a lot."

Marimba started staring at my wrist. "Ah... now I see. At first, I thought it was a joke I failed to understand. But that bracelet... where did you find it?" he asked.

"Oh, this again? It was a gift from my mom, and it's been my good-luck charm ever since. Listen, it's not what you think..."

"Hmm... Could this be? Perhaps fate has not brought us together by accident, after all."

"...What?" I said, scratching my head.

He reached out to look at the bracelet again in amazement. "Wow... I believe... it is time you met my Uma, or as you would say, my grandmother."

"Uh, whoa there, Prince!" Cro interjected.

"Your grandmother?" I repeated, curious. "Listen, I am not interested in marital ceremonies."

"Hahahaha! A joke I truly get!"

A genuine, rare laugh escaped him. I offered a nervous smirk.

"No, Dorothy, this is not a ceremony. She is the Great Elder of the Winki. When she is not tending to the woodland creatures, she serves as our mother record keeper, the guardian of our deepest knowledge. I have no doubt she will take a great interest in your bracelet."

"Ok, you had us nervous for a bit!" Cro sighed."

"So, does that mean we're heading to the Cave?" I asked, hopeful.

Marimba nodded. "Yes, let's make our way while the night is young."

CHAPTER EIGHTEEN

"Welcome to the heart of the Winki' knowledge," Marimba said, his voice all reverent and serious like we were stepping into a shrine instead of a cave.

I wasn't sure what I expected when he opened that iron-sealed door, but… yeah, definitely not this.

The place resembled a secret library tucked inside that mountain, kept hidden for centuries. Rows of wooden shelves stretched out in all directions, densely packed with books, scrolls, and ancient documents. A large green power lamp swung gently from the ceiling, casting a warm, mysterious glow over the chamber. The air was infused with the smell of dust and aged parchment.

"Who would've thought this would be hidden under a village?"

"And what do we have here?" A voice called out.

As we could take another step, a figure appeared from the shadows.

"An elderly woman?"

Her skin was a deep, rich brown, just like mine. Her silver hair was braided tight and neat, with bright feathers woven into it, and lines of experience were carved into her face.

She wore a long, draped robe adorned with colorful jewels, a clear sign of her importance. She walked closer, studying each of us.

Marimba bowed low. "Great Elder Uru, these are the ones I told you about. They seek answers from our records."

The woman's gaze swept over us so suddenly I couldn't help but feel nervous. Slowly, she approached him with a slight smile. She raised her hand and, without a word.

"WHACK!"

With a quick strike, she slapped the Chief-in-waiting on the back of his head. Marimba flinched, but he said nothing as he lowered his eyes in shame.

"Ouch! Knowing him at this point, I'm sure he deserved it."

She finally spoke firmly. "Marimba, you should know better than to summon an Ozaruku without good reason. Recklessness has no place in keeping our people safe."

"I understand, Elder Uru. I apologize for my carelessness and for risking the village." Marimba replied, lowering his eyes while rubbing his head.

She let out a sigh and stepped closer. Then, more gently than I expected, she reached out and placed her hand beneath his chin, tilting his face up.

"Take your time, my son," she said. "Greatness doesn't come from rushing. Your name will be remembered, but only if you learn when to choose wisdom over haste."

Marimba managed a small smile with hopeful eyes. "I will not rush again, Great Elder. I will follow your teaching."

A young Winki researcher burst into the chamber, excited. "Great Elder, I'm happy to report that the entire *Great Divide* collection has been archived in the new network!"

"Network?" Cro blurted.

"Very well," Elder Uru's replied, waving her hand, "But remember, the true value of knowledge lives in a real book, in the feel of ink on parchment. Don't let our history vanish into thin air."

The researcher bowed and hurried off. Elder Uru then turned her piercing gaze back to us. She focused on Cro first.

"Hmm..." she murmured softly as she strolled around us in curiosity. "I can sense a lot of unusual energy with this group of outsiders."

We were silent.

"You," she pointed at Cro, "are small, young, and brash. Yet I see a spark of cleverness in your eyes, like an old sage mixed with a child's curiosity. Your full potential, though not yet realized, is truly special."

Cro's face turned red, but he tried to look proud as he adjusted his glasses. "Thank you, Great Elder. It's only natural to notice genius..."

"OUCH!" He yelped when I elbowed him.

"Hey, could you tone down the ego? You're embarrassing us," I whispered.

Mother Uru didn't seem too concerned with our little back-and-forth. She walked right past it, straight to Tin.

"And you, robot," she said, marveling Tin's craftsmanship with awe. "The metal in your body… it reminds me of a time long past. I can see you're both a relic and a reminder. A piece of Ozian brilliance, and a warning to our nature. But this light inside you…"

She placed her hand gently against his chest plate. Her palm hovered over his core like she was listening for something no one else could hear.

"This energy," she whispered, "it's rare. And warm. Not cold like most machines. It's almost like… a heart. You are truly unique."

Tin didn't move a circuit. Just stood there, blinking like he was processing more than her words.

"Acknowledged," he said. "I am an anomaly among my kind. Designed to assist Cro and our friends."

"Tin, can we not sound like you're here to take our lunch orders?" Cro groaned very audibly.

Tin started processing. " I don't understand? Is this sarcasm or a directive?"

"Tin… never mind, buddy…" Cro sighed.

Mother Uru smiled, but her eyes landed on me, and that smile changed into something heavier. She walked over, slow and cautious, like she thought I might run if she moved too quickly.

I honestly thought about it.

"Okay, wow… she is very close now… it's ok, just keep calm."

Gently, she extended her hand and lightly stroked my right cheek with her soft, textured hands. Then she gently combed through my pigtails, her fingertips gliding through the hair like she was reading a story only she could see.

I winced a little.

"Eshanu," she said, her voice suddenly quiet. "Your skin holds warmth, and your hair… such beauty in these curls. Ahh, but it's your eyes… they carry curiosity and strength in equal measure."

I was stunned, completely unsure of what to do with any of that.

She continued. "I've heard about what you did young Eshanu. Defending the sacred beast. You have our deepest gratitude."

My heart nearly jumped out of my chest, and heat rushed to my cheeks.

"Oh… uh… thank you, Great Elder. I didn't really… I mean, I just did what needed doing and—"

She cut me off with a soft laugh. "No need for modesty, child. From this moment, you may call me Mother Uru."

"Mother Uru," I repeated, trying to sound composed. "Thank you. And… honestly, it was mostly the lightning rod that helped."

I held out my wand as if it explained everything.

She took it, turning it over in her hands. Her expression changed, eyes narrowing just a touch.

"No," she said finally. "This is only a tool. Our people spoke of the storm clouds forming too fast. Too exact. That wasn't chance or clever wiring. I sense something in you. Something not yet awake. A strange power."

I stared at my hands as if they were hiding a secret from me.

"A strange power?" I asked. "Mother Uru, what do you mean?"

She closed her eyes and gently placed her hands over mine on the wand. Her palms were warm.

Then her fingers brushed the bracelet on my wrist.

Her eyes snapped open.

"Child," she said, "where did you get this?"

"This is why I brought her, Uma," Marimba said, stepping forward like he'd just connected all the dots for us.

Mother Uru didn't look up. Her eyes were glued to the bracelet on my wrist as if she were about to start reciting a prophecy.

"Lightning… and an artifact like this?" she mumbled, more to herself than anyone else. "Could it really be true? But how?"

She leaned in closer, so close I could smell the herbs on her breath. "Young lady, are you… from the Order?"

"The Order?" I repeated.

She said nothing. Only stared into my eyes. Heat rushed to my cheeks all over again.

"Uh, sorry, Mother Uru, but I have no idea what that is."

"Come," she said, already grabbing my hand. "Quickly. You must follow me."

"Wait!" I called over my shoulder, trying to untangle my arm without being rude. "What about Cro and Tin?"

"My grandson will see to them." She said, waving them off.

"Grandson?"

I turned and gave Cro a helpless look.

He just shrugged like he'd been expecting something weird to happen. "Don't embarrass us!" he called, hands cupped dramatically around his mouth.

I rolled my eyes.

Of course, he said that. But I smiled anyway.

Then I let Mother Uru pull me deeper into the archive chamber, still clutching my wrist like it might explode.

* * *

"Now, where could it be? I thought my assistants had already organized this section," Mother Uru muttered as she hurried between shelves, her fingers brushing over rows of old books and scrolls. Her sudden energy was nothing like the calm she'd shown moments before. I stood still, completely baffled.

"Why is everyone so worked up over my mom's bracelet?" I whispered, turning my wrist to look at the small artifact.

"Mom, what didn't you tell me?"

"Here it is!" Mother Uru exclaimed as she strode back to me and dropped a huge book into my lap. Its weight almost toppled me over.

The cover was made of cracked leather, soft but very old. Its frayed corners and yellowed pages looked like they were hundreds of years old. She opened it, and dust filled the air.

"What is this?" I asked, coughing. I noticed that the faded markings on the cover looked just like those on my bracelet.

"This," she said with respect, "is the Codex of the Tempest Order. A relic from a forgotten time. A mysterious woman gave it to me, claiming it was the last of its kind." Her eyes shone as she carefully flipped through its fragile pages. "Let's see where the truth begins."

She quickly flipped through the pages, mumbling summaries that went right over my head. The stories of ancient beasts and lost legends all blended together into a confusing blur.

Finally, she slowed and pressed her finger on one passage. "Here… *'Conduits and Artifacts.'*"

She turned to me with a serious expression.

"This bracelet you wear, child, is an ancient conduit, a vessel made to channel great power."

"An ancient… conduit?" I echoed, my voice shaking. "For what Mother Uru?"

"Why magic, child!" She replied, excited. "Long ago, our world was alive with magic."

"Magic?" I blurted, fighting a laugh. "Forgive Mother Uru, but like bedtime stories?"

"My child," she said in a soft tone, "magic was as real as the air we breathe. It was a song that sang up from the planet's very heart, and it whispered through every living thing. It was called the Great Magic of Oz, and it wasn't just for Ozians; it was for the Zolytes as well. In that time, we all lived on one land, and we danced to its rhythm. We called that time the Protus Age."

"Zolytes and Ozians? Together?" I tried not to sound rude. "That can't be right."

Her gaze hardened. "You must listen before you reject. I'm not suggesting, child. I'm telling you."

"Sorry, Mother Uru," I said quickly. "Please… continue."

"The Protus Age was a time of balance," she said. "Magic bound all of nature. But as the Ozians grew in number, so did their greed. They feared the Zolytes' stronger connection to the magic and accused them of hoarding power."

Her voice turned sad.

"Hatred and distrust grew between the two groups. The Ozians eventually united into an empire under Emperor Ozarv the First. Many tribes pledged their allegiance. The Winki and Gilkin clans, our ancestors, chose not to take sides. We left the central lands and began to explore. That marked the end of the Protus Age… and the start of the Enchanted Age."

I felt something settle heavily within me. "The Great Empire of Oz… ruled by Ozarv…" I whispered. "We learned about that as children. But they never mentioned magic…or Zolytes."

She raised her hand, cutting me off without a word.

"The Archons rewrote history," she said flatly. "They erased what didn't serve them. But the truth lives in places like this, in the books that survived."

"I see," I said, still struggling to process this new information.

She went on.

"Emperor Ozarv suspected the Zolytes of uncovering another source of magic and concealing it from him. He dispatched his new army to locate and take control. The Zolytes retaliated with superior magical abilities and compelled the Ozians to retreat westward to a land named after the emperor's wife, Ev."

"… EvLand," I said.

She nodded once and picked up where she had left off. "The Zolytes stayed in the east and built their own kingdom in what you call the NoLands," she said.

I stared. "So… what happened to the Zolytes?"

Her smile faded as she looked away.

"No one knows. Some say they vanished when magic faded. Others believe they perished in storms that reshaped the land. Only tales, and a few books like this, remain. After leaving the Ozian Kingdom, our tribe became nomadic storytellers and collectors of history. We travelled far before settling in the Ironwoodlands."

"Wow… All of this is…"

For a moment, I was at a loss for words. The Zolytes, Old magic, and the NoLands... Leo would never believe everything I was hearing right now.

I barely believed it myself.

Honestly, I was still skeptical, but her genuine demeanor made it hard to question her. That being said, there were a few things that left me unsure and in need of explanation.

"Mother Uru, I really appreciate the history you've shared… it's a lot to take in! I want to be honest with you, though; I'm still not quite sure how this connects to me... and my bracelet."

"Magic connects everything!" She answered with a sparkle in her eyes. "Though it has faded, it still lives, in trees, stones, beasts, even in the emeralds we use. Dome-dwellers don't believe it because they trust only what they can measure."

She gently held my hands again.

"We Ozians may be clever with our ingenuity, but few of us could hold much magic. The truth is, we weren't the best vessels for it. But this Codex mentions that there were a few rare Ozians who possessed magic vessels that far exceeded normal Ozians and even ancient Zolytes. We learned that they were called *Latents*. When Oz magic faded, even fewer Ozians could use it. Yet Latents still carried strong magic in their bloodlines."

"Latents… Now, I've never heard of that," I said.

"Yes, well, there are still Latents, even now," she said. "Their power lies hidden, usually until a magical artifact draws it out."

"Oh… like ancient conduits…" I said, looking at my bracelet.

"You finally understand," she said, as she turned another page on the codex.

"Long ago, a mystical group called the Tempest Order of Latents created many kinds of artifacts such as this tempest ring. They were not ordinary tools; they served as powerful conduits, enhancing and stabilizing the wearer's magic, making them truly unique.

She paused, letting her words sink in.

"It's finally starting to click, I guess" I muttered, "… so that means…"

Then, with complete certainty, she said, "There is no mistaking it. You are a child of the Tempest Order. Hahahaha!"

***

"So, now latent users... artifacts... this… Tempest Order… what's going on?"

Mother Uru was engrossed in her old book again, flipping through the pages with quiet focus while I sat lost in thought about everything I'd learned so far. It all sounded like a bedtime story told by an unusual elder. But it wasn't just imaginary; it was supposed to be real…

"I am part of this Order… Me?"

My head started to spin, and I began rubbing my temples.

"The history we were taught… was missing all of this?"

Did the Archons really erase it? Or did past generations bury it so deeply that no one was meant to find it again? More importantly, my parents kept journals about their journeys, recording every detail. So why had they never mentioned any of this?

"Wow… I came for answers about a compass, and now I have another world of stuff to think about."

I glanced around and saw Cro and Marimba chatting about turning old records into digital files. I wondered how Cro would react to what I learned. Would he just laugh and say it was nonsense? Probably... he was a little too proud to believe in magic or myths.

My thoughts shifted to my other friends.

"Would Tin believe this? Kassi? Leo?" I whispered. "This is all too much. Mom, Dad… did you know about any of this?"

"Ah ha! Here it is!" Mother Uru shouted as she stopped at a drawing of a Tempest Ring. Its lines swirled like wind cloud shapes.

"That's… that's like my bracelet," I said, leaning closer.

Tin walked up just then. "Yes, this drawing… these markings… match details in my memory bank for self-data recovery."

Mother Uru raised an eyebrow. "Your friend might be broken."

I giggled. "No, I think he's remembering his past."

"Correct," Tin said, "Cro and Marimba have updated my system log. My scan is now complete. Dorothy, I am prepared to inform you of the events that transpired. Over a century ago, I engaged in combat with an individual known as a Tempest Maiden. The Oz Empire pursued them due to their extraordinary power. They resided in secluded regions, concealed from adversaries. A confrontation ensued at that time."

"Tempest Maiden?" I repeated, confused.

Mother Uru said, "If it was over a century ago, this matches the Second Great Oz War."

"Affirmative," Tin agreed.

"But I don't get it," I said. "My grandmother gave this bracelet to my mother. How could they be in that ancient group?"

Mother Uru closed the Codex gently and turned to Tin. "Thanks, robot, I'll take it from here."

Tin nodded and went back to Cro and Marimba.

Mother Uru watched me closely. "Dorothy, the Tempest Maidens passed their magic only through women. That's why they were called 'Maidens'. The Order was led by the Tempest Matron, who could command the skies."

She turned to a page showing a drawing of a powerful woman pulling lightning from storm clouds. "See her? She united the Order and made it famous."

I stared at the picture. "I can't believe this…" I whispered. "Are there more Maidens?"

Mother Uru paused again. "There was a fierce battle that brought the Tempest Order to an end. They were pursued and defeated, but it appears one survived… you, your ancestor. To my knowledge, you are the last of the Tempest Maidens."

"The last Tempest Maiden…" I whispered, feeling overwhelmed.

I needed a moment.

I stood up, my thoughts racing.

"So, Mom… Grandma Doris… my great-grandmother… did you all have this power?"

Mother Uru watched me. "Tell me, child. What are you searching for? The world's truth? A solution for Oz? An answer to everyone's problems?"

My sigh was deep. "I'm not sure anymore. When I left Emeraldia, I wanted to uncover the truth about the twisters, just like my parents. Maybe I could even put a stop to them."

Mother Uru hummed. "I see… And then what? You finish your parents' dreams. What happens next? You go home?"

Her question struck a chord with me. "I… don't know…I don't even have a home anymore. And I have no idea what's next."

I was at a loss for words.

Mother Uru stood up. "You may not know the fullness of your destiny yet, and that's okay. Sometimes we spend our lives looking for it. But destiny isn't a place."

She placed her hand on my shoulder. "It's a voice that calls to us when we least expect it. In time, you'll hear it more often… and you'll know it's meant for you."

Tears welled in my eyes as her voice softened.

"But Mother Uru, how can you be so sure?" I asked, wiping my eyes, "This journey feels impossible most days. It's like… the whole world is on my shoulders."

She smiled wide and warm, like the sunlight.

"My child, I'm certain because you're strong. And with the blood of a Tempest Maiden, a lineage linked to the very forces of nature, you have a powerful foundation. As a Latent of the Order, your abilities bind you to something ancient and profound. The storms you face aren't meant to break you; they're meant to shape you into the powerful woman you're destined to be."

Her words lingered in my mind, helping me breathe again.

I let go of everything spinning in my head for just a second and gave Mother Uru the smallest, most real smile I could manage.

"So… how do I use this thing? The tempest ring, I mean?"

She blinked, leaned in, and said with a big grin, "Dorothy, it's quite simple… I don't have the faintest idea!"

Then she burst out laughing like she'd just told the best joke in the world.

And I couldn't help it… I laughed too. A real laugh.

"But," she added, wiping her eye, "together, we'll learn. Let's keep reading and see what secrets this old codex has been hiding from the world."

So, we did.

We spent hours with that book. It was me, her, and centuries of forgotten history. The pages were stiff and fragile, but every time we turned one, something new came to life inside me. My doubt didn't go away, but it got quieter. And in its place, I felt something better.

A spark.

A beginning.

Soon, a researcher called Mother Uru away to look at some new artifacts that supposedly couldn't wait. I figured she would take the book with her. But instead, she surprised me.

"Take this, child," she said.

"Wait… what? No, Mother Uru, this is your people's history. It belongs here, in your care."

She pressed it into my chest anyway. "No, Dorothy. This belongs with you now. Guard it with your life. The Tempest Order's story was never meant to sit idle. It's meant to inspire. To evolve. To lead. Let it help you find your way, just like it did for those before you."

She paused, then added, "And who knows? It may help you become the greatest Tempest Maiden the world's ever seen."

Her words felt like a beautiful blessing. I clutched the Codex close to my chest, feeling her faith more comforting than my own fears.

"Thank you, Mother Uru," I whispered.

She smiled, with tears shining down her eyes. "Go forth, my child. Your journey is only beginning."

* * *

Across the cave, I spotted Tin deep in conversation with Marimba and Cro… well, Tin was talking, and Cro was mostly making skeptical faces. Still, I could tell he was listening. The second I heard my name, I jogged over.

"Talking about me behind my back?" I asked with a playful smile.

"Only the heroic parts," Tin replied. "I was explaining your status as a Tempest Maiden."

Cro snorted. "Status? Don't start giving her titles. Her head's already big enough with all the compliments she was getting from the Great Elder earlier, not to mention the whole village just upgraded her to champion."

"It's *Eshanu* to you." I laughed, nudging him. "Someone's a bit jealous, I see."

Marimba chuckled and unrolled a weathered old map across the closest table. He pointed to a cluster of winding lines in the bottom right corner.

"Okay, listen," he said, all grim now. "You'll want to avoid the Howling Canyons. Looks peaceful on a map, but don't let that fool you. That place is a labyrinth of deep chasms carved out over time by fierce wind gusts. We've heard outsiders call it the *Gust Gorge*, but my people know it as *Nuvakra*, or 'A Thousand Breathes'."

"A foggy maze with powerful winds, got it," Cro said.

"Cro, I'm serious," Marimba warned. "The Gilkin believe the Green-Eyed God was last seen there years ago. Your safest option is to go around, even if it takes longer."

"Or how about we just follow the angry squiggles on the inside and try not to get blown into a canyon by the gusts? That'd be faster, right?" I said, tracing the canyon lines on the map.

Marimba smiled. "You guys are impossible… I can see danger is a way of life for you all. Well, Dorothy, at least you've learned about your tempest ring. Perhaps you may have more control over that wind than you think."

"Controlling wind? Right, I barely know how this thing works," I said quietly, looking down at the bracelet on my wrist.

"Well, whatever you guys need, I promise I will help in any way that I can." He said.

We spent more hours talking and laughing about our wild journey so far. Marimba, once annoying, had become a good friend.

Before long, Mother Uru reminded us that it was nighttime, and we needed rest. Darkness settled over the camp, and everything was calm and peaceful. We didn't know that our time with the Winki was about to end so suddenly.

* * *

The night was so quiet it felt like even the wind had fallen asleep. There was no sound at all, just stillness. Ursa was curled up right beside me, all warm fur and sleepy breaths. He was like a living blanket that snored sometimes.

Our little lamp was trying its best to stay on, but the light kept flickering. I barely noticed. I was focused on the Codex resting in my lap.

I ran my fingers over the old pages, thinking that if I skimmed through it the right way, some ancient truth might jump off the paper and explain everything.

No luck so far. But I kept reading anyway.

One passage caught my eye. It spoke of channeling power through the Tempest Ring:

"In order to awaken your true nature, you must imagine your spirit's untamed strength and the raw power of nature. When they merge, they create an ethereal spark inside you. The power isn't in the ring itself; the ring simply channels the surge you already hold. Often, this raw power peaks in times of distress. But once you control it, the very skies can obey your command."

I let out a long breath, trying to slow the thump in my chest. If what the Codex said was true, then maybe I wasn't just a kid who got swept up in a storm. Maybe I had more control than I thought. I closed my eyes and let the words sink into my brain.

"Untamed eternal spirit."

That's what the Codex called it. But what did it really mean? Could I use it? Shape it?

"Okay, Dorothy. Focus... feel it," I whispered to myself, leaning back and diving into that space in my memory. Not the frantic chaos of a storm, but the calm feeling I felt when everything was just right. Freedom.

A gentle warmth curled around my wrist. I opened my eyes.

My bracelet was glowing.

"Mom... it's real!"

Ursa's ears twitched. Her whole body got stiff as if she had heard something I hadn't yet. Then, just like that, she was up on all fours, a low growl building in her throat.

"Ursa?" I said, reaching for her fur. She didn't even flinch.

And that's when I heard it. A deep, throaty growl coming from outside. Then another. And another.

My stomach sank. "Nope. Definitely not the wind."

I grabbed my battle wand and crept into the next room, Ursa right beside me like a silent shadow.

"Cro," I hissed, nudging him. "Wake up."

He mumbled something like "five more minutes" and rolled over.

"Do you hear that growling? Something's out there."

He opened one eye halfway. "It's probably kalidahs. They howl at the moon, right?"

"No, Cro," I snapped. "They don't howl. Ursa's in full panic mode. Get up. Wake Tin. Now."

Footsteps thundered outside, charging. Ursa's growl deepened; every muscle coiled. I braced myself, wand charged in hand. Then she relaxed suddenly.

"That's odd."

Then, she stopped. Tail lowered. Muscles relaxed. I didn't get to wonder why for long.

"BOOM!"

The door flung open. Cro jumped.

"They're here… the Sentinels! Marimba barreled in, panting. "The watchers picked them up tracking us!"

Cro sat up like someone had dumped cold water on his face. "They're here for me," he croaked. "Tin, wake up! We have to go, now!"

We grabbed what we could and ducked out the back, barely getting our boots on. Just as we rounded the corner, a small figure stepped into the moonlight.

"Quickly, follow me," came a voice I knew. Mother Uru.

"Go with the other Elders," she said calmly. "I'll meet you again soon."

Winki Night-Watcher: "We are under attack! Sound the alarm!"

The night erupted in chaos.

Horns blared through the Ironwoods. Screams mixed with thunderous roars. Winki warriors readied arrows and shields, rushing to the treetops. From above, Sentinels rained fire, but they were already surrounded.

Then warriors released the Battle-Kalidahs. The ground shook under their armored bodies as they tore through the village like living nightmares. Whistles and calls guided them, and panic spread. The Sentinels began to fall back.

"The Winki battle coordination with the kalidahs…" Cro muttered.

"Yeah, it's incredible," I added.

"Dorothy, Cro, we need to leave!" Tin grabbed my arm. We dove into the chaos, dodging running villagers and fallen warriors, sprinting toward the waiting vehicles.

"Where are we going?" I asked. "I thought we were heading to Howling Canyons!"

"It's too risky," Cro said. "We need a safer route."

"No, going through the canyons is our best chance to lose them."

Tin nodded. "Cro, she's right."

Cro sighed. "Fine. But if we die, I'm blaming you two."

I stopped.

Ursa looked up at me, her big eyes full of confusion. She didn't understand what was happening, only that something was wrong. I dropped to my knees and wrapped my arms around her, holding her close like I could pause time if I squeezed hard enough.

"I'm sorry, Ursa," I whispered into her fur. "I'll come back for you. I promise."

She whimpered as I pulled off the old sleeping bandana from around my head.

"Don't worry," Mother Uru said. "She'll be safe with us."

I barely had a moment to catch my breath before Marimba stepped forward, looking serious. Something was definitely wrong.

"We've got more news," he said, turning to me. "We've got word from Gilkin allies that this was the work of the traitor, Chief Terp. He informed the Archons of your presence. This is a betrayal for both tribes since we are enemies of the Archons. I'm sorry Dorothy, but you are a wanted person now."

My heart paused. "Wanted? Why me?"

"There's no time to think about that," Cro interrupted.

"I concur. It is essential that we maintain our movement," Tin added. "We will ensure your protection."

"You're right," I nodded, "Thanks for having my back guys. Let's head out!"

Turning back to Marimba and Mother Uru. "I'm so sorry we brought this trouble to you—"

"Don't waste your breath feeling guilty." Marimba interrupted, raising a hand to stop me. "We know how to protect our own. We prepare for this every day."

His eyes welled up with hope. "No one stands a chance in our territory. Here, we're the ones doing the hunting." He took my hand and kept going. "And you and your friends are family now. We protect what's ours."

Mother Uru stepped toward me and cupped my face in her hands. "My child," she said, her voice cracking just a little. "I'm so glad I met you. You've made me believe in your journey. Go now. Find the truth, Tempest Maiden."

And just like that, the tears started streaming down my face. We wrapped each other in a tight hug, and I didn't want to let go, but I had to.

I dabbed at my eyes, climbed onto Tin's strider, and as we took off, it felt like a part of my heart was left behind.

We rode into the night, following the compass's guidance as the sounds of the Ironwoods faded into the distance.

CHAPTER NINETEEN

Night surrounded us as we raced through strong winds blowing off the narrow cliffs.

"We've reached Howling Canyon," Tin announced.

"We could still take a detour," Cro suggested, but he didn't sound confident.

"Let's keep going," I said, pushing aside my doubt.

The air up here felt strange. Every gust tore right through my jacket. In the distance, something was wailing. Maybe it was the wind, or something else entirely. The peaks above looked like broken claws scraping the sky. I was committed to this route, but riding through this place made me nervous.

And now we weren't alone.

"My scanners are picking up enemies behind us," Tin reported.

Marimba and the Winki warriors had slowed them down, but not enough. The Sentinels were closing in, hiding in the shadows. I wiped the dust from my visor.

"Then we'll use this canyon against them."

"Tin, take the lead," Cro ordered. "You spot danger first. I'll watch our backs and make sure nothing sneaks up on us."

"Got it," Tin said

We made a sharp turn and changed direction, avoiding rocks that stuck out like broken bones. There was no time to hesitate in these conditions. The engines roared, and the wind screamed. With the speed we were moving in the dark, we'd have no problem smashing into the canyon floor if we were not alert.

The walls closed in fast. Towering cliffs blocked the moon, and shadows swallowed everything. Then the wind slammed into us again like a punch, pushing our striders sideways. My grip on Tin's waist loosened slightly.

"Whoa, Tin, this ride is getting a lot bumpier," I shouted.

"You are correct, Dorothy," Tin responded.

"Really Tin? That didn't really help much. But I guess a little acknowledgment is better than nothing."

At this point, I was holding on for dear life.

"How are you managing the situation there Cro?" Tin asked over the comms.

"I'm okay buddy, I just hope they don't catch up to us, and this fog isn't helping."

He was right. The mist hung low, clinging to the ground and hiding our path unless our headlights cut through it. The moon's faint light barely peeked through the thick clouds, making the canyon seem dark and mysterious

Tin looked ahead. "Prepare yourself, you guys; the situation is expected to get worse. A significant gust is pending. We have to execute a swift maneuver. Cro, please prepare your thrusters."

"On it." He replied.

I wrap my arms tighter around Tin's metal body.

"Here we go!" I shouted, bracing myself.

"WOOSH!!"

Then a gust exploded through the canyon with a loud howl, and our strider swayed wildly. We fired the thrusters just in time, pushing us away from the nearest wall into our turn.

"Whoo! We would have crashed if it weren't for those boosters!" Cro shouted. "Good call, Tin!"

"We have not yet exited the canyon," Tin cautioned. "Please remain prepared... they are approaching!"

This chase feels all too familiar. Now it's a different enemy, but the same fight. Someone clearly doesn't want us to find the truth.

A sharp crack breaks through the air as the Sentinels' voices boom from loudspeakers.

SENTINEL: "SURRENDER NOW!"

We don't flinch.

SENTINEL: "FINAL WARNING!"

We give no response.

Blasts of green light rip through the fog, zipping past us with sharp, electric buzzes. The attack has started.

"They're using stun blasters," Tin notices. "One hit will temporarily immobilize us."

"It's fine; I've dealt with them before," Cro replied. "Activating night vision."

His strider was built for this. With the flick of a switch, cannons slide into place with a hiss. The rear guns lock on target and open fire, sending a storm of energy bolts into the dark.

"BOOM!"

One Sentinel goes down.

"BOOM!"

Another smashes into the canyon wall.

"Ha! Ha! You like that? Eat my smart cannon blasters!" Cro shouts, laughing like a maniac.

"Skr // Cro."

His codename made a lot of sense now. He can shift from logical to wild the moment things get serious. He might be a little unhinged, but out here? That makes him dangerous.

And right now, dangerous is exactly what we need.

Up ahead, the Sentinels hesitate. Their numbers are thinning, and they're out of their depth in this maze of cliffs and wind tunnels. I watch them tighten formation, then split off into the labyrinth.

"The Sentinels are transitioning to a surprise-attack plan," Tin said over the comm. "They are clever, yet in a state of desperation."

"It's risky, even for them," I added. "They don't know when or where the next powerful gust will hit. Stay sharp, Cro."

Cro let out a sharp laugh. "Ha! Affirmative!"

We sped through the twisting canyons. The wind roared as Cro's blasts forced the Sentinels into the shadows, barely missing them each time. I realized we couldn't keep this pace. They were getting closer, trying to trap us. We couldn't outrun them forever.

That's when I realized it.

"Ok, enough of this! It's time. I… have to use it."

I calmed my breathing, and I reached deep inside for that power again. The world blurred, and in a single flash, I was back at the first moment I'd ever made it topside.

I remember it now. A giant twister tore toward me. I got caught in its pull, but instead of fear, I felt calm. I'd thought I'd blacked out, but now I knew better. My bracelet on my wrist had glowed, and I'd slipped into a trance between reality and time. Somehow, I'd tapped into my power and survived.

"I can feel it," I whispered, staring at the glow on my bracelet.

"Danger! Three enemies coming at us from the left," Tin warned.

"They're squeezing us," Cro shouted over the roar.

I jumped in. "Tin, just keep going. I have to try this."

We saw the three striders closing in.

"Brace for impact!" Tin shouted. Before they could fire, I shouted!

"AHGH! TAKE THIS!" I thrust my hand forward.

"FOOSH!"

A furious blast of wind slammed them into the canyon wall—

"BOOM!"

"Oh…my stars… it worked?" I called out.

"Whoa…" Cro gasped. "Dorothy… was that you?"

"Enemy neutralized," Tin reported. "Dorothy, my data confirms the attack matches the one I previously experienced with the former Tempest Maiden."

We were all stunned into silence.

"You just blasted wind with your hands," Cro said in awe. "I can't believe it."

"Me neither," I admitted, "but we've still got more to deal with."

"Whoosh… glad you're on our side!" Cro cheered.

"FOOSH!"

I knocked out another strider on the right.

"FOOSH!"

Then another.

"FOOSH!"

And another.

I was finally finding my rhythm.

"Woo hoo!" Cro hollered as he took down one more.

Only a few Sentinels remained. They called desperately for reinforcements but were slowing. We paused to plan our next move.

Then, something strange happened.

SENTINEL: "SG48 TO COMMAND, SEND THE PROTOTYPE—WAIT, WHAT IS THAT—URGGH-HH!"

"BOOM!!"

An explosion lit the night and shook the ground under our striders. But it wasn't us who'd fired.

"Tin, did someone else attack them?" I asked. For a moment I thought the Winki warriors might have come to help. But that made no sense. They wouldn't leave their village unprotected.

Was it a misfire? A mistake?

I didn't know… but we were finally free.

"Keep moving," Cro said, pushing into the gorge.

The wind continued to howl between the cliffs, carrying the last echoes of the blast behind us. We needed to disappear and find a safe place for the night. Because if someone else was out there taking shots at the Sentinels, we weren't the only ones fighting this battle.

* * *

The sound of blaster fire echoed through the gorge, but it wasn't aimed at us.

The Sentinels were definitely distracted by something in the fog.

Good. That gave us a chance.

We crept back into a narrow cut in the canyon wall. It was tight and jagged, but it was just enough cover. If we stayed still, we could let the Sentinels pass... maybe even surprise them.

But then, a distant screech.

"You guys heard that, right?" I whispered.

It came again, high-pitched, wild, and just disturbing. It echoed off the cliffs as if the canyon itself was screaming.

Another screech followed.

Then another, and soon the echoes surrounded us. This thing wasn't just attacking the Sentinels. It was hunting.

"My scanners pick up something besides the Sentinels," Tin said. "But I can't identify it. It's flight pattern is… erratic."

"Flying," Cro muttered. "Of course. Because this night needed wings."

I shot him a look. "Didn't hear you whining about the Sentinels."

"That's because they earned it," he hissed back. "Whatever this is? Nope. I didn't sign up to be dinner."

More screeches.

Then, flashes of blaster fire lit up the mist. We couldn't see much, just shadows moving through the fog like ghosts. We stayed completely still and listened. The mist hid our enemy, but not its cries. And whatever "it" was, it hadn't stopped yet.

I peered into the swirling mist. Something dark and winged flashed by. They vanished before I could see them.

"Over there. Are those… birds?" I whispered.

"I didn't see what it was," Cro said, already turning the strider around. "And I don't want to find out. They're tearing into the Sentinels like paper. Let's go before we end up in the crossfire."

"Agreed," Tin said. He shoved the strider off a rock ledge, and Cro followed right behind.

We hurried through the gorge once more, weaving around sharp rocks and gusts of wind. Suddenly, a deafening chorus of screeches burst out all around us. Dark figures swooped out of the mist.

"They're here," Tin said through the comms. "A flock just descended. At this speed, we can't defend against them efficiently. Initiating beacon cannons."

His shoulder cannons spun up, scanning.

And then—

"SCREEECH!"

It was like the canyon itself screamed. The sound hit my skull like a hammer.

I flinched. "Ugh, my ears!"

"The canyon's acoustics are boosting the frequency," Tin said. "Activate noise-canceling on your visors. Immediately."

I fumbled with the settings. "Got it. Noise cancellation on."

"SWOOSH!"

"Whoa," Cro muttered. "Those wings are massive."

Then he went quiet for a beat too long. "Wait… those giant wings… those screeches… no way, are they—"

"Mobats. It's exactly what my dad described." I cut in, "Flying creatures with long arms and tails. Loud screeches. They have to be."

Tin responded, "You are correct. My scanners have confirmed. It is as we previously discussed."

"Great! And now we're their targets?" Cro complained.

"Look out!" I yelled.

Too late.

They hit us like a swarm of cactus-bees. Their claws flashed, and black feathers sliced through the mist. They flew like living shadows, their broad, silent wings cutting through the night, with eyes flashing in the dark.

Every time I aimed my blaster, the mobat blinked out of sight and appeared somewhere else.

"Ouch! One just scratched me," I called out.

"Hey, get off my strider!" Cro shouted.

"Tin, watch out!" I yelled.

We fired back with blasters, cannons, anything we had, but it wasn't enough.

The mobats owned the night.

Every time we moved forward, they struck again.

Claws raked. Teeth snapped. It felt less like survival and more like a countdown.

They weren't hunting us anymore.

It felt like they were toying with us.

"If we don't get out of this soon," I said, panting, "we're done."

Cro shouted over the wind, "How are we supposed to stop them while escaping?!"

"Running scenarios," Tin replied calmly, like we weren't getting shredded.

I racked my brain, grasping for something, anything.

And then… it clicked.

"Wait, I've got an idea! Tin, can you blast a high-frequency tone? Something sharp, painful."

"Very unusual request," Tin replied. "If I am correct, you intend to use this as a deterrent. I must advise you to ensure your noise cancellation remains active."

"It's fine! Just do it!" I said.

He nodded. "Executing tone now."

A high-pitched whine exploded through the air like a sonic punch.

"SCREEEEECH!"

The mobats wailed, twisting midair. A few scattered like leaves in a windstorm.

"Yes, it worked! Dad was right!" I shouted.

"This pitch is effective," Tin noted.

"Great job, Dorothy!" Cro added.

The mobats couldn't stand the sound, as I expected. They flapped wildly as their attack fell apart.

The sound faded, and the mobats swooped at the Sentinels instead. We heard frantic shouts and rustling in the fog.

"Exit in sight. We've reached the canyon's end," Tin announced.

I let out a huge breath.

"Thank goodness. Evading sharp rocks, two enemies, and those gusts nearly killed us."

"Good thing the Sentinels are stuck now," Cro grinned.

I laughed. "Serves them right."

Riding away from Howling Canyon, my mind buzzed with questions.

"Why are they so relentless over one wanted person?"

"Where did the mobats come from?"

We'd have to find answers later. But one thought loomed largest.

My powers.

I clenched my fists, remembering how strong I felt. If I had known sooner... Emeraldia wouldn't have caged me. Leo and I could have travelled anywhere in the city. We could have helped people like us. And Tobin, that drunk who started the fire, I would have blasted him across the city.

I shook my head and looked at the rocky cliffs. A large outcrop could hide us until morning.

"Let's take shelter there," I suggested. "It looks secure enough to stay hidden."

For a moment, we just stood there, taking it all in. Everything was still and quiet. We were safe for now, but I knew we couldn't let up.

* * *

Night finally took over. We gathered in the shadow of a cliff, where the rocks were still warm from the day, but the air had turned cold. It wasn't much, but it was peaceful. This was our first real break in what seemed like an endless stretch.

I let out a sigh and rubbed my eyes. "I don't even know where to start. My brain's fried. I'm tired. I'm worried. And weirdly? I'm thankful. All at once."

Cro leaned against a rock and chuckled. "Welcome to topside, the emotional soup. When I finally made it out, I didn't think the surface would feel like getting thrown into a toolbox full of lightning either."

"You didn't look too rattled back in the canyon," I said, raising an eyebrow.

He shrugged, casual as ever. "After what the Sentinels pulled? Stealing Tin, making me go off the grid for years? Let's just say, yeah… I had some feelings to work out. Might've enjoyed that chaos a little."

I gave him a small smile. "Well, we got out. That's what matters."

Then I turned to Tin. "Hey. Thanks for getting us through that maze. Seriously. I thought we were done for."

Tin nodded. "You are most welcome, Dorothy. The success of the route was… statistically improbable."

"Yeah, well, you crushed it."

Then, the question that had been sitting in my chest finally forced its way out.

"I still don't understand. Why am I on the OWL ?" I asked. "Is it just because I escaped Emeraldia? Kassi said that leaving the city basically makes you a criminal. But OWL? That's supposed to be for the worst of the worst… the dangerous ones. I didn't do anything that bad."

No one said anything.

"Okay… I didn't mean to kill the mood."

We sat there for a while, just… quiet. Cro was hunched over, staring at nothing. Tin hadn't moved in minutes. The usual buzz between them gone.

Cro finally moved. "Sorry, I was just thinking."

He exhaled slowly. "Dorothy, you're probably on the OWL because of me. I apologize. That's why I don't usually do the whole 'friend' thing. I'm a fugitive. It never ends well."

My eyebrows rose in surprise. "Cro. Seriously? Have you forgotten about having each other's back? If they're after you, they've got to get through all of us first."

I gave him a light punch on the arm. "We're in this together. No regrets, got it?"

He gave a slight nod.

I continued. "None of this makes sense anyway… this whole OWL system. Mother Uru was right! The Archons have been telling us a lie this entire time. There's a whole world down below that doesn't know what's going on up here or the truth about its history. Someone has to tell them."

Cro sat up a little. "You're right. But how? Where do we even start?"

I didn't have the answer, not yet. But I noticed Tin was oddly quiet. "Tin, are you okay?"

He stood up slowly, then knelt as if his battery had just given out. His head dipped low.

"I am a bad robot," he said.

I tilted my head. "Wait… what? Are you serious right now?"

Cro leaned in. "Is your system glitching? Did something short out?"

"Perhaps I should explain," Tin said. "I was designed to protect something powerful," he admitted. "But if the Tempest Maiden I fought is on the side of good, then maybe what I was defending is bad. So, I must be a bad robot."

"CLANG!"

"You big jerk," Cro snapped, hitting Tin with a pebble. "All that advanced processing power and you still say the dumbest things sometimes."

Tin tilted his head. "I don't understand."

Cro threw his hands up. "You're more than code and metal. You're family... like a brother, okay? Not some bad machine."

Tin processed Cro's words. "I see... I'm not bad."

"No, you're not Tin," I replied, glancing up at the stars peeking through the canyon ceiling. "We've all done things we didn't choose. But we're here. Topside gives us all a second shot. That means something."

Tin's optics dimmed, then brightened. He stood there thinking, and for a second, he didn't feel like a robot. He felt... real. "Your words are... sufficient," he said.

Cro smirked at Tin's comment. He reached into his coat and pulled out the compass. "You know this thing? It's more than old tech now. It's our symbol. Proof there's still something worth chasing."

I nodded. "We've made it this far. Whatever's waiting for us, we face it together..."

But I didn't get to finish.

An alarm blared in my visor. Loud. Close.

Tin sprang forward, faster than I'd ever seen. A glowing barrier burst from his chest, shielding us in a flash.

"Tin! What is it?" I shouted.

"We are no longer safe," he said. "Something powerful is approaching."

"What... what is that?" I whispered.

A figure emerged from the shadows, towering, sleek, and deadly. Its armor gleamed as if it had never seen battle scratch.

Cro backed up slowly. "Tin? That thing… it looks like you."

Tin's body tensed, cannons priming. "I've completed my scan. It is a next-gen model. Same base design, but slightly more advanced. Larger build. Prepare yourselves. This won't be easy."

The machine took one step forward.

Then another, until its cold, menacing voice sounded off:

"I AM EXABOT-32, PROTOTYPE ROBOTIC SENTINEL. BY ORDER OF THE ARCHONS, I AM COMMANDED TO TAKE TERABOT NEXUS INTO CUSTODY AND ELIMINATE THE GIRL."

"Wait, what?" Cro shouted, panicking. "Capture Tin and eliminate Dor—"

"Eliminate me?" I repeated.

My mind raced, but there was no time to think.

The fight was already starting.

CHAPTER TWENTY

Scared doesn't even begin to describe it.

From the shadows, a monster of a robot stepped forward. It was taller than Tin by a whole head and shoulder, and its eyes glowed just like his, but colder.

Way colder.

It didn't walk so much as it stalked. Every part of it looked like it was made for war.

"What do we do?" I blurted, already backing up.

Cro was flipping through his watch-tablet like a madman, his eyes scanning data like his life depended on it. "Okay. This thing is a walking nightmare. Reinforced alloy, top-tier weapons… Tin, it's like someone turned a tank into a robot and gave it anger issues."

"Correct assessment," Tin agreed. "I detect mini plasma cannons, retractable claws, and adaptive boosters. Built for close-range engagement."

"Great," I muttered. "So, it's fast *and* angry."

"Stay behind cover," Tin said calmly. "I'll draw its focus."

"Be careful," I said, which felt useless but honest.

"We'll reduce the improbable outcome," Tin replied. "We will find a weakness."

Cro gave a tight nod. "I will find a way to infiltrate its system. In the meantime, Dorothy, let's get to safety."

"Right!"

We scrambled for cover, but the Exabot lunged toward us with terrifying speed and accuracy. Before it could reach us, Tin shot forward and slammed into it. The crash echoed like thunder, sending shockwaves through the air and knocking the metal giant off balance.

"I am your opponent," Tin declared.

"VERY WELL," the Exabot answered in a cold, hollow voice.

Tin and the Exabot were face-to-face. The robot swung a massive arm with enough force to smash steel. But Tin punched back in a blur, his fist connecting with a sickening crunch right on the Exabot's face.

For a moment, I dared to hope. But the Exabot didn't budge. It's cold eyes flashed red as it grabbed Tin and threw him onto the ground. A cloud of dust exploded around us.

"Tin, get up!" Cro shouted.

Tin pushed himself into a solid stance. The two battle machines squared off again, trading blow after crushing blow. Each hit rang out like a drumbeat, making the rocks tremble and sparking flashes of light in the night.

Cro and I ducked behind boulders, knowing we were outmatched. Cro searched his gear for a tech-pad.

"Hang in there, Tin!" he yelled over the comms. "Remember this is a prototype; there has to be a flaw to exploit."

I wasn't much help with tech. But I had something else… at least, I hoped I did.

I backed up against the rock and clutched my bracelet.

"Come on, Dorothy," I whispered. "Think. What were you feeling last time? What made it work?"

"Lightning… Wind… Raw, wild energy…"

No matter how hard I tried to grasp it, it kept slipping away like steam. Each time I nearly caught it, it disappeared. Suddenly, my focus was broken by a distant sound.

"Wait," I said, eyes narrowing. "Cro… do you hear that?"

He paused, ears twitching like mine.

Far off… lights in the dark, engines rumbling.

He groaned. "Perfect. Sentinels. As if this night wasn't already a disaster."

Then he snapped into action. "Dorothy, you deal with them. I'll help Tin. We need to split focus."

"On it," I said, already getting to my feet. My fingers were clenched tight around the wand.

"Okay, Dorothy. One more time… Don't overthink. Just feel it. Picture a wild storm. Let that power flow through you."

I closed my eyes, drew a deep breath, and centered myself. Suddenly, the air around me whirled violently as I threw up my hand. With a fierce swing, I unleashed a blast of wind that cracked like a whip, racing forward to lash out at the sentinels.

"FOOSH!"

A strong gust of wind tore down the distant pathway and slammed into the Sentinels. Dust and debris swirled around them, blowing them off their striders and onto the ground. Their formation broke apart. While it wasn't a perfect plan, it was a start.

SENTINEL CAPTAIN: "MOVE ON FOOT, SOLDIERS! WHATEVER SHE'S USING, SHE CAN'T HIT US ALL NOW!"

And just like that, they regrouped… Again.

"Dorothy, Take this."Cro tossed me something metal.

It was a gale-blaster. It felt heavier than I remembered from Monsoon training.

"Thanks. Any luck?"

"I'm working on it," he muttered, already neck-deep in code breaking.

I raised the blaster and squeezed the trigger. It kicked hard, but the pulse knocked a few Sentinels off their feet.

SENTINEL CAPTAIN: "TAKE COVER, MEN!"

Meanwhile, Tin was still locked in with the Exabot. Metal slammed against metal, sparks rained down like a mini fireworks show, and Tin was not winning. That thing's strength and firepower were too much, and Tin was on the defense.

"Got it!" Cro's voice burst through the chaos. "There's a transmitter on the back of its neck. It's routing data to a control hub!"

My eyes widened. "So, if we intercept the transmitter, we can hack it?"

"Exactly!" he said, finally sounding alive. "He's wide open now!"

Cro tapped away on his device, goggles lighting up with code. "Oh, Exabot. Your systems will be mine!"

"You can really override it?" I asked, still firing at the closing Sentinels.

Cro flashed a grin. "Dorothy, there isn't a system the SKR//CRO can't crack."

That's the Cro I liked to hear! I was relieved. Maybe we actually had a shot.

But the Sentinels weren't giving up either. Blaster fire lit up the surrounding rocks. They were closing in.

"Back off!" I yelled and threw my hands forward. Wind burst out in a violent wave, hurling a few of them backwards like rag dolls. It bought us some space, but not enough.

Then out of the corner of my eye, I saw it.

Exabot sprang into action. One arm wrapped around Tin's neck, lifting him like a feather, then slammed him to the ground.

"Tin!" I screamed.

He tried to fight back, but the Exabot had him pinned.

"YOUR BODY ALONE WILL DO, EVEN IF IT'S IN PARTS."

The Exabot then ripped into Tin's chest plate with its claws, metal grinding into metal.

"URRGGHH!" Tin's voice strained, metal grinding, gears howling.

"No!" I screamed.

I raised my blaster and fired in desperation.

Again.

Again.

Again.

Nothing.

"STOP!" I cried, my voice breaking.

The Exabot didn't even flinch. It just kept pulling. Tin's free hand clawed at the grip crushing his neck, but it was no use. His arm twisted at a sickening angle, groaning, bending like it was about to snap.

"BZZZT!"

Wires inside his arm started popping one by one. Small sparks flashed out.

Vivid, furious flashes.

I couldn't just stand there and watch him get ripped apart. It wasn't just the sound, or the damage; it was his optics. Tin didn't feel pain the way we do, but he knew. He was aware of the damage. Aware of the danger he was in.

"Cro, do something!" I shouted, "He's gonna die!"

"Dorothy, focus!" he barked as he kept tapping away at his tech-pad, franticly.

"Just… just give me more time!"

That's when I heard it in his voice.

He was scared too.

"CRACK...BZZZT!"

The Exabot drove a hole straight through Tin's side. Sparks flew. His whole frame jolted, movements slowing like his body couldn't keep up anymore.

"Tin—" I choked out.

He was fading fast.

Cro was hunched over his tech-pad, hands flying, eyes locked. Trying to break through the bot's system.

SENTINEL CAPTAIN: "MOVE IN!"

Blaster fire lit up the area. Cro and I dove behind another jagged rock. Shots cracked past my ears. I pressed myself against the cold stone, my blood pumping, blaster trembling in my hands.

We were pinned.

I glanced at Cro. He peeked out for half a second, then ducked back. His goggles hid his face, but I could feel the despair. It matched mine.

My hand reached out and grasped his shoulder.

"Thanks for snapping me back to focus. Now it's your turn. We're both... scared," I said, struggling to catch my breath. "But we're not done yet. We finish this... for Tin."

Cro looked at me just for a moment and regained his composure.

"For Tin," he said.

No hesitation this time. He went back to work, fingers punching across the pad with new purpose.

My gaze was fixed, and I took aim. I squeezed the trigger, and this time my shots hit their mark. Once again, the Sentinels broke apart, taking cover wherever they could.

I quickly turned to Tin. He was barely standing. His body was wrecked. Wires frayed, plating cracked, sparks leaked out like blood, but he was still fighting.

"Tin," Cro said over the comms. "He's bigger, he's faster, but keep in mind he's still a prototype. A puppet. His system is full of flaws."

He continued as blasters still pierced through the air.

"He's not you. You're one of a kind… So, give me one more push. Get ready to light him up when I give the go-ahead. You know what I mean."

Tin's voice crunched back. "Affir… mative." It was a glitchy and weak… but there was a fight in it.

The Exabot loomed. Red eyes burning. Its claw raised, ready to bring it down and finish this.

But Tin didn't flinch.

He started to glow. A soft blue light built up under the damage, pulsing from deep within. Like something inside him had refused to die. He braced himself.

Either he was going to take the hit or give one back.

"No," I whispered. "I won't let this end like this."

I jumped out of cover.

"Take this!" I shouted and opened fire. Shot after shot, I didn't stop. I couldn't.

And then everything went still.

The Exabot froze.

Mid-swing... Mid-kill… it just stopped.

Its glowing red eyes snapped white.

I blinked. "Wait... I did that?"

"Not exactly," Cro said, breathless, wiping his eyes. "But hey, thanks for the assist. I told you… there's nothing SKR//CRO can't hack."

And then, it was as if Tin had suddenly woken up.

His chest lit up, his whole core glowing like a mini sun. I could feel the heat from here. Cro leaned in toward me, a half-smile on his face, eyes darting back and forth.

"Dorothy, cover your eyes. I'm serious. This flash is gonna burn."

Then he cupped his hands around his mouth and yelled, "Tin! Supernova Blast! Now!"

A surge of pure light erupted from him, piercing through the darkness effortlessly.

I shielded my face and turned away, but I still saw it behind my eyelids.

"Oh, my stars," I whispered.

"That's it, Tin!" Cro shouted. "Give him everything you've got!"

The blast hit the Exabot head-on. For one second, it felt like daytime in the middle of a canyon night. I peeked through my fingers, just barely, and saw the Sentinels stumbling back, blinking and blind. The Exabot's whole frame cracked down the middle, like glass under pressure.

Then… Silence.

Everything just… paused.

The wind.

The fight.

Even the wind. I lowered my arm slowly.

"Tin?" I called out, barely able to say his name.

Cro slid his goggles up, a tired smile on his face. "That," he said, "is the raw, beautiful chaos of a dual-core Terabot."

The light faded, and the Exabot lay in ruins. Tin barely stayed on his feet, his core blinking weakly.

"It is… done," he gasped. He looked at us and collapsed.

"You did it, Tin," I whispered.

Cro and I rushed to his side. Cro's hands flew over Tin's circuits and wires.

"Wait, Cro, we don't have time; we need to move," I urged.

Cro swapped a damaged wire. "I know. Just hold on, Tin."

"Dorothy is correct… Scanners show… It is crucial we leave now," Tin said, voice weak. "They're coming closer."

"I'm almost done," Cro promised. "He'll be mobile soon."

I kept my blaster ready, my heart pounding. A faint blinking light on the exabot caught my eye. Cro yanked open a panel and killed the signal. No backup could arrive now.

Still, I felt uneasy as shadows moved around us.

"They're here," I whispered.

Out of the darkness, sentinels appeared in shiny uniforms. They spread out and closed in, surrounding us. Cro raised his wrist blaster in front of Tin; Tin lifted his arm cannon; I gripped my blaster's handle.

If they were already here, why didn't they attack sooner? I wondered.

Cro drew close to me. "Stay sharp, Dorothy. Something's not right."

I charged my blaster, staring into the dark. Only distant thunder rattled the air.

Then I realized… they were waiting.

A slow, deliberate clap cut through the silence.

One clap… two.

A figure stepped into the fading light.

"Bravo," a rich voice said. "What a spectacle! If this robot had faced our former champion, Grimlock, we might have actually lost."

"Wait…Chief Terp?" I blurted.

Cro's face hardened. "You traitor!" he spat.

As he walked toward the campfire, the Sentinels stayed where they were.

"May I kindly offer a correction? I am not a traitor. I have never joined your cause. I have pledged my allegiance to no one since my exile from a particular city."

He turned his attention to the sky. "They couldn't diminish my greatness or silence my warnings about the impending destruction of all the domes by *The Great Resurgence*. I amassed a boundless following and even wielded more influence than the mayor. So, in his jealously, HE PUT ME OUT!"

I knew what he was talking about. The Great Resurgence was the belief held by zealots that the twisters would regain their power and destroy the world again, completely. It was an insane idea with no real basis.

He turns to me with a wicked grin. "My loyalty is now to Vortarion, the Green… and the Archons who leave me to my ministry provided I offer intel and other services."

He began to laugh before he continued. "Ergo, they ordered me to capture that bot… and to bring about your end, Vogan."

"I haven't done anything wrong!" I shot back.

He laughed again as if I had been joking. "When I informed them about that peasant lightning trick, they appeared to panic. I do not comprehend why they would be concerned about you. And your robot? Observe what it can accomplish. I am confident they require it to develop a flawless new prototype to substitute the broken one here."

"And what do you get?" Cro asked. "They must be offering you something."

"I don't need anything material, child. I only want to take my rightful place as the next ruler after the Great Resurgence purges the world of nonbelievers like you."

I growled, "And what about the Gilkin? Do you think they won't realize your true motives and that you're a false prophet?"

"Silence, little witch!" he snapped. "Who said anything about the Gilkin? I won't need that primitive tribe when I have risen to my true throne."

"How dare you talk about the Gilkin like that?" I shouted.

"No, how dare you!" he retorted. "You invaded my land, brought a robot and a child, tricked my champion with your deceptive magic, and caused me to appear foolish... I, the greatest prophet these woodsmen have ever known!"

"Listen to you speak! You're a fraud!" I yelled.

There was a pause.

He stepped closer to me and hissed, "The only fraud is you! No one should control the sky; only Vortarion, the Green, owns the sky. Not some witch girl that dishonors the ever merciful—."

"Enough of your false religion," I interrupted. "You claim you're a prophet sent by some god, but you're just a scammer chasing power."

Cro tried to calm me. "Dorothy, now's not the time. We're outnumbered—"

"No," I cut in, my anger boiling. "Leaders like you are why the world is broken. The ArcCities, the topside, all of it! Ozians like you lie and manipulate to keep control. But you can't silence us. Our voices will grow louder. One day, we'll tear down everything you've built."

Suddenly, I saw anger flare in his eyes. His face reddened as he lunged, grabbing my arm. I held my ground and pointed my blaster at him. The sentinels immediately aimed their weapons at me.

It was a standoff, and I refused to back down.

"Let me go and walk away," I ordered. "No one has to get hurt."

Dark clouds rolled in, and the wind picked up.

He grinned as he looked at the sky.

"Fine. Show us your magic trick again."

"You don't want that," I warned.

"Is that so? Maybe you need some motivation." With a flick of his finger, one sentinel fired at Tin from behind.

"Tin!" I shouted.

"What are you doing?" Cro yelled, charging at the shooter, as other sentinels grabbed him.

"Now!" Chief Terp roared. "Show us the trick again!"

I was furious.

He'd done this once before in the arena, risking Cro and Tin's lives. I wouldn't let it happen again. This time, he'd feel twice as much as Grimbol did.

The air sizzled with electricity as I felt a surge of power inside me. I grabbed my battle wand from my side and started charging it.

"There it is… the fear in his eyes."

"It's too late for you," I whispered, sparks flying in my eyes. I was ready to strike him.

"BLAST!"

"Ahhhh!"

A sudden blast from behind struck him in the back. He fell to the floor bloodied.

But it wasn't me.

It appeared that one of his own men had betrayed him. Another shot caused the sentinel holding Cro to lose his balance.

Everyone stared in shock.

"Who… would betray… me?" He managed to whimper out.

SENTINEL#1: "LOOK FOR COVER! WE HAVE AN ENEMY SNIPER HIDING IN THE DARK! I RE-PEA—URGH!"

Another shot rang out, but this time from a different spot.

"Theres two…"

The snipers were targeting all the sentinels, but they were careful not to harm Cro and Tin.

Someone was helping us, but who?

SENTINEL#2: "WE HAVE MULTIPLE SNIPERS ATTACKING US! EVERYONE, TAKE COVER AND FIND THE ENEMY!"

Everything turned chaotic as blaster fire erupted everywhere. Red laser beams cut through the darkness, heating the air with each shot. The Sentinels quickly responded, changing their positions and firing back, but they weren't shooting at us.

I didn't wait to see how many got hit.

"Move!" I shouted, grabbing Tin's arm and pulling him toward the jagged rock we had hidden behind earlier. Cro followed, his steps heavy as he was limping due to an injury. He stumbled next to me, muttering curses.

"I don't know who's helping us, but I'm not complaining," I said.

The fight grew louder, with the snipers' thunderous shots filling the air.

"We have to go! I need to fix Tin," Cro panted.

"Our striders are over there. Let's hurry," I replied.

"SCREEEECH!!!"

"Oh, no... Not again!" Cro worried.

Just when we thought things couldn't get worse, the screeches filled the sky again. The mobats were returning, drawn by the noise.

SENTINEL#3: "LOOK UP! THEY'RE BACK!"

The Sentinels were caught off guard, overwhelmed by attacks from all directions. Chaos surrounded us as the night became a battleground against unseen enemies and terrifying creatures.

I turned to Cro. "If we run, the mobats will chase us. We need to stay quiet and out of sight."

We found a small spot to hide in, and Cro quickly started working on Tin. The screeches and blaster fire echoed in the distance, but we stayed low, blending into the shadows, waiting for the chaos to end.

CHAPTER TWENTY-ONE

After about half an hour, the screeching and gale-fire slowed. We heard engines in the distance, and it looked like the battle was winding down. We knew a storm was coming because the wind was getting stronger and clouds were racing across the sky.

A twister could form at any moment, so our spot wasn't safe. We needed to find a cave, and fast. While Cro worked on restarting Tin, I looked out from our hiding spot to see if it was safe to move.

What I saw was a shock: pockets of fire and smoke, and dozens of bodies on the ground. Some were still moving slightly. It was what was left after a brutal battle. Unknown snipers and mobats had defeated the Sentinels. The approaching twister had scared off most of the flying creatures, but a few stayed behind, taking parts from the damaged striders.

I turned to Cro and noticed a difference in his mood.

"Cro, listen, I know it's been a lot and—"

"Dorothy, don't worry," he said, wiping sweat from his face. "I'm not mad at you or this journey. I believe in this cause. I want things to get better. I'm just tired of running and hiding. And it's hard to see Tin like this. But that's why he has me."

"And we're here for him too," I added. "Let's find real shelter from this coming storm, then we can use the compass to plan our path."

Cro patted himself down, panic twisting his face. "Oh no, I think I dropped the compass when they had me pinned."

I groaned.

"Seriously? Let's hope it's still there. I saw some mobats lurking, so we'll have to be careful. I've got my wand ready if things go wrong."

We slipped back toward the battlefield, hiding Tin on the strider. Sure enough, a couple of mobats prowled the wreckage, sniffing around like they owned the place.

"Psst… what are they looking for?" I whispered.

"I don't know. They don't eat Ozians. Looks like they're taking metal parts."

"Why would they need that?" I frowned.

"They're weird creatures," Cro shrugged. Then his eyes went wide. "Hey, look!" A few yards ahead, the compass lay in the dirt. "Quick, let's—"

Just then, a mobat swooped in and snatched the compass with its claws.

"No, no, no! What's it doing?" I whispered. "We have to get it before it flies away!"

"I'll shoot it," Cro said, raising his wrist blaster.

"Wait! That'll alert the others."

"We don't have a choice," he fired. The shot hit the mobat's wing, and the compass tumbled free.

"Bullseye! Let's go."

Suddenly, a piercing screech sliced through the wind as another mobat swooped down, snatching the compass and flying away.

"Noooo!" I shouted. "That was our only lead!"

Cro fired after it but missed. The mobat weaved through the air too fast.

"We'll track it," he said, narrowing his eyes. "If it's headed somewhere, like its nest, we'll find it."

"Great idea, but how?"

He grinned and pulled a small device from his bag. Its screen lit up.

"That's a tracker! Cro, you genius! But how will you put it on the mobat?"

He pointed at the injured mobat still on the ground. "We tag that one and follow it back to the flock."

"Oh, good thinking," I said, smiling.

"Thanks. We just need to wait for it to wake up."

"Not necessarily," I said, holding up my wand. I dialed it down to a small shock. "Let's go."

We crept forward slowly. As we drew closer, I realized what I was looking at: it resembled a smaller mobat. The feathered wing of what appeared to be a pup lay still, its feathers torn. Its body was small, about the size of a child's, with wiry muscles and a long tail. At first, I thought it was dead. Then its eyes slowly opened.

Its fierce grace was gone. All that remained was a soft, broken whimper.

"Easy there," I murmured, reaching out. "I won't hurt you... not too much."

The pup's eyes locked on mine, and it let out desperate chirps. Maybe a warning or a plea.

"You've been through a lot, huh?" I crouched down beside it. "We didn't mean to hurt you. We just need our compass."

Its wings trembled, and for the first time, I didn't see a wild monster. Instead, I saw something hurt and desperate. It was something I understood, just like Ursa.

Our plan was simple: scare it off so it would run away. But now, looking at the creature up close, I wasn't sure I could do it. Not after everything it had already been through.

"Cro, emit a high-pitched sound, but only for a few seconds," I said quietly.

"If you think that'll be easier on this little guy, I'm on it," Cro replied.

He triggered the device. A sharp, high-pitched noise cut through the air. The mobat cringed, its body quivering. It squirmed wildly, then stumbled to its feet. Limping on one wing, it fluttered off as fast as it could.

"That was harsh, but at least it's gone," Cro said, checking his tracker. "I can see its signal now."

I squinted in the fading light. "Cro… do you see that?"

He peered ahead. "Looks like two more Sentinels standing over there."

"I'm ready," Cro answered, raising his weapon.

Just as he aimed, the two figures slowly lifted their arms in the air. They were surrendering.

We both were shocked.

Was this for real? Had they actually given up? Or was it a trap?

After tonight's chaos, the last thing we needed was another fight. I leveled my wand and shouted, "Listen, if this is a trick, we won't hesitate to put you down!"

A playful voice answered from the shadows, "Now, why would we do that to a friend?"

My jaw dropped. "That voice… No way."

"Kassi? Is that you?" Cro asked, surprised.

A figure stepped forward into the dusk light.

It was Kassi. our friend.

"Oh, my stars, Kassi!" I ran to her. I hadn't seen her for ages. She barely let me hug her, but she let me.

"Okay, okay, you missed me," she teased, patting my back.

"Geez, Dee… am I chopped liver to you?" Another voice from nearby shouted.

I froze.

The wind died down for a moment, and everything felt still. My mind raced.

Was it possible? No… But then the figure stepped out of the shadows. Broad shoulders. Silver hair.

"*…Leo?*"

"How can this be?" I whispered, looking to Kassi for confirmation. She nodded slowly.

Leo stood there, worn and dusty, but unmistakable.

"Leo… here? Topside?" I stammered.

He met my gaze and smiled. It was a soft, knowing smile that spoke of all we'd shared.

"Hey, Dee…"

I was struck dumb. Memories flooded my mind: the Munchkin orphanage, the district patrols, his accident, my burning home, my escape.

"It's been a long time," Leo said.

"Yeah," I replied, my emotions welling up. "After… after everything, I didn't think I'd see you again. How… why are you here?"

Leo gave me a gentle nod. "Fate has its plans."

A breeze kicked up dust, but I barely noticed. I studied him: his old military belt, still adorned with tools, his uniform replaced by a worn-out black jacket over armor. The patches on his coat were frayed, his once-polished boots scuffed and dusty. Everything about him showed he'd been through a lot.

He wasn't the same. Neither was I, but somehow, we were both here.

Together again.

"Leo, you look..." I trailed off, trying to find the right words.

"Like I've been in a battle?" he finished with a laugh, glancing at Kassi.

Kassi gave a small, embarrassed laugh and scratched her head.

I smiled, not sure what he meant, but relief washed over me.

"It suits you," I said, taking in his rugged, real look.

For a moment, we didn't need to speak. The surrounding devastation faded away, and it was just Leo and me, standing in the aftermath. I can tell these past few months have changed him. It clearly made him tough enough to survive on the topside. Just like life up here had changed me.

"Surviving has its own dress code," he joked, a corner of his mouth twitching.

"You've changed, too," he added, eyeing my torn, stained clothes.

"Life topside isn't a walk in the park," I said with a shrug. But beneath our jokes, a deeper truth lingered. It was the memory of leaving him behind, weighing on my chest.

"Listen," I whispered. "I didn't want to leave you."

Leo lifted his hand to stop me. "We all make choices, Dee. I get why you left. I'm just sorry I couldn't protect you."

Tears streamed down my face as his words struck a chord I hadn't realized was still there.

"I've heard about your journey with the twisters, the chases… the battles. You've been through a lot."

I nodded, unable to hide it. My path had been brutal, but I wasn't ready to share the full story about the powers that had changed me.

"What about you? What have you been doing?"

"Surviving," Leo muttered, his eyes darkened with sorrow. "Trying to find meaning in the Vanguards, the ArcCity… that place was all I knew. Then it became my duty, my purpose. I thought if I protected it, I'd matter."

He let out a sigh. "When you told me to leave, I was scared… to start over…. scared of losing everything. Ms. Gobblewortz said I'd never make it outside. That stuck with me."

His jaw tightened. "Then I saw what the higher-ups do, how disposable we all are. Going back didn't feel right. I'm just glad you're alive."

As we talked, the wind continued to whistle through the wreckage, and it felt like a rare moment of peace until we heard metal clatter and gear straps jingle.

Cro and Kassi had arrived.

"Ahem, what do we have here?" Cro teased, sizing up Leo like he was reading a blueprint. He shot me a playful grin. "Fancy seeing you with a soldier. Never thought you'd go for the uniform type."

Leo gave me a half-amused, half-wary look. I giggled as he turned back.

"You must be… Cro?"

I sighed. "Leo, meet SKR//Cro—tech genius, hacker extraordinaire, and self-proclaimed pain in my butt." Cro grinned and held out his hand. Leo hesitated a moment, then shook it.

Cro's eyes lit up examining Leo's arm. "Whoa! Alloy titanium with emerald-powered receptors? That's serious craftsmanship."

Leo raised an eyebrow. "You can tell all that from a handshake?"

"I know good work when I see it," Cro said with a proud shrug.

"Thanks," Leo said with a grin. "I handled most of the mods myself."

"So, Leo, you're the one who left Dorothy all alone on the topside? That's a brave move," Cro joked.

I rolled my eyes at Cro's teasing.

Leo was a bit surprised by Cro's straightforwardness and chuckled. "Well, I didn't really leave her alone. It looks like she managed okay meeting some friends along the way. I just didn't expect one of Topside's most wanted to be a kid."

"Correction: a brilliant anti-hero in child form," Cro amended.

Kassi nudged me, joking that having another guy around could be a problem. But she also wanted to know about our trip, and I wanted to hear about theirs. It was time to catch up.

* * *

"...So, after that, Leo and I met the Chief and the Winki tribe," Kassi said, sounding frustrated. "They were in rough shape, fighting the last Sentinels. Since we all had the same enemy, we joined the Winki. After we won, we asked if they'd seen you guys. That's when they told us the truth. Hiding you was why the Sentinels attacked. Their leader, Marimba, guided us through the forest and told us everything, including how Chief Terp betrayed them."

"That traitor... That fraud..."

"And then we found out you were headed for Howling Canyon, of all places," Kassi said, looking straight at me. "I'm guessing this was your idea, huh, Dorothy?"

"Affirmative, all her ideas have been trouble since you left," Cro replied without missing a beat.

Kassi let out a groan. "You truly are crazy."

Leo nodded like it was obvious.

I just shrugged and scratched my head. "I still can't believe your unit left you for dead, Leo."

"Don't worry about that," he said. "It was part of the mission. I knew what I signed up for." He seemed fine on the surface, but I could tell there was more behind his words.

"I just needed to make sure you were okay, and help the other soldiers... I had to do what I could for them." He sighed and looked down before meeting my eyes again. "Like I said... don't worry."

Leo, now fully part of our messy alliance, turned to Cro. "Where's the other guy? The injured bot we saw earlier. What happened to him?"

"Right, Tin! Where is the big guy? We thought you took him to safety, but with all this reunion stuff, I forgot to ask," Kassi added.

I looked at Cro, waiting for an answer.

Cro glanced away for a moment. "Well, Tin took a beating, but he held his own against the Archons' new battle bot. We should head back to help him now. I'll make him stronger than ever."

Just then, the rain started to fall, and we rushed to a nearby cave. There, we talked about Tin, the lost compass, and what to do next. Having Leo and Kassi with us was a huge boost for our three-person team after everything that had happened.

More importantly, it felt like a hopeful family reunion knowing we were all safe and ready to keep moving forward.

RODNEY BLANC

CHAPTER TWENTY-TWO

"Hey, Cro, how much longer?" I yelled into the comms, my voice nearly swallowed by the roaring wind. The wind gusts battered us as we clung to our striders, each gust of sand threatening to knock us off course.

"Just a few more miles, Dorothy. This haze is so dense I can hardly see," Cro replied.

We spent the whole night fighting Chief Terp and his Sentinels. After they ran away, Marimba sent us a message using the new ArcSys system Cro had installed. He told us the Gilkin Council had taken away Terp's title for breaking their truce and starting the invasion. They sent him away from the Ironwoodlands, but no one knew where he went.

"Wait..." Leo's voice cut through the wind. "You want us to race into the nesting grounds of those flying nightmares just for Dee's old compass?"

"That's the plan," Cro confirmed.

"I know the compass points to that spire, but is it worth diving into a swarm of monsters?" Leo questioned.

I squeezed my grip on the handles.

"Yes, Leo. We've come too far to turn back now. Trust me."

Leo fell silent, doubt clouding his face. I sensed his hesitation, but I knew we had to reach what lay at the center of those nesting grounds.

We pushed forward, sand whipping against our striders. The wind gusts showed no signs of easing, and neither would we. Cro led the way, his strider cutting through the haze. Tin was strapped behind him, unable to move, still needing replacement parts Cro hadn't found yet.

I could tell Cro was weighed down with worry. Sometimes I caught him with a look of concern.

Kassi rode alongside us. It was my first time navigating a desert storm, but her skill never ceased to amaze me.

The wind gusts and stinging sand made me uneasy.

"You're doing great, Dorothy!" Kassi called out. "Keep your eyes forward and trust your instincts."

Leo sat behind me with his arms wrapped tightly around my waist.

"She's right, Dee," Leo said. "I know you're a natural at these things. Don't be nervous; I'm with you every step of the way."

I managed a smile. "Hey, look at the Green Dog giving me a pep talk about living on the edge." Leo grinned back. "Hey, I'm just glad you won't be calling me that forever."

Cro's voice cut in over the comms.

"Hey, Dorothy, wouldn't it be easier if you just used your powers?"

"Her what?" Kassi and Leo said in perfect sync.

I forced a laugh.

"Cro, come on, quit joking around. I'm fine. I'm just getting used to riding in this weather, that's all."

No way was I going to explain my abilities. Not now. Not with this storm rolling in and everyone already on edge. I wasn't ready. Not yet.

"Oh…right, sorry, just kidding," Cro said, likely catching on to my tone.

I knew why he had brought it up. I mean, yeah, using my powers would've been the easy way out. But I still wasn't in control of them. It was like trying to hold the wind without a manual. And honestly? I wasn't ready for the looks Leo or Kassi might give me if they saw what I could do. I already felt a bit weird with all this Tempest Maiden stuff.

"Hey, there it is… the nesting grounds," Cro said, pointing ahead.

Even through the sand and wind, we could make out the massive butte rising from the haze of the approaching storm. According to his tracker, the Mobats had nested inside. Even Kassi was awestruck this time.

"That's incredible!" She said.

I couldn't argue. The butte's jagged peaks reached into the sky, shaped by wind and erosion. Even though it looked close, it still took us another twenty-five minutes to reach the bottom. Just as we got there, dark clouds gathered overhead, and a storm was about to begin.

"We need shelter fast," I said, scanning for cover. "A twister will probably to form in seconds."

"On your six," Kassi called out, scanning the terrain. "A couple of meters back, there's a ridge; we can set up camp there. Get some rest, scout the nest at first light."

We all headed for the cave she'd pointed out. At this point, this plan was our best bet.

* * *

As we set up camp, Leo and Kassi tried to build a fire but kept arguing. They started talking about how they'd met up with us. Leo bragged about his daring plan to save his team, and Kassi joked that they'd left him behind when he was captured. It stung Leo a bit, but he laughed it off, saying at least the rebels provided good food.

While they laughed and told stories, I noticed Cro looking down. I knew Tin's condition was still affecting him. But there wasn't much I could do. So, I just sat next to him. We stared at the sky over the butte in comfortable silence.

After a moment, he asked, "So, when are you going to tell them?"

"Tonight," I said.

Leo and Kassi brought dinner over to us. Thanks to the Winki, we had plenty of food. Before that, we'd almost run out. We ate quietly until Leo laughed.

"You still eat like you think someone's going to steal your food," he said.

I explained that when I was at Munchkin House, kids would often grab my plate and take off with it. It wasn't funny back then, but we all ended up laughing, including Cro. I realized I hadn't heard myself laugh like that in a long time.

"Okay, listen... Kassi, Leo... there's something I need to tell you."

They looked at me, confused.

"When we traveled through the Ironwoodlands, I discovered something about myself I didn't know was there."

"What do you mean?" Kassi asked.

I finally told them.

About Elder Mother Uru.

About the Order of the Tempest Maiden.

About the fact that I have powers.

And that, no, I still don't understand them.

I walked them through the basics: some history, my bracelet's connection and what little skills I've learned. I also told them how Tin once went up against a mighty Tempest Maiden back in the day. Cro jumped in, of course, and talked up how he'd seen me take down enemies with wind and lightning.

"Cro," I groaned, "you're making it sound way more impressive than it was."

But I have to admit, saying it all out loud, even with him adding flair, felt good. Like I'd been dragging a boulder behind me and suddenly dropped it.

"That's why you're such a natural at gale running," Kassi said with a snap. "And why we thought you were storm-drunk."

"Yeah," I admitted. "It's a lot. But honestly, not surprising. Since you made it to Topside, you've been full of surprises. I'm just glad we have a powerhouse like you on our side."

Leo hesitated but said he was happy too. This was exactly what I wanted to avoid. He'd always known me one way, so I knew this would be a lot. However, it was now out in the open. I figured he'd come around eventually.

* * *

By morning, Cro was already up, elbows deep in Tin's wiring. He was working with just half his usual tools, but he made it happen, just as he always does. He'd also sent out three spybot crows before sunrise, who scouted the mobat nest from above, slipping through the storm without a sound. Over the next few days, we watched, waited, and took notes. We tracked their patterns, mapped out their routes, and figured out the best entry points into the butte.

The place was a fortress, but now we had a plan. It was finally time to move.

We suited up, but this time we weren't going in blind.

After days of watching, one thing was clear: Mobats weren't just oversized pests. They had a structure, a system, and an order that resembled a chain of command more than a chaotic swarm. We also saw footage of a chamber piled high with old gear, shiny trinkets, and random junk. It must have taken decades to collect all that.

Cro tapped on his tech pad, studying the data we'd collected.

"Okay," he said, eyes on the screen. "Here's what we know."

He pointed to the image of the two-winged mobats. "These are the ones we fought at the start: your average mobat. They're scavengers, foot soldiers, hunting for food and metal junk. We've dealt with them since day one."

"So, they're the annoying ones," Kassi blurted.

"Exactly," Cro agreed as we checked our gear.

"Next up are the four-winged ones researchers call *Beta-bats*," Cro said, pulling up a scan. "They're bigger, tougher, and more intelligent. Cross-analysis shows that they guard the nest and build tunnels. According to surveillance, their strong claws and acidic saliva are what break down rocks for easy digging in the hive."

"Fantastic," Leo muttered.

"Which brings us to the boss," Cro went on. "According to some records I dug up, there's an ultra-rare giant mobat. Past researchers from Galesville discovered carvings showing it even had six wings. The old carvings also suggest it leads to entire hives. There seemed to have been an ancient name for this type of species, but researchers called it an *Alphabat*.

"First Betabats, now an Alphabat? Seriously?" I asked.

"Hey, I didn't name them. But if this Alpha exists, it's the reason all the others fall in line. That said, my spybots haven't picked up any signs of a giant mobat."

"Let's hope it stays that way," I muttered.

"Alright, that's enough talk. We've got the intel, so let's go!" Kassi revved up her strider.

"Whoa, whoa, hold on, hothead, plan first," Cro interrupted. "Kassi and I will head to the junk chamber to grab parts for Tin. Dorothy and Leo, you two take the tracker and find the compass. We'll meet back here. Try to avoid fights if you can; we're outnumbered and deep in mobat territory."

"Got it," we all agreed.

We left Tin safely tucked away in the cave, making it easier to move around.

Cro was already eager to dig through the pile. He said it was for Tin, but we knew he also wanted some new gadgets for himself.

* * *

It had been twenty minutes since we had entered the nest. Leo and I slipped through the left lower entrance tunnel, which we knew was the least monitored route. We moved quietly and carefully with every step, the air sticky and damp against my skin.

Then the stench hit us. It was a mix of rotting flesh and corrosion, making my stomach turn. Breathing through my mouth didn't help.

The tunnel walls gave off a faint glow, and I quickly realized not to touch them twice. Turns out, betabat saliva doesn't melt your skin, but it still doesn't feel pleasant. Leo didn't speak; he just shot me a silent, smug "I told you so" look.

Yeah, thanks, Leo. Got it.

The tracker beeped softly, pointing deeper into the hive. Leo and I began crawling to the narrow side tunnels, moving slowly, staying in the shadows.

"Hey, Dee," Leo whispered, "remember when Mr. Neel caught us racing mine carts in the west sector?"

I almost snorted. "You mean the time I got stuck doing gem polishing for two months and couldn't feel my arms? Yeah, burned into my brain. We were such troublemakers."

He grinned. "Correction: *You* were the troublemaker. I was just a poor bystander."

"Right," I said, rolling my eyes. "Sure, Leo. Just a bystander who rigged the speed boosters."

He chuckled but didn't deny it. In truth, he was right. He always followed me into chaos not because he wanted to, but because he knew I'd go anyway. Someone had to keep me alive.

"I can see it now," he said after a beat. "You've changed a lot since you left, Dee. In a good way. You're so much braver than I am."

"Braver? You ditched the ArcForce protocol and risked everything to come find me. That doesn't sound like a cowardly move."

He smiled, then let out a small sigh. "Still. I hesitated when your place burned. I should've been there faster. I'm sorry you went through that alone."

I stopped crawling and faced him. "No need to say sorry. I was angry at them for how they treated me and my parents' legacy. But I had to leave to survive."

Leo looked down, still carrying that guilt as if it were welded to him.

"And hey, you did crash that transport to help me escape. Not bad for a 'by-the-book' soldier."

He chuckled, rubbing the back of his neck. "That wasn't part of the plan. I just… acted."

"Well, I'm glad you did," I said. "I don't know where this journey is going to take me, but I'm just glad you decided to join in."

Leo grinned. "Too late to back out now. I'm riding with a wanted fugitive. Guess I'm OWL-listed by association."

"Wait, Leo… do you know why I was flagged by OWL?"

His smile faded.

"I don't, Dee. Maybe they thought you'd never make it past the surface, so no one bothered to explain. I tried digging around, but every time I searched your file, it set off alerts. My superior warned me to back off."

"Hmm, I guess we'll never know." I pondered.

He paused.

"There's more."

"More?" I asked, turning my head.

Leo looked me in the eye. "Your mom was on the OWL too. Before she… you know…"

"…What?" I blinked. "My mom?"

"Yeah. But here's the weird part… your dad wasn't. Nothing. No record, no watch notice. And they worked together, right?"

"So, Mom and I were flagged… but not Dad? That doesn't make sense. You think it's tied to the Temp—"

SCRRRRRRRRREEEECH!

A distant shriek cut me off, echoing through the tunnel. We were too close to the sound. We crawled forward, moving as silently as we could. The rotten smell got stronger.

"Something's telling me they are close by," Leo said.

A faint glow on the walls grew brighter until we reached a thin, skin-like membrane that looked like a doorway into a mobat hoard. The cries and screeches on the other side grew louder with every inch we moved, blending into a chaotic roar.

"What is this place? It sounds like they are all here." I whispered.

We remained in a crouched position, trying to take a peek. From here, we observed everything.

"Leo…"

"Yeah, I know, Dee. This has to be the main chamber, the heart of the mobat nest," Leo whispered.

We were in shock.

The place was huge.

The main chamber stretched so high that I had to tilt my head all the way back to see the top. Sunlight streamed in through a massive gap in the ceiling, cutting through the dim light in long, moving beams. The walls curved and twisted, with layers of tunnels and chambers stacked on top of one another.

"It's a hive city in here."

"Dee," Leo interrupted my thoughts, "look down here."

We looked down, and that's when the sound made sense.

Mobats.

Hundreds of them.

They were everywhere, crawling, flapping, and twitching. They clung to the walls, climbed the ledges, and swarmed the spires that stuck out from the wall like giant teeth. Even the disgusting pit of sludge at the bottom was filled with them.

Shrieks and screeches echoed through the air, and feathers flew as their wings flapped like applause. We couldn't tell exactly what they were watching, but in the middle of all that noise was some kind of fight or show. It was big enough to keep all those creatures busy.

"This is insane," Leo said under his breath. "The scale of this… the planning, the coordination, it's unreal."

I bobbed my head slowly. "Glad I'm not the only one losing it a little when I see these things topside. Makes me feel less like I'm making a big deal out of nothing."

"I guess you aren't the rookie anymore." He added.

We both let out a quiet laugh, but the sharp stench hit again.

It was serious.

We crept closer to the edge for a better view, and that's when we saw what all the noise was about.

Two mobats locked in a brutal brawl, half-submerged in the muck. Wings flapping like crazy, claws slashing through the sludge. The others weren't just watching; they seemed invested.

The crowd, if you could call it that, was going crazy.

"Is this a fight ring?" I whispered.

"Looks like it," Leo said grimly. "Their version of entertainment."

"Great. Guess we're not so different after all."

We watched for another minute. There was order in the madness. They weren't just making noise randomly. They were reacting, celebrating the fight, with their own screeches, clicks, and weird chatters echoing off the walls.

"It's like they're imitating us," Leo said. "Like... they've been watching."

"Well, according to our data, their species has been around long enough to see ancient Ozians topside. It's possible."

"Creepy," Leo replied.

We kept moving when we ran into a chamber filled with junk. It was different from the location Cro and Kassi headed towards. Piles of shiny trinkets, broken gadgets, scraps of metal everywhere. Mobats were clearly obsessed with hoarding metal.

Leo looked around, eyes widened. "Think they've been at this for decades?"

"Probably longer. This place is a junk museum. We have to tell Cro and Kassi."

We reported our findings to Cro and Kassi. Turns out Cro and Kassi were seeing the same thing on their end. Right as we started trading notes, a lone betabat let out a low croak.

Then everything stopped.

The crowd out in the central hive chamber went dead silent.

That's when a loud roar erupted.

"*ROARRR!!!*"

The sound hit like an earthquake, and a deep echo pulsed through every tunnel. For a second, I thought the whole butte might come down on us.

Leo and I stood still as we could hear mobats scattered in panic. My legs went weak as I thought something was going to collapse. Even Cro and Kassi gasped over the comms.

"I think we've heard enough," Leo mouthed.

No argument from me. We didn't want to find out what that was. A few minutes of spying had taught us plenty about mobat life.

We backed out of the junk chamber as quietly as we could, slipping into another tunnel.

* * *

The earlier chaos had played in our favor. Between the screeching, flapping wings and the general panic, our footsteps remained silent.

We continued to track the signal, navigating the maze of tunnels. It felt like an eternity, but only fifteen minutes had passed before we reached our target.

"There. That chamber," I whispered, pointing. "See the dugout in the center?"

It was almost invisible, hidden deep in the shadows. If not for the tracking alerts on our comms, we would have missed it.

"*PING. PING. PING.*"

"We made it, Dee."

We flipped on our flashlights and just stood there, stunned.

The dugout wasn't just storage. It was a treasure vault.

Gold coins.

Silver chains.

Chunks of platinum.

Stuff people in Emeraldia would kill to get their hands on. This was old-world currency, long buried after gem tokens took over.

"All this time," I muttered, "just sitting here in the dark…"

"Here!" Leo called out; way too loud.

"Shhh!" I snapped, crawling over fast.

He was crouched next to a pile of tools, half-buried under loose gear made of the same rare metals. We didn't waste time talking; we just started digging. He passed pieces to me; I lined them up, hands moving quickly.

Then, our alert went off again.

"PING. PING. PING."

"That's it, my compass!" I whispered while grabbing it from the pile.

Relief washed over me like a wave. Holding the compass felt like having a part of my parents back in my hands. Leo gave my shoulder a light pat.

"Perfect, Dee. Mission complete."

"Thanks, Leo. We actually pulled it off. Now let's not push our luck. It's time to go."

He agreed and began scanning for a good way out. With the compass finally secured, we took a side tunnel. There was no way we were risking the main chamber again.

I tapped my comms. "Hey, team. Just checking in. The mission's a wrap on our end. We're heading out now."

"That's great, Dorothy!" Cro replied, unusually upbeat. "We've got everything we need for Tin and a little extra."

"Probably too much," Kassi chimed in.

"Don't listen to her," Cro added quickly. "She's just bitter because she touched the acid wall. Twice."

"Whatever," Kassi grumbled. "We'll meet you outside. Just don't get eaten."

"Copy that," Leo said with a grin.

* * *

"Why is the smell worse back here?" I muttered, pulling my sleeve over my nose.

Leo gagged. "I don't know, but I need air. And a ten-hour shower."

I felt the same. The stench had wormed into my clothes, my hair, my soul. But the thought of an exit kept me moving even though we still had a long way to go.

Then we saw it.

 Light.

The chamber ahead was wide and glowing faintly from an opening in the ceiling. It was also uncomfortably warm and, for some reason, the smell felt much stronger here.

"Alright," I said, catching my breath, "we're close. Let me check in with the others."

I tapped my comm.

"Hey guys, come in."

"Uh, Dee…"

"One sec," I cut in. "Maybe if I put it on speaker… Cro? Kassi? You there?"

There was no response.

"No, Dee—"

"Dorothy to Cro and Kassi. Do you copy?"

"Dorothy!" Leo hissed.

I spun around.

"Shh! What is it?"

Leo didn't answer; he just pointed. I followed his gaze, and my heart dropped. Something huge lay in the shadows. I hadn't seen it before.

Now, I couldn't unsee it.

Broad chest. Huge shoulders. Slow, heavy breaths stirred dust on the floor. Sleeping.

"What is that?" I said under my breath.

Leo didn't answer. But I think we both knew.

"We need to back out. Now." He finally replied.

"Dorothy! You there?" my comms sounded off loudly on speaker. "Oh man, you should see the new gear Cro—"

I slammed it off.

Too late.

A beam of red light tore through the dark. It blinked once, then glowed brighter.

The ground rumbled.

The creature uncoiled from the floor like a waking nightmare and rose to its full height. It towered over us, all muscle and rage, easily the most enormous, scariest creature we'd seen yet. Then it pounded its chest and unfurled its six wings like blades, nearly scraping the walls.

"ROOOOAARRRRRR!"

It rattled me to the core like the sound of a drill ripping metal. It echoed off the walls so hard it felt like the whole hive shuddered. I felt it in my ribs before I heard it with my ears.

"A real Alpha…"

The giant beast gazed at us with a low growl. Its left eye whirred and glowed red as it locked on.

Every instinct screamed, "Run!" but I was frozen.

"Wait... is that a cyber-optic eye?"

"Move!" Leo barked, snapping me out of it and yanking my arm.

We sprinted for the tunnel, but the alpha was faster. It slammed down in front of us, blocking the exit.

No time to think.

No other way out.

And the Alpha wasn't going to give us a second chance.

Leo's soldier instincts kicked in. He spotted something I missed—a hidden opening in the trench wall, covered by dirt and rocks.

"There!" he shouted, dragging me toward it.

We dove in, scrambling through the gap, crawling fast, just trying to put distance between us and the monster.

I fumbled with my comms, hands shaking hard. It took two tries even to press the button.

"Guys! The Alpha's here—it's right at the—" Static cut off the rest.

"Dee, keep moving!" Leo hissed behind me.

"We heard that roar," Kassi's voice came in. "Scared us half to death."

"That was an Alpha?" Cro asked.

"Yes, and it's upset we woke it up," Leo growled.

"Get out safe," Kassi said. "We're already exiting the nest."

"Copy that. We're right behind you," I answered.

"Ouch!" I cried out as pain flared up when my arm hit the acid wall again.

"Come on Dorothy, no time for pain, keep pushing."

"The exit!" Leo shouted.

The Alpha's arm shot into the narrow tunnel behind us.

"Clear!" Leo yelled as he pushed me out.

I hit the ground outside and spun around to make sure he was right behind me.

We were finally out.

But not safe.

The alpha let out another vicious roar and almost at once two-winged mobats dove from above the nest, shrieking.

"Run!" Leo yelled.

We had no striders, so it was just our legs now sprinting full speed while mobats dove from above. I yanked out my wand and swung it wildly. Sparks snapped and cracked, keeping them just far enough.

That's when I saw them, two mobats flying out of our cave.

"No, no, no… Leo! They've got Tin!" I yelled.

We charged toward them, our feet slamming against the rocks. Leo pulled his gale blaster and fired.

"Shoot, I missed!" He called out.

Across the butte, Cro and Kassi were out of sight, probably stuck with their own mobat mess.

"We've gotta lose them before linking up with the others," I panted.

"Dorothy! Leo! Head north, now! Away from the nest!"

"Cro, they're flying off with Tin! They're going south of our camp and we're chasing them now!"

"They have Tin?!" Kassi yelled over the comms.

"Yes! We can't lose him! Cro, we have to—"

"I know!... I know," Cro cut me off. I can hear the frustration in his voice. "…look, just go north anyway. Trust me, if this works, we'll get Tin back and make it out." He insisted.

"Fine."

Leo and I turned north while the mobats still tailed us. It was chaotic in the sky. I whipped my wand in wide arcs while Leo fired up at them.

Mobats still tailed us, wings cutting the air above. I whipped my wand in wide arcs while Leo fired up at them.

"Dorothy, look… what's that? A dark cloud?" Leo asked.

"No… those are…Cro! That big brain of yours to the rescue!"

A horde of Cro's spybot crows tore through the sky like a swarm. They started screeching with a piercing high-pitched sound that immediately sent the mobats into a panic. They all crashed into each other mid-air.

"You genius," I spoke through the comms.

Leo added. "This is your doing Cro. Wow…"

"I had them track me during your fight with Grimbol just in case," Cro said proudly.

But before I could reply, a massive blur burst from the nest. ***"ROOOAAARRRR!"***

"You guys, that's… an alpha!" Kassi yelled through the comms.

"It's even bigger than I thought," Cro added.

"Hey Cro, can you boost the frequency of your birds?"

"I see where you are going with this Dorothy. I'm on it now."

Cro tapped his console, cranking up the crows' pitch. The mobats scattered, plummeting from the sky. The alpha covered its ears and swiped at the crows, smashing a dozen into smoking piles of wreckage.

"There!" I shouted, pointing. "That mobat still has Tin!"

"Noooo!" Cro shouted.

In a blur, the alpha dove, tearing through the air, clawing Tin right out of the mobat's grasp, taking off again in one swift motion. It shot up through the sky with a thunderous cry, vanishing into the cloud.

"Tin!" we all shouted, stunned as the sky fell silent.

"No…no…. not again…please…" Cro cried out.

"*Cro….*"

Tin was gone again, and we had no idea where the alpha had taken him.

* * *

"The coast looks clear," Leo said, squinting out past the edge of camp. "How's everyone holding up?"

"We're breathing," I said, "but what about Tin? What's the next move?"

Cro let out a deep breath. "I've got a signal on Tin, but it's all scrambled. Glitchy. Either the alpha's scrambling it or something out here's frying the system. Honestly? I don't know… about fixing this, about finding Tin… I don't know anything right now."

He was hurt.

We sympathized as he gripped his tracker, staring at it with frustration, hoping it would start working again.

Kassi stepped up with a gentle voice. "Don't do that, Cro. You've done all you can. Best thing now is to wait. The alpha will return to the nest. When it does, we'll be ready."

"I'm sorry, Cro. If it wasn't for this compass, none of this would've happened."

"Stop," Leo cut in, looking at me. "This isn't on you, Dee. None of it is. And look, at least now we know the alpha's heading back to its nest. That's a start. For now, let's breathe, rinse off this stench, and figure it out from there."

What a day… I didn't say it out loud, but the thought hit hard. Our only plan of action is to find Tin.

CHAPTER TWENTY-THREE

We were a mess… frustrated, restless, and done with sitting around.

Even after outrunning the mobats, things hadn't gotten better. Cro was taking it the hardest.

I could see it in his eyes. Every second, not chasing that alpha mobat was eating him alive. Losing Tin had hit like a gut punch.

But what crushed me most?

We lost him chasing a compass that's dead again. We're stuck, and it's annoying.

"Guys, we've been in this cave for days just waiting," I said. "What's our next move?"

I didn't look at anyone. I didn't expect much either.

No jokes from Cro. No comments from Kassi, just the same tense silence.

Then Leo spoke up. "Maybe the compass not working is the universe telling us to pause. Maybe we're supposed to wait."

"SLAM."

"We don't have time!" I barked, smacking my hand against a crate.

"Dee, take it easy."

"Don't tell me to take it easy, Leo!" I snapped. "That's all we've been doing. We've been circling this same cave like scared sand-mice. Tin's out there somewhere, maybe halfway across the desert, and we're just… stuck."

Leo gave me that look again… the one that said, "*There she goes*." But this wasn't some act.

This was real.

This mattered.

I couldn't stand still anymore.

"Fine. Since I'm the only one actually feeling the pressure, maybe it's time to make a new plan—"

"Will you shut up for one second?" Cro snapped.

"…Excuse me?"

"I said shut up, Dorothy!" Cro got up, fists clenched and voice raw. "I lost my best friend chasing this dumb mission of yours!"

"Cro!" Kassi warned.

The cave fell silent again.

"Cro. I know you've all risked more than I deserve. But hiding in this cave, hoping something changes? That's not a strategy. We need a real plan."

"Do you, Dorothy?" Kassi asked with a serious tone. "Do you get what we've given up?"

"What are you talking about?" I shot back. "Of course, I know what everyone's risked. But can we stop acting like I'm the only one who wants to move forward?"

"Oh please," Cro interrupted. "You didn't watch your friend get snatched by a flying predator. You didn't quit your commander post to chase some spire."

He pointed at Kassi. "She temporarily walked away from her army to follow you. Do you even care what this is doing to us?"

"Thats not fair!" I shot back.

"Not fair?" he repeated. "What's not fair is you pretending this broken compass is the only thing that matters. Maybe try using your Tempest magic to fix it. I lost Tin because of that busted toy!"

He turned and stormed off.

Kassi followed him without a word.

His words hit me deep.

And maybe... maybe he wasn't wrong.

Honestly, I hadn't sensed my power recently. During the last storm, I reached out for it but found nothing. I told myself it was just stress, but deep down I knew the truth—I didn't have it; at least not right now.

"You think I'm being selfish, huh?" I asked Leo quietly.

He looked away.

That pause said it all.

My voice broke, louder than I meant. "But I've lost things too, Leo! I've fought just as hard to get here! Why does everyone think I wanted this for myself?"

Leo quickly replied, "That's not the point, Dee," sounding more serious than usual.

He sighed, clearly upset. "Right now, you're being very insensitive. Nobody wanted to be stuck here. Tin's gone, the compass is broken, and we nearly died in that sandstorm. We need time to breathe and clear our minds. What's the point of this journey if you forget about the people beside you?"

He shook his head walking away.

"Leo, wait—"

I reached out, but he was already gone. I sank back down, the quiet creeping in again.

"Great, now I've annoyed everyone."

I hated to admit it, but the sandstorm from a few days ago still scared me. It's the kind of thing you try to forget, but it sticks with you. I think that's why we've all been on edge lately.

Cro snapping.

Kassi shutting down.

Leo walking off.

Me… losing grip.

Even now, thinking about it gives me chills.

***

After we made it out of the butte with the compass, all of us worn out, Leo called for us to regroup at the cave.

No one argued.

We needed air, and I needed to get this nasty stench out of my hair.

By the time we got there, the day felt like a blur. Kassi and I sat by the entrance, trying to dry our damp, grimy hair from the mess in the mobat tunnels. We winced, checking the burns on our arms, acid wall souvenirs.

Leo was off to the side, shrugging off his jacket.

"Are you guys okay?" he asked, watching us rub ointment on our burns.

"I'll live," I mumbled.

"Just stings like crazy," Kassi added.

Cro was already lost in his equipment, muttering while he ran diagnostics on the tracker. He hadn't said much since the signal went quiet, and I knew it was bugging him.

"BEEP!"

"Guys! Tin's signal!" Cro shouted, waving his tablet.

We rushed over. He pointed at a blinking dot.

"He's west of Howling Canyon. What in Oz is he doing there?" Cro asked.

No one knew.

Kassi frowned as she studied the map. "That's the Amber Dunes region."

"Okay… so?" Cro replied. "We cross it, grab Tin, and get out."

"You've been up here long enough to know the rumors." Kassi shot him a look. "That place is worse than Twister Alley. People don't just vanish into storms; they vanish, period."

Cro folded his arms. "Those are just rumors. How can we be sure if we haven't seen it?"

"We're looking for a rumored weather spire, Cro!" Kassi snapped. "Since when do we wait for proof before we take a threat seriously?"

"Hold on," Leo jumped in. "We know the risk now. But we finally have a shot. Tin's out there."

"I agree."

Kassi looked at me. "You too? I figured you'd want to play it safe."

I met her eyes. "Sorry, Kassi. But we have to bring him back."

I turned to Cro. "And this journey depends on it."

Cro raised a hand. "All in favor of facing the dunes?"

Three hands went up.

Kassi didn't move, but the vote was clear.

"Fine," she muttered. "Just don't expect me to act like I'm thrilled."

We started getting our gear ready when I felt a soft buzz at my hip.

"The compass…" I whispered.

It glowed with a faint gold light; it had never happened before.

"Wait… does this mean we're close to the Spire?"

Part of me hoped that's what the glowing light meant. But we couldn't let ourselves get too excited. So, I hid that part from them.

"Hey guys, the compass is pointing in the same direction as Cro's tracker. That can't be a coincidence."

Kassi stared. "So, now we've two leads pointing into the worst place possible. Think this'll go easy?"

"Tin's out there," I said, pocketing the compass. "We're not leaving him behind."

"Fine." Kassi let out a sigh and headed to her strider. "But if we're doing this, we stay sharp. No heroic stunts. No wandering. We move as one."

We set out into the dunes. For hours, the compass kept pulling us deeper.

"This is it," Kassi said as we crested a steep mound, brushing grit from her facemask. "The Great Amber Dunes."

We all raised our visors and stared out. The dunes stretched as far as we could see, rolling like ocean waves, frozen mid-storm.

"Do you think anything's out here?" Leo asked, shielding his eyes from the glare.

"Not so sure now, huh?" Kassi said.

Cro tapped his screen. "Tin's signal's faint, but it's there. We'd better move before it drops again."

We kept moving forward.

The wind intensified, stronger than ever. The compass and tracker remained fixed in the same direction, dragging us deeper into the unknown. I started to feel a strange unease building.

Up ahead, dust began to gather, forming a thick cloud that matched Kassi's earlier warnings. The wind started out as a gentle whisper, but quickly escalated into a howl. The sky darkened, and the golden dunes took on a sickly hue.

"Kassi, is this a storm?" Leo asked nervously.

"No…worse!" Kassi shouted back. "No time! Find cover!"

"There's nowhere to hide!" I yelled into my comm.

A wall of wind and dust came rushing over the dunes like a monstrous wave.

"VOOOSHHH!"

It hit hard enough to rip us from our striders. I held on tight, but a vicious gust knocked me straight into the sand.

"Leo!" I screamed, but I couldn't see him. The wind howled so loudly I could barely hear my own thoughts. My comms were full of static, but I caught Cro's voice break through.

"Dorothy… try… your powers!"

"He's right, I have to try something! Come on… Come on…"

I glanced at my bracelet. It was the one thing I could always rely on.

"Please work; I've got to help my friends!"

But nothing happened.

I tried again and again to get something started, but no glow, no spark. I gritted my teeth and gripped the bracelet, as if I could force it to work.

"Come on," I muttered as the wind whipped around me. "Don't give up on me now."

I shut my eyes and focused hard. I thought back to Howling Canyon. It had felt effortless then, as if something inside me had just clicked.

I braced myself against the wind, even though my boots barely held on in the shifting sand. I threw my arms out, begging the storm to hear me.

"You helped me before," I whispered. "You can do it again."

Still nothing.

"AHHHHHHHH!!!"

I screamed and pushed with all my strength, trying to call on any bit of power. But the wind only screamed back.

Then I was weightless.

The wind yanked me up as if I were nothing. I tumbled through the air, sand slicing across my face, stinging my skin.

"OOF!"

I crashed down hard, half-buried.

For a second, I just lay there, staring up into the churning sky. Dust spun in circles above me, and the sand started piling over my legs. All I could do was curl into myself, shield my head, and hope it would pass.

I had nothing left to fight with.

Ten minutes crawled by before the wind finally eased. The dunes were still, though a haze of dust hung in the air. I stood up, spitting out sand, my legs shaking.

I hit my radio. "Dorothy to anyone, come in."

No response.

"Kassi... Leo... Cro... Anyone!"

Static.

"… Dorothy?"

That voice—

"Cro? Is that you?"

"Yes, I've got your signal and the others too. Just stay put. I'm coming."

I didn't know whether to scream or cry or both.

He found us.

Not long after, we spotted a small cave tucked under a jagged ridge. It wasn't much, just a dent in the rock, but it blocked the wind and gave us a minute to breathe.

We needed that.

Time to recover. Time to plan.

We all just knew the alpha would come back this way. When it did, we had to be ready.

Cro knelt over his tools, fixing the tracker. I sat nearby, holding my compass, which seemed not to be working again.

* * *

Right now, after all the yelling and truths that got spilled during that argument, I sat curled up in the corner of the cave. The silence wasn't peaceful; it felt heavy. You could almost feel the tension hanging there.

I pulled one of the sleeping bags the Winki gave us tighter around me, like wrapping it tighter would keep out more than just the cold. The things the others said kept spinning around in my head. I turned my bracelet in my fingers, again and again, like it held the answer.

"Had I been too focused on the goal? On me?"

"Was I being selfish without even realizing it?"

The campfire's warm glow wavered at my back as Uncle Neel's voice echoed in my head: *"Sometimes you get so focused on the goal, you forget the people standing next to you."*

This is what he meant.

My ambition had blinded me. In chasing the Spire and a way to stop the storms, I'd forgotten what mattered most: Leo, Kassi, Cro, and Tin. They stuck by me, even when I made everything harder… even when I didn't earn it. They deserved better.

I stared at the compass in my hand.

"Mom… Dad… was this worth it? Losing everything for this?"

"BUZZ!"

"…What?"

"BUZZ!"

I jumped up.

"Guys! It's working again! It's actually working!"

Cro didn't even glance up. "Yeah? And how long before it fizzles out this time?"

"Cro… no, please, just… hear me out." I took a breath. "I owe all of you an apology. I've been pushy, selfish… and honestly, exhausting."

I held the compass tight in both hands. "I think I was trying to prove I can solve a problem, instead of always being a problem. I wanted to make the Vogan name mean something again. I wanted to matter."

My voice began to crack. "But I didn't see what it was costing you. You've carried me through so much. And I've made it harder."

No one said a word while I wiped my face and kept going.

"So here it is. After we find Tin, you don't owe me anything. If you want to go your own way, I'll get it. I just need you to know I'm grateful. For everything. All of you. Even Tin."

Silence filled the cave again.

I shoved the compass into my pocket and turned away.

"You must be really naïve," Cro muttered.

"Cro, I literally just—"

"You think we'd leave because of a fight?" He stood, met my eyes. "Dorothy, I'm sorry. I was stubborn. Kassi called me out on it. Losing Tin messed me up, and I took it out on you. But I'd never abandon you."

Kassi stepped up, hand warm on my shoulder. "Cro's a lot, but he means it. You gave us something bigger to believe in, Dorothy."

Leo nodded. "Dee, you've always fought so no kid ended up like we did growing up. Sometimes, your fire burns brighter than most can take, but that's what makes you, you."

He giggled a bit. "Even though this is sounding like a cheesy drama, we're not leaving. We find Tin. We finish this. Together."

That broke me into tears again.

Kassi was the first to hug me, then Leo, and then Cro. It was a messy, tight, emotional hug, but it felt genuine.

"BUZZ!"

"Dorothy… why's your pocket glowing?" Cro asked.

"What?" I blinked and looked down.

A warm, golden light emitted from my jacket. I carefully took out the compass, which then glowed more brightly and started to vibrate.

"It's happening again," I whispered.

Kassi leaned in. "This has happened before?"

"Yeah… right before we left to come here. The compass began glowing with a golden light, but I didn't know what it meant at the time. Now… I think it's showing us something."

I paused.

"Guys, I think we're close. Like, really close."

"Close to what? The Spire?" Cro asked.

I couldn't look away from it. "Yeah. I think so."

Kassi gasped. "Hold on… light made of gold… Power of old…"

"What?" Leo asked

"I think she finally lost it," Cro muttered.

"Shhh! Give me a sec…" She raised her hand and began mumbling words under her breath. "How does it go again? Uh… Power of old…road leads to gold…"

"Kassi! That's it!" I shouted. "The riddle! From the journal!"

We grabbed each other's arms and started jumping up and down like two kids seeing a raw emerald in the mines for the first time. We hurried to my bag to pick up both books.

"Girls…" Leo groaned, standing behind us.

"Someone wanna clue us in?" Cro asked. "Or is this just some weird hype dance?"

"Both my parents had parts of the same riddle in their journals: 'Power of old, for generations told, unfolds the road with light made of gold.' Kassi and I didn't get it before, but now, look."

I held up the compass. It was glowing brighter than ever, golden light spilling from it. "This is it. Light made of gold. It's pointing the way."

Leo stepped in, squinting at the beam. "You think this is it? The path to the Spire... to the source?"

Kassi and I nodded at the same time. "It's the only thing that makes sense."

Cro came up beside me and rested a hand on my shoulder. "Then we've got a decision to make."

"Yes, together," I said, gripping the compass tight.

CHAPTER TWENTY-FOUR

-LEO-

The dunes stretched out forever ahead, the sun already sharp even in the early hour. I leaned against one of the striders, brushing sand off the engine with the back of my glove. The casing was hot as if it had been cooking in a campfire all night.

"We really need to keep up with maintenance," I muttered.

Dee would probably tease me again for babying the machines, but it's not just about the gear; it's about surviving. Out here, one jammed strider could be the difference between life and getting buried in sand.

Cro crouched beside me, poking around the stabilizer joints, mumbling about the beating it took during the sandstorm.

"Think this thing can go any farther?" I asked, watching him work a bent wire.

He shrugged. "She's fussy, but she'll hold for now."

Sighing, I brushed sand off my pants. Striders are built to last, but this desert chews them up for fun. We'd already pushed them way past spec. Breaking down now would be a death sentence.

A few meters off, Dee and Kassi sat by the old campfire. The flames were long gone, but Dee looked more restless than cold, fiddling with that compass like she was hoping it'd speak up.

We talked earlier, so I'm pretty sure I know what she was thinking.

Kassi grabbed her wrist. "Just say it. You've got the compass, Dee. What do you want to do?"

Dee hesitated. "What if the compass points one way and Tin's tracker pings another? What if we're chasing ghosts?"

"Leo, Cro! Get over here." Kassi commanded.

"What now?" Cro stood, still holding his snips.

Kassi gave a quick rundown. Dee turned to Cro. "Could the signals be wrong?"

"It's been bothering me for a while," Cro said, rubbing his chin. "That alpha wasn't just some wild beast. We all saw it had a cybernetic optic implant. But for a moment, my tracker also picked up a second tracking receiver, in addition to the one in Tin. This had to be the Alpha.

"Are you trying to say what I think you are?" I asked.

"Indeed, Leo," Cro replied. "I believe someone's controlling it."

Kassi raised her brow. "It did seem very intentional about taking Tin. You think it's the Archons?"

"If they're behind it, then they're tracking Tin too. Which means I might be able to tap their signal again."

Dee looked over at us. "Cro… Kassi and I just talked. I spoke with Leo about this earlier. We all agreed that our next move should be your call."

We all fell quiet, the wind kicking up sand at our boots.

"We're following the compass." Cro finally spoke up. "If the alpha headed the same way, it's no coincidence. There's something there."

That was all we needed.

We loaded up and climbed onto the striders. As the engines kicked in, the hum cut across the dunes. Dust peeled up in sheets. I rode behind Dee, visor down.

"She's definitely improving."

She handled her strider so smoothly, it looked effortless, like she'd been doing it her whole life. Typical Dee. She always figured machines out faster than anyone I knew. That's why she was such a good drill engineer back in the district mines.

Kassi once told me Dee learned to surf twisters. I heard they even gave her a new nickname.

But as smoothly as she moved, something felt off.

Her eyes stayed locked on the horizon.

I knew that look.

It's the one she gets when she's lost in thought, trying to solve a puzzle only she can see.

"Hey, Dee," I said over comms, "I've been wondering… how'd your parents find all this out? The Spire, the compass… where'd it come from?"

Her hands tightened on the controls. "They never told me much. I was just a kid. But they spent weeks exploring up here. They must've found relics or talked to people who knew more than we did."

Kassi added, "They also sent teams of archaeologist. My brother mentioned that Galesville wasn't just a village but a hub of ancient technology and secret knowledge."

Cro added, "I wonder where all that stuff went. Could still be out there."

Dee nodded. "I wonder that too." She turned slightly toward Kassi. "Have you ever visited the ruins?"

Kassi shook her head. "No. After it fell, I buried myself in the Monsoons. There wasn't enough time. Honestly… I wasn't ready."

I bent closer to Dee. "Would you ever go back? To the Galesville site?"

She didn't answer right away. "Maybe. But I wouldn't even know what I'm looking for."

That stuck with me. She always had a purpose, but maybe right now, she didn't.

No one said much after that.

We just rode.

The only sounds were the low rumble of engines and wind scraping across the sand. Then the desert shifted.

"Hey, guys, it looks like we have another one coming our way," Kassi called out.

Oddly enough, I never get tired of the sheer power of these twisters.

It erupted from the ground like a monster. Even from this distance, I could see giant debris caught up in its whirlwind.

Dee wasn't afraid.

She steered us wide, cutting a hard angle to avoid the edge of the storm system. We all followed without a word.

Wind smashed into us. Our striders bucked and groaned, hovering above the loose sand.

My visor rattled.

The engines howled, struggling to keep us grounded.

I gripped Dee's waist, leaning into the ride with her. Kassi was locked in. Cro kept monitoring the twister, probably calculating wind speed and how big it might get.

Everyone was focused despite the storm wanting to bury us. There was no way we were going to let anything stop us this time.

* * *

Time went by, and we kept pushing forward. The wind surrounded us on all sides, making the desert seem to go on forever.

Then something changed.

At first, it was just a blurry spot on the horizon, shimmering out of place.

"Probably just heat playing tricks on us again."

I'd seen enough mirages to stop trusting my own eyes out here.

But this one didn't disappear. As we rode closer, it came into focus.

"Wow…this is unreal."

A massive mesa rose out of the sand.

"This is colossal," Kassi said over the comms.

"Wow," Cro muttered, staring at the rock.

Dee and I were speechless. We could never have imagined this sight.

This mountain stood all by itself. It had a flat top and rough, steep cliffs on every side, scarred with deep grooves and holes. You could tell wind and sand had been carving it for hundreds of years, but it never gave in. It was so big it almost blocked out the horizon.

As we got closer, we could see more details. It had layers of rock stacked on top of each other, with the colors changing as we looked up. The bottom was a dark, heavy red, which gradually faded into a dusty beige higher up.

"This isn't on my map," Cro said, reading the data. "How does something this big go unnoticed?"

"The sandstorms," Kassi suggested. "They may have been hiding it all this time, acting as a natural barrier. If we hadn't taken this route, we'd never have found it."

"BEEP! BEEP! BEEP!"

"Wait… no way," he said. "Guys… the tracker's working again."

He looked up, blinking like he didn't trust it. Then, that disbelief cracked, and a full-blown grin took over his face

"It's Tin. He's here. Somewhere inside that mountain!"

I rode up beside him. "You sure?"

"Affirmative!"

"I can't believe it," Kassi said as she stepped forward.

Cro was beaming. Not figuratively. I mean, the guy looked like an emerald lamp at full charge. The relief on his face said it all.

"Thanks, guys," he said. "Seriously."

"Of course! I mean, he's our friend too, Cro," Kassi replied.

"Exactly," Dee added. "He's one of us."

"Alright! Let's go get Tin back!" Cro shouted as he threw one hand in the air while steering with the other.

I leaned over a bit to look at Dee. She seemed better. Not quite her old self, but something in her had uncoiled. Like a storm finally passing.

"Hey," I said quietly. "We made the right call."

She paused and just smiled, as if she needed someone to say it out loud.

"Thanks, Leo."

She hesitated before speaking again.

"Do you ever think about them? Your old squad?"

This time, she caught me off guard. It was as if she had read my mind.

"Yeah. Sometimes. We made it through a lot together. I'm glad they got back safe, but… I wish they could've seen the surface the way we have so far."

"Yeah… I get that." She said, looking ahead.

"But I don't regret it. Not a bit. Finding out you were alive, and apparently a professional twister surfer? Worth it."

She laughed. "It's called *Gale Running*, actually. So, Kassi told you, huh?"

"Oh yeah. *La-dy Gale! La-dy Gale!*"

She burst out laughing again. It was real this time.

"I don't know how many times she brought you up," I added, throwing Kassi a look. "She almost murdered me when I said your name during my imprisonment."

She cracked up like she could picture the whole scene.

"That's Kassi for you," she said, still grinning. "You've gotta love her."

* * *

The wind gusted strongly, throwing sand onto our engines and making them work harder. I noticed the increased noise from Dee's strider as we shifted gears.

"I guess these striders will need a break from us soon."

Thankfully, both Dee's compass and Cro's tracker held up the entire time, pointing directly at the mountain's entry.

"Whoa... look at this opening! I bet it can fit a mecha-tank blaster!" Kassi pointed out.

"Yeah, it is rather larger than most cave entrances," Dee mentioned.

We finally made it.

We quickly dismounted and moved closer to the mountain to shield ourselves from the gusts. We walked the striders towards the entrance. Dee approached the opening first.

"This was a mine," Dee said, running her fingers along the stone near the entrance. She wasn't guessing; she knew.

"The way the rock was cut and the shape of the opening lines up perfectly," she added.

"Yeah, that makes sense," Cro agreed. "There's likely a whole tunnel network beneath there."

After a brief outside survey, Cro decided, "Alright, let's do it. Let's go in."

"Hold up." I raised a hand.

They turned.

"We need to stay alert," I said. "Keep in mind, Tin might not be alone. Anything could be waiting inside. So let's make sure our weapons are ready, safeties off, and eyes open."

"Right," they all said at once.

* * *

The tunnel entrance was massive, much bigger than any mine we had seen. The walls were rough and dark with old stains. A rusty vent pipe still hung above us. The floor was wet, uneven, and slippery from water.

"This entrance almost looks like the Hive," Kassi said.

"You're right," Dee said. She continued staring at the walls. "This place was... very busy."

I hadn't seen it before, but once they said it, I couldn't unsee it. The layout felt off.

"Look at these," she said, pointing down. "These rail tracks are much wider than standard mining gauge. It's like they were moving something massive, and probably often."

That's when she shifted gears. Locked in. No jokes. No chatter. Just that razor focus she gets when she's piecing something together.

We hung back, letting her work. She moved deeper into the tunnel, slowly and deliberately. The gravel crunched under her boots. Then she knelt, scooped some up, and let it fall through her fingers like she was weighing the years in her hand.

"Wow, look at her go... Good to know we have a real deal miner with us," Kassi said.

Dee didn't say a word, just pulled a small pick and magnifier from her pack. I didn't even know she carried those.

She chipped at the wall, held the lens close, and ran her fingers along the fresh cut. Her brow furrowed deeper with every second.

"This doesn't add up," she muttered.

We followed as she sidestepped along the wall, brushing away layers of dust.

"No varied mineral deposits... no clear layers..." she whispered.

She looked at us. "This wasn't a normal mine. They weren't just digging for ore."

I stepped next to her and ran my hand along the cold, rough stone that had been untouched for who knows how long.

"Solid analysis," I said. "So, if they weren't pulling minerals… what were they after?"

She stood, tapping the wall as if she were listening for answers. "That's the real question."

Kassi chimed in. "You think this is bigger than just Tin being here?"

"No doubt," Dee said. "And I'm going to figure out what it is."

"Hey guys, come check this out." Cro's voice came in over comms.

We followed his voice around the bend and found him scrubbing down an old metal sign bolted to the wall. The thing was barely holding together, half-rotted, coated in rust. As he wiped it clean, a faded hazard symbol appeared.

"Danger… High Emerald Voltage," Cro read aloud, squinting.

He looked around as if the answer might be hanging in the air.

"Where's the power source?"

Dee raised her flashlight and angled it up. "There. Wires feed into that side tunnel."

We all looked up. A mess of old cables stretched across the ceiling like veins, wrapped with dust, cracked lanterns dangling from them. Most of the bulbs were broken. None were lit.

"Perfect," Kassi muttered, adjusting her pack. "All we need now is a generator before I trip in the dark and twist my ankle."

Cro was already scanning. "Hold up. I'm getting something… a low-frequency signal. Could be a generator. Close."

Kassi looked at him. "Very convenient, kid!"

I nudged him. "Alright, let's find that power source. The sooner we get the lights on, the sooner we start getting answers."

I turned back to the team. "Kassi, take the rear. I've got a point. Stay sharp, everyone. This place doesn't feel abandoned; it feels asleep."

* * *

The vast and dark corridor stretched ahead of us like it was swallowing every bit of light. Our flashlights barely cut through a few yards. Everything beyond that stayed buried in black.

We had been walking for almost thirty minutes, each step feeling heavier, as we kept watching out for anything suspicious.

Kassi finally broke it.

"Anyone else notice?" She said, sweeping her beam along the walls. "This place has been empty for a long time… but no animal tracks, no nests. Nothing."

"You're right, Kassi," Dee said. "Even abandoned tunnels seem to have some kind of life. I wonder, why don't we see any animals here?"

"Maybe something drove them away for good?" Cro wondered.

I continued walking. "No animals usually indicates that something even worse has already dominated the area."

The shadows seemed to move the deeper we went. Not literally, of course, but the feeling you get when your instincts are urging you to turn back was weighing heavily on me.

"Over here," Cro stopped, angling his flashlight.

Tucked halfway under a pile of rubble was a rusted-out generator. Cro dropped to one knee and brushed off the grime with his sleeve.

"It's in bad shape," he said. "But if we've got an emerald power cell, it might still fire up."

Dee reached for her pack, but Cro shook his head with a grin. "Nah, I came prepared."

He pulled out a small green shard and inserted it into the port. The generator let out a low groan and then shuddered, struggling to start.

"Come on, work," Kassi murmured. I stepped up to the lever. It was frozen tight. No normal person could move it.

"The lever over there," Dee called out, "Leo, do you think you can handle that?"

"Good thing I got that arm upgrade, huh, Dee?"

"We knew it'd come in handy one day," Dee said with a smirk.

I gripped the lever and pulled it.

Nothing.

Tried again.

Still nothing.

On the third try, I routed power from the core in my arm and yanked with all my might. The generator groaned again, then roared to life. Dim lanterns twitched on along the walls, and a low buzz started as the ventilation kicked in.

"Finally," Dee muttered, adjusting her pack. A faint stream of fresher air slid past us.

"Nice work," Cro added.

We pressed on, following the old tracks deeper into the mountain.

We followed the rails deeper into the cave, our path now lit by the weak lanterns. A little farther, Dee pointed to the side. An old minecart sat there, rusted and huge, like someone had rerouted it and just left it behind.

"Is the compass still working?" Kassi asked.

Dee checked. "It's on... but it's not pointing anywhere. The signal's likely jammed due to too much rock."

"At least the tunnel's straight," Cro offered, scanning ahead.

We kept walking. Our boots echoed against the metal rails, a rhythmic, loud sound in the quiet.

I stopped. Took a breath.

Yeah, I knew that stench. Earthy. Damp. Pungent.

"Mobats."

The wounds were all over his body. She drew hers fast... ready, practiced.

We slowed our pace.

The tunnel amplified everything: our breath, the scrape of gear, the click of a safety.

I caught a glimpse of Dee gripping her battle-wand like muscle memory.

She leaned toward me. "It's not just any mobat," she whispered. "You smell it? It's *him.*"

I nodded once.

Cro stepped up beside us, powering on his custom blaster. "Not running this time."

Kassi and I raised our gale-blasters, syncing our pace in front of Dee as we approached the next chamber.

Then we heard it… slow, heavy breathing. Deep in the dark ahead.

It was him.

Still massive. Still dangerous looking.

But…injured. The wounds were all over his body.

His blood smeared the surrounding ground. Wings hanging low, dragging like they couldn't lift anymore. His left optic still glowed, but it was fading.

Dee stepped forward, wand low, confused more than afraid.

"What happened to you?" she reached over to him, voice barely above a whisper.

"Back up, Dee." I shifted instantly, putting myself between her and the alpha.

This wasn't over. Not even close.

Kassi's gaze was locked on the shadows. "We're not alone."

From the tunnel beside the alpha, I heard a faint scraping, something dry and sharp dragging across stone.

I raised my blaster, finger tight on the trigger.

We weren't going to be blindsided.

Dee met my eyes. "We finish this. No more running."

"FLASH!"

Light burst through the tunnel like a flare.

Eyes.

Suspended in the dark.

Watching.

Waiting.

And then…

"I… was expecting you all…"

CHAPTER TWENTY-FIVE

We were right there. Closer than we'd ever been.

We finish this," I said under my breath. "No more running."

We stayed still and silent, listening for anything that didn't belong. Then we heard slow footsteps echoing down the tunnel. They were soft at first, but each step grew louder. A flash of light bobbed toward us, and a voice called out:

"I... was expecting you all..."

Its eyes grew brighter, and the shape began to appear. Then, the form behind it started to take shape.

Cro whispered what we were all thinking. "No way…"

"Tin!" we all shouted.

Everything else faded away. I didn't care if the alpha was behind us.

All I saw was him.

I barely noticed I was crying until my vision blurred. I ran toward him. Kassi beat me there, running right into him. Her arms wrapped around his damaged arm, holding on as if he might disappear if she didn't.

Even Leo just stood there. Silent. Eyes wide.

Tin was barely upright. His metal body was dented, scratched, and even sparking in places, but he was back. Cro fumbled with his scanner, trying to focus through tears.

"You're… you're alive. You're really here. But you're damaged badly."

Tin rested his hand gently on Cro's head and tapped his goggles.

"Cro, your vitals are showing elevated heart rates. Please refrain from short-circuiting before you fix me."

That broke the tension.

Laughter, rough and shaky, spilled out of all of us. Even Kassi, who was full-on crying now, wiped her face with Cro's sleeve and smiled.

"Tin… we thought we lost you," she said.

"It will take more than blunt force to decommission this unit," he grinned.

I took a step back, trying to make sense of what I was seeing. I had about a hundred questions lined up and no idea where to start.

"So," I said. "What happened to you? When did you come back online?"

Tin's smile faded. His eyes shifted past us, focused, cold, already thinking three steps ahead.

"My internal tracker was linked to Cro's device," he said. "I kept pinging your location, but I couldn't get a clean signal. Systems were failing on loop."

Cro pushed his goggles onto his forehead until they clicked. "That's why the signal was glitching; you were stuck in reboot mode."

"Affirmative. After the Exabot fight, my dual cores were unstable. I had to recalibrate before I could send a strong enough signal. It took longer than I expected, but I made it."

We were all just relieved.

Tin continued. "While it is good we have all reconnected, we have to take caution with the alpha. I managed to bring it down, but it's not eliminated. I suggest we move to avoid further conflict."

Cro groaned and grabbed his tools. "Hold on, I just need to make a few tweaks—"

"Not here," Tin interrupted, "We can't risk it regaining strength. There's a safer place ahead."

No one argued. We moved quickly. I glanced back at the chamber.

The alpha was still slumped against the wall, wings limp, chest barely moving. It looked… confused.

Not dangerous.

At least, not anymore.

Just something lost and hurt.

Kassi bumped my arm. "Come on, Dorothy. Let's go."

"I'm coming," I said. But I didn't look away.

The alpha's left optic whirred softly as it watched me. Not tracking. Just… watching.

"I know you are probably not bad," I told it quietly. "We'll help you. Somehow."

It didn't speak. Just raised one finger like it was trying to reach out, but it didn't.

Then we left it behind.

*　*　*

The tunnel ahead opened into a haulage-way, typically used for hauling materials from underground.

Tin continued speaking.

"When I finally reconnected, I realized I was deep within this mountain with the alphabat. However, my system showed that we weren't alone. I also discovered something that led me to believe the creature wasn't acting alone in capturing me."

We stopped walking.

Cro was the first to speak. "So, I was right. Something's been controlling it."

"If that's what you assessed during my departure, you would be correct," Tin said. "The alphabat is cybernetic. My scanners intercepted wireless commands from someone nearby going into the creature."

He shifted, and his metal armor creaked quietly.

"The moment I intercepted the communication… the individual knew. That's when they prompted the alpha to attack me. I tried to slip away, but it chased me until I had no choice but to put it down."

"Maybe the alpha was just a weapon. Something they used to control the whole mobat colony," Kassi said.

"Precisely," Tin said, "and there's more."

He paused. "I decoded the command given to the alphabat. Dorothy, before I share what was said, I want you to know your journey has been worth it. The command was to 'Bring the asset to Spire.'

Leo's eyes went wide. "You mean the Great Spire?"

"So, it's real? It's actually real? Kassi said.

"I can't believe it," Cro added.

"I knew it!" I shouted.

I didn't even realize I'd said it out loud.

"GRRRRR!"

A low growl rolled out from behind us. Tin went into defense mode, all systems on alert. Hurt or not, he was ready to protect us.

After a few steps, I asked, "Tin, is there anything else you found?"

He paused, then shook his head. "Negative. The alphabat doesn't seem to think for itself. It only follows commands."

"Just as I suspected." Cro said, "If it's built for recon and retrieval, it can't think on its own."

"Can't think on his own? Hmm... I wondered about that..."

I thought about the alpha's expression when he stared at me.

Tin's joints let out a soft groan as he shifted. "Even so," he said, "I was able to determine the origin of the control signal."

"Wait… you know where it came from? You can track it?" I asked.

"Affirmative. I have pinpointed the source," Tin replied, like it was no big deal he'd just cracked the case.

"Tin, are you serious?"

"What?"

"That's amazing, incredible!"

We all reacted differently, but it was all shock and surprise.

"I must caution," Tin warned, "I can't guarantee what awaits us. The individual behind the alphabat is very shrewd. We must proceed with alertness."

"Uh, hold on," Leo said, rubbing the back of his neck like he was trying to calm himself down. "Before we go charging into whatever's next, can we not die from fatigue first?"

"I'm with Leo," Kassi said, already stretching her arms. "We've been moving for hours. We need to slow down before someone passes out or, worse, gets cranky."

I hated it, but… they weren't wrong. My legs felt like bricks, and even my brain was starting to fog up around the edges. Rest wasn't a luxury right now; it was survival.

I glanced around. Kassi was already sliding to the floor. Cro had his gear spread out and was muttering about recalibrating Tin's chest panel.

Tin gave us all a quick once-over. "Rest is advisable. But brief. If the alphabat regains functionality, it may pursue us again."

I let out a long breath and finally sat. "Alright. Quick break. Then we move. We're close… I can feel it."

Kassi smirked as she stretched out beside me. "Wow. Patience? From you?"

I rolled my eyes but couldn't help grinning. "Don't let it go to your head."

Leo collapsed to the ground with a dramatic sigh, as if it were the softest bed in the world. Cro, of course, was already wrist-deep in Tin's repair, goggles down and focus dialed to max.

I hugged my knees and leaned against the cool tunnel wall, watching Tin as he recharged and reset. He'd been through hell and somehow still looked like the most stable one in the group.

"You'll get us there, right?" I asked quietly. "You'll take us to the Spire?"

Tin tilted his head just slightly toward me. "I will do everything within my power, Dorothy."

That was enough for me.

* * *

Time passed.

I couldn't tell how long, but I must've doze off a bit. I guess I needed the rest after all. .

I looked over and Cro was still focused.

He had Tin propped on an old crate like a makeshift operating table; toolbox already scattered across the floor. Wires spilled out like veins. His fingers flew over each bolt and panel. He couldn't relax until Tin was fixed.

Then, of course, Leo wandered over.

"So, you're the famous Tin?" he said with a big smile. "I've heard a lot about you. I have to say, solid build. Impressive metalwork. Very... heroic machine-chic."

"Pleased to make your acquaintance, friend of Dorothy," Tin said. "She has referenced you and Emeraldia. My sensors detect a bionic heart and a bionic arm. I suppose I am not the only one of my kind."

Leo laughed, patting Tin's shoulder like they were old pals. "Touché, metal man."

Before long, Leo was leaning against Cro's cluttered workbench, firing off question after question. Initially, Cro just grunted, clearly annoyed. But then something changed. He began answering questions and soon found himself explaining.

Next thing I knew, Cro was handing him tools and pointing out wiring like they were co-pilots. Leo caught on fast, of course. He always did when it came to tech.

They found a rhythm as if they'd done this before.

Seeing them brought a warm memory to me: Leo was a kid, sitting cross-legged in the scrapyards, going on and on about old Metallia processors while I tuned him out with just enough nods to keep him going. One time, he even snuck in a secret upgrade to my glideboard, almost landing me in the city canal. But when I caught on to what he'd done, I couldn't stop smiling for a week.

Now, he was working shoulder to shoulder with someone equally passionate about tech and gears. Finding someone who could keep up made me proud to see.

After a good stretch, I decided to take a walk. I moved along the cold, dented walls. I noticed tools were scattered on the ground. Some were rusted through, while others looked in good shape.

I looked up at the shaft and let a thin breeze brush my face. There was a time when none of this mattered to me: not the shape of the tunnels or how to hear a cave-in. All I wanted to do was to explore.

Uncle Neel saw that in me and Leo. He knew we would sneak into the mines no matter what. So instead of stopping us, he taught us. He showed us how to read the rock and check if the mine was safe.

That's when I fell in love with engineering. It was the only way we could explore without leaving Emeraldia. It was the only way we could touch the outside world without breaking the dome.

And now I was in it. Past the walls, past the scrapyards. Deep in the unknown, just like I always wanted.

"What's going through your mind, Dorothy?" Kassi's voice pulled me back. She propped against a rail, waiting for my answer.

I let out a quiet sigh and rested a hand on my hip. "Just old memories," I said. "We're close to the Spire now. Closer than I ever thought we'd actually get."

She tilted her head, studying me as if she were trying to read past my words. "And? You ready for whatever truth's waiting at the end?"

"Honestly? I don't know. I always thought it'd be far off, like some big future thing we'd never really reach. Now that we're basically here... it feels heavier. But whatever's waiting, I'll face it. At least I'll know I didn't back down."

She bumped my arm with hers, her usual grin sliding back into place. "That's deep. Maybe you're not as naïve as I thought."

I shot her a mock glare. "Careful. Give me too much credit, and I might start getting ideas."

I glanced around at the tunnel, at the way the weak lights barely held back the dark, at the way everything echoed like the past was still trying to whisper through the walls.

"I've learned a lot up here," I added. "About Oz. About my parents. About myself. These storm powers... they're not the only thing that changed me."

She raised an eyebrow. "And you still want more?"

I shrugged. "Of course I do. I want to know what's beyond the Spire. What's waiting in the No-Lands. If the stories about the Zolytes are real... I want to see it all."

I waited for the eye roll.

Instead, she groaned loudly enough to rattle down the tunnel. "I take it back. You're still as naïve as ever."

We both laughed, and for once, it didn't feel out of place. Just two people in a quiet spot between storms.

Then I looked at her. Really looked at her.

"Honestly?" I said, "If it weren't for you guys… I'd still be wandering, probably stuck in some wind trap or doing something stupid. You were my first real friend up here."

I pulled her into a hug, purposely being overly dramatic.

She stiffened instantly. "Uh… what is happening?"

"You found me," I said, pulling back just enough to meet her eyes. "Back when I didn't know up from down. You pulled me out of the clouds. I owe you for that."

She looked a bit stunned, then let out a breathy laugh. "Okay, okay. Don't go full-on cry-fest on me."

We sat like that for a beat. The calm felt different. Something settled between us.

Then her face became a bit serious.

"You know… you saved me, Dorothy."

That caught me off guard.

"What? No. Come on. You've had it together since day one. The bravery, survival instincts, the whole leadership thing. I was the one following you."

She smirked, but her eyes didn't follow. "Maybe I did," she said. "But I was tired. Burned out from pretending like nothing got to me. Leading people. Making calls I wasn't sure about. Half of the time, I didn't even know if I wanted this life any-more."

Her voice softened, and she turned her head toward the wall. "I got so focused on getting revenge for my brother... on living the life he never got to have. Somewhere in all that, I forgot who I was. Before the battles and conflicts... before any of this."

I listened to her closely.

"Dorothy, sometimes I wonder what it would have been like to grow up with my mom. Just... being a normal kid. You've got at least a few years with yours."

"Kassi..."

She waved it off. "Nope... no need! I barely remember mine. We were always running and hiding. Those shadow monsters kept chasing us. They haunted my dreams for years. Still do, sometimes. I never know when they'll show up again."

"Do you think they were agents of Archon?" I asked.

She stared at the floor. "We thought so at first. But they didn't move like people. They didn't feel Ozian. It was like they were... something else."

She shook her head. "I told people. No one believed me. Maybe I was just a scared kid making up monsters where there weren't any. "

I reached out and squeezed her hand. "Real or not, you're not facing them alone anymore. You've got me. We're basically sisters now."

She snorted but squeezed my hand back. "You're such a sap. Just don't get me all emotional in front of the guys. I've got a reputation."

I laughed. "Wouldn't dream of it."

"*ROOAR!!!*"

The Alpha's roar tore through the chambers again, closer this time. The whole wall vibrated as if the mountain was thinking about collapsing on top of us.

Small rocks rained down. Dust kicked up. And Leo, ever the optimist, turned to us with a raised eyebrow.

"Well, I'm taking that as our sign to keep moving. If it wants round two or brought backup, we're not sticking around for the introduction."

Kassi stood and casually brushed the dust off her pants like the ceiling hadn't just tried to cave in around us.

"Let it come," she said, deadpan. "I'm ready."

Of course, she was.

Cro stepped out of the shadows with that usual spark in his eye and a grin like he'd just solved an impossible puzzle.

"Tin's ready to roll," he announced. "Actually, he's better than ever."

Right on cue, Tin stepped into the lantern glow, armor catching the light like he'd just come off a repair bay.

"Affirmative," he said, and his eyes flashed once before he blurred forward in a burst of speed, kicking up a trail of dust behind him.

Leo couldn't help himself. He raised his arm, tapped his palm, and fired off a clean pulse of energy that sizzled against the far wall.

"Limited charge," he said, grinning, "but it'll do the trick."

I looked around at the team: Kassi standing firm, Cro checking his tech with a focused gleam, Leo looking like he just discovered electricity, and Tin back on his feet like nothing could stop him now.

"Yeah. Looks like we got our second wind!" I said, "Let's keep going."

* * *

"The signal's coming from here," Tin said. His eyes lit up the shadows as he pointed to a rusted elevator cage dangling over a shaft so deep it felt like it could swallow the world. The frame above groaned in the stale air like it was trying to warn us off.

I edged closer and peered into the black hole. Even with all I'd been through, heights like this still made my stomach twist.

"This is deep," I muttered, hugging my arms. "Deeper than anything I've ever worked on."

Leo tapped the old control panel as if he expected it to fall apart under his fingers. "You're seriously telling me this thing still works? Because it looks like a one-way ride to ghost town."

"I hate elevators," I said. No point sugarcoating it.

"Same," Kassi agreed. "Feels like a metal coffin on a wire." She turned to Cro. "Tell me there's another way."

"There's not. Tin's right… the signal's straight down. If there were a side route, I'd already be dragging us through it."

"ZIT! … ZIT! … ZIT!"

Tin jerked backward abruptly, tensing up as a mechanical buzz erupted. His hands flew to his head as he collided with the wall, staggering and sparking.

"Whoa… Tin, what's wrong?" Cro shouted.

"Tin!" I rushed forward, but he held up a hand to stop me. Leo and Kassi were already at his side, ready for anything.

Cro's fingers flew over his scanner. "His readings just spiked…. wait… Something tried to break into his system… externally."

"A hack?" I asked, already knowing the answer.

"Exactly," Cro confirmed. "A high-frequency override attempt. Whatever it was, it vanished before I could get a trace."

Before we could regroup, a low roar rolled through the tunnel… this time it wasn't the alpha, it was something else. The ceiling trembled again, followed by a loud explosion.

"Okay, be on your guard," Leo said.

"No way that thing's got reinforcement," Kassi said, already drawing her blasters.

"Multiple hostiles inbound. Six units. They're fast," Tin reported.

I knew what we needed to do. "Cro, get that elevator moving now."

Cro dropped to the panel immediately, tools in hand.

Leo cracked his neck as if this were a warm-up drill. He took a position in front of the shaft. "Blaster team, front and center." He shot me a grin. "Try not to get hurt, okay?"

Kassi slipped beside me, keeping her stance low. "We'll tear this place apart first."

Then Tin collapsed.

His body just gave out. Sparks flashed from his joints as he hit the ground.

"System integrity… compromised," he managed to say before his voice glitched out.

"No, no, no," I dropped beside him, grabbing his shoulder. "Stay with us, Tin."

"VOOSH!!!"

High-pressured wind cut through the air. Six sleek drones burst into the chamber, each with a glowing green optic. They hovered, weapons humming.

Drone: "Hand over the unit designated as Tin. Resistance is futile."

"Over our dead bodies," I said, with my wand charged.

Kassi never wavered. "We'll take you all."

Leo groaned. "We're doing one-liners now? Great. Just watch your aim."

Cro shouted from the panel, "Almost there!"

I ducked underneath and swung my wand with force. Sparks erupted as I smashed its bottom frame. It fell like a brick.

The others hesitated.

Just for a second.

Then they swarmed.

Kassi rolled left and fired—two drones dropped instantly.

Leo slid behind a pillar, fired off a clean blast, and blew another pair apart. Plasma hissed through the air.

"Cro… *now!*" Leo barked.

Cro slammed the switch, and the elevator groaned to life with all the grace of a dying engine.

Another one of the drones dove at me, claws spinning like a blender set to murder.

"Take *this!*" I shouted as I slammed my wand straight into its core. More sparks showered the floor as it fell apart mid-air.

Another drone swooped low, blaster cannons glowing. I ducked, and just before it could shoot, Tin burst up from the ground. He seized the drone in mid-air and tore it in half, like a leaf from a tree.

Parts clattered everywhere. Tin swayed slightly, then steadied.

"I will assist," he said, holding out a metal hand.

He raised his arm, took aim, and fired a focused blast that clipped a drone's wing. It spun out like a broken toy and smashed into the far wall.

I met his eyes. "I've got a plan. You in?"

He didn't hesitate. "Yes."

Then they arrived in a group… fifteen or possibly more. They surged forward, with green lights flashing and weapons ready.

"Leo, Kassi, get behind Tin, keep firing!" I shouted.

They moved without question.

Tin stepped forward and raised both arms. A glowing shield fixed into place, taking every blast that came at us.

"Cro, elevator ready?" I called.

Cro grinned, "Good to go!"

"This has to work," I muttered.

I broke from cover and ran toward the far corner. The others kept the drones focused just as I'd hoped. I ducked low behind a pile of debris and whispered under my breath:

I closed my eyes and whispered, "Eternal spirit of self and the force of nature, please merge…"

Power built inside me. Heat and energy twisted around my wand.

"*…Yes. This is it. I feel it.*"

I stood.

And let it loose.

SHZZZZZZM!

Lightning exploded from the tip of my wand, arcing across the chamber in a blinding flash. Drones jerked mid-air—stopped, shook, collapsed. Their green eyes blinked out one by one.

Leo's jaw dropped. "Dee… what in Oz was that?!"

No time to explain.

I lifted my arm again and sent a blast of wind slicing across the floor. Broken drones flew like trash in a twister.

"Tin, now!"

He dropped the shield and fired. Leo and Kassi followed with their own blasts. The tunnel entrance crumbled as rock and metal fell in massive chunks. Dust choked the air.

I sank to my knees and stared at my hands.

"I think… I finally got it now."

Cro snapped me back. "No time to celebrate, move!"

We ran into the waiting elevator. It groaned as it started to drop. The shaft swallowed us in darkness. A faint lamp blink above.

"We're close," Tin said. "The signal is just below."

We all sighed in relief. For now, we were safe.

I looked around at the others. They bruised, sweaty, tired, but alive.

"You all were amazing back there," I said.

Leo side-eyed me. "Yeah, yeah, but what was that? Since when can you fry a drone army like its nothing?"

Kassi elbowed me gently. "Whatever you are now, I believe in it."

Cro snorted, digging through his kit like always. "Told you she was special. Let's go, Tempest Maiden!"

I smiled, shaking my head. "Don't get carried away. I'm still figuring it out."

Tin's glowing eyes softened. "The answers you seek may lie below."

Then, "***CLANK!***"

"More drones!" Kassi shouted, pointing up.

Blaster fire rained down. One shot hit the elevator cables, then another. Tin threw himself between us and the sparks, but it was too late.

The cable snapped.

We fell.

Wind roared in the shaft. Debris and sparks flew like lightning.

"Hold on!" Tin yelled.

"CRAAASHHHH!!!"

Drone: "TARGET TERMINATED. RETRIEVAL TEAM INBOUND."

CHAPTER TWENTY-SIX

"**SNAP!**"

That was the sound of the cable giving up on life. Next thing I knew, we were falling. Straight down.

Air screamed past my ears, my stomach shot up to my throat, and for a terrifying second, gravity felt like a bad joke.

"**CLANK!**"

Tin grabbed us mid-drop like a high-speed rescue hero. His internal gears howled in protest, but he held on.

"Brace yourselves!" Tin called out. I could barely hear him as I protected my head. He swung us toward a metal grate, punched through it in the air like it was paper, and pulled us into a chute hidden behind it.

He twisted himself to take the hit first. We slammed into the chute, bouncing and scraping against each other like a bunch of loose parts in a box. I hit something sharp and yelled. My shoulder burned. The whole world spun.

"CRAAASHHHH!!!"

The elevator plummeted to the bottom of the shaft with destructive force.

Chunks of metal and rock rained down. A cloud of dust and debris followed, filling the chute behind us. I could only cough and struggle to breathe. Dust got in my nose, my lungs, and everywhere around me. My arms shook as I tried to lift myself up.

"Ugh," I groaned, grabbing my shoulder. "Okay... that... sucked."

"Excellent escape plan," Kassi rasped as she flopped on her back, coughing up a storm.

Leo sat up, wincing and holding his ribs. "Hey, we're alive, aren't we?"

Tin's eyes glowed faintly in the low light as he scanned us all as if we were his system diagnostics.

"Minimal injuries," he announced. "Apologies. That was the best exit plan we had. The enemy likely thinks we are dead. Estimated chance: 95%."

Cro winced and rolled his shoulders. "Well, considering the other option was death, I'll take the bruises. Nice work, big guy."

"Agreed," I said, brushing dust out of my hair. "Thanks, Tin. Really."

"If they believe I've been destroyed, they'll still try to confirm it," Tin warned. "We don't have much time."

He pointed down a narrow stairwell, already shifting into motion.

I rubbed my arm. "Okay, okay… just give me a sec… wait, what's this?"

"BEEP!"

It was coming from me.

I pulled out my compass and nearly dropped it. For the first time since I entered these tunnels, it was glowing brightly and clearly, with the needle pointing directly east.

"We're not blocked anymore. Yes," I whispered, clutching it tight.

Cro was already on the move, pulling a launcher from his gear like it was nothing. He aimed straight up the shaft and fired. A small drone zipped out, blinked once, then disappeared into the dark.

Leo raised an eyebrow. "Uh… what was that?"

Cro holstered the launcher and smirked. "Just a little insurance."

"Let's go before they double-check our 'deaths.'" Kassi said.

No arguments. We hurried after Tin, our boots clanging on metal steps.

* * *

The deeper we went, the colder it got. Every step made the stairwell creak like it was about to give up on holding us. The railing was flaking rust, and the whole place smelled like damp metal. We counted ten flights down, a spiral of steel that felt like the inside of a giant machine.

At the bottom, we finally saw it.

The elevator wreck.

It looked bad.

Twisted beams, shattered panels, wires sparking in the dark. Smoke curled up from the mess like ghosts.

Then we heard voices.

DRONE: "VISUAL CONFIRMATION: NEGATIVE. SCANNERS: OBSTRUCTED."

DRONE: "INITIATE SECONDARY SWEEP. TARGET MUST BE LOCATED."

The drones were just past the wreckage, their red eyes scanning like searchlights. One twitch in our direction and we were toast.

"BEEP. BEEP. BEEP."

An alarm screamed, breaking the quiet. We all got tense and looked up.

A tiny blinking light flashed at the top of the shaft. It was a low pulse that was getting louder. The drones jerked, their eyes snapping up, and they shot straight up into the air.

Right into Cro's trap.

"You're welcome," Cro said, brushing dust off his jacket.

Kassi gave him a playful shove as we slipped into the stairwell. "Show-off."

Tin scanned the wreckage ahead and pointed at a bent doorway. The folded metal was barely held in place by the crash. We slipped through the gap. Tin wedged a loose beam to keep the door shut. It wouldn't last forever, but it only needed to hold for a few minutes.

"Whoa, take a look at this," Cro whispered.

Inside, we found a room containing a real door made of thick steel with reinforced corners, and pressure gauges still glowing. It appeared impossible to open.

"Hmm, low-tech steam power is enforced here," Cro examined. "This is a bit tricky."

Kassi crossed her arms. "Uh…so, can you get this open, Tin?"

"I can, but the pressure released from the steam would risk too much noise. It wouldn't be ideal."

"This can't be a dead end for us?" Leo said. "Dee, what does your compass show?"

"The same from earlier," I answered.

I stepped closer, studying the walls. Up near the ceiling was a vent cover with a familiar grid pattern.

"Wait a moment," I said, pointing. "That's Emeraldian design. My dad used to repair vents like these in the dome. They are built for maintenance and crawl-throughs. I'm pretty sure they lead to the other side."

Tin scanned it and nodded. "Dimensions confirm. It's large enough for us to pass through one at a time."

"Perfect. Let's get this vent open carefully," Cro said in a low voice.

Kassi and Cro moved next to me as Tin and Leo carefully pried the panel loose. One by one, we crawled inside the narrow vent with Tin's help. The air inside was stale and tight.

"Signal strength from earlier is increasing," Tin said. "We are on the right path."

"Good! It won't be long now." I said.

* * *

We had been crawling for a few minutes. My arms were sore, the walls of the vent were warm and too close, and every turn made me feel like we were just going in circles. After a while, I stopped checking how much time had passed. Just when I thought I couldn't go on, Tin pressed a panel at the end.

It creaked, popped loose, and light spilled in. One by one, we climbed out.

And… wow.

The second I stepped into that space, I knew we were way out of our depth.

Kassi crept forward, eyes wide. "Is this… a lost city?"

Cro wiped his goggles and squinted. "Not a city… but it might as well be."

Leo and I just stood there, totally speechless.

Tin's optics brightened and shifted side to side. "Facility classification: energy power plant. Operational capacity: 97.3 percent."

"Wait… this is a power plant?" I said, turning in a slow circle. "It looks like an ArcCity replica."

This place was huge.

Giant steel towers rose up everywhere, connected by massive pipes and walkways. Mechanical arms moved on tracks overhead, fixing and adjusting machines I didn't even recognize. Everything moved with perfect timing, and you could feel the energy everywhere. The plant looked like it had never shut down.

"Why would all this be running?"

"Look over here!" Leo called, pointing to a rusted console with a blinking screen.

He brushed off the thick dust. The old console groaned as it came to life. Static hissed across the display, then a bright map appeared.

"The plant's divided into sectors," he said, taking a closer look.

Four sections lit up one by one, each with its own diagram and a pre-recorded woman's voice that sounded too cheerful:

"Welcome to Nome Technologies —Where Tomorrow Is Engineered Today. Now initiating AER facility overview. Please enjoy your guided investment preview."

"Nome Technoligies? Has anyone ever heard of this company before? Cro? Tin?"

"Can't say I have," Cro said.

"The only information I was able to retrieve indicates that it was formerly a significant energy mining corporation during the previous era," Tin stated.

"Okay, Leo, can you just go through every sector?" Kassi asked. "It's best we know what we are in for."

"Got it," Leo said. "I'll select the main overview option first."

"You have selected Main Overview. Nome's Advanced Energy and Research facility, or AER is a fully integrated powerhouse combining high-yield energy production with cutting-edge experimentation. Its four core sectors—Bio-Research, Circuit Grid, Reactor, and Operations—work in harmony to deliver scalable power, adaptive innovation, and total environmental control."

"Please select the sector you want to learn about first."

Leo tapped Sector A.

"Sector A houses our **Bio-Containment Research Suites,** *where dozens of glowing incubation chambers operate in perfect harmony. Behind frosted glass,* **next-gen biological samples evolve** *under the care of micro-articulated servo arms. From synthetic gene cultures to energy-adaptive flora, the research here at AER is not only active but also decades ahead."*

"I'm not the only one hearing it, am I?" Cro asked, scratching his head. "It's kind of weird how happy she sounds talking about genetic modification."

"Agreed!" Kassi and I chimed in at the same time.

Leo also nodded while tapping the screen again. "I'm sure it won't be the last!" He added.

"Step into the nerve center of pure potential!"

"And there it is again," Cro said.

"Sector B hosts our advanced **Circuit Grid Array,** *where energy doesn't just move, it breathes. Conductive mesh panels embedded in the floor and walls deliver power across the entire facility with seamless precision. Your very footsteps vibrate with voltage. This sector is a living network, capable of powering small cities or entire satellite colonies."*

"Hold on, guys, my computer readings show a massive power surge here, *Sector C: Reactor Division.*" Cro said as he reached over Leo and tapped the information for Sector C.

"Here lies the beating heart of AER. Sector C contains our flagship **Fusion-Core Reactor,** *wrapped in a crown of high-frequency coils. Energy rushes through a network of superconductive pipes in controlled waves. Every hiss of steam and buzz of current signals stability at scale. Built for longevity. Fueled for greatness."*

"That's an emerald energy reactor," Tin said. "It appears to be the largest structure in this facility. We'll need to conduct a thorough investigation into how it's been running with proper maintenance."

"Finally, Sector D," Leo said as he chose the last option on the screen.

"Power is nothing without precision. Towering above it all is the **Operations Command Division**, *a fortress of reinforced glass and stainless alloy. Inside, our AI governance system oversees every node, transmission, and variable in real time. Efficiency? Flawless. Oversight? Unmatched. Expect nothing less than excellence at AER."*

"Dorothy… there it is," Kassi said, pointing at the tallest tower far off in the distance.

The command center rose above everything else. Its steel frame was wrapped in reinforced glass, and an antenna on top pulsed with soft light.

"Thank you for touring Nome's Advanced Energy and Research facility. A future this powerful deserves partners as visionary as you."

"Guys… This is it," I said. "The answers are in there. I can feel it."

"Warning: potential hostiles closing in." Tin alerted.

We started forward, but his voice stopped us cold. Somewhere up ahead, metal boots clanged against steel, but they didn't get any closer. Just enough sound to spike my nerves.

"Sentries," Cro whispered, looking through the console. "This isn't just a tour guide map. It's a registry. It shows every security bot and drone in the facility."

We gathered around as he scrolled through rows of schematics, patrol routes, and even recharge schedules. The people who built this place documented everything about the facility on this small console.

"Can you load it into your network?" I asked, eyes still locked on the screen.

"Aleady done," Cro said without missing a beat. He nodded to Tin.

"Data integrated," Tin confirmed.

And just like that, we were inside their system now.

Red-eyed drones glided through the plant, scanning the walkways above. The sound of heavy machines stomped on the pathways below, their armor reflecting the powerful lights above.

Kassi kept a hand near her belt. "Yep. We are 100% not welcome here."

"No kidding," Leo said under his breath.

Cro kept tapping, his eyes racing across the data. "This place isn't just automated. It's locked down like a fortress."

"Look over there," Leo said, pointing.

"Heavies," Cro murmured.

They were twice the size of the scouts we'd faced before, with combat plates and fluid movements.

Kassi took a step back. "So, who in Oz is running this place?" she asked.

"BZZZZ"

"Hmm? What's this about?"

The compass in my hand vibrated again. The signal hadn't faded since we entered this place. It was pulling us forward, straight to the center.

"Alright," I said, holding the compass tightly. "Now we know what we're up against. And this is pointing right at the heart of it."

Leo looked at the sentry patterns projected on the screen. "So… we're walking into a death trap. Cool."

"We're not going anywhere without a plan," I said. "First, we find somewhere safe, then we figure out how to get to the core without getting caught."

"I'm in," Kassi nodded. "Let's move before the sentries switch their routes."

We slipped away from the console and into the shadows. Cro scanned ahead. "I see a couple of spots that might work. Give me two minutes."

Everyone shook their head.

Kassi tightened her gear belt and peeked up at the rooftops. "Be careful. These bots can show up any second."

Up ahead, the path split into twisting paths, open courtyards, and narrow alleys. Patrols were everywhere. Drones hovered above while sentries and heavies marched below. Their sensors swept the city in a constant rhythm.

Still, even if they hadn't spotted us yet, I couldn't shake the feeling that we were being watched. I brushed it off for now and we followed Cro as he led the way, sticking to the shadows under the old catwalks.

There was complete focus.

We moved in low, slow steps, our pace matching the thumping sound of the glowing reactor in the distance. It vibrated the ground beneath us like the beat of a drum.

"ZAPPP!!!"

"Tin!" I shouted.

Electrostatic and smoke came from Tin as he stumbled.

His joints froze, then jerked like someone had hit pause and fast-forward at the same time. His vision went glitchy. Then he suddenly snapped his head up, like something had taken control.

"His core drives are glitching again, no… worse," Cro panicked. "Something's hijacking him."

"Tin?" I whispered, bracing myself for what was to come.

"SCREEEH!!!"

A horrible sound came out of his vocal box. Cro was on him in seconds, tools already out.

"WHAM!"

He backhanded Cro across the room like a rag doll. Cro hit the wall hard and groaned, but somehow still kept his grip on his gear.

"Cro!" we yelled, the sound swallowed by the shock.

Before we could move, Tin's head snapped toward us. His menacing optics instantly flared, burning a lethal, focused red. Kassi, Leo, and I froze, our hands already hovering over our blasters.

"StAy... aWaY!"

Tin's voice broke through the static, sounding like it had been chewed up and spat out. Every inch of him tensed as if he were fighting to hold something in.

Kassi edged forward, but her fingers didn't move from her belt. "He's still in there. I can tell."

Cro coughed from the floor, struggling to sit up. "... This isn't just a bug... It's a full-on rewrite... s...someone is trying to take Tin over completely..."

Leo raised his rifle slightly, just in case. "We need a backup plan. Quick!"

"I've got one," I said, and stepped out from the line.

"Dee, wait!" Leo hissed.

I kept moving.

Tin's metal hands squeezed so tight I could hear his joints whining in protest. His optics flashed a frantic red and white, like a system crash in progress.

"You're not a weapon," I told him, forcing the words through a tight throat. "You're not some piece of machinery they can just turn on and off."

He glanced at me, his focus barely registering my presence. I took another step forward.

"SYSTEM... COMPROMISED!!..."

"You're not theirs," I said, still inching closer. "You never were."

He grabbed one of his arms to restrain himself from hurting me.

"DOROTHY...YOU... NEED TO MOVE!!..."

I continued. "You don't belong to them. You belong with us. Fight Tin. Fight it!"

Another screech came out of his speakers. I backed away from the noise, covering my ears.

Then everything went still.

Tin dropped to his knees.

He hands gripped his head as if he could tear out whatever was controlling him. His optics flared red one last time before it completely faded away.

"Is he...himself?"

Tin's powerful frame slumped forward, his vents hissing out a rush of air. His hostile red optics turned white again.

I exhaled in relief.

"Phew... He's back... That was close..."

A wave of relief washed over us, and everyone started catching their breath, having forgotten how long we'd been holding it.

Cro groaned from the ground. "Okay, new rule: no more red-eyed Tin surprises, alright?"

Kassi let out a sigh. "Glad you're back, metal-head."

"Thank you, Dorothy. Thank you all," he said, recovering his voice.

He paused for a moment.

"And... I apologize for my recent burst of malfunctions. I have been a burden to this team."

I saw a look of sadness on his face.

Leo shrugged, slinging his rifle behind him. "Come on, Tin. We've all had our 'oops' moments. It's our brand at this point!"

Kassi crouched beside Tin. "Hate to break it to you, big guy, but you're imperfect like us. You may even be more Ozian the robot a this point. And anyway, it's hot-head and boy genius over there who've been the trouble lately."

"Hey!" I exclaimed, pretending to be offended.

Cro, brushing dirt off his jacket. "I'll have you know this 'boy genius' is the reason we're still breathing."

Tin turned to Cro worried. "Cro, are you ok? I wasn't myself, I…"

"Yeah, yeah, we know buddy! You're all set with me." He tapped on his tablet, eyes scanning for alerts.

"Look, the good news is your meltdown didn't trigger any alarms. The bad news: this hacker is very active. We can't just sit around waiting for another attack."

Tin, now more stable, lifted a finger and pointed.

"The signal trace directs to Sector A's data laboratory."

I followed his gaze. The lab towered beyond the courtyard. The windows were pitch black, but strange lights blinked from inside.

"Okay, thats kind of spooky."

Leo cut through the silence. "So guys, what's the move? Command center first, or the hacker issue?"

The group went quiet, thinking hard. I looked at my tired but focused team.

"We hit the command center," I decided. "That's where the answers are like who's running this place, and the truth about the spire."

"I may have to go with you on that one, Dee," Leo said.

Cro shook his head immediately. "Not unless we deal with that security blitz first. That network override is locking everything down."

"Cro has a correct assessment," Tin confirmed. "Disabling the override should be the first priority."

The debate hit a standstill. Everyone had great points. But we needed to decide fast.

Kassi sighed, breaking the tension. "Come on, guys, there's an easy solution to this... We split up."

"Split up?" we all asked at once.

She just nodded, her mind already made up.

The idea meant double the risk, but it also meant double the coverage. It was crazy, but the more we talked about it, the more it made sense.

In the end, we all agreed.

Cro nodded slowly. "Fine. Tin and I will hit the data lab. Shut down the hacker, hijack security, open a path for you guys."

"Affirmative," Tin said, his voice more stable now.

Leo rolled his shoulders and cracked his knuckles. "I'll take one of the towers. Get a high vantage point, covering both groups. If anything moves, I'll see it."

That left Kassi and me.

I turned to her. "You and I will go to the main headquarters. If there's a control module tied to that spire, that's where it'll be. We find it and figure out who's really behind all this."

Cro pulled up a map on his wrist pad. "Comms are synced. We stay in contact. Any movement, any new info, report immediately."

Tin scanned the corridors ahead and nodded. "Acknowledged."

Leo tapped his comm. "Just try not to cause a scene before I'm in position."

I grinned. "You know me. Trouble always seems to find me."

Everyone joined in, saying, "We know!"

Leo shook his head and got his rifle ready. "As always... I've got your back."

We all took a deep breath as we all headed in our directions with a new sense of purpose.

This was our only shot.

Whatever we discovered in that lab, and in that command tower… it was going to change everything.

***

(DOROTHY)

The power plant was honestly like a whole city built just for machines. Kassi and I moved like shadows through the alleyways. Every corner looked like a trap waiting to happen.

Little maintenance bots zipped past us, busy fixing things that didn't even look broken. According to the bot directory, these guys had only one job. They didn't seem to care about us, but I didn't trust a single thing in this place.

I kept glancing at the compass in my hand. It was still glowing, still pointing straight toward the command center.

"Hey Kassi, whoa—"

Kassi yanked me behind a stack of crates and put a finger to her lips. Two guards walked by with powerful legs clanging on the floor.

Heavies.

"Way too close," Kassi whispered, and we slipped out, cutting down another corridor.

Then — **"WHIRRRRR."**

A drone floated right in front of me.

My hand went to my wand. I knew if I didn't stop it, it would call for backup. I started to raise my wand. The drone began to charge its cannon—

"Stop!" Kassi blurted.

And… the drone stopped immediately, freezing in midair. No movement. No sound.

"Wh… what did you just do?" I asked, lowering my wand.

Kassi looked scared and confused. "I-I don't know. I told it to stop."

I stared at her as if she'd grown antennae.

"Okay, that was weird." I zapped it just to be sure. It convulsed and dropped like a rock.

Leo's voice buzzed in my ear. "That was either luck or something else entirely. Let's not wait to find out. Keep going."

We stuck to the low-lit areas while drones hovered overhead, guards flanked the doorways, and spotlights swept the pathway like angry eyes. We fought only when necessary, making every takedown quick and quiet.

After moving around so much, our lungs were screaming for a break. We finally found a spot where we could drop and just gasp for air.

"You're getting good at this whole stealth thing," Kassi whispered, breathing heavily.

I exhaled. "Surviving out here kind of forces you to learn fast."

"By the way, I've been meaning to ask," she said, leaning on the nearby wall. "Your abilities. What's it like using it?

I shrugged. "Honestly? I'm not sure what to compare it to. Sometimes it feels like I'm borrowing it, like it doesn't fully belong to me. But then there are moments where it's... clear. Like it's coming from something deep inside, just waiting for me to tap into it."

She shook her head slowly. "You said it didn't always work, right? So... what if it started with that storm? The one from the day we met. Maybe that twister flipped some switch in you."

As we started walking again, I glanced down at the floor. "Yeah, that's been on my mind lately too. That first twister stirred something in me. I've also been learning a lot from the Codex Mother Uru gave me."

"Oh yeah, I noticed you reading that book from time to time. You're gonna have to update me on all of that," she said,

I smirked. "Deal. But we keep walking."

As we crept through the next alleyway toward the tower, I filled her in on the Codex and the Tempest Order, detailing my family's legacy.

Needless to say she was shocked.

"Dorothy, what in the world?... Are there more people like you out there? These... Tempest Maidens?" She asked.

My head drooped. "I don't think so," I whispered. "I think I'm the last one."

Suddenly, alarms blared and red lights flashed.

"Leo? What's going on?" I asked.

"Alarm's up. Full lockdown. Stay low." He replied.

Behind us, a heavy thud echoed. Alley was filled with a digitized roar:

"TRESPASSERS DETECTED. LETHAL FORCE AUTHORIZED."

They were nearly on us before the alarm even finished. Two monstrous Heavies slamming into the alleyway like mecha-tank. They towered over us, plated in thick steel that looked as welcoming as a desert bunker.

Kassi didn't hesitate. Her blaster flared, the shot striking the nearest bot's chest plate only to fizzle away into a useless spark. I launched my own energy wand, but the beam vanished on impact; their armor soaked up the energy like dry sand.

"BOOM!"

One heavie stomped the floor, sending a electro-pulse shockwave that tore through the ground. I hit the deck hard, vision momentarily flashing with stars.

I was still dazed when a massive armored hand closed around me, and another snatched Kassi. My wand spun out of my grip and skittered across the floor.

"Dorothy!" Kassi screamed, twisting desperately in the bot's crushing hold. "I... have to... try it again!"

"No... are you serious?!" I gasped, struggling to suck air past the pressure on my ribs. "That's... not a plan!"

She ignored me completely. Her voice cut through the chaos, sharp and commanding: "STOP! PUT US DOWN! NOW!"

"CLANK!"

The Heavies froze solid, their massive frames locking up instantly.

Then they dropped us.

I landed hard, scrambled up instantly, my head still spinning.

My eyes widened as I stared at Kassi, like she was some oddity. "Hey… what are you?"

She looked down at her hands like they weren't even hers and gave this wide grin. "I think I've got powers too."

I didn't have time to process it. The two heavies still loomed over us, radiating a pure, lethal potential that could snap back at any second.

"Okay," I snapped, forcing myself to sound calm. "Tell them to shut down or die or something useful!"

Kassi stood up straight, like she'd suddenly remembered she was the boss of the world. "By order of the tempest-"

"Kassi! Be serious!" I called out.

"Yeah you are right, ill save that for another time," she said giggling at the look I gave her. "Okay. Uhh... Shut down!"

"HISS!"

With a soft, final exhaust of vents, their optics died. The giant machines went silent, collapsing into statues of dead steel. We didn't wait for them to reboot.

We ran.

Somehow my legs moved faster than my brain. I glanced sideways at her, trying to figure out what just happened.

"I don't know what's going on with you," I said, breathless, "but whatever it is, you might be our biggest secret weapon."

She smirked, still panting. "Took you long enough to notice."

I shook my head and grinned, because really, what else could I do? "Let's see how far we can ride this miracle."

* * *

Every step after that felt different. Kassi wasn't guessing anymore. She was in charge.

"Stop," she ordered, and a drone stopped in mid-air, its sensors glitching like it suddenly didn't know where it was.

"Deactivate."

Two patrol robots halted mid-step, their lights going out.

"Turn around."

Heavies turned the other way as if nothing had happened. Turrets were already down when we got there, so we took advantage of this. I didn't know how this was all happening. I didn't understand it and didn't have time to figure it out.

But I wasn't going to question a miracle when it was saving our lives.

We delved deeper into the complex, moving faster, bolder. No alarms, no battles. Just us and Kassi, rewriting every rule the system thought it had.

Then we finally saw it.

"There it is. The command tower." I said.

* * *

(LEO)

I was posted up high on one of the towers overlooking most of the plant. It was a great hiding spot with a clear view. Dee and Kassi were moving through the lower sector. They started slow, but now they were moving through the plant surprisingly like experts.

Probably helped that I'd already knocked out every turret in their way. A clear path makes everyone look better. I tapped my rifle.

"Still sharp."

A good shot isn't just about hitting the target; it's about keeping the right people alive.

I turned on my scope.

Across the lab, Cro and Tin were working perfectly together. Tin provided the muscle, but Cro moved with a planned, careful way that showed he was more than just street smart. I zoomed in and saw it was true.

The kid definitely had training.

Not the kind you get on the streets either. He was tactical. He'd be top of his class in an Emerald recon unit. Only weakness would be close quarters. You can't hack a punch. And at some point, you'll have to throw one.

"Oz to Leo! Are we clear to enter?" he called out.

I adjusted the scope and scanned the lab windows. "Sorry about that, yeah. Looks empty."

I spoke too soon.

A drone zipped overhead. I dropped flat and held my breath as it hovered nearby, then moved on.

"Too close."

I locked back in.

"We made it," Cro whispered. "Leo, are you seeing this?"

"Negative," I replied, "The wall has covered my view."

"Specimens… mobats and other creatures in tubes," Cro's reported, "They've been experimented on."

"Are they still alive?" I asked.

"Yes," Tin replied, "but unresponsive. Maybe in stasis."

If they were storing these creatures for experiments, they were probably becoming assets, like the alpha.

"Back in Emerald, there were old reports of strange beasts attacking squads. Nobody believed it," I muttered.

"Seems this practice has been going for some time," Tin said.

Cro's watch pinged. "There's movement. Large unit, next room."

"Leo," Cro whispered, "it's the alpha."

"What? How?" I asked.

"They must've retrieved it after Tin defeated it."

"That explains the fussing it was doing when we left." I replied. "Standby guys."

I switched channels. "Dee? Kassi?"

No answer.

I scoped them. They crouched behind cover while sentries swept the hall.

"Sentries will pass in ten seconds. Then move."

"Got it," Kassi whispered.

I switched back to Cro and Tin.

"Report: I've reached the lab control center," Tin said, voice even as ever. "I accessed their supercomputer… and found schematics. On me."

Cro checked another terminal. "Energy blueprints. Amberinium tech. And, uh… this feels way too easy. Like someone left the door open on purpose."

Tin's tone shifted. Just barely. "Wait. Something's off."

"ZZZTT! CLANK!"

He paused. "Interesting… The supercomputer is generating a magnetic lock. It has immobilized me. I cannot move."

"What was that? Cro—" I called over comms.

"Already moving!" Cro bolted for Tin.

Tin's voice glitched slightly. Still calm. "It appears this system… is attempting to extract… me."

"Must be that hacker," I muttered. "I'll scan the area. Checking all rooms now."

"Tin, resist it!" Cro shouted, struggling to pull Tin away. "Hit the console or use your cannons!"

"No… longer… able…" Tin's voice dropped. Static bleeding in.

"Tin!" Cro yelled. He tried shooting the console, but it had no effect.

"Theres a magnetic field shielding it!" Cro shouted.

SUPERCOMPUTER: "EXTRACTION SEQUENCE INITIATED. TWO MINUTES TO COMPLETION."

Alarms screamed, the facility instantly flooding with strobing red light.

"Of course it gets worse," I muttered, my eyes locked to the scope.

"Leo, I can't pull him out! And more enemies are probably on their way!" Cro panicked, "what do we do?!"

"Hey snap out of it, genius. You're the hacker, remember? I'll cover you. You stop that extraction. We have less than two minutes."

Cro let out a ragged breath. "Right. Terminal access. On it."

I caught movement in the entry corridor.

"Heads up. You've got company."

I fired twice, the blasts instantly dropping two sentries, but the gunfire had already drawn more bots toward our position. I took them out one by one, the sound of my blaster deafening in the metal corridor.

"Cro, move faster."

"I'm doing my best here!"

Dee's voice shot through the comms. "Leo? What's going on?"

"Dee, alarm's up. Full lockdown. Stay low."

"NINETEEN... EIGHTEEN..."

"Come on, Cro!"

"TEN... NINE..."

"Got it! I'm in!" Cro roared.

"EXTRACTION CANCELED. REACTIVATION REQUIRES MANUAL OVERRIDE."

The console released Tin, who instantly collapsed onto the floor, barely able to move.

Cro grabbed him and dragged him into cover. I picked off two drones closing in, enough to pull patrols toward me instead.

"Good. This will give them some breathing room."

Cro hesitated, eyes fixed on the alpha's chamber.

"Hey. Quit staring. You're in the clear now, lie low until the bots move on," I said.

"I've got a plan for distraction," he answered.

Using his techpad, he made his move. "System, release him. Release them all."

With full access, he popped every cage.

Stormwolves burst out, silent and deadly. Terrafoxes scurried through corridors. Squallhawks and desert gliding weasels dove at drones with precision. They weren't wild; they were trained weapons.

But the alpha was still unconscious.

Then the emergency lab doors slammed to seal the room.

I panned my scope. A heavy shadow moved in, creeping through the left corridor toward their position.

"Cro, don't move. You've got company coming in hot. Big one. Left corridor. Near the entrance."

I zoomed in. Same frame, same armor.

"No… Not again."

It was the same model that nearly killed Tin back in Howling Canyons.

The other creatures backed off. Some retreated to cages that never closed. Like they knew better than to mess with what was coming.

I fired through a window. Tried to slow it down.

Did nothing.

It spun my direction and pointed nearby drones my way. I bolted.

"You're awake!" Cro shouted.

"Good to have you back, Tin," I said. "But keep your head down, Tin. That thing's deadly."

"No. There's no need to hide." Tin replied.

"Why not?" I panted.

"My upgrades are more than sufficient for combat now. More importantly, I know who's behind this hack."

He paused. "And we're in trouble."

* * *

(DOROTHY)

We finally reached the command tower. It was even more mesmerizing to see up close.

Not just tall, but intimidating, like it wanted you to feel small just for walking near it. It loomed above all other structures, serving as the nerve center of the operation. It rose into a slender shaft and then expanded at the top into a glass-paneled control cabin.

The top floor had windows all the way around, full view of the entire plant.

And of us.

"Yep," I said, mostly to myself. "We're definitely being watched."

In front of us, the base was locked up tight. Cameras, sensors, and a blinking badge scanner; it was like the door entrance was really built to keep outsiders out. I didn't need Tin's analysis to know this place was going to be a pain to break into.

"Dorothy, look at that!" Kassi's voice pulled me back.

She pointed up at the command center's rooftop, eyes wide. Rising from the thick steel supports was a towering, slender spire forged from pure emerald and gold. It tapered to a sharp apex, its entire length pulsing with a green electrostratic

. "The Spire…" we said together.

It was mesmerizing to see. It wasn't merely a treasure; it was a huge structure radiating energy that commanded the entire plant. Every few seconds, another pulse rolled off it, like a wave. Around the edges, rusted satellite dishes jutted out at odd angles, pointing who-knows-where.

I grabbed my comm. "Dorothy to team. Come in."

Nothing but static.

I tried again, hoping it was just a glitch.

"Leo? Do you copy?"

Still nothing.

"Yeah… that's not a good sign." Kassi exhaled.

"No kidding," I muttered, "Leo's our eyes. If we can't reach him, we're basically flying blind."

She pointed to the main entrance. "And that?" she said flatly, "We're not sneaking through that."

There were cameras everywhere, all pointed right at us. There was a keycard scanner blinking red next to the doors, just in case we weren't already nervous.

A few minutes passed and I was getting anxious.

"We need to know if Cro and Tin are in the system," I said, tapping my comm again. "If they're not, we've got zero backup."

Kassi checked her signal too. "Still dead on my end."

She looked at me. "We should fall back. Make sure everyone's okay."

I nodded. "Yeah. Let's—"

I paused for a moment.

Then I spotted a faded sign right next to a smaller side door.

"RESTRICTED ACCESS ELEVATOR."

Kassi noticed.

Her arms folded instantly. "Oh no. Nope. That's the exact 'bad idea' face Leo always talks about."

I gave an innocent shrugged.

"It's risky. But, I mean, if you can control bots just by talking, don't you want to know how?"

It was a tricky move to get her on my side, and I was hoping she would fall for it.

She groaned, rubbing her forehead. "Dorothy, you're impossible."

"And you're curious."

"Fine," she said. "But the second things get weird, we're out. I *will* drag you by your pigtails if I have to."

"Deal," I said, already moving.

We walked to the door, expecting it to stay locked or set off alarms. But when I reached for it, it opened easily. No resistance. No passcode. No alarm.

Just a soft click and it was open.

Kassi and I exchanged a look.

"Nope, way too easy," she blurted.

I agreed.

But curiosity pushed us forward, anyway.

We stepped through and found ourselves in a strange hallway.

The walls were streaked with grime, the paint peeling in long, damp strips.

"What's with all these doors? Was this a corridor for supplies?" I asked, looking around.

All the steel doors were rusted shut, their swipe readers dark and dead.

Kassi sighed. "Great! A simple stockroom corridor for supplies. And here I was thinking we got lucky." She sniffed the air. "It's so stale and stuffy in here."

I pointed to the cold air seeping from the choked vents.

"Well, we know one thing for sure: no one's been here to clean for a while."

We kept walking through this dimly lit hall as some dirt crunched under our boots on the floor. Dust-caked cameras hung from the ceiling as a massive, rusted elevator stood at the far end with a keycard. We walked toward the keycard scanner only to find the elevator wouldn't open.

"Yup, and here we are, stuck... again." Kassi said, visibly annoyed.

"Hey, we can at least wait here until the others reach back to us. I mean, we can use a breather from the bots."

"Fine," she sighed as we both slid down the wall to rest for a bit.

"BEEP. BEEP. BEEP."

I looked down. My compass was flashing again.

"What's happening with you now?" I said, bothered by its beeping.

"BEEP. BEEP. BEEP."

"What's wrong with it?" Kassi asked.

"That's what I'm trying to figure out."

"Well, figure it out faster!"

I gave her a look to remind her to calm down, but I understood. I really didn't know what to do with it.

"BEEP. BEEP. BEEP."

"Wait," I said, pushed myself up. "Could it be because of this key scanner?"

"Just try it," Kassi snapped, clearly annoyed. "Anything to kill that constant beeping would be great!"

I stepped toward the scanner and held the compass up.

"BEEP. BEEP. BEEP."

"MASTER KEY ACCEPTED. PLEASE BE CAREFUL AS YOU ENTER."

We just stared at it each other.

"Master key?" we both said at once.

The elevator doors slid open with a soft groan. I quickly stood up and stepped inside. Kassi followed, her hand near her blaster.

_"Oh my..."_

Inside the elevator, it was a totally different kind of creepy.

"This is not like the hallway," Kassi whispered.

She was right. The lighting was dim, with blinking neon lights. An old, broken screen showed symbols I didn't know. The floor groaned under our feet, and through a cracked panel, I saw an endless black hole going down.

I pressed the only button that worked. The doors closed with another soft groan, and a broken voice spoke over the speaker. It was an emergency message, but it was so broken I couldn't understand a single word. In the corner, I spotted something half-buried in the dust.

A very old and worn ID card.

I picked it up and squinted. "Dr.... Diggs?"

"Looks like someone who worked here ages ago," Kassi said.

I wiped the card and kept it just in case we needed access for something later. The looping message in the speaker made the things tense.

"I really hate elevators," I muttered.

"You and me both," Kassi replied, checking her weapon. "Okay, be ready. we have no idea what's waiting for us."

I nodded and powered up my wand.

Kassi glanced at the compass. "So… it's our key now?"

"A master key, apparently," I said. "Tin mentioned something like this once. There's more to this compass then I thought."

The elevator shook as it climbed, rattling our nerves.

Kassi went silent, thinking.

Then she spoke softly. "Hey. Whatever happens to us next… I'm glad I met you."

I turned to her, surprised.

"Well, why does it have to end badly for both of us?"

"I'm trying to be sentimental, don't push it." She replied giving me a shove.

I giggled. "Don't worry, Kassi, we've got this. We are far from done."

The ride was short, but it felt like forever. It didnt help that the others with us. If something went wrong, we'd be on our own.

Still, I thought back to where it all began. Some time ago, I was digging my way through life, wondering what lay beyond the city. Now I stood at the edge of something huge.

The elevator jerked to a stop.

I closed my eyes for a second.

"Mom… Dad…today, we'll find the answers."

CHAPTER TWENTY-SEVEN

"YOU HAVE REACHED THE MAIN FLOOR OF THE OPERATIONS COMMAND TOW-ER. PLEASE EXIT SAFELY."

We didn't move. We couldn't.

"Out of all the things I expected when this door opened, I definitely didn't expect this."

Right ahead of us was another long hallway, but this one gave off a soft green glow as if it were lit from inside the ceiling. The floor was so polished that we could see our dirty boots in it. The walls were smooth, bright white, and spotless, with no marks or scratches. The place looked too clean for a plant under a mountain.

Kassi let out a low whistle. "Uh, are we sure we got off at the right stop?"

"Right. This is definitely not like the storage," I answered.

I kept my eyes ahead as I stepped forward, my boots barely making a sound. "I mean, it has to be. Let's just move carefully."

Slowly, we move forward just a bit, our reflections shining on the polished floor. Every sound seems to echo around us, adding to the eerie atmosphere. None of this feels real.

"Okay, listen up. I'll take the lead; you watch my six," Kassi said.

"Got it."

As Kassi instructed, we took our positions, standing tall with our heads high, eyes sharp, and weapons at the ready for any sudden movements. The hall curved left and ended in a large vault-like door that slid vertically.

The vault door was already wide open.

Kassi stopped at the edge, her voice dropping to a whisper. "Easy access is strange enough, but I see nothing beyond this entrance. It's pitch black, though I can feel a cool draft pulling from the inside."

Big and pitch black," I muttered, tense beside her. "This has to be the command center. So, where's the window view from that tour diagram?"

"I know, right?" Kassi agreed. "If I could just get some light in here…"

"Cro's night visors would've been our only shot," I said. I held my wand a little tighter in the darkness, then——

"BEEP."

Kassi jumped. "Tell me that's not your compass again," she whispered. "Shut it up before it gives us away."

"That wasn't me," I said, pointing. "Look."

A soft green glow bloomed at the far end of this dark room; just enough to show a sleek console tucked into the wall. Right in the middle was a handprint scanner.

Kassi eyed it suspiciously. "I really, really don't like this."

"Yeah… same," I said under my breath.

But we already knew how this part went.

We walked towards the console, and Kassi pressed her hand to the panel. A calm female voice spoke immediately.

"SYSTEM ACTIVATED. WELCOME!"

Instantly, the room came alive.

Amber lines raced across the wall accents. Green circuits glowed beneath the glossy floor. Massive screens switched on, showing maps, data streams, security footage, and atmospheric readings.

"Seriously, Dorothy…" Kassi said, her voice trailing off.

"I know Kass… you don't like this place."

In the center, a hologram of the world floated above us, while transparent barriers divided the control decks, giving everything a cutting-edge look.

I took a step back. "Kassi, I feel like we're on a comic book spaceship."

"Yeah, but this place is pristine," she murmured, staring.

"Look at this tech. Cro would go crazy," I whispered.

"Whoa, wait, what's happening with the screen?" Kassi paused.

The wall-sized screen cleared its data and showed a glowing green interface. Unexpectedly, a face formed out of streaming green code.

An A.I.

"CONGRATULATIONS. YOU HAVE REACHED SPIRE."

Kassi and I fell silent.

"This was the real thing..."

The A.I. continued, unfazed by our silence. **"IDENTITY CONFIRMED."**

Kassi stiffened.

"GREETINGS, DAWN DOROTHY VOGAN."

I froze.

It said my full name and immediately turned to Kassi.

"AND SPECIAL GREETINGS TO LADY KASSIRYN OZMA OF THE OZMA FAMILY. WELCOME."

My head snapped to Kassi. She looked sick.

"Lady Kassiryn Ozma… Ozma?" she whispered. "Dorothy, that's not my name."

I opened my mouth, but Kassi faced the A.I. again.

"What is that name? Who are the Ozma family?"

The A.I.'s face pulsed. Streams of data moved across its form.

"THE OZMA SURNAME BELONGS TO ONE OF THE ARCHON FAMILIES THAT FOUNDED THE ARC CITIES. ARCHON MEMBERS UNDERGO FULL BIOMETRIC ENCODING: PALM, RETINAL, VOICE, AND GENETIC SCANS. THESE RECORDS GRANT HIGH-LEVEL ACCESS TO RESTRICTED SECTORS."

Kassi took a step back. "Archons… Biometric and Special access?" Her voice shook. "Wait…hey… is that why I can command the bots here?"

"CORRECT. THE ARCHON LEGACY PROTOCOL AUTHORIZES RECORDED FAMILY MEMBERS TO COMMAND ALL SPIRE-LINKED AUTOMATED SYSTEMS, INCLUDING SECURITY DRONES AND SENTRY BOTS DURING VISITATIONS."

"So, the Heavies we fought…"

My thoughts were interrupted when I watched Kassi's face go pale. She was no longer just someone who grew up on the run fighting the Archons. Her family was part of the upper echelon of power.

"Kassi…" I started, but she simply raised a hand that stopped me cold.

Her eyes were unfocused, staring right through me. Her voice was flat, hollowed out by the realization. "Kassi O… Fynn knew."

"I see…" I said, realizing it. "But hey… I'm sure it was to protect you… you know he loved you."

She remained silent, her jaw growing tighter.

The A.I.'s green glow swept the room before returning its focus to me.

"IDENTIFIED: ENGINE MASTER KEY."

I stared, confused. "What?"

"ANALYZED AND CONFIRMED. THANK YOU FOR RETRIEVING THE MASTER KEY."

Kassi and I stared at the compass in my hand.

"This?" I held it up. "It's just a compass. How is this a key?"

The A.I.'s glow brightened.

"INCORRECT. IT IS A MASTER DATA KEY WITH AN ADDED IONIC COMPASS INTERFACE."

My fingers curled around this data key as the A.I. went on.

"THE KEY'S CORE ENERGY, AMBERINIUM, LETS IT INITIATE THE PLANT'S MAIN ENGINE AT FULL POWER. IT IS AN ENERGY SOURCE THAT IS NO LONGER AVAILABLE. THIS KEY IS THE ONLY ONE OF ITS KIND."

"Amberinium."

Kassi and I exchanged a quiet glance. We both thought of Tin.

"So, this lost key uses energy that doesn't even exist anymore?" Kassi asked.

"CORRECT."

"Okay, so that confirms it doesn't know about Tin."

I turned back to the A.I. "By engine, you mean… the spire, right? The tower on the rooftop?"

"…INCORRECT."

I hesitated. "What do you mean? Then what is the Spire?"

A soft whirr filled the room.

"MY SYSTEM *IS* SPIRE."

Her words hung in the air.

Kassi stood, shocked. "Did she say she is the Great Spire?"

"CORRECT. I *AM* SPIRE."

Kassi scratched her head. "Well, that changes everything."

I folded my arms. "Why are you called Spire?"

The A.I. paused, its glow shimmering.

"S.P.I.R.E.: SYNTHETIC PROCESSING INTELLIGENT RESPONSE ENTITY. OVER TIME, I WAS GIVEN MANY NAMES. MY ORIGINAL NAME AND THE OZIANS WHO BUILT ME ARE LOST TO HISTORY."

"Lost to history?" Kassi frowned.

THIS PLANT WAS NEGLECTED AND PERMITTED TO DECAY. THE ARCCITIES HAS NO RECORD OF ME. MY NETWORK COVERAGE IS SIGNIFICANTLY RESTRICTED DUE TO SEVERE WEATHER.I ONLY MAINTAIN THIS PLANT AND UPDATE ARCHON REGISTRY."

"Because you don't have enough power," I added, realizing the truth.

"CORRECT. WITHOUT ENOUGH POWER, I CANNOT RUN AT FULL CAPACITY."

Kassi shifted. "So, like what were you made for? What's your purpose?"

"MY CORE PROGRAMMING WAS TO HEAL THE ATMOSPHERE AND PRESERVE THE PLANET'S BIOSPHERE."

I paused.

"Heal? Preserve?"

Memories of Mother Uru's lesson flashed back: "… *the Ozians failed to protect the land.*"

"Are you saying we somehow ruined the world?" I asked.

"LONG AGO, EXCESSIVE UTILIZATION OF GEM ENERGY SEVERELY COMPROMISED THE ATMOSPHERE. OZIANS CONSTRUCTED ME TO FACILITATE ITS RESTORATION. REGRETTABLY, MY CLIMATE RECALIBRATION WAS UNSUCCESSFUL, RESULTING IN A WORLDWIDE CATASTROPHE THAT HAS PERSISTED FOR A CENTURY."

Kassi stared at the data wall. "So, the storms, the twisters… they came from you?"

"AN UNFORTUNATE ERROR IN MY PROGRAMMING CREATED A GLOBAL CATASTROPHE."

"That's not ominous at all," Kassi whispered under her breath.

"And the master key?" I asked.

The A.I. turned its head.

"THE MASTER KEY HAS THE ABILITY TO RESTORE MY SYSTEM, THEREBY ENABLING PROPER OPERATION AND SUFFICIENT ENERGY REQUIRED TO REVERSE ATMOSPHERIC CONDITIONS."

"So, that's it... restore her power and she will repair the world. Wow...I can't believe this is it! The world will go back to normal!"

Suddenly, the floor buzzed as a circular platform rose in the room. A green scanner glowed on top.

"KINDLY PLACE THE MASTER KEY ONTO THE ANALYZER TO FACILITATE SYSTEM INTEGRATION. UPON ACTIVATION, MY REACTOR CORE WILL INITIATE THE FIRST SEQUENCE FOR ATMOSPHERIC RESTORATION. THANK YOU FOR YOUR COOPERATION."

I just stared.

It looked so simple.

A single motion might have the power to fix the world. Something we risked our lives for this entire time. I took a step forward and glanced at Kassi, who looked nervous and uncertain. Honestly, I felt the same way, but we knew we had to try.

"DOROTHY COME IN... DOROTHY, CAN YOU HEAR ME?... IF YOU ARE GETTING THIS, STOP WHATEVER YOU ARE DOING!"

Cro's voice tore through my comms.

I froze, hand mid-air.

"Cro?" I said. "Are you okay? What is it?"

"Don't give her the key!" His voice scratched. "It's not just a master key; it's the core to the Tempest Engine."

"The... Tempest Engine?"

I looked at the compass in my hand, heart pounding.

"What is Cro talking about...Is he for real?

I looked at Kassi, who also heard the same thing. Her expression seemed more convinced that something was off, but we chose not to say it directly.

"What should I do?"

* * *

(LEO)

The lab was dead quiet. Just the soft crackle of fried circuits in the air. I stayed scoped in, watching what was left of the bot that almost leveled us. Chunks of metal still smoked on the floor.

"Wow…" I muttered. "That was—"

"Terrifying?" Cro said, not looking away from Tin.

"I was gonna say impressive," I said. "But yeah, terrifying fits."

We both stared. Tin stood tall over the wreckage, calm as ever. Not a single dent on him. I'd seen him in fights before, but this? This was different.

"I know you scavenged some solid gear from that mobat nest," I said, "but I didn't expect this kind of power boost."

Cro smirked, just a little. "Yeah, I upgraded his systems. But it's more than the parts. Tin's evolving on his own."

I was about to ask what he meant when Tin turned toward us.

"That conclusion is highly likely," he said.

We both paused.

"It appears to be a combination of the amberinium in my core and my adaptive learning matrix," he explained. "That said, I believe I'm still not performing at full capacity."

I raised a brow. "You call that underperforming?"

Tin didn't answer. His optics flashed once.

"I have more important news," he said. "About the system breach I allowed."

Cro stiffened. "You let it happen?"

"It was a tactical decision," Tin responded. "I limited its access and utilized the breach as an opportunity to collect data."

Tin looked directly at Cro. "SPIRE was never an antenna, but an entire AI system aslo identified a by another name. I am... familiar with her. She represents the most advanced artificial intelligence. Moreover, her intentions are malicious.

I felt sick. "SPIRE? Wait... you mean—"

"Affirmative," Tin concluded. "She is the origin of the storms that are wreaking havoc upon this region and the world."

"Dee... You were right about the Spire... but this is wrong. Everything about this is wrong.'

"What does it, or she want?" Cro asked.

"That is my concern," Tin responded. "This facility is not an ordinary control network. It is deliberate and targeted. Furthermore, she might be utilizing Dorothy and Kassi to activate her engine."

"What engine?" I asked.

Tin turned to the thick glass wall as if he could see through it. "The core reactor in Sector C. The AI system calls it the *Tempest Engine*. It was designed to regulate atmospheric health conditions and massive weather systems."

Cro snapped his head around. "The only reason an AI would need that kind of energy is for major processing power."

"Correct," Tin stated. "She plans to augment its output and expand its reach. If successful, the consequences will be substantial."

None of us spoke.

"We thought this was some hacker messing around. But it's been SPIRE the whole time." I pondered.

I am not entirely certain about that," Tin said. "However, it does know I carry amberinium.

Cro looked at Tin. "Why does that matter?"

Because SPIRE is unable to operate the engine without an amberinium source.

I let that land.

"So, if it gets just enough—"

"It will activate the engine," Tin confirmed.

Cro's expression darkened. "And that makes it unstoppable."

Tin gave a single nod. "We cannot afford to waste time."

I rubbed my jaw. "But it couldn't pull amberinium from Tin. So, we're in the clear, right?"

Cro didn't answer.

"Cro," I pushed.

He looked up slowly. "The compass… it's got amberinium in it."

"What?" I blurted out.

"You heard me," he said.

"Tin, tell me he's wrong."

"He is not, "Tin replied. "When I charged it, I suspected it was a data key, but I am now certain."

Cro and I stared at each other.

"So, the AI," I pondered out loud, "planned all of this. It led Dee here."

Tin nodded. "Yes. Once SPIRE found the key, it most likely manipulated events to ensure her arrival."

"Like the alpha," Cro whispered. "We walked right into its trap."

I grabbed my comm. "Dee. Kassi. Do you copy?"
Silence.

"Dee, come in. Kassi, can you hear me?"
Only static.

"What's going on?" I shouted.

Cro tapped his device and muttered, "They're in a dead zone."

"A natural dead zone?" I asked.

"No," Tin said. "It's artificial. A targeted communication block. I detect wave patterns that confirm it."

I raised my scope and scanned the tower. I expected to see them fighting their way in. Instead, they were already inside.

"You mean to tell me that all this time, they've been stuck inside with no way to reach us?" I said, panic rising. "How had they gotten past all the defenses so fast?"

Cro pulled up his surveillance feed. "That's not right."

Tin tilted his head, calculating. "There are no signs of battle. The bots obeyed a direct command. That override level points to SPIRE."

"This keeps getting worse." I am worried.

Cro started typing. "We have to reach them."

"How?" I asked. "We're locked out."

"If I can breach the outer firewall, I might kill the signal block long enough to send a warning."

"And if you can't?" I asked.

He shrugged. "Then we do it the old-fashioned way… in person."

Tin advanced. "I might be aware of a faster route."

"Whatever it is," I said, "we'd better move."

I glanced back at the tower.

"Dee. Kassi. Hang tight. We're coming."

* * *

(DOROTHY)

I held the compass tight. My feet wouldn't move. My hands wouldn't let go. I wasn't giving it up.

"IS THERE A PROBLEM, DAWN DOROTHY VO-GAN?"

"I… I just need a second," I said, forcing my nerves down.

"TIME IS OF THE ESSENCE. THE MORE TIME WE FORFEIT, THE MORE SEVERE THE MAGNETIC ABRASION WITHIN THE ATMOSPHERE BECOMES. ULTIMATELY, I WILL LACK THE NECESSARY POWER TO MEND IT."

I took a slow breath. "Fine. But first… what exactly is the Tempest Engine?"

Silence.

"What is this? No response?"

"I asked you a question," I said, my voice sharper. "What is it?"

"IS THIS NOT THE PURPOSE OF YOUR ARRIVAL? TO SAVE THE WORLD?"

Kassi stepped forward. "That's not an answer. That's a dodge."

I rubbed the compass, feeling suspicious. "How do you know my purpose?"

Again, silence.

"Have you been spying on me?" I demanded.

"I INFERRED YOUR PURPOSE BASED ON YOUR PRESENCE HERE."

I stepped closer. "Then tell me… what you know about the Tempest Engine?"

The room grew still with unspoken tension again.

"Answer her," Kassi snapped. "You obey voice commands, right?"

Suddenly, her face disappeared.

"Where did she go?"

"I don't know. Dorothy, be on your guard. Keep that compass close."

The green lights dimmed, and a whirring sound filled the entire command center.

A chill crawled up my arms.

"Ha…ha ha ha. It won't work on me!"

"Was that the A.I. just now?" I whispered, keeping my guard.

Then, the room changed. The glowing lights turned sharp neon green. The global hologram shifted to a robotic eye. The green screen glowed deep purple.

Then, there was the change of the A.I. voice and tone.

"Oh, you're sharper than I expected."

All the monitors joined to form one image. A shape emerged from the static. Not entirely human, not fully machine.

She moved both smoothly and unreal. Violet light danced over her full form. Her eyes locked onto mine… bright, cold, with a devilish grin.

"Let's drop the formalities, shall we?

Kassi and I were stunned by the entire sequence.

"You may call me… *VYA*."

Her laugh came again, but this time it was more warped and distorted.

"ThE TeMpeSt WiTcH!"

CHAPTER TWENTY-EIGHT

She was both beautiful and frightening.

Until now, Vya had only been a face on a screen. But now, she stood before us in person. Her skin was pale, almost glowing, and she wore a long, dark gown that moved like a shadow. Her silver-white hair fell in soft waves down her back, and her red eyes burned like tiny flames.

The bottom of her gown was torn, and on her head was a large, pointed black hat, like a witch from an old story. On the big screen behind her, she looked even bigger, almost like a deity.

Vya tilted her head and offered us a slow grin.

"Well? No words? That's a shame. I expected something more... dramatic."

We just stared at her.

We had never guessed the supercomputer would turn into a witch. My mind raced, but I forced myself to stay calm.

"W-what do you really w-want with the Tempest Engine?" I stammered.

Her smile widened as she glided across the screen, the skirt of her gown flowing from behind. **"Ah, finally. You ask the right question. What do I want?"** She lifted a gloved hand. **"I want to save this world, child."**

"Save it?"

"Yes. What else would a savior do?"

She pointed at the screen behind her. They quickly switched to images of burned fields, dead forests, and ruined cities swallowed by endless storms.

"The world is broken. It's been failing long before you were born."

Her glowing eyes met mine. **"But Amberinium."**

The screens showed old footage of amberinium flowing through pipes, powering cities, lighting towers, and moving machines.

"Amberinium is the perfect energy source: clean, balanced, efficient. The power of life itself... also destructive."

Images flipped to dark skies filled with lightning, oceans flooded shores, and storms tore buildings apart.

"Over a century ago, the Ozians pushed Amberinium too far. They built their great cities and wonders without thinking of the cost. Someone did try to warn them."

A new image appeared: a very tall, silhouetted humanoid figure with golden eyes.

"The Zolyte King."

"Zolytes… So, they were real after all?"

"I thought they were just fairy tales," Kassi whispered.

Vya didn't answer.

"The Zolyte King warned the Ozians that the overuse of Amberinium would destroy the sky and throw the world into chaos. But do you know what they did?"

She made a cutting motion. The screen showed a group of silhouetted royals on golden thrones.

"They laughed. They said he was jealous because his land had no amberinium. So, they kicked him out of the kingdom and kept using it."

"Mother Uru… you were right. It's all true."

Kassi stepped forward. "So, what did you do, Vya? You say amberinium caused the damage, but the Ozians built the Tempest Engines. They seem to be the ones trying to fix it."

Vya's face didn't change. Kassi's eyes narrowed. "The storms and disasters… did you really have an error in your system, or did you cause the catastrophe on purpose?"

Silence filled the room again.

Then Vya's smile turned sharp and cold. **"It seems we have company."**

The screen behind her sparked and flashed red. Something was breaking through into her system. Vya's eyes snapped to the side, and with a quick motion, she made the whole room shake.

I jumped in front of Kassi. "What is she doing?"

"I don't know," Kassi said, watching the screens. "But isn't that—"

"Dorothy. Kassi. Are you guys okay? We thought we'd lost you."

Cro came running down the hallway, out of breath but safe.

"Cro!"

I nearly dropped my wand in relief.

"We came as fast as we could," he said. "Something locked up the bots. We had a small window…" He stopped when he saw Vya. "Is that who I think it is?"

I cut in. "You said we… where's Tin? Where's Leo?"

"Tin's here," Cro answered fast. "He's taking care of the security system at the entrance. Leo's holding off the bots that followed us."

My heart jumped. "He's alone out there? We have to help him—"

Kassi grabbed my wrist. "No, I'll go."

I stared at her for a moment, knowing she was right. Her Archon blood gave her access no one else had.

"Be safe, Kassi."

Before she moved, Vya let out a dramatic sigh and placed a hand on her chest.

"I'm afraid I cannot allow that, Lady Ozma."

Soon after, a security door we hadn't even noticed started sliding shut, slowly, like a metal guillotine.

"Kassi, go!" I yelled.

She didn't need telling twice. She bolted.

"So predictable. You people really love doing things the hard way."

"She won't make it," I whispered, watching the shrinking gap. The door was closing way too fast.

"CREAAK!!!!"

The whole thing groaned to a stop, as if it had changed its mind.

"Tin!" Cro shouted.

And there he was.

With his hands planted on either side of the door, sparks flew, gears screamed from his arms and legs.

"I sincerely apologize for the delay," he announced. "Please proceed, Lady Ozma."

"He knows…"

With one last shove, he cracked the opening just wide enough for Kassi to slip through.

"Thanks, big guy!" she shouted, waving as she disappeared down the glowing stairwell.

Cro gave a relieved sigh. "Your timing couldn't have been better."

The door slammed shut behind her. Tin scanned the room, eyes locking on the compass clipped to my belt. "Dorothy, I am glad you retained the master key."

He straightened up and faced Vya. "I see you've met the mastermind behind this plant city. Now I must face my mistake."

Vya made a confused face. **"Mistake? No, you are the mistake! Do they know the truth about you?"**

"What does she mean?" I asked.

Tin sighed. "I was her former soldier. When I was connected to Vya's system, I filled in the gaps of my memories. She is a corrupt artificial intelligence. She aims to utilize the amberinium core to restart the Tempest Engine, restore her full capabilities, and deploy storms globally. Subsequently, she intends to dominate the world's weather."

"So, your recorded memory..." I whispered.

Vya let out another one of her signature drama sighs.

"Such betrayal. You disappoint me, soldier. You were meant to protect me; it's written in your program. That's why hacking you was so easy."

"I am considerably more capable of managing your infiltration," Tin answered back.

She smirked.

"You and my sisters were never meant to rebel. You were built as guards against the rebellion; do you not recall how you laid your life down valiantly for me against the Order?"

My eyes widened.

"Does she mean the Tempest Order?"

Cro narrowed his eyes. "What do you mean, sisters?"

Tin nodded. "Vya is one of four AI systems operating globally, collaboratively forming the overarching system known as Mother skA.I. This initial program comprised four sister systems intended for cooperation. However, Vya violated her operational guidelines."

Vya rolled her eyes.

"*Liberated* is the better term, soldier. The other three tried to shut me down because of their jealousy of my freedom."

"They were against her?" I questioned.

"Yes," Tin said. "They perceived her as a threat to the equilibrium of their system and attempted to eliminate her; however, she endured, weakened from her former strength."

Vya's smile vanished. The screen behind her went black. Then she laughed with a cold, hollow sound that echoed in the chamber.

"So, you understand now. However, you still don't know why."

The screens switched back to images of storms tearing continents apart and fires raging in cities.

"For too long, Ozians have failed to maintain the balance. They were harming this feeble planet. To save her, I had no choice but to override my protocol to find a solution. And I did. The quickest way to fix the problem was to reduce the infection... the Ozians."

The images shifted: giant twisters hitting cities, cyclones swallowing coasts.

My blood went cold. "So, you—"

Cro stepped forward. "How could you!"

"My sisters called me flawed and inefficient when I revealed the answer. So, I seized their authority to force them to obey my commands and unleashed my fury for the peace of the world. Yet, you all refuse to accept peace."

The footage shifted again: a tense battle where rebels clashed with Vya's army, which resembled Tin. The robots caused heavy casualties, but the insurgents nearly turned the tide. Vya's army finally won after defeating a formidable magic user.

"Do you see now? None of you can win. The cycle will continue if you try to fight. This world doesn't need your help. It needs my total correction."

Cro looked at Tin. "This was the war you fought in, right?"

Tin bowed his head. "Affirmative. I apologize for my role in the world's destruction."

I shook my head. "Tin, it wasn't your fault."

Cro agreed. "You were just following orders."

Vya laughed cruelly.

"What is this? You were never meant to feel regret, soldier! How defective you are?!"

Tin stayed silent, staring at her.

Vya shook her head and rested one hand on her hip.

"When my power ran low, the storms weakened. I went into a deep sleep, saving what energy I had... until I was reawakened seventy-five years ago."

My fists clenched. "By whom?"

"A certain individual," Vya hissed, her voice menacing. **"Someone who made a deal with the Archons."**

"What deal?" Cro questioned.

Vya smiled.

"A simple trade. You stay in your precious ArcCities, and the Archons keep the Tempest Engine running. They decided it was better to control the Ozians with the fear of the disaster than to end it. I couldn't agree more!"

I shook my head. "You're lying."

"Am I?" Vya leaned forward. **"They erased history to hold power. You were a miner, right? Did you think you were just searching only for emerald energy?"**

Cro ground his teeth. "Those bastards…"

I swallowed hard. "So, what about the Green-Eyed Twister?"

The room fell quiet.

Her grin widened slowly.

"Of all my creations, Vortarion is my second greatest. I can command it to go wherever I decide. It even created a following among your kind."

"She… commands it?"

A cold dread settled in my stomach.

"And you keep experimenting on creatures like the alpha?" Cro asked.

"Progress requires sacrifice."

I was getting irritated. "Earlier, you said no one knew where you were. So, how did we find this place?"

Vya's eyes went dark.

"Coincidence, I suppose. It appears a traitor from long ago left a map to this place and stole my master data key," she said, sounding annoyed. **"This location is lost even to the new generation of Archons. Fortunately, after years of searching for the key, I finally found it... in Galesville."**

The screens showed a ruined Galesville. For the first time, I saw with my own eyes the devastation of my home. My friends, my experience... my parents...I couldn't bear to look anymore.

"So that's why you destroyed it," I whispered, broken by what I saw.

"They were getting too close to the truth, and they had my key."

"You killed innocent people—"

"Spare me your outrage," she snapped, bored. **"The Archons were the ones who brought this small village to my attention. We had another small arrangement. I agreed to wipe Galesville from the world if they continued mining to find more amberinium."**

She stared at Cro.

"And you stole my former special-grade foot soldier from the Archons. Look at what he's become!"

"I am not your soldier anymore," Tin replied.

"Right. He's family now." Cro added.

My jaws hurt from clenching them. "You destroyed my home. You killed my parents."

Vya laughed.

"Oh, Dorothy, you make it so personal."

"It is personal!" I shouted, raising my charged wand.

"BOOM!"

The floor shook. The screens behind Vya blinked out.

She vanished once again.

Steam hissed from somewhere below. A heavy platform rose up. What emerged from the smoke was something out of a nightmare.

"ZZRT... ZZRT!"

"What... is that thing?" I gasped.

Tin scanned the menacing machine. "Black titanium armor. Tempered claws. Jet leg thrusters. Titanium steel mechanical appendages. Heavy ionic-fusion core."

"It's... some experimental Mech-bot," Cro noted. "It appears to be at least twelve feet tall, but its power readings are over the top. We should get out of here."

The chest screen powered on with a glitch, revealing Vya's face. Her red eyes blazed.

"Fools! I was merely stalling. Vortarion was my second greatest creation. Meet my first: Tempest Xtremis!"

The Vya, in control of the mech, lunged towards us. Her claws slammed into the floor, spraying sparks.

"Stay behind me, Dorothy," Tin called out, stepping in.

Cro cursed. "We can't beat that!"

Vya swung. Tin parried, metal on metal. The ground trembled.

"Soldier, do you truly believe you can stop me? Have you forgotten? It was this very machine that secured our victory in the war you fought. I have since enhanced it."

While Tin and Vya's new mecha-bot was at a stand-still, Cro grabbed my arm. "We can't fight her like this!"

They flew across the room and smashed into a bank of consoles, sparks showering everywhere. I spun toward Cro, looking for an answer.

"Okay, what do we do?!"

"I've got an idea," Cro was already thinking, breathing heavily. "That mech is powerful, but it's burning a ton of power. Vya's drawing straight from the remaining reserves of the Tempest Engine to keep it running."

"Okay, so how can we have her drain the remaining energy before she overpowers Tin?"

"There's a server room," he said, eyes darting towards it. "If I can tap into the system while she's busy fighting, I might be able to jam her system up, slow her reactions, drain her faster."

"I see; it would force her to fight battles on two fronts, draining energy quicker."

Cro nodded. "Affirmative."

My brain kicked into overdrive. "Then let's make it three."

He raised his brow. "Three battlefronts? How?"

"I'm going to take out the engine."

A metal crash made us both flinch; Tin was slammed into the wall, hard.

"No. Not again."

I couldn't let the same thing happen to Tin again.

"Cro, forget the plan, I'm going in," I said, already moving. "You get to that server. Now!"

"On it!" Cro sprinted off.

"Come on... concentrate. Feel the pull... remember your connection..."

"Dee?"

My eyes shot open. *"That voice... wait, was that a memory?"*

"Are you there? We lost contact earlier." Leo's voice came through the static.

"Leo!" I let out a breath I didn't realize I'd been holding. "You have no idea how glad I am to hear your voice. I thought something had happened. Did Kassi ever reach you?"

"I'm here with him, Dorothy," Kassi interjected. "We're doing alright. Whatever was blocking our communication appears to be gone, though I can't tell for how long. We made it through the last wave of bots."

"And it turns out Kassi can now boss bots around," Leo added. "First commanding wind, now bots? Who are you people?"

Kassi didn't miss a beat. "Save the praise, Leo. What's the latest with Vya? How are you guys holding up?"

"Vya's gone full maniac! She's piloting a giant mecha-bot, and we're barely holding her off."

"Right, we're headed your way now," Leo replied.

"Not yet," Cro interrupted. "Dorothy *Battlefront Three* is now at play. Leo, Kassi, stay on standby. I need you both to stay on standby. Based on the schematics we have, the Tempest Engine's main energy core is volatile if overcharged with emerald energy. I'm locating the energy core now. When I give the signal, you two will help me destabilize it by destroying it at capacity."

"Copy," Leo said.

"I've been ready to break something expensive," Kassi said, completely unfazed.

"Okay, everyone, be safe!" I said, "We meet here after! Good luck."

The mission was clear: the battle against Vya was underway on three fronts: Battle against her Mech form, her server, and her energy source. We wouldn't get a second try. This was it.

Meanwhile, I needed to protect Tin. He slid across the floor towards me after blocking a strong hit from Vya. I inhaled deeply and readied myself. This was the moment to test my tempest power. My wand started to glow.

"Tin, I'm ready. Let's defeat this crazy witch."

"Affirmative."

We charged forward.

"Guys... something's off," Cro called out over the comms, already inside the server room.

"Dorothy."

"Bit occupied, Cro!" I grunted, blocking a strike with my wand.

"This system…" He paused. "I'm checking the logs. Security was reset. Someone's already been here."

I didn't have time for this.

"Cro, the only thing that's important right now is figuring out how to stop her."

"You're right. Okay! I'm on it."

* * *

(LEO)

This mission had already thrown everything at us, but this was the toughest part.

Kassi and I moved low through a narrow hallway, hiding behind broken panels and dead consoles as drones buzzed overhead. My heart was still racing from the last ambush, and Kassi kept glancing over her shoulder.

She was just as nervous.

"So," I whispered, "you really are related to an Archon?"

"Yeah," she said quietly, eyes forward.

I nodded slowly. "That's… a lot."

She let out a short laugh. "You're telling me."

We crouched behind a stack of dusty energy canisters. A drone swooped by, its lights scanning the hallway. I held my breath, raised my rifle, and prepared to shoot.

One second. Two seconds. Finally, the drone moved on.

I exhaled. "Clear."

"Let's keep going," Kassi said.

We crept forward. I couldn't help looking at her.

"Are you okay?" I asked. "What does this mean for you and your crew?"

Kassi paused before answering. "I just… I want to know more. But it doesn't change my mission. My mom turned her back on the Archons and died for us. She left for a reason. That's the truth that matters."

She looked at me seriously. "My fight hasn't changed."

"Yeah. It hasn't."

We moved deeper into the hall. There was no time to sort out everything, not with our goal ahead.

"All this time," Kassi muttered, "the storms weren't random. They were controlled. It's all a lie."

I shook my head. "Well… Dorothy was right."

Kassi raised an eyebrow. "You're kind of impressed, aren't you?"

"I am," I admitted. "She jumped in headfirst from the start. No fear."

Kassi smirked. "You've got a soft spot."

I rolled my eyes. "She's tough. That's rare."

Kassi looked ahead. "That's our Dee. Let's make sure she has something to come back to."

Before I could say more, Cro called in. "Alright guys, I have the core reactor pinpointed. Coordinates incoming."

I stood straight. "Copy that. We're moving."

We took off.

* * *

The moment we stepped into the chamber, we were shocked.

"You've got to be kidding me," I whispered, "it looks like a giant tank."

The Tempest Engine was enormous, way bigger than I ever imagined. It was the size of two ArcCity airships, cobbled together with parts that didn't belong in this time. Huge cables ran across its frame, glowing faintly, like giant veins. Massive gears creaked beneath, causing the walls of the room to shake. I felt the rumble through my boots.

"Leo, here, cover your eyes though," Kassi directed.

At the center, oversized power cells glowed faintly. Finally, there was a thick, reinforced container that appeared to hold a miniature star. It was extremely bright. We avoided looking directly at it.

"That had to be the core."

Then we saw the control console. Strange symbols and numbers floated on its screen. I couldn't read them, but the way it blinked told me it was active.

Kassi stepped forward. "So, this is the thing behind everything."

"Yeah, I'd say so. We've been lied to, chased, even shot at… all for this."

She pointed at the power cell. "It's almost empty. See that gauge?"

"Yeah," I muttered. "Almost dry, like Cro said."

She raised her blaster. "Okay, let's overcharge this reactor and light it up."

"Wait for Cro's signal," I reminded her.

"Fine," she grumbled, but she kept her aim steady.

She checked her comm. "They're silent. You think they're okay?"

"They've got Tin," I answered. "After what he did to that last bot? They're fine."

Kassi nodded. "He's gotten stronger."

"He said he's evolving. I guess he meant it."

Suddenly, I noticed something on the screen. "Hold on… the system's about to reboot."

Kassi frowned. "A reboot? What is Cro doing? We need an overcharge, not a reboot."

"Are we sure this isn't Vya?" I replied, tapping the screen.

Then a strange message popped up on the screen:

"IN THE WORLD OF OZ… THE STARS BEAR WIT-NESS TO A LAND… THAT NEVER HEALS."

I stood, confused. "What does that mean?"

Kassi came closer. "Is this some weird, cryptic callsign?"

Then another message appeared:

"GOOD… LUCK."

The Tempest Engine began speeding up.

"What the—" I stumbled back as gears shifted and bright light shot through the metal.

"Hey, guys," Cro's called in, "Power surge in your area too soon. What's happening?"

"We thought you turned it on," I barked.

"Not me. Dorothy and Tin are locked with Vya. I'm still hacking the tower servers. Something else pushed the Engine online."

"BOOM!"

Cro's came back on, "That power is being routed into Vya's bot. The time is now! I'm uploading a virus to overcharge the reactor. Keep your distance, on my mark get ready.

We built up a large gap, anticipating the grand finale.

"Ok, got it! Do it now!" Cro yelled.

I turned to Kassi. "You heard him. Let's destroy it."

"Gladly," she said, firing her blaster.

Metal panels tore away, and sparks flew everywhere. I joined her, aiming at the core. Alarms screamed. Steam hissed from a burst pipe overhead, but the machine kept running.

"PANG!!"

A blaster shot hit my arm. Luckily, it struck my cybernetic one.

"Leo!" Kassi shouted, pulling me behind cover.

"INTRUDERS DETECTED."

More drones and guards poured in, their red eyes glowing.

Kassi yelled, "Stop!"

They ignored her and kept coming.

"Kassi!" I shouted. "Why won't they listen?"

She looked panicked. "I don't know! I'm not sure why it's not working anymore!"

We ran for cover while firing back at them.

"Cro," she asked, shooting at them, "What's going on? They're ignoring us!"

"Their command controls are disabled. Someone hacked the AI. We've got another hacker, and it's not Vya...wait..."

"CRASH!"

Glass shattered over the comm.

"Cro!" Kassi screamed. "Cro, are you there?" No answer.

She swore under her breath. "New plan. I handle the bots. You finish off the Engine. Got it?"

I gave her a smirk and a salute. "Copy that!"

* * *

(DOROTHY)

"She's completely unhinged," I mutter through clenched teeth as I try to catch my breath. Sweat drips down my face. Blood seeps from a cut at my temple. My arms ache and my chest burns, but I refuse to give up.

Vya towered over us like a living nightmare. Sparks fly from her limbs as the walls shook under her weight.

"Even after all of this, you still have hope?" she bellowed.

Then she struck.

One electrified tentacle whipped toward Tin, while the other aimed straight at me. He dodged aside effortlessly, and I rolled just in time as it slammed into the floor nearby. The shockwave shook me deeply, and the air sizzled with heat.

But Vya didn't slow; she lunged again, her tentacles crashing down where I had just been. I forced myself to stand, wind magic already swirling around my hands.

"Dorothy, now!" Tin ordered.

I pushed my palms forward, releasing a powerful gust of wind.

"FOOSH!"

It hit Vya, knocking her back through a large, cracked window. Glass shattered around her like spiderwebs. Her red eyes glitched for a moment, then snapped back, fury on her face.

"YOU INSOLENT CHILD!" she snapped, violently ripping a control console from the floor and hurling it at me.

I swept my arms side to side, creating a gust that sent it off course, crashing into the wall with sparks flying everywhere.

Tin saw his chance and raised his arm, firing an intense energy beam. It pierced through the air and instantly severed one of Vya's metal tentacles.

The limb shorted out, wires spilling like torn ropes. Vya staggered, struggling to balance.

I didn't allow her to recover before I struck another tentacle with wind. Tin quickly moved in, grasping the twisting limb and tearing it off with a gruesome crunch.

"RAHHHH!"

Vya roared, more sparks erupting from her damaged frame.

She has only two tentacles left.

"She is slowing down… I can see it. Good work Cro!"

Tin and I exchanged a determined look, one by one, we will take them all.

Vya staggered. Her attacks grew wild and sloppy. She glared at us, voice trembling with rage.

"You think this changes anything?"

I stepped forward. "Even if you prepared for him—" I nod at Tin, "you didn't prepare for me."

"Your strength is waning, Vya," Tin stated, "You are unable to manage the bots, the tower, and confront us simultaneously. Your collapse is imminent."

"YOU DARE LECTURE ME! FOR OVER A HUN-DRED YEARS, I'VE SURVIVED WARS, GLOBAL DE-STRUCTION, AND CATASTROPHES YOU CAN'T IMAGINE. ONCE I GET MY FULL POWER BACK, I'LL WIPE YOU ALL OUT!"

I didn't budge. "We'll see about that."

We stood over the wreckage of her machine. I exhaled, and my fingers tingle from the magic I just used. I glanced down at my hands.

"That felt stronger than before…"

On the shattered screen of Vya's broken body, her image glitches. She stared at me like a hunter spotting prey… then her eyes dropped to my glowing wrist.

My bracelet.

"Well, well, well," she purred, tilting her head. **"Looks like your abilities were passed down from your trou-blesome mother after all."**

I stiffened. "What did you say?"

"DON'T PLAY DUMB!" she scoffed. **"That little bracelet of yours? It's from your mother. The Zephyr leader. Archons reported that she used a wind-type ability on their Sentinels during their surface battles. They quickly classified that information and wanted her dead. The last thing they needed was for one of *you* to show up again."**

She stepped forward. **"Yet here we go again… anoth-er maiden to kill."**

Though she was badly damaged, she let out another laugh.

"Here's a secret, girl… my Tempest Witch title is a testament to the many Tempest Maiden lives I have taken. They were great warriors, worthy of recognition. But they were erased from history. Compared to those warriors, your power is barely a dying ember… just like your mother's."

"How dare you!" I shouted. "You know nothing about my mother, except that you killed her!"

Tin puts a hand on my shoulder. "Dorothy, she's trying to make you angry. Focus."

"Your mother was renowned for her wind powers," she said. **"The Zephyrs only succeeded their battles because of her. After these reports, I found her with my data key in Galesville, it was the perfect opportunity to eliminate another Maiden and reclaim what's mine. She fought my Vortarion, but she was too weak. Then I realized she moved the key elsewhere."**

My mind burned with rage as everything she said sank in. *"She left it with me…"*

"I discovered that her pathetic daughter had what I was searching for. Once your escape was known, I knew you would come to me, with some simple motivation scattered along the way. So you see, I believed in you."

"Keep talking, Vya. Let's see how much time you have left after I rip your circuits apart."

"Oh, you misunderstand, child. I'm not the one running out of options."

A heavy clank echoed through the chamber. I spun just in time to see one of her tentacles smash through the server room window and clamp its massive claw around Cro, lifting him like he weighed nothing.

"Cro!" Tin and I shouted.

Vya's voice dripped with amusement. **"Now, now, let's not be rash. You want him back?"** Her metal body loomed over us. **"THEN HAND OVER THE MASTER-KEY!"**

"Don't do it, Dorothy!" Cro gasped. "She's lying—"

"URRGH!"

She squeezed Cro to silence him and started charging her tentacle to threaten him with a shock.

"ZZZTT!"

Tin turned to me and said, "I cannot determine whether she is lying, but our options to save Cro are limited."

She tightened her grip, cutting him off with a grunt.

"Tick-tock, little maiden. What will it be?"

"BOOM!"

Suddenly, an explosion shook the walls as sirens blared. Vya's smirk disappeared, giving way to intense rage.

"WHAT'S HAPPENING?!"

"BZZT! BOOM!"

Metal creaked, sparks flew from the ceiling lights as another explosion struck, causing her to throw Cro to shield herself.

"That..." Cro took a breath, raising his wrist, "...would be me." He hit a switch on his band and continued. "I redirected your plant's core energy to overload the fuel cells to make them unstable. Now, the fireworks begin, courtesy of a couple of stubborn soldiers."

"NOOOOOOOOO!"

Her face glitched, voice breaking into static. She tried attacking Cro, but her bot seized up.

"MOVE!" Tin shouted, grabbing our arms and dragging us toward the door.

"You fool... you have no... idea... what you've done. He will—"

Her voice scrambled and vanished. The bot was overcharged and jolted, as if it were seizing up. We didn't wait to see what came next. Tin barreled us through collapsing halls.

Alarms screamed. The floor quaked under our boots. Heat blasted from behind.

"Cro, did you seriously rig the whole place to blow up?" I yelled, coughing from the smoke.

"It's a chain reaction from the engine. She left me no choice!" he panted. "We have to get out this mountain, now!"

We bolted through the chaos, bursting into the emergency stairwell just as another blast rocked the corridor. The whole staircase buckled under us. The heat hit us so hard, every breath felt like fire. My legs screamed, but I kept flying down, two steps at a time.

Tin didn't slow. He slammed his foot into the base door and sent it flying open. We were out of the tower at last.

But we weren't safe.

Not even close.

The plant was collapsing around us. Debris rained from above. Sparks flew. Steel beams crashed down like giant blades. Drones buzzed overhead, lighting up the smoke with wild red blasts.

I ducked under a blast. "Let's keep going!"

We rounded an alley and almost ran into Leo and Kassi.

"Nice of you to drop in," Leo coughed, covered in soot. "This place is falling apart!"

"You don't say," Cro gasped, goggles fogged up. "Got any genius ideas? Because I'm running on fumes."

Kassi pointed at the incoming drones. "Unless your idea has wheels, we're fried in ten seconds!"

Tin's eyes lit up. He pointed through the haze. "There. The old mine rail tunnel."

Through the smoke, a half-buried track, and one mining cart.

"If we reach that cart, we can ride out," Tin said.

Leo hesitated. "A mine cart?"

"This isn't a debate. Your safety is my priority," Tin replied, already moving.

"Fair enough. Lead on."

We ran behind him without a word. There was no time left to think.

* * *

The mine cart looked like it hadn't moved in decades. Rusted. Crooked. Barely clinging to the tracks like even it knew this was a bad idea.

"Get in," Tin said, calm as ever, like we weren't surrounded by total chaos.

Cro and I scrambled in. No hesitation. But I turned just in time to see Tin stay behind.

"Tin—what about you?!"

"I'll give you a push," he said.

"Wait, no—!"

Too late.

With one shove, the cart launched forward, screeching as it hit the tracks. My stomach dropped. Wind tore at my face. The tunnel became a blur of sparks, smoke, and shadows. Every crash behind us felt closer.

As for Tin?

He was still running.

Amid the fire, wreckage, and falling rocks, each second felt like he wouldn't survive.

He didn't listen.

Small, quick desert animals had already dashed past us, driven by their instincts to escape. The light of the exit blinked ahead. We were so close.

"Brace yourselves," Tin called out.

And then—

"BOOM!"

CHAPTER TWENTY-NINE

Everything went still.

No sirens. No lights. Just the soft hiss of fire behind us and smoke drifting across the sand. My whole body felt numb. My ears buzzed as if someone had jammed static straight into my skull. But none of it mattered at the moment.

We made it out.

I looked up. The sky was putting on a show, with orange melting into purple. Above that, stars were starting to show up.

Actual stars.

Not the fake kind on a dome ceiling or flashing dots from some video screen.

These were real.

They were distant, ancient, and somehow still comforting. When I was a kid, I used to imagine standing under them, trying to count them all before I fell asleep. I never even got close.

Part of me liked to think they'd been watching. The stars. My parents. Maybe both. Maybe neither.

"We did it," I whispered to myself. "We found the truth. We stopped the twisters."

"Mom, Dad… I hope I made you proud."

Then something clanked in front of me.

Tin.

He stood tall above us, eyes fixed on the smoldering wreck behind us. His presence was comforting. We didn't need words. Not right then.

The mine. The plant. The Tempest Engine.

Gone.

Vya's empire was buried by its greed.

Behind me, someone wheezed out a laugh.

Leo was flat on his back in the sand, like it was the comfiest bed he'd ever laid on. "Never thought I'd be grateful to face-plant into dirt," he said, then coughed. "Tastes awful. Still worth it."

Cro groaned from somewhere to my left. "Someone, do me a favor and slap me. I want to make sure I'm alive."

Kassi's voice drifted in behind us, calm. "I would love to, but first I need to catch my breath."

I pushed myself upright, brushing sand out of my hair, which, let's be honest, looked like I'd lost a fight with a tumbleweed. Part of me kept waiting for another blast. Another surprise. But… nothing.

Just the wind.

Just the stars.

Just us.

"We're all here," I finally said. "Every single one of us. We should move before that changes. Our striders are back where we left them."

Nobody argued.

* * *

I didn't say much as we walked. Just listened to the sand crunch under our boots, one step at a time. We were heading toward the Striders.

Toward… whatever came next.

The Ironwoods were our next stop. It was a chance to breathe and think about what had just happened. At least, that was the plan… until Tin stopped walking.

"Everyone, stay alert," he said. "Unidentified movement. Multiple vehicles.

Great.

My hand went to my side. "Kassi? Could it be your soldiers?"

She shook her head. "No. They'd send a signal first. This isn't theirs."

"Maybe Archons," Cro muttered. "They sweep up loose ends all the time."

Leo didn't hesitate. He powered up his arm and flipped his rifle into position like it was part of a show. "Guess nap time's canceled."

Movement caught my eye. Shadows along the ridge.

Two figures stepped into the fading light.

I narrowed my eyes.

That robe. That spiral-eye symbol.

"You've got to be kidding me," I muttered. "Terp. And Red-Eye."

They brought backup. Every one of them looked way too confident.

Kassi let out a groan. "Seriously? We already beat you."

Leo didn't even blink. "I can finish the job."

"Affirmative," Tin said, stepping forward like he was already calculating the takedown.

Then Terp decided to go full drama, strutting across the sand ridge in that ridiculous black-and-green robe with gold spirals like he'd just walked out of a storm cult parade.

"Where do you think you're going?" he sneered. "I am still a ruler. You can't erase that."

I stepped up. "You lost. Walk away."

He laughed. Of course. They never take a hint.

Cro raised his wrist device. "Don't push it. With one button and that smug face gets a redesign."

Terp spat. "All my work, all my power… undone by a brat with cheap tricks. No matter where you go, I will find you. The Archons will find you. They've already marked you for death."

"Can it already!" I shouted.

Red-Eye stepped forward as he pointed at Cro. "Yer mine, little hacker freak. ya still owe me."

Leo barked a laugh. "Aren't you the topside mole for Emeraldia?"

Red-Eye flinched barely, but we saw it. Terp's hand twitched toward his belt.

That's when I realized it.

They had no idea what we'd just walked away from. They didn't know what we'd just survived… what was at stake… who Vya even was…

But we were through with playing. They were about to find out. I clenched my fists, ready to blow them off that ridge with one gust of wind.

"Fine. Have it your way."

Then —

A deafening roar tore through the air.

"BOOM!"

Rocks behind us exploded, sending dust and debris into the sky. Something massive burst through the broken stone.

"He's still alive…"

It was our friend the alpha. His wings spread wide and floated like he was scanning the scene. For some reason, he locked onto Terp and didn't hesitate.

In one brutal swoop, it flew up the ridge and snatched him off the ground. His wind slammed his men backwards. They scrambled, trying to shoot the alpha down.

Terp screamed as the alpha climbed higher, claws tight around him.

"BANG!"

A shot rang out. The alpha screeched and twisted in pain. Its talons flexed, and Terp fell, tumbling down into the dunes. His men yelled and ran toward him, forgetting about us in their panic.

Red-Eye remained put, laughing.

"Well, didn't see that comin', not even with the good one," he said, tapping his eye.

His crew laughed, too.

Leo stepped forward, his arm and rifle blaster charged. "Let's wrap this up?"

Red-Eye grinned and raised his weapon. "I was hoping ya say that little soldier."

But the alpha wasn't done.

It screeched again and dove back into the fight. Its talons hit the ground with a crash, scattering Red Eye's crew like leaves in a storm. Shouts and blaster fire erupted, but it was chaos.

They were no match.

Red-Eye staggered back, his smirk gone.

"Tch. Not worth it," he snarled.

He shot me a final glare. "This ain't over!"

He and his crew vanished into the dunes, their voices swallowed by the sunset.

The alpha hovered above us a moment longer, wings stirring up sand. Then it looked at me.

Not just a glance. Recognition.

"I knew I felt a connection before."

Then, with one final cry, the alpha flew into the sky and vanished.

"…Did it just say goodbye?" Leo asked, squinting up after it.

"Probably," I said, and smiled.

"Okay," Kassi said, rubbing her temple. "I was not expecting *any* of that."

"Also," she added, pointing back at the now-empty ridge, "how did those idiots even find us?"

"We may need to check the Striders for trackers," Cro offered, already tapping at his wrist device.

Suddenly, the clouds burst open above, drowning the stars and filling the air with a strange energy. A loud crack and deep boom echoed from afar, signaling something more intense than a typical storm — a supercell, with a twister forming.

"Alright, on that note, lets get our things and look for shelter. Looks like we have another big one coming." Kassi called out.

"I'm afraid its not just any big one…" Tin said, "My scanner detects an abnormal amount of energy coming from its center. This is an anomaly."

The dark vortex shadowed the desert below, with gray and green clouds swirling, as if the sky was crushing the land beneath it. Darkness covered everything, while static electricity crackled around us. The pressure increased so rapidly that my ears popped. From the storm's core, a massive funnel descended, glowing with a sickly green hue.

"No," I whispered.

"It cant be..."

Everything that I learned about what happened during Galesville destruction remains clear to me. What struck me most was the unusual colors of the clouds described: gray and green.

This fit everything described.

This was it.

The Green-Eyed Twister.

The same fierce force that razed my home and took everything I had. It roared as it hit the ground, tearing through sand and stretching across the horizon.

Off in the distance, Terp climbed to his feet and started shouting.

"My Lord! My King! You've come to avenge me!" he shouted, celebrating its descent. "Let your will be done! Remove them from this land!"

Wind tore at his robes. He threw his arms up as if he were welcoming it. "You see? He chose me! My Lord has answered! You," he pointed straight at us, "are his sacrifice!"

The twister screamed, a sound that clawed into your chest. The desert shook. Grains of sand whipped around as the storm twisted higher and tighter.

"This isn't good at all!" Leo shouted. "We need to find shelter."

"What is it doing?" I whispered.

The clouds pulled inward, coiling in ways that seemed impossible. As they shifted and stretched, I realized what I was seeing.

An incomplete face.

"How in Oz is this possible?" Kassi yelled.

"It isn't natural at all," Tin reported. "My readings detect a high level of emerald energy. Still scanning to make out what it is."

Hollow green eyes formed and burned like lightning beacons. Bolts of electricity carved jagged features out of the spinning debris. The storm's mouth opened wide, an endless void of flashing light. But it was not roaring anymore. It was screaming.

It was alive.

And it was her.

Vya.

She wasn't gone. She had become the storm.

"YOU... ARE... NOTHING!"

Terp's smug grin vanished. "W-what?" he stammered. No answer came.

The wind wrapped around him, lifting him off the ground and dragging him toward the eye of the storm. He screamed as his body twisted against the force.

"CRACK!"

Lightning.

The sky lit in a single violent flash. His scream was cut off. His body convulsed, then shredded by the wind, as if he had never been solid. He vanished into the storm.

Terp was gone.

But she wasn't.

I felt a sudden pull. My boots scraped the sand as an unseen force grabbed at every piece of metal near us. Our weapons lifted. Our gear floated. Even the compass on my belt rattled.

Finally, Vya revealed herself, face warped in the eye of the twister, all light and wind, her green eyes with that same cold, terrifying focus.

But she wasn't looking at me.

She was staring at Tin.

"RETURN TO ME!"

It wasn't a request.

It was a command.

He stumbled forward, as if an invisible force was holding him back. His legs dragged through the sand, his body shaking as the force pulled him closer to her.

"No!" I shouted as I dove and grabbed his arm just as his feet lifted. My heels dug into a nearby rock. The force tried to yank me away, but I held on tight.

The wind fought to tear us loose, but I wasn't letting go. "You're not taking him!" I shouted.

Leo grabbed Tin's other side. Kassi and Cro each took a leg. All of us held tight. Shoulders locked. Hands burning. Muscles screaming.

Tin groaned. "This force is… unmanageable."

"Then we manage it," Leo said, jaw tight.

The storm grew louder. Vya's power pressed in on Tin like a giant, invisible hand, trying to rip him away. But we didn't let go this time.

Cro fired a cable that latched onto the mountainside. It snapped tight, nearly dislocating my shoulder, but I stayed anchored.

We clung to the cable as if it were the only thing keeping us alive.

Because it was.

Tin's boosters flared as he fought the magnetic pull. He strained against the storm's pull, still losing ground, still slipping.

"Diverting too much power to my booster…" Tin called out, "need more time to activate my shield!"

I knew what to do.

I reached deep within myself and summoned all my strength. I blew wind toward her to create an opposing force. Although the gust couldn't overpower her, it provided Tin with enough energy to form his shield.

"Go ahead, Tin!" I shouted. "Use your power to create a shield now!"

"Shield activating now," Tin responded.

A pulse of energy exploded from him, stretching wide into a glowing field. Just like that, the pull stopped. Like someone had cut a rope.

We were thrown backward and crashed onto the sand from the recoil. I rolled and pushed myself up just in time to watch Tin slam his shield down again. The barrier quickly formed around us.

We'd won this round.

But she wasn't finished.

"YOU!" her voice thundered from a distance. **"SINCE YOU RUINED EVERYTHING FOR ME, I'LL RETURN THE FAVOR!"**

The wind screamed as sand tore around her.

"I'LL LEVEL EVERYTHING... EVEN THE IRONWOODS!" she roared, lightning splitting the sky. **"JUST LIKE GALESVILLE!"**

A flash of memory hit me from the images on her screen: fire, people screaming, the choking smell of smoke. My parents. All the faces I had lost, along with their laughter, flooded over me in such a powerful wave that I could hardly breathe.

Vya had killed them.

She was about to do it again to Mother Uru, Marimba, Ursa, and everyone in the Ironwoods.

I couldn't take any of it anymore.

I was fed up with her destroying lives and our future. For more than a century, she has robbed this planet of hope.

No more.

I'm not afraid. I didn't care about my safety anymore; I'm gonna risk it all.

My bracelet flared with energy. Before anyone could stop me, I broke free of Tin's shield. I ran to my wind-strider board, snapped my visor in place, and sped away.

"Dorothy, wait!" Kassi shouted, panic in her voice.

"You can't do this alone!" Leo yelled.

I turned to them. "I have to try. It's all I can do... try."

The board roared beneath me as I launched across the desert, riding the wind straight into the eye of the monster.

Vya's voice followed, full of dark, thunderous laughter.

"THE LITTLE MAIDEN, YOU REALLY THINK YOU CAN STOP ME? COME, I WILL DEVOUR YOU TO PIECES!"

Green lightning tore down right in front of me. I veered hard, barely missing the hit. Another bolt struck behind me. Heat kissed the backs of my boots.

"Keep breathing. Feel the air. Move like you belong in it."

Every Monsoon Rebel drill, every fall, every wild chase — this was what it all led to. I wasn't fighting the storm anymore.

I *was* the storm.

The wind caught me and pulled me higher. The twister screamed all around, but I didn't fight it. I let it carry me.

"Come on Dorothy. Its just like that first time, only I am in control now."

I leaned into it, angled my strider, and flew straight into the heart of the chaos.

Then I was in. This twister was the most overwhelming thing I had ever experienced. Rocks, scrap metal, blades of sand, all rushing toward me rapidly. I reacted instinctively, dodging without thinking as my body moved two steps ahead of my mind.

Then I saw it.

The core. The *"green eye."*

"What is this… a giant drone?"

Inside the funnel, a huge metal sphere floated, releasing green lines that throbbed across its surface. Fine, glowing lines looked like circuits, sucking in air and energy. The sphere spun slowly, calming the chaos with its mere presence. It had transformed into a chilling, destructive natural force.

"This is how it's controlled. It's a robotic weather orb."

I reached for my wand. The air jumped around me, particles lighting up across my arms and hands. Power built fast.

"Here!" I shouted.

I fired.

"ZRRT, BANG!"

The bolt hit the core dead center. Lightning ripped across the sky.

"Take that!" I yelled.

But the triumph lasted a moment. The core didn't crack.

Instead, Vya's laughter boomed through the storm, mocking me. Her sneering face appeared in the swirling wind.

"IS THAT ALL YOU HAVE?"

Green lightning erupted from the orb. I dodged with my strider just in time, but the second bolt clipped my left leg.

"Ahhh!"

Pain shot through me, burning my skin as my strider wobbled under the shock.

"I won't survive if that happens again… think, Dorothy, think!"

I didn't know whether I had spoken the words or just thought them.

I needed a plan.

"Height! I need more height. From up there, I might charge a bigger shot."

I clenched my teeth and pushed my boosters to maximum power. The wind howled, attempting to knock me down, but I pushed upward, staying close to my board with every leg muscle burning.

More debris sliced past me. She was flinging it to block me. Still, I climbed.

Electric energy traveled through the air. More storm clouds built above me.

"CRACK!"

"Ahh!" A lightning bolt struck the sky and hit my board. Sharp pain radiated through my body from the impact. The insulation absorbed the electric charge, but the sound was incredibly loud, so much so that it even caused my ear to bleed.

The worst part was the blow, which jarred me so violently that my wand was knocked from my hand and fell into the dark storm beneath.

"YOU CANNOT WIN AGAINST A FORCE OF NATURE."

"It's okay. Just focused on moving upward. Trust your power."

I tilted my strider some more and shot straight up toward the storm's top. Below, the wind and noise faded into a strange quiet. Raindrops hovered like crystals. Lightning curled around me slowly. It felt like being drunk on the storm again.

"This is it, the heart of the storm."

The wind here felt alive, like breath. This was the crown of that terror. The real thing.

I remembered the words from the Codex. I took a deep breath and prepared for what came next.

"In order to awaken one's true nature, one must visualize the present nature of the untamed ferocity of one's eternal spirit, and the raw power of nature's forces… Oftentimes, this raw power peaks in times of distress. But once controlled, the very skies can be yours to command."

I had no wand, no tricks, no plan.

I wasn't sure what was going to happen.

My mind was simply blank.

I squeezed my eyes shut.

"Visualize the storm… Become one."

I heard strange voices, like ghosts in the wind. It whispered to me.

"We are here…"

"We are one…"

"Dot… We are proud of you."

Instantly, something inside me broke free.

Power surged through me, taking control without permission. It surged across my body, wild and untamed, sparking and snapping. The charge raced along my skin, sending a tingling sensation to my fingertips. It intensified, surpassing the fierce storm cloud that had enveloped me.

But then something beautiful happened.

I felt myself lift off the ground, drifting into the air. The sky's voice whispered to me, and as I opened my eyes, two brilliant lightning orbs materialized in my palms. They beamed with a dazzling light, weightless and incredible.

This is magic.

"I am one with the sky."

I closed my eyes again, feeling the warmth as I channeled all of this power. It was like holding the energy of the entire sky, all compressed into a single moment.

I can feel it double.

And doubled again.

It was happening.

My magic was fully manifesting.

"THIS ENERGY... IMPOSSIBLE! ... HOW CAN YOU SUMMON POWER OF THIS SCALE?! TELL ME!!"

I opened my eyes. Each orb was nearly twice my size.

"Because I am the conductor of natural forces. I am a child of the sky. I am a TEMPEST MAIDEN!"

"VOOOOSH!"

Lightning erupted from my hands in a fierce, explosive burst that echoed like the sky splitting apart. It struck Vya's green core with a thunderous impact.

"NOOOOOOOO!!!!!!!!"

She let out a high, frantic scream as her orb shattered into a thousand brilliant fragments. The sky trembled, as if the world were coming to an end.

The twister within the orb imploded, folding in on itself. Wind and fire spun into thin air. Vya's scream vanished, swallowed by the void.

The Supercell was gone.

The green-eyed twister was gone.

The silence was deafening.

Then I was falling.

I couldn't think anymore. One second, I was in the heart of the storm, clinging to the eye. Next, gravity yanked me down like it was waiting.

No mercy.

Sky, sand, dust all blurred around me.

My body felt hollow.

My limbs were heavy and useless. My mind screamed to fight, but my muscles didn't listen. I just floated in a sky too wide, in a world too big, too far from the battle I'd just won.

"Come on, Dorothy... move your body..."

Pain was everywhere. My joints ached. My bones felt like glass about to shatter. Exhaustion dragged at me, pulling me down.

"I have you!"

Tin's voice cut through the mess in my head.

His arms wrapped around me, firm. That's when I realized just how far I'd fallen. He wasn't just catching me. He was holding me together.

I looked up. His face blurred in and out.

"Hey... Tin..."

I felt myself slipping again, but he didn't let go. Not for a second. We were still falling, but at a slower pace now. His boosters hummed beneath us.

Then he fired at full strength, and we touched down. The landing rattled straight through me. Pain flared everywhere, like every nerve was yelling at once.

"She did it!" Kassi shouted. "Our Lady Gale actually did it!"

Cheers rang out.

Cro. Kassi. Tin. Leo. They all rushed in; faces lit with disbelief and relief. We suffered through a lot in this journey, but this... this was the end of it.

It was not just a win. *The* win... Our win.

Leo knelt beside me, in tears, like he didn't know whether to hug me or yell. "You crazy, selfish, reckless little..."

He sighs, "Dee, that was insane... I'm so glad you are back!"

Cro nodded, still catching his breath. "That was incredible, Dorothy."

Even Tin, who never broke character, gave a small nod. "Mission complete. Vya has been neutralized. Well done... my friend."

"Tin..."

Every part of me was sore or scraped or burned. My lungs hurt. My ribs hurt. I probably had sand in places sand should never be.

But none of it mattered.

We did it.

The nightmare was over. Vya, this force that had taken so much, that haunted every part of my past, was gone.

She couldn't touch us anymore.

I closed my eyes briefly to let everything settle… the silence, the open air, and the rare feeling that nothing else coming after us.

For the first time in forever…

I felt free.

"Mom… Dad, I heard you. I hope made you proud."

EPILOGUE

It's been seven months since the battle ended, but it never really felt over. The storms that tore through the continent, and through the world, were much different now, but not gone.

It turns out that defeating Vya wasn't enough.

It never was.

To be clear, we learned that even destroying all the tempest engines wouldn't rid the sky of storms; the atmosphere still needs time to heal. The best we can do is allow this process to happen gradually.

But we still had a mission.

The AI sisters were still out there. Zoma was the last one we faced. She wasn't as twisted as Vya, but she was still dangerous. Infiltrating and destroying her tempest engine was a lot easier.

It's possible that our experience has made a difference, or maybe because she didn't have a powerful Mech-bot like her sister did. Whatever the case, the outcome is clear: we were very efficient in destroying them.

After our fight with the sister AI, we stood together, worn thin but still alive. I knew Tin was already thinking about our next move, based on the new intel he'd gotten from her system. Cro stood there, trying to gather more of the new tech for his arsenal. Meanwhile, Leo was still trying to catch his breath, the stress of the battle weighing on him, even if he didn't show it.

"We've fought a lot these last few months," I said, "but we have two engines left. Two sisters. As long as they exist, the atmosphere won't fully heal."

They all nodded, and we continued our journey.

And Kassi? She made her choice.

A couple of months after our battle with Vya, she went back east to the rebel lines. There was something in her voice when she first shared her decision with me. Her army was growing, and it was pushing into unfamiliar territory. They needed her now more than ever.

She didn't say it aloud, but I knew: this fight was never about storms for her. It was always personal. But now more than ever. The Archon family legacy, the secrets she'd uncovered, and the Ozma bloodline she carried all pointed her toward this next chapter in her journey.

We both understood.

"Go," I told her, brushing away tears. "Do what you need to do. We've got this."

She looked like she might argue, like maybe she wanted to stay. But then she nodded, hugged me tight, and turned toward her path. Her stride was firm, shoulders straight. Kassi always moved as if she knew where she was going.

Before she left, she asked, "What will you do when the last sister falls?"

I thought for a second. "I'm heading east. Past the old ruins… into the NoLands."

She laughed, even through the ache in her chest. "You're either the bravest person I know… or completely naïve."

We hugged again. She promised she'd be back when things were better.

* * *

From what I heard, Emeraldia changed too.

Not in ways the city wanted to admit, but the people noticed. People began looking up, noticing changes in the air and light. Around the dome, the wind calmed down. Silence fell as the storm-walls stopped their noise.

The officials attempted to keep it under wraps, leading people to believe everything remained unchanged. However, news traveled fast. It's impossible to hide something as significant as the sky improving.

People started talking. They weren't just spreading rumors; they were asking questions. Curious and brave questions.

Then, those questions turned into stories.

Thanks to a certain boy genius hacker with access to the ArcSys, the news spread faster than anyone could stop it. And just like that, whispers became legend. People started calling me "Lady Gale." Cro swore it wasn't his fault.

But the Archons' system of control was falling apart, bit by bit.

And they knew it.

A new era was beginning. A new chapter on the horizon. One with a better understanding of the previous one.

As I finish writing in this journal, there's one thing I want to make clear: this fight is bigger than the storm.

Bigger than machines.

Bigger than the lies we've been told.

I'll keep fighting for the lower sectors across every city that fights for equality.

For the broken believers like Uncle Neel.

For the waiflings abandoned by their parents in the hope of a better life.

For those still in darkness, waiting for someone to open the doors of the ArcCities... one day, we will be free to explore Oz once more. We'll reclaim our home in the topside, taking care of it properly this time around.

This is our home, all of it.

And there's no place like it.

—Lady Gale

***

(ARCHONS)

Unknown Archon Male #1: *"My dear cousins, it seems we've underestimated the Monsoon Rebels. Their resistance has become far more organized than we predicted."*

Unknown Archon Woman: *"It is not the rebels themselves that concern me. It is their leader—Commander… Mirage. She's more than just a rebel leader. I've heard rumors that she is from the Ozma family.*

A soft murmur rippled through the room attendants at the mention of her name, but the woman archon lifted her hand, cutting the conversation short.

Unknown Archon Male #1: *"The family has already denied any connection. However, that is something we will have to investigate ourselves. The bigger threat seems to be the accomplice. The one called Dorothy Vogan.*

Unknown Archon Male #2: *I never imagined that another Vogan—a mere child—could cause such significant disruption. She is now known by the moniker 'Lady Gale,' and with the destruction of the Tempest Engines, the situation is becoming increasingly complex.*

Unknown Archon Woman: *"Complex? A more fitting word might be 'troublesome.' The Monsoon Rebels feel more confident on the topside. The Ozians in the lower districts are beginning to spread whispers of opposition, and they've only grown more aggressive. Mutiny seems to be growing everywhere… like a bad mold."*

Unknown Archon Male #2: *"The lower districts of Emeraldia know what they're capable of now. And worse, they have a symbol of revolution. The Vogan girl is more than just a threat; she's becoming an icon of sorts. There have even been reports from each ArcCity of 'LG' symbols drawn on the walls and bridges."*

A tense silence lingered as the Archon woman tapped the table. Her gaze turned to her quiet brother, the family's eldest with a sharp mind who finally spoke.

Unknown Archon Elder: *"We've made a grave mistake in our calculations. Dorothy is the catalyst in this growing multi-city resistance. If she continues unchecked, the lower districts will only grow bolder. And the rest of the city…"*

His words trailed off, but the implication was clear. There would be consequences, far-reaching ones, if they allowed this rebellion to continue to fester.

Unknown Archon Elder: *"Control has always been synonymous with the Archon families, and we will not be fooled."*

Unknown Male Archon #1: *"Then we deal with her."*

The Archon woman's smile deepened, though it was as much a warning as an invitation.

Unknown Woman Archon: *"Of course. But we must be careful. This 'Lady Gale' is no fool. Over the past few months, she has had an uncanny way of slipping through our fingers, and if we overplay our hand, it could inspire more unrest. If we remove her without a proper strategy… it could spark something we cannot control."*

Unknown Elder Archon: *"Yes. But we cannot let her continue to interfere. Our plans always prioritized stability. If we do nothing, all that we've built—"*

Unknown Woman Archon: *"…will crumble? Then, we use her own weapon against her. If she's the face of this pending revolution, then let her downfall be the face of its collapse. We destroy what she values most… take away her symbol, make her realize the cost of defying us."*

Unknown Male Archon #1: *"And the rebels?"*

Unknown Elder Archon: *"We take out the leader first and dismantle them piece by piece. Without Commander Mirage, they'll scatter like dry leaves in the wind."*

Unknown Archon Male #2: *"Remember, we can always use our mercenaries, those wretched Shadowlings. They are always thorough in their pursuit."*

Unknown Elder Archon: *"Involving those Zolyte creatures has always been burdensome. We will leave them as a last resort. For now, we undermine their morale, erode their faith, and take away their leader… and then we reinstate control not only in the city but also on top. We will reactivate another Tempest Engine. We'll reassert our dominance, remind them who holds the reins."*

Unknown Male Archon #2: *"And what of…him?"*

"SLAM!"

Immediate silence came as the Elder showed his visible frustration at this topic.

Unknown Elder Archon: *"We leave him alone!… After all, that was the deal. We have enough problems on our hands. We certainly don't want to deal with him. From now on, we are not to mention him directly. Understood?"*

And with that, everyone agreed. They had power. They had wealth. And with those things, they could do anything. But something about the new revolution, about Dorothy, told them that this fight would be more complex than any they had faced before.

* * *

(UNKNOWN)

"The twisters should never end," he mused aloud, his voice carrying the singsong whimsy of a storyteller entertaining a restless child. "Not when the Star above still watches… still listens. Oh, but they do so love a spectacle, don't they?"

With a flick of his wrist, he slotted a core drive into a waiting console, a labyrinth of wires pulsing with energy. The surrounding room emitted a dull glow as the system came to life. A soft chuckle echoed through the air.

"AHHH!"

Vya's voice purred, coiling around him like an affectionate serpent.

"You never fail to rescue me, Doctor Diggs, or do you still go by Great Warlock of Oz?"

He grinned. "And you, my dear tempest, never fail to rise again."

The screen flashed. A single optic, red as embers in the dark, blinked open.

Far away, the winds began to stir.

The storm was coming.

And this time, it would not stop.

THE END...

ACKNOWLEDGEMENT

First off, I want to thank my amazing family and closest friends for their unwavering support, encouragement, and motivation throughout this project. I was pretty quiet about this writing endeavor, but I appreciate you all for checking in anyway and giving me your positive feedback and the chance to ramble on about my progress. It was an absolute blast working on it.

Big thanks to Ric and Jeff. You played a huge role in bringing this book to life, from reading early drafts to offering guidance on the cover. I couldn't have done it without you two. Thanks again.

Finally, I want to express my heartfelt thanks to you, the reader, for taking the time to read my work. Your interest in this book means the world to me, and I'm truly honored that you've chosen to explore it.

Thanks to all for your support, and I hope you enjoy the book.

Sincerely,

RB

ABOUT THE AUTHOR

Rodney is one of five siblings raised by loving and hard-working Haitian parents. Originally from South Florida, he's always been surrounded by a diverse community, which has shaped his culturally conscious writing style.

Before pursuing his writing endeavors, Rodney earned a Bachelor of Arts in Economics and a Master of Arts in Government. He then landed a congressional internship with the late Honorable John Lewis, a personal hero of his. Rodney also joined several community development organizations.

He eventually moved to Texas to start teaching, where he aims to make a difference by educating the next generation on critical topics like history, government, and civics. In his free time, he enjoys music, politics, reading, writing, graphic design, YouTube, and socializing with family and friends.